Praise for

Austin Grossman's
You

"A razor-sharp comedy.... A smart meditation on the nature of gaming. Grossman, who has designed video games, brings experience but more importantly abundant affection to describing this world—the welcome recognition of the one Dungeon and Dragons enthusiast for another, the surreal happiness that comes from mastery, the semi-ironic clinging to juvenile aesthetics."

—Kate Tuttle, *Boston Globe*

"Some of the most startling, acute writing on video games yet essayed."

—Tom Bissell, *Harper's*

"*You* confirms Austin Grossman's status as a major talent. Grossman isn't just chronicling the rise and fall of a company, or of a character, or even an industry. Rather, he uses *You* as a tool to pry open the mystical center of what art is, what games are, what fun is, and how they all mix together. A novel that both uplifts and entertains, and reframes the world we live in and the things we do in it. Easily one of the best books I've read this year."

—Cory Doctorow, *Boing Boing*

"A celebration of video games and their creators.... Grossman invites us into the world of video games, introduces us to the people whose lives revolve around them, and makes us feel right at home."

—*Booklist*

"Austin Grossman combines videogames, advanced technology, and suspense into one crazy page-turner."
— Caitlin Cress, *Kansas City Star*

"*You* is set in the late '90s, and anyone who played PC games in that era will have an instant fondness for the games Black Arts is developing. But while nostalgia is one of *You*'s appeals, it's not what this book is about.... *You* is more about friendship and relationships between its characters than the technology that surrounds them."
— Kevin Nguyen, *Grantland*

"*You* is the story of a generation discovering and creating its own 'incandescent mythology.' I've rarely been this sad when a novel was over."
— Stefan Raets, Tor.com

"A work of fiction dedicated to the folks who create the worlds millions of people lose themselves in every day."
— Evan Narcisse, *Kotaku*

"I highly recommend this novel to anyone who is fascinated by the mechanics of storytelling, and the way fantasy shapes our perceptions of reality."
— Annalee Newitz, i09.com

YOU

Also by Austin Grossman

Soon I Will Be Invincible

YOU

A NOVEL

AUSTIN GROSSMAN

MULHOLLAND BOOKS

LITTLE, BROWN AND COMPANY

NEW YORK   BOSTON   LONDON

The characters and events in this book are fictitious. Any similarity to real persons, living or dead, is coincidental and not intended by the author.

Copyright © 2013 by Austin Grossman

All rights reserved. In accordance with the U.S. Copyright Act of 1976, the scanning, uploading, and electronic sharing of any part of this book without the permission of the publisher constitute unlawful piracy and theft of the author's intellectual property. If you would like to use material from the book (other than for review purposes), prior written permission must be obtained by contacting the publisher at permissions@hbgusa.com. Thank you for your support of the author's rights.

Mulholland Books
Little, Brown and Company
Hachette Book Group
237 Park Avenue, New York, NY 10017
mulhollandbooks.com

Originally published in hardcover by Mulholland Books / Little, Brown and Company, April 2013
First Mulholland Books paperback edition, April 2014

Mulholland Books is an imprint of Little, Brown and Company, a division of Hachette Book Group, Inc. The Mulholland Books name and logo are trademarks of Hachette Book Group, Inc.

The publisher is not responsible for websites (or their content) that are not owned by the publisher.

The Hachette Speakers Bureau provides a wide range of authors for speaking events. To find out more, go to hachettespeakersbureau.com or call (866) 376-6591.

Library of Congress Cataloging-in-Publication Data
Grossman, Austin
    You : A Novel / by Austin Grossman.—First Edition.
        pages cm
    ISBN 978-0-316-19853-0 (hc) / 978-0-316-19854-7 (pb)
    1. Video games industry—Fiction. 2. Computer hackers—Fiction. I. Title.
PS3607.R666Y68 2013
813'.6—dc23   2012039730

10 9 8 7 6 5 4 3 2 1

RRD-C

Printed in the United States of America

To everyone making games.

For they are actions that a man might play,
But I have that within which passeth show...

—WILLIAM SHAKESPEARE
HAMLET

SWORD IN ONE HAND, BLASTER IN THE OTHER!

REALMS OF GOLD is the ultimate in computerized interactive entertainment, brought to you by your friends at BLACK ARTS STUDIOS!

FOLLOW the adventures of FOUR ETERNAL HEROES through INFINITE WORLDS in the greatest INTERACTIVE experience ever forged.

In FANTASTICAL ENDORIA, LIVE the struggle to rebuild the world in the wake of the SHATTERWAR, as the THIRD AGE of the world draws to a close.

In the TWENTIETH CENTURY'S COLD WAR, match wits with the spymaster KAROLY in the thrilling world of *CLANDESTINE*.

In the FAR FUTURE, forge the destiny of the human race in a WAR for the GALAXY in *SOLAR EMPIRES*.

- Mind-blowing graphics in Real Time and Three Dimensions.
- Choose from one of four Characters: Warrior, Mage, Thief, or Princess.
- Groundbreaking simulation technology makes the world come alive as never before.
- YOU determine the story! YOU choose your own Destiny!

MASTER THE REALMS!

BLACK ARTS STUDIOS ADVERTISEMENT

GAMELORDS MAGAZINE, MAY 1992

YOU

PART I

THE ULTIMATE GAME

Chapter One

"So what's your ultimate game?"

He made it sound like a completely normal question, and I guess in this context it was. My long afternoon of interviews had come down to these two strangers. A tall guy, twentyish, with an angular face and graying hair pulled back in a ponytail, who enunciated everything very precisely, as if speaking into a touchy voice-recognition program. The other one was slightly over five feet tall, with long, Jesus-like, wavy dark hair and a faded black T-shirt that read CTHULHU FOR PRESIDENT; WHY SETTLE FOR THE LESSER OF TWO EVILS? It was from 1988.

"Right." I swallowed. "So, how exactly do you define that?"

None of the questions was what I expected. Most of them were esoteric thought experiments, "How would you turn *Pride and Prejudice* into a video game?" and "If you added a button to *Pac-Man,* what would you want it to do?" Conundrums like "How come when Mario jumps he can change direction in midair?" And now this one.

"You know, the game you'd make if you could make any game at all," the long-haired designer explained.

"Forget about budget," the short guy added. "You're in charge. Just do anything! Greatest game ever!"

I opened my mouth to answer and then stopped. It was obviously a throwaway question, a way to close out the afternoon on a fun note. And so it was weird that my mind had gone blank when it was the one question I should have known the answer to, given that I was interviewing for a job as a video game designer.

I'd spent the past few hours in a state of mild culture shock. I'd arrived forty minutes early at the address the office manager gave me over the phone, an anonymous office complex at the far limit of the Red Line, past Harvard and Porter, where Cambridge gave out entirely, lapsed into empty lots and restaurants on the wrong side of Alewife Brook Parkway, and then into wetlands, brackish water, and protected species like sweet flag and pickerelweed.

Beyond the wetlands were the forested hills and the suburbs Arlington and Belmont and Newton where I grew up. Alewife was built to be the point of exchange between Cambridge and the true suburbs. It was also home to the acres of office space demanded by high-tech companies spun off from academic research and funded by the Department of Defense, IT training schools, human resources offices, real estate companies, and tax attorneys. Coming back here felt like I'd made it to the big city and now was on the verge of drifting back out into the nowhere beyond. This was where Black Arts Studios set up shop.

This particular building was apparently designed in the early eighties, while the Department of Defense was still funding blue-sky tech companies. The heavy glass doors led into a three-story lobby and courtyard with a fountain, pastel Mediterranean tiling, and incongruous broad-leafed faux-tropical foliage. It had a humid, greenhouse smell even in the oddly chilly spring of 1997; the frosted skylights let in a perpetually dim half-light. About half the office space looked empty.

Black Arts was on the third floor. There was no sign or number on the door, so I wandered back and forth along the balcony until I saw a piece of paper with BLACK ARTS written in black Magic Marker taped to the inside of a glass window reinforced with chicken wire. There was no doorbell. Through the square of glass I could see an empty reception area, and behind it an open doorway leading to a dimly lit office.

I wasn't exactly comfortable in a job interview, and what made it worse was I already knew these people — pretty well, actually. We'd met when we were in high school together, fourteen years ago. Now I would be asking them for work, in the company they started. Darren and Simon were the cofounders. They'd been friends since as long as anyone could remember. Simon I remembered as small and dark-haired, round-faced, with olive skin that never seemed to see the sunlight. He wore checkered shirts and corduroys and never seemed to quite come into an adult body — at fifteen he could have passed for twelve. He was supposed to be smart but for some reason didn't take any advanced classes. Pathetic, but so dorky as to almost round the corner into menacing. People claimed he built pipe bombs and had hacked a kid's grades on the school computer once. They laughed at him, but not to his face.

Darren was taller and horse-faced and passably athletic. He ran track one year, but when he got to high school he grew his hair out, dropped the athletics and the honors classes, found an old army jacket and wore it all the time.

They were a fixture, short and tall, two different flavors of loser. You'd see them walking home every day, Simon's hands shaping the air. What did they talk about? Comics, movies, inside jokes held over from the fourth grade? Another teen friendship, another tiny mysterious universe.

I met them in an intro to programming class, and six years later they were legends, the two burnout kids who founded a computer game company and got rich. But even the money wasn't as alluring as the idea that they'd made video games their jobs, even before anybody knew that games were going to turn into an industry, an entertainment medium as big as the movies — bigger, if you believed some people. Simon and Darren made money out of — well, being awesome, essentially.

Don and Lisa went with them, too — got rich, stayed, won. Meanwhile,

I went on to an English degree, a year of law school, an internship at a doomed newspaper in Dallas, sublets in Cambridge, Queens, Somerville, San Francisco (a new start!), Austin, Madison, and imminently, nowhere.

Simon never graduated from college. He was killed four years ago, in a ridiculous accident that resulted in security cameras being placed inside all the elevator shafts of all the buildings on that particular campus. He wasn't even a student there.

People were already starting to talk about him as a genius on a par with Bill Gates and Steve Jobs, and about what he might have done if he lived. The software he left behind was still state of the art in some ways, even though he wrote it way back in the eighties, before video games were in 3-D, before CD drives, before photo-real graphics. It was called the WAFFLE engine, a witches' brew of robust world simulation and procedural content generation, the thing that powered Black Arts games first, to critical success, then to profitability, then to becoming a runaway phenomenon. It was still under the hood of every game they made; it had a weird genius x factor to it; it had never been surpassed or even duplicated. Before Simon died he was working on a project that he claimed would the next generation of the technology. He used the word *ultimate* more than once — in fact, right there in the title of his proposal (it was meant to finally get him his BA from MIT; they'd as much as offered it to him, but he never followed through): "The Ultimate Game: A Robust Scheme for Procedurally Generated Narrative." There had even been a press conference, but no copy of the proposal had ever been found. The idea — the Fermat's last theorem of video game technology — lingered on at Black Arts.

I should say, people have had the impression Simon killed himself, or else died as part of a game. That was the way it was reported in most of the papers. "A 'Gamer Death' on Campus," as if there were such a phrase. More than one dipshit psychology professor said things like,

"It's not uncommon for these self-identified 'gamers' to lose the ability to distinguish between what is a game...and what is reality."

First of all, this is a viewpoint that is frankly idiotic. People who play games don't get killed or go crazy any more often than anyone else. It's just that people point it out when they do. Second of all, Simon was a person with a vocation, one of the few people I've ever met for whom this was unmistakably the case. He wasn't out of touch with reality, he was simply opposed to it. Third of all, fuck reality. If Simon didn't like the world he grew up in, he has my wholehearted support and agreement. I went to his funeral, as did his many friends. They were not any kind of checked-out gamer fringe; it turns out a dude in a kilt who introduces himself as "Griffin" can be honestly, normatively upset that his friend got killed in a ridiculous accident.

When I heard that Simon had died, I tried to find something appropriate to feel. What I did feel wasn't flattering. We hadn't been friends since the early 1980s. I was still young enough to feel the death of someone I'd known as a novelty. Like it was one more aspect of Simon's eccentricity, or his genius. One more place Simon got to before the rest of us. I felt sorry we'd been out of touch, sorry because we'd both vowed to do the impossible, and it was the only vow I'd ever made, and I hadn't done it, and Simon — well, that was the thing. I was partly there because I wanted to know what exactly happened. How far Simon had gotten.

I let myself in. I smelled fresh paint; I could hear somebody laughing.

"Hello?" I called into the darkness.

A teenager in a black T-shirt looked out. He was built on a funhouse scale — my height but twice my width, a fat kid with the arms and chest of a linebacker. "Oh, hey. Are you Russell?"

"Yes, that's me," I answered, relieved.

"I'm Matt. Hang on." He turned and yelled down the hall. "He's here!"

He waved me inside, into a room that turned out to be almost half of the building's third floor. It was a dim cavern, kept in semidarkness by venetian blinds. From what I could see it was mostly open space. Soda cans and industrial-size bags of popcorn had accumulated in the corners, along with a yoga ball, stacks of colorfully illustrated rule books, and what appeared to be a functioning crossbow. It looked like the aftermath of a weekend party held by a band of improbably wealthy ten-year-olds. In fact, there was a man curled up under one desk in a puffy blue sleeping bag. A young woman in a tie-dyed dress and sandals was sitting against one wall, typing on a laptop, ignoring me, her blond hair done in elaborate braids.

While I waited for Matt to come back, I looked at a wall of framed magazine covers and Game of the Year awards. I went over to one of the computers, which showed what I thought at first was an animated movie of a space battle, but when I touched the mouse the camera panned around the scene, and I saw it was a functioning game, a fully realized environment navigable in three dimensions. I hadn't been paying much attention to video games for a few years, not since I'd graduated from college. Did they turn into something totally different when I wasn't looking?

I was born in 1969, which was the perfect age for everything having to do with video gaming. It meant I was eight when the Atari 2600 game console came out; eleven when *Pac-Man* came out; seventeen for *The Legend of Zelda*. Personal computers were introduced just as our brains were entering that first developmental ferment of early cognitive growth, just in time to scar us forever. In 1978, kids were getting called out of class in the middle of the morning. A woman from the principal's office (whose name I never learned) quietly beckoned us out two at a time, alphabetically, and ushered us back in fifteen minutes later. When our turn came, I went with a boy named Shane. I was tingling a little bit just with the specialness of the moment, the interruption of routine. We were led down the hall to sit in one corner of the school secretary's office in front of a boxy appliance that turned out to be a computer. It was new, a Commodore PET computer.

The PET's casing was all one piece, monitor and keyboard and an embedded cassette tape drive forming a blunt, gnomic pyramid. It was alien, palpably expensive, and blindingly futuristic in a room that smelled of the mimeograph machine used to print handouts in a single color, a pale purple—a machine operated in exactly the same manner as when it was introduced in the 1890s, with a crank.

The lady sat us down and quietly walked away. Shane and I looked at each other. I don't know what he felt, but there was a realization stirring inside me. They didn't know what the machine was. They'd been given it, but they didn't know how to use it. It didn't do much. It didn't understand swear words or regular English. It played a couple of games, *Snake* and *Lunar Lander*. After fifteen minutes she led us back to class and brought out the next two kids, who would also type swear words into it.

But it was probably the most generous and the most humble gesture I received from an adult in the sixteen-year duration of my schooling. The woman was simply leaving us alone with our future, the future she wouldn't be part of. She didn't know how to do it or what it was, but she was trying to give it to us.

As we grew, the medium grew. Arcade games boomed in the late seventies and eighties and gave rise to video-game arcades themselves, built in retrofitted department stores and storefront offices, making money in twenty-five-cent increments, floods of quarters warmed with adolescent body heat. These were the cooler, dumber cousins of the quiet, hardworking PET. Video games had the street swagger and the lowest-common-denominator glitz of pinball machines refracted through the seemingly ineradicable nerdiness of digital high tech.

I was older when I started going to arcades—eleven, maybe. I relaxed in the warm, booming darkness of the arcade, the wall of sound, and the warm air, smelling of sweat and teenage boys and electronics. The darkness was broken only by neon strips, mirrored disco balls, and the lighted change booth. Looking around the arcade was like seeing thirty Warner Bros. cartoons playing at once, shown ultra-bright and overspeed.

The state of the technology meant characters were drawn on 8-by-12-pixel grids, a strangely potent, primitive scale. Dogs and mailmen and robots became luminous pictoglyphs hovering in the dark. The cursory, dashed-off feel of the stories seemed to have opened a vein of vivid whimsy in the minds of the programmers and engineers of this first wave. The same limitations threw games into weird, nonperspectival spaces. Games like *Berzerk* and *Wizard of Wor* took place in bright Escher space, where overhead and side views combine.

And the dream-logic plots! Worlds where touching anything meant instant death; where mushrooms are friends and turtles are enemies. In each one I felt the presence of a deep logic living just offscreen, each one a bright painting telling a not-quite-explained story: Why am I a plumber fighting an ape for a princess? Why am I, a lone triangle, battling a fleet of squares? Who decided that?

And adults hated to be in there. It gave them headaches and made them look stupid when we all knew how to play and what to do because we were growing up with a technology whose buried rules made sense to us. In the swirling primordial mix of children and teenagers, hormones and technology were combining to form a new cultural idea. Some days I spent up to three hours in the arcade after school, dimly aware that we were the first people, ever, to be doing these things. We were feeling something they never had — a physical link into the world of the fictional — through the skeletal muscles of the arm to the joystick to the tiny person on the screen, a person in an imagined world. It was crude but real. We'd fashioned an outpost in the hostile, inaccessible world of the imagination, like dangling a bathysphere into the crushing dark of the deep ocean, a realm hitherto inaccessible to humankind. This is what games had become. Computers had their origin in military cryptography — in a sense, every computer game represents the commandeering of a military code-breaking apparatus for purposes of human expression. We'd done that, taken that idea and turned it into a thing its creators never imagined, our own incandescent mythology.

One summer in middle school I finally got an Apple IIe, a beige plastic wedge with computer and keyboard in one piece, along with its own nine-inch monochrome monitor. I discovered the delinquent thrill of using copy programs like Locksmith to duplicate copy-protected games on 5.25-inch floppy disks and the trick of double-siding a disk by clipping a half-moon out of it with a hole puncher.

The idea of simulating an alternate world had taken over thousands of otherwise promising minds. It was the Apollo program for our generation, or maybe the Manhattan Project was a better analogy. Because everyone wanted to do it, and every year it got faster and better. I could feel it, the chance, the generational luck of being born alongside a new artistic form, the way Orson Welles was born at the right time to make *Citizen Kane* and define the greatness of a medium. It was a chance to own the artistic revolution of our time the way Jane Austen owned hers and D. W. Griffith owned his.

When I ran a game, the splash screen would give the name of the hacker who cracked it, names like Mr. Xerox, the Time Lord, Mr. Krac-Man. Who were these people who cracked games? Who made them, for that matter? How on earth did you get that job?

It was time to find out. It was time to say something. I had an audience of four or five people now. People had been shuffling in and out of the conference room all day, to listen or ask a few questions. All men, though, until Lisa, the third founder of Black Arts, came in. She looked as I remembered — pale, with a big forehead that made her look like a cartoon alien. She'd ditched the flowery dresses for a tentlike oversized black T-shirt. I remembered her from high school, from car rides home at two or three in the morning. In winter she drove with the window rolled down and the heat going full blast.

"The Ultimate Game," I said. "I can do just...anything?"

They nodded. I felt ridiculous. Was the Ultimate Game the one in which I ride a hundred-foot-tall pink rhino through the streets, driving my enemies before me? The one where the chess pieces come alive and talk in a strange poetry? Is it just the game where I always win?

"Relax, guy," the short guy said. "It's just whatever you're into. Your game."

It was hard to say what was so particularly odd about the two of them. Maybe it was that even though everything about them screamed "loser," they didn't seem to care. In fact, they carried themselves like kings in T-shirts.

"So...okay, okay. You're playing chess, right, but all the pieces are actual monsters, and when you take one you have to...actually fight... it?" Why were they looking at me that way?

"You mean like in *Archon*? For the C64?"

"Um. Right." Lisa scowled even a little more. A bearded guy at the back rolled his eyes, as if in disbelief at what a loser I was; he was wearing a jester's hat. It had come to this.

I'd wanted to say, but couldn't, that what I really meant was the way it felt getting out of the car on that chill September morning, first day at Dartmouth, first day when I had a chance to be a new person and get it right this time after the hell of high school. How badly I wanted that moment back. Simon and Darren had chosen to be, well, awesome, and I hadn't, I'd been a good little soldier and tried to be an adult, and up until today I'd forgotten that woman and the PET computer and what it felt like to be offered the future.

Before I left I had to stop off and see Don, the company's fourth founder and current CEO. Unlike the other employees, he had an actual office, a side room with a picture window looking out on the dark expanse of the work area.

"Good to see you again." He shook my hand firmly, a grown-up hello. "KidBits, right? How've you been?"

He was even taller than I remembered. He'd grown a beard, which suited him.

"Good, good. Is Darren around?" I asked.

"Still in Nepal. He's the same guy he was. So you really want to work here?" he asked. This was the moment I'd rehearsed more than any other, actually done it in the mirror. Eyes averted, I slid into the faux-casual delivery.

"I kind of do, Don. Law's getting a little boring — I'm on to the next thing, you know?"

"Design? Programming? Assistant producer?"

"Design, I guess. Or producing. I'm not sure. My programming's as shitty now as it ever was."

"Did Jared ask you the ultimate game question?"

"Yup. It was a good question."

"It is, isn't it? I guess we'll call you."

"Thanks, man." We shook hands again.

On the way out Lisa brushed past me, apparently on her way back from the snack machine. "Nice one," she said. "Archon." They didn't have things like Asperger's in the eighties; probably they'd have given her something for it.

"Thanks," I answered. "See you later."

I wanted to linger and get more of a look at the games, but there was no pretext for it, so I let myself out into the chilly evening. Outside, I kept on thinking about the game, the game this would be if my life were a game. The lamest computer game of all time.

"You are standing in a half—empty parking lot beside an

office building in suburban Massachusetts. The interview is over, and the sun is setting. What do you do next?"

LOOK

"You can see cars turning on their headlights as they crest the hill of Route Two and start the slow plunge toward Cambridge, then stack up through the Alewife traffic circle. It's getting cold. You have nowhere to be."

INVENTORY

"A worn leather wallet.

"Directions to the office, written on the back of a flier for an open-mike poetry reading.

"A navy blazer. You were incredibly overdressed this whole time."

WEST

"You walk along the bike path. You pass behind seafood restaurant. Most of the land around the parking structure was never developed. Lilac, small oaks, and tall grasses grow out of control here. Where exactly do you think you're going?"

WEST

"You can barely hear the highway behind you, and soon it fades out altogether. You can still see the sun through the branches overhead.

"Oddly enough, you find railway tracks crossing the path. Since when was there a railway line here? It hasn't been used in a long time, but you follow it anyway. The walking keeps you warm. Oak seedlings are growing up from in between the ties. In some places you can barely find the rails among the dirt and leaves.

"Sooner or later you'll round a bend and find Mass Ave. and catch a bus back into Cambridge and that will be that. No idea. Why, you think, did you have to play this character anyway?"

WEST

WEST

WEST

"God, you'd walk forever if you thought it would get you out of here. The tracks take you uphill, and then you see, through a line of trees, a swing set. It's the back of an elementary school.

"And that's when the memory hits you, the thing that's been bugging you the whole time. It's been years since you thought of it, but it comes back all the way, breathed in like the burnt-carpet smell of the car Darren used to drive you around in."

Chapter Two

The five of us as we were then. Darren, a hyperkinetic burnout. Lisa, dark, inward, wry. Don watching everybody else in the room. Simon, pale, distracted, intense in a place you couldn't reach. He was smart, really smart, math-in-his-head, perfect-scores-without-trying smart, the way I fantasized about being. I could be valedictorian of my class—and I was—but I would never come off that way, the way he did. He just didn't seem to care that much about it. He didn't even take Honors courses which made it doubly annoying.

We all were friends although not in the way where anyone wanted it said out loud. Our project was finished, at least the letter-grade part of it. Maybe we kept meeting out of habit, or not wanting to go back to our respective homes again. We'd go to pointless movies or on Friday night expeditions into Cambridge or to a stupid street fair or bowling. We were too young to get into a bar or a proper rock show or anything else remotely cool.

Sophomore year, definitely, early spring. Darren held an ice cube to his ear and the rest of us waited around in his garage. It was an extremely ordinary evening, and we were wasting it in an ordinary way.

"Can you feel anything?" Simon asked.

"I don't know. I don't even know if I can. Let's just do it." Darren's voice trembled just a little.

"Okay."

Simon lit a match and ran it up and down the needle. "Where does it go?" he asked.

"Just in, like, a normal place. Do it already."

"Okay, okay." Simon fidgeted. His hand was shaking. "Just turn your head toward me. Hold still."

He bent close; their heads were close. A convulsive moment, and Darren cried out. "Shit!!"

"Jesus, you moved."

"It fucking hurt! I'm going to do just one more minute." He put the ice back on. Water dripped a little pink onto his Rush T-shirt. "Just do it right this time."

"Don't move."

"It's going to wear off!" Darren said.

Simon pushed, hard. There was a very slight popping sound.

"It's through!" he said. Darren started to reach up and Simon grabbed his hand. "Don't touch it it's through it's through. Don't touch it."

"Okay. Okay. Okay." Darren shook his head. "Let me look." He looked in the mirror and nodded. He'd gotten a beer from somewhere and sipped it, holding the cloth to his ear.

Darren's parents' room was above the garage and they always kicked us out around ten, and we needed to get out before they asked what was wrong with the side of his head. So we drove around for a while, but we didn't even have a plan, so as usual we ended up at Hancock Elementary. It was still cold, but Simon spat on his hands and climbed one of the swing set's metal legs all the way to the top, cold rusty steel burning against the palms of his hands. He hung there a few seconds, then dropped heavily into the sand, having made his point.

We climbed a low brick wall, then hoisted ourselves onto the school's flat tar-paper roof.

"Why are we doing this?" Lisa asked.

"Life experience," said Darren. "Shh!"

A car passed down the road at the far end of the field, and we all lay down until it was gone before climbing down.

"Jesus this is boring," Lisa said.

"So what do you want to do?"

"I don't know. Something...God, something that doesn't suck."

Go to college? I don't know what I would have said. We looked out across the back parking lot to the chain-link fence and the woods beyond. I remembered how in the fall we'd ordered a Japanese ninja star from a mail-order house that advertised in the back of an issue of *Alpha Flight*. It came in a padded envelope, wrapped in plastic and stiffened with cardboard, return address a sporting-goods store in Alabama, five dollars and ninety-eight cents plus three fifty shipping. It was a shiny metal disk incongruously inlaid with a flower pattern looping around the central hole. There was a booklet showing, in sequential black-and-white photographs that seemed to date from the 1960s, how to hold it by one of its arms and hurl it with a sidearm motion. Which when Simon tried it sent it first into the grass, and then curving up over the chain-link fence and into the woods. We kicked through damp leaves looking for it until it was almost dark. It must still be there, I thought.

I honestly don't know who brought up the issue of the ultimate game. It was just one of those topics, like whether the plot of *The Terminator* makes sense, or if magic can ever be real, or if it would be better to have a robot girlfriend or a real one.

But at some point we got around to the question of what would be the most amazing video game you could possibly make. It had a bunch of different names — Real *D&D,* the Dueling Machine, the Matrix. The word *holodeck* hadn't been invented yet, not until *Star Trek: The Next Generation* happened four years later.

Darren jumped on the question. It would have to be in 3-D. No, maybe it would all be holograms, like they had in the chess game in *Star Wars,* or Larry Niven's novel *Dream Park,* or maybe something weirder, like *Neuromancer,* wired into your skull.

"You'd do things just by doing them!" Darren said. Simon nodded vehemently, sharing the same dimly imagined picture. An electronic world springing up around us, a neon Eden.

"And you could do anything you wanted," Don added. "You wouldn't just follow a track. If you wanted to go on adventures you could, but you could stay home, or talk on the phone, or get a job if you wanted."

"Why couldn't there be a game where…" I began, and everyone started in. It was always the question — why couldn't there be a game where you could solve problems as you would in the real world? Cut the ropes holding a bridge up, or start a forest fire if you needed to, or make friends with a monster instead of fighting it, or go out into the forest and catch a horse and tame it, and then you could ride around? Why couldn't there be a game where you could go exploring or go into a town or be evil instead of good, or kill the king and take his place?

The conversation was edged with frustration. If only the hardware would get faster, or interfaces would get better, or graphics, or if only time itself would just go faster so they could get to the future already. At the time, even *Wolfenstein 3D,* our earliest crudest harbinger of real-time 3-D gaming, was nine years away.

But, Simon argued, forget about the technology challenges, the full-body interface, the 3-D display, all the inexhaustible problems of graphic detail, counterfeiting the bottomless complexity of human facial expressions, interpreting natural human speech beyond the subject-verb pidgin used in traditional text adventures. Let those problems be solved or not. It doesn't matter. There was still and always would be the problem of storytelling. You — you in the game — *should* wake up in a world with total choice. Go searching for a legendary jewel, stay home and make paper dolls, or run out into the street and punch a stranger in the nose. Somehow the computer copes. In a normal game, a real game, you couldn't do it. The world is a narrative channel, a single story that you can follow but never escape. Or maybe there's an open world, but only a specific range of actions you can perform—you can punch strangers in the nose but you can't talk to them; you can't make a friend or fall in love. Or you can talk to strangers but they can only say a few things—they're not really people, just shallow repositories of canned speech. At some point, sooner or later but usually very, very soon, the world just runs out of stories it can tell. And every time you run into that point, there's a jarring, illusion-breaking bump that tells you it's just a game.

What is the thing we need?

There's a story, but you choose what it is and make it yourself, and the world is full of tools for doing that. You can follow the path into the forest if you want, or you can turn around, go home, and cut the king's head off because you decided you always hated the old bastard and you're sick of this story and want to be someone else for a change. Cut the forest down, use the wood to build the highest possible tower, and reach the sun. Build a dam and try to flood the kingdom and kill everybody, then let the water out and collect all the treasure. Maybe that's not a great story, but it's yours. What was wanted was the storytelling engine that kept building the world as you made your choices, and made sure that it felt like a story. That when you picked up the phone and dialed that number, you reached a widow in distress or a private detective agency that was hiring. Or if you walked outside and broke a branch off a tree and tied a string to it and walked until you got to a lake, the third fish you caught would have in its stomach a ring engraved with strange writing.

And all the time, you'd be rapt, absorbed in the story in the gently paradoxical, bootstrapped state of semibelief that video games can create, where you're enough outside yourself to be someone else and enough in yourself to be living the story as if it were real life. It might be a naive way to think about computer games, but it doesn't make the need for it any less real. And it was impossible to make, but they'd already started and impossible was no reason not to go on a bit further. *Realms 1.0* was just the beginning: they would build and build into *2.0* and *20.0,* into cities and kingdoms and systems within systems and interfaces within interfaces and princesses and starships and submarines and grassy fields and volcanoes and floating cities and laughing gods and blackest hells and on and on, because you were never satisfied, ever, and you didn't have to be because there would always be something else there over the next hill, beyond the turning in the road, down the dark hallway and into the next room, and somewhere in there you'll escape at last, escape yourself and forget and forget and forget and live in a story forever.

We drove around town until it was past midnight. It was then that I first clearly remember Darren declaring, "We have to do this." This was our rebellion. We could walk out on reality itself and the raw deal it gives even the luckiest of us. Fucking leave it and go on an adventure. In the dark of the station wagon I couldn't see faces but I felt sure everyone had the same thoughtful expression. Everyone knew and nobody had to say it. How Simon's mother was kinda crazy and poor, and Lisa's parents were rich but had no interest in her whatsoever, and Darren was terminally pissed off at the world, and how I — well, no one ever seemed to be able to put a finger on it, but I was never going to be as happy as I was supposed to be. Everyone had a reason to want out.

People with any sense of the dramatic would have shared a drink or said a vow, cut their palms and made a blood pact. Spoken or not, it's the only vow I ever made, or ever would, the only true moment of lunatic ambition. But it didn't seem to matter — who needed to share blood when we'd shared the exact same thought from the moment we saw what a Commodore PET could do?

Like the Lumière brothers seeing the flickering image of a locomotive pulling into a railroad station and sensing the enormity of the moment, we recognized that this miracle illusion would be currency of the imagination of the next hundred years or more.

And so, two weeks after the interview, I rented an apartment and dragged my futon, computer, and a box of books left over from college back to Massachusetts. I was an entry-level game designer, whatever that was, earning thirty-five thousand dollars a year. I guess in the end they couldn't not give it to me.

I thought about mailing the Dartmouth alumni magazine, but I'd told them about law school, and before that about the Fingerlings Improv troupe, and before that about an internship in L.A. at a talent agency. I didn't even tell anyone I was going for an interview as a video game designer. I didn't want to see the blank looks.

What had been a long, uncalculated slide into the fourth or fifth tier of academic standing finally flipped over into outright free fall. Who gets expelled from anything? Salvador Dalí. Buckminster Fuller. Woody Allen. Robert Frost. But they'd done it with considerably more style. And I wasn't properly expelled, only put on a mandatory leave of absence. I'd simply sat there and watched it all float away. It was stupid that my parents had paid for it, for the lawyer they thought I was supposed to be — that I'd "told" them I would be.

This was me giving up on any sort of casual panache, any pretense that I'd be one of the up-and-coming best and brightest I'd been emulating less and less successfully since — when? Changing majors for the third time? Earlier?

Who knew? But this was the moment I publicly stopped pretending to be cool. Rhodes, no Marshall. There would be no *Sex and the City* bar-hopping, no making partner, no Central Park view. I scrubbed the uneven floor of my new apartment, the odd snaggletoothed nail shredding the wadded-up paper towel, letting the dream dissolve.

No one had cleaned the apartment in what seemed like a decade. I bought four rolls of paper towels and a spray bottle of dangerous-smelling cleaner. I sat on the floor and sprayed along the baseboard and onto the yellow-and-white linoleum. I kept spraying until it soaked into the caked-on dust and hair and brown whatever it was and turned it darker and soft. The wadded-up paper towels turned into a soft, soggy pile. I found a paintbrush caked with grime, shards of glass, peanut shells. Halfway through I realized I should have bought rubber gloves, that I was probably poisoning myself, but there was no point in stopping. Around midnight I'd wiped down the floor and all the fixtures; it didn't look clean but it looked like if you started now it would be a normal enough cleaning job. I tried to count how many apartments I'd been through since college, but there had been too many three-week sublets to keep track of. One more, anyway.

The mystery wasn't how my life had failed to come together — why I didn't stick with things, why days and weeks seemed to vanish under the sofa, why I was always telling my six-month friends I'd found an internship or entry-level job at a newspaper or theater or paralegal firm and I was moving to San Francisco or Austin — the mystery was how it was any different for anyone else, how other people managed to stay in one place and stick it out.

I e-mailed my parents with my new address, the same as always — when I visited at home I'd see my name in my mother's address book over a long column of crossed-out addresses and phone numbers. They sent presents — books and shirts — and birthday cards that said things like, "We're so proud of your new internship," and "Here's to great things this year!" Here's to training myself to pick locks. Here's to learning to speak with a British accent from a set of four CDs I found in a used bookstore. Here's to friendship. Here's to failure. Here's to the Quest for the Ultimate Game.

Chapter Three

Nobody gave me a schedule; it was more like a standing invitation to come over and hang out. The Monday after I moved in I tried going to work, and came in at nine in the morning. I sat on a beanbag chair just inside the door until a tall, fiftyish woman with short blond hair stopped by and introduced herself as Helen, the office manager. She took my picture with a digital camera and moved on. I read an old role-playing game manual, long lists of possible mutations you could choose. I decided that in the blighted future to come, it would be cool to have insect wings, and made a note to start saving up radiation points now.

After a while Matt noticed I was there and rescued me. He looked about fifteen, and must have been older than that but was still plausibly younger than the *Realms of Gold* franchise itself. On second viewing he was still disconcertingly large; his face seemed to widen from the top downward, like that of an Easter Island statue. He was an assistant producer, it turned out, a catchall workhorse position.

Black Arts was mostly the one big room, so we walked the perimeter, passing the wall of trophies and plaques: Game of the Year 1992, Game of the Year 1994. There was an early company photo, with Simon glowering at the extreme left, only three years from death. A poster showed the Milky Way galaxy with four enormous faces looking down on it, along with the words: *Solar Empires III: Pan-Stellar Activation*.

"Mostly people are on break from shipping *Solar Empires,* that's why nobody's here." He stopped at a U-shaped formation of maybe a dozen desks. It was mostly empty. "This is the design pit, where you'll be."

The short guy from my job interview was at a desk, playing a version of *Doom* modified to have Flintstones characters instead of space marines. He was wearing a top hat.

"Hey," he said without looking up. "I'm Jared."

"We met," I said.

"I guess Russell's going to be working on the new thing," Matt explained.

"Wait; what's the new thing?" I asked.

"It's still secret," Matt said. "Darren will tell us when he's ready."

"It had better not be space. I'm so fucking sick of space." The voice came from the other side of the divider, an older man, bald, who wore a leather vest over a dark blue button-down shirt, like a Radio Shack manager who moonlighted as a forest brigand. I'd noticed him as we passed because his monitor showed a 3-D image of a brick wall, and he'd been sitting there pushing the camera a quarter inch to the left, then a quarter inch to the right, over and over, watching for some infinitesimal change.

"The market wants sci-fi, Toby," Jared said.

"I'm so fucking sick of drawing planets." He slumped in his chair and went back to tapping the arrow keys.

"Here's where you'll be sitting," Matt said. "We've got your work machine set up."

I'd had only one computer since freshman year, a Compaq Presario with a 486 CPU and a thirteen-inch monitor that at the time had looked like the last computer that ever needed to be made. The off-white slab felt expensive and contemporary and powerful. But over the next four years the white casing acquired smudges and Rage Against the Machine stickers; it sagged and slowed under the load of next year's

word-processing software and the cumulative weight of cat hair clogging the cooling vents and being shoved under too many cheap desks in
too many low-rent apartments, only to be yanked out three months
later. I hated that machine.

Matt explained that the computer in front of me had a 200 MHz
Pentium MMX processor, 32 MB of RAM, a 2 GB hard drive, a 12x
CD-ROM drive, a fifteen-inch monitor, external speakers, and sub-
woofers. It was built for the overspecced world of 3-D gaming, and
viewed all lesser tasks with an appropriate contempt.

Matt showed me a file called RoGVIed.exe, and suggested I "play
around with it." I shrugged and said, "Sure." When he was gone, I
clicked on it.

For a few seconds there was nothing, then a torrent of text scrolled
by, too fast to follow. Then the screen blanked, then showed only the
Black Arts logo for about a minute. Just when I thought the computer
had frozen on me, the screen changed to a startlingly complex collection of buttons, widgets, icons, and maps. It was like a mad, complicated puzzle box, but I knew I'd found something—one of their
treasures.

I was feeling a little terrified, but also thrilled—however tentatively,
I'd pulled back the curtain on this dorky reality. I knew this must be
the game editor, the designer's basic tool, the thing that lets you do
everything a designer does—build the geometry of the levels, place
monsters and people and objects in it, put in any traps and surprises
and, generally speaking, create a world in which you can menace and
persecute anyone fool enough to enter. Here were the nuts and bolts of
the world.

Only . . . I'd expected it to be a high-tech piece of wizardry—a 3-D
display, rotating cubes and graphs and blue-green numbers. This—this
thing looked like crap. No one had ever spent time making the editor
pleasant to work with, and in fact its ergonomics were almost abusively

wrong. The screen was divided into four quadrants, with no indication of where to begin or what they represented. Each had functions accessed through dozens of unreadably tiny icons, many of them virtually identical but for a pixel here and there, most of which had only the vaguest relationship to their functions. It must have been intuitively obvious to somebody, but I was lost. What was the question mark for, and why would I click on it? What was the snake for? The semicircle? The tiny automobile? And why didn't anybody write any of this down?

No one was paying attention to me, and I slowly realized that this was their equivalent of job training—leaving me alone with a computer and a game editor just to see what I'd do. Like dropping a delicate tropical fish into a new aquarium—they'd come back in a few hours and I'd either be swimming around or floating at the top of the tank.

I poked at a few icons experimentally, but nothing seemed to happen. People were throwing me glances every once in a while; I saw Don peering out of his office at me. It came to me, gradually, that I was undergoing a test, a deliberate one. Not for technical literacy, because there was no way I could have learned this ahead of time. It wasn't supposed to make sense. It was a test of character—could I sit with this patchy, buggy, undocumented piece of software and learn it by trial and error and not freak out, not be reduced to tears or incoherent rage? They wanted to know how much frustration I could stand.

The truth was, though, that for the first time in a very long time I was being given a test that made sense to me. I clicked, a section of map highlighted. I clicked somewhere else, I noted the result. I didn't worry about making a mistake. The editor was designed with a perversity that shaded over into cruelty, but I sensed that once I learned its rules, I could live with it.

I learned by trial and error. I figured out how to raise and lower pieces of floor, to place blocks and monsters, how to apply colors to the terrain and objects. I learned that trying to save over a file with the same name crashed it to the DOS prompt.

The screen froze, and somebody walking past said, "Did you right-click in the 3-D window? You can't do that." I learned that clicking Save As while you had a piece of terrain selected meant you had to reboot. I learned that nobody ever clicked on the button labeled SMART MODE. Nobody knew what it did.

There was another test. At first I thought there was no manual whatsoever for how to use the editor, until I realized that the manual was the people in the room with me. You learned when it was okay to ask — you waited for a coder to launch a long compile or export, as signaled by a trip to the candy machine. You learned to distinguish the "I'm taking a break" stare (usually accompanied by a sigh or chair spin) from the "I'm thinking really hard" stare (straight ahead, or angled roughly fifteen degrees upward) and the "I'm really screwed up and angry" posture — elbows on desk, hands gripping head.

And you learned whom to ask. Todd was the nearest UI/tools guy but he was perennially cranky, so talk to Allison if she was around, or catch him when he's just coming back from lunch, and always phrase the question so it sounds like you screwed up and are just looking to be rescued, not like there's something actually wrong with the editor.

It must have been around two in the afternoon when I started to relax. Bug fixes were for the customers, the soft, lazy civilians who only got the software after it was finished and boring and safe. Real game developers worked with real software, the kind that broke a third of the time unless you knew exactly what you were doing. The next time I went to the kitchen for a bag of Skittles, I did so with just a hint of world-weary swagger. Of course the editor crashed all the time. Why on earth wouldn't it?

College was one long series of missed cues and indecipherable codes for me. Other people followed invisible markers to their appropriate clubs and majors and activities. Other people seemed to know which dorms meant what, which parties to go to, and what to do there. The knowledge was all there for me to pick up, but other people had some faculty of observation, patience, and fluency that let that knowledge adhere to them.

Whatever long-latent cognitive ability was involved, it had perversely decided to activate for me here in the land of the geeks. It was my brain stem's way of letting me know I was basically home.

Don instant-messaged me on the third day, well into the afternoon, as if only just remembering I'd been hired. The company had its own internal chat network, shitty and home-cooked, just like the editor. Everything you read was in yellow letters on a bright blue background, and there was no way to change it.

DON: Hey it's Don. How are you doing so far?
ME: Fine, good. Playing with the editor.

I'd gotten to the point where I could change terrain a little, save and load files, and make primitive shapes and not crash the editor too often, but that was it.

DON: Turns out we need you up to speed for early next week, level geometry, objects, scripting and all that—sound cool?
ME: Okay...
DON: Anyway, ping Lisa and she'll give you any help.
ME: Okay. Hey, what's the next game going to be?
DON: That would be telling.

He rang off. I looked at the personnel web page in the vain hope there would be another, different Lisa there. There were about a hundred people listed, most with a first-day photograph showing a stressed-out grin. Lisa was listed as a tools programmer on the *Solar Empires* team. She had somehow avoided having her picture taken.

Just as I'd gotten my bearings I was being pushed into another, subtler test—I'd gotten myself this far, but I now had to open an unsolicited online chat with this senior employee who had never liked me anyway, to tell her I'd be ruining her afternoon schedule so she could explain to the new guy what everyone else in the building already knew.

I took a few moments to breathe, then reopened the chat program. It's not that I disliked the people who'd known me in high school, exactly. But I didn't feel like explaining what I was doing there. Or why I hadn't talked to them in years. And most of all I didn't feel like seeing them. I'd gotten rid of the person I was in high school. I didn't want to see the people who'd known me that way.

ME: Hi. This is Russell Marsh.

I got to watch the cursor blink for about ten seconds before the reply came.

LMcknhpt: Hi.
ME: So I got hired and so I work here now.
LMcknhpt: So I know.
ME: Don said to ask you to demo some editor features for me?
    Sorry to bother you, I need to get up to speed quick.

Another twenty seconds ticked by, unreadable. Was she distracted? Or, more likely, was she opening another chat window to yell at Don? Or was she just marking time to indicate how annoying she found this?

LMcknhpt: Okay. Come by @ 5 and we'll work it out.
ME: Thanks. I really appreciate this.

LMcknhpt: You're a designer now?

ME: Yes.

LMcknhpt: See you then.

I wondered why she was even still here at Black Arts. I remembered the no-girls-allowed clubhouse feel of the arcades; it must have been hard work to find a place here.

Then again, I thought, everybody has a reason.

Chapter Four

Lisa Muckenhaupt's cubicle was socketed in at the far back corner of the *Solar Empires* sector of the office. *Realms of Gold* is only one of Black Arts' three franchises. It has a science fiction and an espionage series as well, each set in its own separate universe. As I passed an invisible line in the cubicle ward, the decor shifted from foam broadswords and heraldry and other faux-medieval tchotchkes to a farrago of space-opera apparatus. A LEGO Star Destroyer was strung from the ceiling, along with an enormous rickety mobile of the solar system, its planets as big as softballs. I saw ballistic Nerf equipment and a six-foot-long, elaborately scoped and flanged laser rifle.

The decor was something other than simply childish. It was more like a deliberate, even defiant choice for a pulp aesthetic, holding out for the awesome, the middle-school sublime of planets and space stations, the electrical charge of nonironic pop, melodrama on a grand scale.

Lisa herself was the person I remembered, tiny and now in her late twenties. Lost in what seemed like an XXXL Iron Maiden T-shirt. She was vampire-pale, jet black hair pulled back in a ponytail from a broad, pimply white forehead. Her face narrowed downward, past a snub nose (her one conventionally pretty feature) to a narrow mouth and chin.

"Hi."

"Hi," she said. There was to be no handshake, and I didn't know where to look. Her cubicle was unadorned, except for a pink My Little

Pony figurine to the right of her monitor. Ironic whimsy? Childish? Dangerously unbalanced?

"How've you been?" I asked.

"Fine. My dad died. If that's the kind of thing you're asking about."

"Oh. Sorry."

"It was a while ago," she said. I'd forgotten the curious way she talked, a thick-tongued stumbling rhythm, in a hurry to get the meaning out. It suggested some cognitive deficit somewhere, but one that she'd been richly compensated for elsewhere in her makeup, a dark Faustian logic to her developmental balance sheet.

"Can I ask you a question?" she said suddenly.

"Sure."

"Why exactly are you working here?"

"I needed a job."

"There are a lot of jobs."

"You know, I don't actually have to explain this you."

"Uh-huh. Well, I don't have to explain how the editor works, either."

"You remember the 'Ultimate Game' thing, right? That conversation?"

She sighed. "Yeah. I remember. I haven't thought about that for years. That was a weird time for me."

"Do you think it's — well, I just kept thinking about it. How I was trying to memorize contract law and you guys were off having fun. How stupid is that, right?" I gave a gusty attempt at a laugh. Saying it out loud, especially to a real programmer, it sounded even more childish than I expected. I remembered how Simon had made it seem like a near-mystical quest; Darren made it seem like the chance of a lifetime.

"It was a fun idea. But until it comes along, this is the latest build of WAFFLE, set to *Realms* mode. Did you end up taking any more programming?" she asked. As she talked she shut down what she was doing—I glimpsed spaceships drifting between planets, in orbit around a double star.

* * *

"Two semesters of C," I told her. But we both knew I was no Simon. I could see her features harden a little. She'd have the extra work of gearing all the explanations to a nontechie.

"All right. We won't do scripting language for now. I'll just load a level," she said. She ran the editor—her setup had an extra monitor with a monochrome display—and as the editor ran it showed a long series of status messages.

The editor screen appeared, split in four parts. She piloted the camera around, zooming over chasms and through walls. We passed a group of goblins standing motionless, each with a swarm of tiny green numbers hovering over its head. Time had stopped, or, rather, had not yet been turned on. There were extra objects visible in the world—boxes, spheres, cartoon bells, and lightbulbs—hidden lines of influence, pathfinding routes, traps, and dangers. I was seeing the world as game developers saw it.

"You got through changing terrain, right? Placing objects?"

I nodded. I hadn't, quite, but I'd decided already to stop admitting things like that, to just add them to the list of things I'd figure out later. I had to just keep assuming I was smart enough for this job.

"That's the 2-D texture library, object library, terrain presets, lighting…" She toggled through a series of windows full of tiny icons that looked like candies on a tray.

"There's really no manual for any of this?" I asked.

"I never have time, and the spec is always changing anyway." Did she write all this?

"This is the creature library. Just select one, then click on the 2-D map to place it. Shift-click to bring up its behaviors. Scripting, conversation, patrol routes, starting attitude." She clicked, and clicked again faster than I could follow. A tiny dragon appeared, frozen in the 3-D window; a corresponding dot appeared in the map window.

"So is that…" I started.

"It's a bad guy. Okay so far?"

"Sure," I lied.

"So viewing options now. You can cycle through the four versions of the world." She backed the viewpoint up into the sky, then whip-panned to focus on a small fort in the middle of a forest, a single round tower, and tapped the space bar.

"Wireframe." The screen instantly darkened to a black void where the tower stood, now revealed as an octagonal tube drawn in precise, glowing straight lines, triangular and trapezoidal facets in a night-black void. "Like in *Battlezone*. Back when you were gaming, probably the first 3-D game you saw."

She tapped again. "Unshaded polygons." The glowing lattice kept its shape but became an opaque crystal formation, sides now solid, a world of pastel-colored jewels that shone in a hard vacuum. Atmospheric haze is a high-tech extra.

Another tap of the space bar and the blank jewel facets filled with drawn-in detail. The tower walls were now painted to look like stone-work, expertly shaded to indicate bumps and ridges.

"Textured polygon. Like a trompe l'oeil painting, if you took that in college. Whatever you did in college."

"English."

"Wow," she said, toneless. "I'm going to zoom in a little — when we get closer it swaps in a high-res texture to give it more detail," she said. As the camera moved in the stones of the tower blossomed with moss, cracks, crumbling mortar.

"Beautiful," I said.

"Smoke and mirrors. It looks real but there's a million little tricks hold-ing it together," she said. I couldn't tell from her tone whether she was proud of the illusion of reality or contemptuous of the cheap theatrics. "Okay, now last year's big hack — textured polygons, but with lighting."

A final tap of the space bar and the tower was brushed with shades of darkness that gave it definition and, somehow, the impression of weight. The light came from just above the horizon, a sunset, and the hills beyond the tower faded away into dimness.

"Didn't it just get darker?"

"Lighting isn't about making it brighter, it's figuring out where the shadows do and don't fall. It's easy to just light everything—you're just not checking for darkness. What's tricky is looking where the light source is and when it's blocked."

In the upper right corner of the screen, I noticed the letters FPS, followed by a flickering number. It bounced around between thirty and forty, with occasional jumps into the sixties. When Lisa added the lighting effects, the number tumbled into a single digit and turned red, and the view seemed to stutter instead of panning smoothly.

"What's FPS?" I asked.

"Frames per second," she said after a moment. "How many times the view updates every second. When it gets below thirty, everything starts to look jerky."

"Like it's doing now?" I asked.

"Yeah. It's having to draw too many lit polygons. It has to do other stuff, like update positions of objects and play sounds and do AI calculations and all that stuff, too, but graphics are always the big drain. It's all about getting those polys up on-screen to make everything detailed and pretty. The more polys you draw the better it looks, but then the frame rate slows down. Fewer polys, higher frame rate."

"So who's putting all those polygons up there?" I said, intuiting the answer.

"You are. You're a designer, you build the world they have to draw every second. So you know when you're in a meeting and there's a guy who's just looking at you with this twitchy, barely controlled hatred every time you open your mouth? That's a graphics programmer. Every bright idea you have is putting more polygons on-screen and making his job harder. Every time that number on the screen goes below thirty, everyone can see that his code is slow and therefore he is not smart."

"Good to know."

"That guy's entire job is to keep that frames-per-second number above thirty and green. Every time you put in too many trees, or make a room too large, or put five dragons in the same room, it's going to turn red."

"Then if I'm a game designer, what's my whole job?"

"I don't really play games, so I don't know," she said. "From what I gather, it's to keep adding stuff to the world until that number gets to exactly thirty-one."

"I thought it was to make the game fun."

"I don't know what that means, though," she said. She was watching me carefully as she spoke. As if maybe she was hoping I knew a secret everyone else had forgotten.

Chapter Five

I sat down at my desk and tried to remember everything Lisa did. Now that I knew about frames per second, I could see the number drop every time I made a room bigger or more complicated, the point of view lurching like a stick-shift car with a novice driver. That's why everything felt claustrophobic, because every cubic foot of space meant more polygons. That's why the player was stuck in underground corridors all the time — it was just the easiest thing to draw.

I browsed around the network directories, looking for something to do, snooping at folders. There was an Art/Assets server with gigabytes of images and 3-D models, thousands of them, and a little viewer that would show the model on the screen by itself, hanging in a starry void. I chose a file at random and opened it: a bird-headed knight on horseback. The next, a black London taxi. The third, a silver-metal rifle with its circuitry burned out. I wondered who the bird's-head knight was. The files went on and on, thousands of them, as if a whole library full of weird stories had been shaken and these were the random objects that fell out. A wooden cross; a china teapot; a sarcophagus. I'd stumbled into the great storehouse of their toy multiverse.

I clicked and a 10' by 10' by 10' cube appeared, lit as if by a candle flame. It was textured as the default plain stone wall. Click and click and you're digging out a corridor, rooms, cube by cube. Paint on textures, stone or wood or dirt or lava. You can build what you like, nothing weighs anything and it's all infinitely strong. You can build pillars of dirt, metal, lava, water. I built a few rooms and corridors, dropped in a few monster spawners, treasure, and the rest, then flipped into game mode to see what it felt like.

Back in the game, I could see how this could get frightening. It was one thing to see a map of the place. It was another to be fifty feet belowground, down there in the dark, in a world silent except for distant running water, and…footsteps. A figure emerged from the darkness at the end of the corridor. A walking skeleton, animated by who knew what necromantic fires, ambled toward me. I stepped to the left to let it pass, keeping my eyes on it. To conserve polygons, it was built like a paper doll, a picture of a skeleton mounted on a single plane that slid around the dungeon shuffling its feet, pretending to walk. I felt bad for it. It wanted so badly to look like it was in 3-D. Up close I could see how low-resolution it was, too, just a bunch of pixels in jagged lines, like the side of an Aztec pyramid, just a graphic pretending to be a skeleton.

As if angered by my pity, it stopped, turned to face me, and clicked into a new set of animations — it was hostile! Its mouth opened and closed soundlessly. It drew its sword and made a chopping motion. The screen flashed red. It hit me! Being a game designer didn't make me special or invulnerable.

I dove to the game manual to see how to defend myself, but it was too late: my health bar was falling away in chunks. The sword had a gold hilt and a fleck of red at its base — a thumb-size ruby mounted in the pommel. Was the skeleton rich once? Were these the bones of a king? No time to wonder; another flash and my in-game point of view fell over and dropped to the ground. I watched the skeleton's feet, seen from behind now, walk off into the darkness in bony triumph. Someday it would be a real boy. I noted in passing that the skeleton had stolen my sword and two gold pieces. Up close, I could see that the floor was a pattern of black and brown pixels.

"Uh, yeah, you wanted to turn on invulnerability there," Matt said, walking past.

I started again, this time working from empty space. I built a pillar, just a stack of blocks. And another pillar, then an arch connecting them, then a line of pillars. I built a second line next to it. I added more pillars, then a roof and a tower, until it became a cathedral, a cathedral to the undead god-emperor Russ'l the Dreadlord. I built a hundred traps to maul or ensnare or disintegrate passersby. Then I built the hell where Russ'l put those who defied him. Feeling a bit ashamed, I created an elaborate garden where Russ'l met petitioners seeking his blessing. I noticed it was four twenty-five in the morning, and I was crouched with my face inches from the monitor, my back oddly twisted and locked in place. I was in pain and needed the bathroom and I was happier than I could remember being for at least a year or two.

I walked home, newly unable to make sense of the world, or perhaps able for the first time to see through the trick of three-dimensional space. Three-dimensional space was not at all what I thought it was. It was just a sort of gimmick, nothing more than a set of algorithms for deciding what shapes you can and can't see and how big they look at a given distance, whether they're lit or in shadow, and how much detail shows. When you could write a computer program that did the same thing, it didn't seem so special. I walked in a new reality, the airless dark 3-D world of Massachusetts, and the ultimate game seemed just a twist of thought away. Maybe I was there already.

Chapter Six

I had only been at Black Arts a week when I saw the bug for the first time. I was trying to clone a level out of a forgotten RPG (*Into the Kobold Sanctum*) just to see if I could do it. It was an underground fortress improbably embedded in the base of a gigantic tree. You never saw the tree itself, just its roots as they wound in and out of the corridors and chambers. At the center was a hostage, your sister, and you were racing to free her. In reality she couldn't be killed, the suspense was fake, but players wouldn't know that.

I was in the rhythm of tweaking a few triggers, flipping into the game, playing through the level until something broke, and flipping back to tweak again. I passed a guardsman half-embedded in a cave wall, flipped to the editor and pumped him a few grid points, then restarted.

Immediately I heard the sound of combat down the hall. Was something off? I'd run this section a dozen times. I ran down the hall, this time passing only dead and dismembered guardsmen. The halls were silent. I reached the main hall, where a goblin king should have been sitting, a bound maiden at his feet. Instead, the hall was a sea of dead bodies. The king who couldn't be killed lay dead in front of his throne. Far at the back of the hall, I saw two figures fighting, and in a moment one was dead. The other was my sister, a black sword in her hand, and there was a moment when she turned, ready to go for me, and I felt an irrational panic, like very little I had felt before in a game. The eerie, substanceless mannequin approached, her black pixel eyes swelling to an inch wide on the screen, and all at once her death animation began. She arched her back and then threw herself violently to the stone floor. Like any dead creature in a game, she spawned her inventory, a few coins and the sword, which promptly disappeared. Before I could stop myself, I shut the computer off, all the way off, powered down.

I booted the computer back up and ran the editor. Both the king and the woman were flagged immortal. I ran the level again, three more times, with no trouble.

It was remarkable, terrifyingly remarkable, and deeply uncanny, the way a broken simulation always is; something about it suggested a brain having a stroke, an invisible crisis in the machinery. It had lunged up momentarily from the depths of the code base, a flash of white fin and gaping mouth seen for an instant, then gone again.

I was going to the kitchen to shake the whole thing off with a bag of Sour Patch Kids when Don's voice came over the paging system.

"Could I have everyone join me and Darren in the conference room for a second?"

"Holy shit," Matt said across the cubicle divider. "Darren's back. It's the new game."

We shuffled in. Don stood at the far end of a row of tired, puffy faces, bad haircuts, a long conference table populated with Diet Coke cans.

At least half of us were wearing iterations of the company T-shirt; I could see four or five versions of the Black Arts logo. Lisa leaned against a wall at the back, eyes closed. She wore the company T-shirt, too, in a tentlike XXL edition.

Don and Darren stood at the front. I hadn't seen Darren for at least six years; he'd started wearing a sport jacket over his T-shirt and ripped jeans, Steve Jobs–style, but otherwise he looked exactly the same — sandy blond hair, wiry build, and slightly messianic stare. I remembered being a little dazzled by him in an older-brother kind of way. It wasn't just me; he had that quality for nearly everybody—he had this taut magnetism. I avoided his gaze. I didn't think he ever liked me, even before I bailed on the game world.

"Thanks, everyone. Thanks. I only have a couple of things to cover," Don said. "Darren and I want to just get everybody oriented." For a manager, he didn't seem that comfortable as a speaker. He was used to Darren handling it.

"Number one, we shipped *Solar Empires III*. It's selling... pretty well so far, and CGW's cover story is going to come out next week, which should give it a boost, and a little bird told me we're a contender for the Best Strategy Game award from *Electronic Gaming*." There was some cheering—people were still buzzed with whatever they'd gone through. Lisa didn't bother clapping. Neither did Toby. He really did hate outer space now—planets, comets, gleaming battleships aloft on the solar wind like golden cities, the whole empty lot of it—but there was a much wider market for it than for fantasy.

"Second thing. Darren and I talked this week since he got back from Nepal, and we roughed out a couple of big decisions for the company.

"First off, we're entering into a partnership with Focus Capital, which should stabilize things a bit after last year's rough spot."

"What's the next game?" Jared called out.

"Right. The market for science fiction gaming is pretty good right now..." The room went a bit quieter. I saw Matt's knuckles actually whiten on the edge of the table. The romance of simulated space exploration had palled over three months of eighty-hour workweeks. "But we're going back to fantasy. We're going back to the *Realms*. Darren's working out the details, but it looks like we're back to the Third Age. Darren?"

Real cheering this time, and questions, everyone talking over each other, Dark Lorac, Endoria, conversation interfaces and hit location, something about the White City.

Darren stood up. It was the first time I'd heard him speak in years. I wondered if he knew I was there; I felt the urge to duck down. All of a sudden I felt ashamed at coming back, like I still wanted him to like me.

"Hi, guys," he started. He spoke quietly, and everyone shut up instantly. "So what's the Third Age about?"

He stopped and let the silence go on a little, the room completely still now; he had a knack for making eleven in the morning feel like a primal midnight. The lights dimmed a little — Matt was standing at the switch. Darren looked around the room at each of us. The screen behind him lit up, showing a series of screenshots from what I supposed were past Black Arts games: at first just a few characters and dots on a black screen, then a hypercomplex board game, fading forward to real images.

"The First Age is long gone, a fallen legend. The Second Age, a magical war that shattered the world. Now the Third Age. Four heroes battling for a thousand years, and for what? Simon's notes don't say. It's up to us," he said, and paused. Darren was good at this.

"I want you all to think about the Third Age, everything that happened there, the fall of Brennan's house, Dark Lorac. How does the Third Age end? I mean, how did it end for you? What did you find at the end of a thousand years of struggle in the dirt and the rain, and what did you do with it? Were you brave? Did you win or lose? What did it take out of you?"

On-screen, the capsule history had gone to 3-D, a view of a warrior fighting wolves alone in a snowstorm. I thought about it. What was Darren's story? What was Simon's? Was he brave? Did he get what he wanted?

"It's the end of the Third Age, people. You are going to slay gods." A burst of applause, which Darren let run for a few seconds, then continued on. He had more coming.

"The ads talk about the technology. We'll say it's the fastest, most realistic graphics yet. We're probably going to beat Carmack at id, we'll beat Epic for sure. But it's 1997, and games are about as realistic as they're going to get, right?

"Think again. Big news, we're throwing out all our old graphics tech, which means...a couple things. We're ditching the Ukrainians, for good"—a modest cheer at that—"and we're bringing in a fresh take on it. I've got a little surprise."

Toby perked up a little, and then I saw Lisa. Her expression had changed very little, but her normally pale face was red almost to the hairline. She was watching Darren with what some might call nervousness, but it was more like hunger.

"I've been talking to a new person for this," Darren said, and I saw Lisa's posture straighten, flexing like a cat waiting to be petted. "We're about to announce a partnership with NVIDIA, to be the flagship product for their next-gen graphics card. We're going to get direct access to the software guys as well as their hardware team."

I saw Lisa react. Her lips made the tiniest possible "no." Otherwise her features didn't change, they just went entirely slack, as if in shock. You would have to have known her a long time to catch the change. I thought I was the only one seeing it, until I saw Don's eyes on her. Darren worked the room, but Don watched it.

Darren showed us a series of new screenshots. A waterfall with sunlight shining through it, forming a rainbow. A garishly lit nightclub where a generously proportioned, lingerie-clad woman danced on a pedestal, lit by multicolored spotlights. A domed temple with arches and gleaming black marble floors. The images looked like they'd taken a supercomputer a hundred hours to draw; they looked incredible.

Darren ticked off the list of features. "Translucency, curved surfaces, colored lights. Everything from a gamer's wet dreams, all in real time. Bloom, specular highlights, insane poly counts, level of detail, all running at sixty frames a second, solid as a fucking rock. This is it, people."

* * *

We were, yet again, looking across the threshold to the next thing, another phase change. Everything new this year was already becoming old, sad, and pathetic. Darren understood this so well. We were going into the future and he was taking us with him. We were the smart kids again, rich in the currency of our peculiar nation, foresight.

"And...number three," Don said. "Scheduling." Darren gave a quick nod, then ducked out the door while Don took us back into the mundane. Lisa followed behind Darren.

"We're going to have about eighteen months for this one. We'll be reusing a lot of tech, but it's still going to be tight. Matt, could you —" Matt hopped up, and Don handed him a page of printout. He started sketching out a grid on the whiteboard on the wall.

Horizontally across the top, he wrote six items: PREPRODUCTION, ALPHA 1, ALPHA 2, ALPHA 3, BETA, and RTM.

At the right-hand edge, he wrote three words, arranged vertically: PROGRAMMING, DESIGN, and ART. These, I knew, were the three core disciplines of video game production. There was also production, which meant tracking the schedule, the budget, and doing a thousand other things, such as organizing translations for foreign publication, keeping in touch with publishers, and generally figuring out what on earth was going on at any given time. And then there was quality assurance, or playtesting, devoted to finding mistakes in other people's work. No one was ever very fond of QA.

Don explained the schedule carefully — we'd have eighteen months for this, which put sharp limits on how much new technology we could create. I got the feeling this made the programmers feel a little pissed off. Working from the sheet, Matt began adding deadlines for each of these in neat, spiky handwriting. As Don talked us through the dates, I gradually picked up on rough meanings of the other terms.

Preproduction: planning the product and scheduling the milestones. As it would in a prolonged dorm-room discussion, the phrase "wouldn't it be cool if" played a major part. Endless circular debates, pie-in-the-sky speculation. Lots of features that would be cut later for scheduling reasons.

Alpha phases 1, 2, and 3: building the game. This part was longer than the others put together, for obvious reasons. For most of this period, the game was going to be nonexistent or broken and decidedly unfun, and everyone would regret everything they said during preproduction.

Beta meant that the game, theoretically, was done except for all the many, many problems and mistakes and omissions.

RTM stood for "Release To Manufacturer," when the finished master disk would be sent off to the publisher (note: we did not have a publisher). The publisher would do its own testing, and either accept it or send it back to have the problems fixed.

Of course none of these phases or deadlines would happen cleanly; there would be slippage and temporary solutions that would be fixed later, or, more often, become permanent. There would be interdependencies, times when art or programming couldn't move forward because design hadn't said what it wanted yet; or design couldn't build its levels properly because art hadn't produced the models or programmers hadn't implemented the necessary features. It would be a dizzying creative collaboration that often took the form of a drawn-out, byzantine war of intrigue.

Preproduction started Monday. It was starting to sink in that this would be our lives for the next eighteen months. It was April then; it would be June when we started alpha 1 while my law school friends would be at graduation parties, the start of a lazy summer before moving on to New York or Palo Alto or New Haven, while I stayed behind in this made-up career. It would be June again when we got out of alpha 3, a year of my life gone, and it would be early October of next year when we reached RTM, and getting cold, and my life would be different in ways I couldn't imagine yet.

Chapter Seven

I took the bug to Matt.

"In *Realms VI*?" he said. "It's possible, I guess. But it's probably already DNF'ed."

"DNF?"

"Do Not Fix."

"Why wouldn't you fix a bug if you knew about it?"

Matt sighed. "Okay. So *Realms VI* has on the order of a million lines of code. It's not going to be perfect, but it has to be shipped. At some point the producer and the leads sit down and go through all the existing bugs and prioritize according to various totally subjective criteria. How often it happens. How bad it is — where the top end is, like, 'Game crashes, hard drive is erased, user catches fire,' and the low end is, 'Yeah, the text in that Options menu could be a more eye-catching shade of blue.' Fixability, i.e., how loudly and effectively are the people tasked with repairing it going to complain.

"So these bugs are assigned priority numbers, but there's a cutoff, and anything below that point is marked DNF, Do Not Fix, and officially closed. Ship it. So it's, like, bugs that almost never happen, or are tiny aesthetic problems, or only come up when you have this or that shitty off-brand video card — it's not our problem. Oh, and bugs that are part of a tricky section of code, so when you fix them you'd probably end up making new and worse bugs."

"Okay, but what if this bug was pretty weird and noticeable?"

"Well there's another category of bugs that don't get fixed, which is the ones that only ever happen once, and those are marked NR, No Repro."

"Wouldn't you fix it anyway, just in case?" I asked. Before answering, Matt gestured me to roll my chair a little closer.

"So I came up through playtest, so...here's how it looks from that perspective. The fate of many, many bugs runs as follows: a playtester spots it once or twice, logs it in the database with a tentative classification — art, programming, design, or unknown. The report includes instructions on how to find the bug and make it happen again, but some bugs don't happen reliably. Sometimes they come and go for whatever reason — there's a little mystery there. But it goes to the bug meeting, where the lead for that area assigns it to a team member, who may or may not have caused it. Doesn't matter.

"So now the team member has to fix the bug, and they're cranky because it's a brand-new bug and they haven't budgeted time for it and they're going to be late for something else. So first thing they do is run the game and see if it reproduces. If it doesn't happen on the first or second try, some guys will slap a No Repro on it, kick it back to playtest, and go on to their next bug."

"Do they think you're making it up?"

"You have no idea the contempt people hold toward playtest. You see the logic — everyone else's job is to get the list of active bugs to zero, except us, whose job is add bugs to the list. So people just kick bugs back all the time. And some of them are pretty hard to verify, and you've got to figure out that the bug happens only if the game tries to autosave while you're actively wielding a plus-three glass dagger and there are exactly four lizard men within three hexes. And then walk into a meeting and do it with — I'm not going to name names, but they're literally standing over you, staking their reputations on the idea that this bug absolutely cannot happen, that it is literally technologically impossible."

"So I guess you're not in play test anymore."

"Not for this one, no. I guess that's the grand prize."

There was nothing going on the rest of the day except other designers speculating about what more Darren had planned. I found a database showing records of bugs from previous projects, all closed and confirmed before shipping, but the records were there. I sorted for the ones that weren't active, strictly speaking, but neither had they been fixed. The DNFs.

I searched around a little in the No Repro pile. It turned out there was no one bug exactly like the one I'd seen, but a few that might have been similar: "King Aerion dead when should be unkillable, WTF"; "Level three, dragon already dead when I arrived"; "Goblin children massacred? Why???" None of them repeated, and they could have been part of the same underlying bug or three entirely separate bugs.

They could have been minor coincidences. I knew by now that a simulation-heavy game was unpredictable. A monster could wander too close to a torch and catch on fire; then it would go into its panic-run mode and anything else it bumped into might catch. Or a harmless goblin might nudge a rock, which then rolls and hits another creature just hard enough to inflict one hit point of damage, which then triggers a combat reaction, and next thing you know there's an unscheduled goblin riot. The blessing and curse of simulation-driven engines was that although you could design the system, the world ran by itself, and accidents happened.

They usually didn't, because the game didn't bother to simulate anything too far from the player in any detail — it would slow everything down too far. But maybe the game was having trouble deciding what not to simulate. Each one was marked No Repro, so maybe it just never happened again.

* * *

I noticed that most of these bugs belonged to the same person, LMcknhpt. I sent Lisa a quick e-mail with the subject line "RoGVI bugs 2917, 40389, 51112."

> Got something similar. Did this ever get figured out? Just
>   curious.
> Yours sincerely, &c.
> Russell
> Assistant Game Designer
> *Realms of Gold* Team

The reply came a few minutes later.

> Re: RoGVI bugs 2917, 40389, 51112
> Nope. Couldn't repro any of these, sent back to Matt. Probably
>   in data.
> Lisa

That "probably in data" was an ever-so-slightly dickish sign-off. What she meant to say was that the code was working fine, so it must be the designer who screwed up—he just forgot to flag the king as unkillable, or he put a rock in the wrong place, or routed a goblin's patrol path through a lit torch.

I wrote back, "I triple-checked the data. Want to see?" but she didn't respond at all, except that five minutes later, the bug database had sent me three separate automated messages.

> RoGVI bug 2917 has been reassigned to you by LMcknhpt
> RoGVI bug 40389 has been reassigned to you by LMcknhpt
> RoGVI bug 51112 has been reassigned to you by LMcknhpt

Where was the bug? How did I even start thinking about fixing something like this? A bug could be in either of two elements of the game, data or code, or it could be in both.

Something horrible was lurking in memory or code or whatever forsaken in-between region of space it lived in, and it was messing with our game. But bugs don't happen without somebody making them, by stupidity or negligence. All I had to do was trace it back to where it lived. The first step, as everyone knew, was to find the version where it first occurred — the crucial change, an added feature or an attempt to fix some other problem, which had been copied from version to version ever since. So far I hadn't even found a version where it didn't occur, but there must be one. I'd just have to go back far enough.

Chapter Eight

I slept late the next morning, sat for a half hour over cereal and coffee before wandering over to work, shirt untucked, past midday traffic, people with regular jobs already heading to lunch. No one minded. I lost myself in reading through old computer game manuals, role-playing game modules, design documents, even the italicized flavor text on game cards (*CORRELLEAN REMNANT* (5/4) / Submarine movement / *The regiment fought on as the waters rose; they never stopped*).

Black Arts made role-playing games, strategy games, first-person shooters, even a golf game. But if there was one constant in the Black Arts games, it was the Four Heroes. They were — I think — based on the ones in *Gauntlet,* but you couldn't say for sure because they were the same four heroes you found in almost any video game that featured four heroes, anywhere:

(1) A muscular guy with a sword
(2) A bearded guy in a robe
(3) A skinny guy with a knife
(4) A sexy lady

Whether you thought of them as Jungian archetypes or a set of complementary game mechanics, they'd been around almost since the beginning. Black Arts mixed and matched them depending on the plot of a given game, but they kept the names the same. It was part of the brand, and people cared a surprising amount about them.

The history of Endoria was divided into three ages, which had in common the fact that the world of Endoria was completely fucked.

Of the First Age comparatively little is known, other than it was an age of near-divine beings, heroes, Dreadwargs, and tragedy. Games were never set directly in the First Age; it was just used to explain strange objects like the Hyperborean Crown and the Brass Head, which emanated from the gods and wizard kings of this era. A creeping darkness overwhelmed the Great Powers, and the world descended into warring kingdoms.

The Second Age: That was when the four central heroes made their first appearance: Brennan the warrior, Lorac the wizard, Prendar the thief, and Leira the princess. I had no idea what happened other than that it ended with a gigantic war involving practically everybody.

The Third Age, where *Realms* games are mostly set, was the era of rebuilding, the long struggle for the restoration of the world.

Third Age Endoria was a dangerous place; it wasn't noble, it wasn't mystical, and it wasn't especially dignified. Dwarves lied; elves slit throats. The land was a chaotic mess of factions and cultures and species. Different languages split the world, Coronishes and Zeldunics at each other's throats. Rival deities and pantheons played games with the world, spawning curious groups like the Antic Brotherhood, which served the chaos daemon, Quareen, and the Nephros Concordance, with its vast and mysterious wealth. Different schools of wizardry competed for supremacy: Horn Adepts were masters of illusion; Summoners and Divinomancers were like cosmic hustlers, making deals with unseen entities, playing powerful forces against each other, always trying to come out ahead. Pyrists and Infomantics clung to their disciplines like addicts; Necromancers, like engineers of a rotting eldritch calculus.

The world was dirty, as if in that tournament all the shiny, high-fantasy idealism had been hacked to pieces and ground into the mud of the Second Age.

The Four Heroes' lives continued, through sequel after sequel. There was no fictional justification for their extended life spans — did they have identical descendants, or did they just live a long time, as people in the Old Testament did? No one explained. Prendar was half elf and half human, and Lorac was a wizard, so they might plausibly have extended life spans, but even this was pushing it. (This was to say nothing of their twentieth-century and far-future analogues, for which no rational explanation suggested itself. *Realms* had a ludic dream logic of its own.) The Four Heroes were more like actors in a repertory company than stable characters. Nearly every story needed to fill one or more of their roles, "fighter" or "wizard" or "thief" or, well, "generic female person," and they always showed up and did their bit. Sometimes they were a little older or younger than they were in previous games.

Were the characters supposed to remember everything that happened to them? If I asked one of them, would it know? It didn't seem like it — most of the time they seemed paper-thin, just empty things you steered around the world to get what you wanted. No way to ask them, and no point to doing so. They weren't even people; they were half people, you and not you, or the half of you that was in the world.

The Heroes met, adventured together, betrayed one another, reconciled, and even married (choice of Leira and Brennan or Leira and Prendar; I went with the latter). Lorac recovered the Staff of Wizardry and became the evil Dark Lorac for a while. Leira and Prendar ended up leading an army against the other two, and even had a son.

The Lich King rose, the last Elven Firstcomer died, and her knowledge was lost forever.

And of course they explored about a thousand dungeons and had a thousand adventures. There was the urban conspiracy one. The icy northern one that explained the elven tribes, the one about the swamp-lands, the one about the dwarven empires, the weird plane-traveling one, the forestlands, the drowned ruins one, the vampire one.

The Heroes saved the world and acquired vast riches, as one does, but when next we would meet them they were always back to square one, broke and first-level. We wouldn't have it any other way.

After that…things got weird. If you paged through enough rule supplements and unofficial spin-offs you could find rules for almost anything—rules in case characters dimension-traveled into the Old West or postapocalyptic Earth, for example.

The Soul Gem turned the time line back on itself, stretching and looping it forever. The Heroes even turned up in the First Age from time to time. Rumor had them fighting in the final siege of Chorn, or seeking out Adric from his wandering years and putting him on the path homeward. People said Leira's child was Adric's and was the true heir to the crown before he fell. Or that one day the far-future heroes Pren-Dahr, Ley-R4, Loraq, and Brendan Blackstar would travel back in time to save the Third Age, or perhaps doom it, whatever that means—people are always dooming things in fantasy. The Third Age kind of doomed everything anyway.

As I thought of it, the First Age was like childhood, years of long-ago upheaval, trauma, and unbearable longing, during which our characters were formed.

The Second Age was high school. Battle lines were drawn, alliances hardened into place, strategies tested, scars acquired. The crimes committed in this Age would fester for millennia.

And the Third Age was everything after, when we went our separate ways and order was restored but nothing quite forgiven or forgotten. There was also a Fourth Age no one much bothered with, which marked the retreat of magic into mere legend and superstition and the ascendancy of humankind—i.e., the time when we grew up and got boring and our hearts, generally speaking, died.

I gathered there was a certain amount of armchair quarterbacking in the lower ranks of Black Arts, about how we were a little too loyal to the *Realms of Gold* thing. Don still believed the franchise had legs, that with the right game behind it, *RoG* could be as big as *Final Fantasy* or *Warcraft,* with bestselling tie-in novels, conventions, maybe a movie. But for now it was just another medieval pastiche, a sub-Narnian, off-brand Middle-earth, waiting to be a forgotten part of somebody's adolescence, all the knights and ladies and dragon-elves left behind along with high school detention and Piers Anthony novels.

On the other hand, there were, out there, players who genuinely cared about the third Correllean dynasty, who read the cheaply ghostwritten tie-in novels, who were emotionally invested in the war against the House of Aerion, and who considered the death of Prince Vellan Brightsword in the Battle of Arn to be an event that genuinely diminished the amount of goodness and light in the world.

But it wasn't as if Black Arts suffered from an exaggerated reverence for its own intellectual property. Maybe at first, but all the high-fantasy gravitas in the world wouldn't survive the sight of Lorac hiking up his robes to nail a tricky hardflip-to-manual transition in *Pro Skate 'Em Endoria: Grind the Arch-Lich.*

The four crowded awkwardly into the skate shop.

"What are we doing here?" Brennan said, gazing around at racks of boards and skatewear.

"I think it's important," whispered Leira. "I think we're here for a reason."

Lorac scowled. "This is humiliating."

"Shred regular or goofy-foot?" asked the teenager behind the counter.

"Regular?" Brennan said uncertainly. Leira and Prendar shrugged— regular would be fine. After an agonizing pause, Lorac replied, "Goofy."

The skate shop attendant showed them an array of possible T-shirts. Lorac chose a black one. He was a necromancer, after all.

They found themselves in the parking lot of Franklin Delano Roosevelt Elementary.

"Skate!" cried the arch-lich. "Skate!"

Brennan scanned the others' faces grimly. "Aye. We will skate."

They learned to ollie and nollie and heelflip and air it out and, yes, grind. Prendar kept an eye out for cop cars while Leira tentatively worked out half-pipe moves in a concrete spillway to a grunge-and-speed-metal sound track. Lorac had promise as a tech skateboarder; Brennan went in for vert. When perfected, his double-handed Decapitation-Vacation 360-degree grab raked in a huge bonus.

They improved. They got licensing deals and won competitions. And there really were moments when GtA-L came mind-bendingly close to working. Prendar gliding through the suburban gloom, elf ears glimpsed for a moment under a streetlight, then just a shadow as he rounded the corner of a Safeway and disappeared. Lorac closed his eyes a moment as he rolled down the long hill toward downtown, felt the sun on his face, set aside, for the time being, his long years of study, the price of his arcane knowledge, the doom waiting for him. He ollied to grind the curb, nollied into a 360 to land clean. He grinned.

When Leira managed a handplant on the edge of an abandoned public pool to the cranked-up sound of surfpunk guitar, it almost made sense of the insanity, her body extended almost vertically in the last light of day, her arm straight on the lip, supporting her body, her back arched against the sunset, orange light glinting liquid off the centuries-old katana strapped to her back and pouring over the grass that was poking through the concrete, over the trash piled against a sagging chain-link fence.

"Skate! Skate, or taste the wrath of the arch-lich!"

That night as I was falling asleep I noticed a light through the crack under the cheap door dividing my apartment's two rooms. At first I thought the refrigerator door hadn't closed, but when I looked, I found that the Four Heroes of Endoria had showed up to visit.

It was unexpected, and I wasn't set up for company; in fact, I had exactly one card table and one folding chair, which Lorac the wizard had claimed. They were a striking quartet, larger than life, angular in the way of computer models.

Their glowing, pixelated forms took up a surprising amount of room. Brennan was nearly seven feet tall, and his broad shoulders seemed to swallow up the entire kitchen.

"What are you doing in my kitchen?" I asked them.

"My friend, the time has come to embark on our quest," he said in the smooth baritone of the semiprofessional voice actor who recorded his dialogue.

I guessed, sure, we were friends, in a way.

"You are the chosen one," said Princess Leira, who leaned against the sink. She had the requisite Amazonian figure, full red lips, and jet black hair. She had bright eyes and a mouth that drooped at the corners, which gave her smile an appealing, sheepish quality. She wore a traveling cloak, which was a relief; some of her costumes were pretty revealing.

"Chosen for what? What quest?" I asked. "I don't understand. Am I supposed to find something?" We were always finding things in games. Rings, books, crowns.

"You're the one we need," said Prendar the thief, a tall, pale half elf with sandy red hair and black eyes. "A man of courage and strength, but also guile."

I'd never seen an elf up close before. From a distance they were graceful, elegant beings, but from a few feet away Prendar was vibrantly inhuman. You'd think an elf would have a cute snub nose, but his was long and beaky. Maybe it was his human father's. I'd never heard the word *guile* used in a conversation, either.

"Russell, we entreat your help," intoned the magus. "Our worlds are in great danger, and only you can save them." His cloak stiff with whorls of gold thread, Lorac spoke with a theatrical old-guy quaver.

He was an Arabian Nights character, an exotic older man with a Levantine cast, a thin, crooked nose, and a neatly trimmed beard. His staff was too long, and he brushed the dusty lighting fixture with it. "Sorry."

"But you're the Heroes," I said. "It doesn't make any sense for you to talk to humans."

"We're all in the game, Russell," Leira said. "We're characters, but you're the player. We need you."

"A great danger is coming," said Brennan. "Greater than any we have ever faced."

"Beware Adric! Beware the grieving blade!" Leira whispered breathlessly.

"Just play the game, asshole," Prendar snapped, and drew on a cigarette.

"Wait...what game?" I said. "*Realms VI? VII?*"

"The Ultimate Game," sing-songed Lorac. He began to laugh. They must have gotten a really good voice actor. Looking closer, I saw that his staff had a small animal skull on the end of it. It might have been a ferret's. The ferret's eyes glowed.

I fell asleep again, and this time dreamed I was still at work but there was an extra office marked Secret Projects, and I went in and found Simon there where he'd been all along and he told me how he'd built the Ultimate Game and it was just a golden ring, and he said he'd already spoken the wish and tomorrow the five of us would wake up and be fantasy adventurers together like I'd always wanted. I'd get to be the elf. I started crying right then and there, I just thought, what a relief, because I remembered now how much I wanted it. How had I forgotten that?

Chapter Nine

Hey, Matt, are there any magic swords in the *Realms* universe?" I asked.

There was no reason for preamble; Matt got thrown these questions. Black Arts didn't have an archivist. The closest we had was Matt. He did the research to find out what make of Soviet tanks rolled into Berlin in 1945, and what breed of horse a Knight Templar might have ridden. He was consistently cheerful, and he was Black Arts' biggest fan. He'd read every comic book and novel adaptation and was an authority on the past and future histories of the Black Arts multiverse. Although for all I knew, he made up the answers on the spot.

"Oh! Well." Matt thought a moment, then drew a breath. "I mean, there's the usual ones, plus one, plus two, that kind of thing. There's flaming swords, ice swords, vorpal. Silver, not really magic, but it interacts with those systems. There's Sunshard, pluses against undead. Daemonsbane—obviously—a bunch of other...banes, giants, and stuff. You can make one out of star metal if you have the right equipment, that's pretty good. There was a place you could find a vibro-sword from *Solar Empires,* that was just in as a joke. And, well, there's the Rainbow Blade, has a bunch of different effects."

I was impressed, by his humility, if nothing else. He always talked as if he were ticking off the obvious points everyone knew.

"Are there any evil swords?"

"Evil...swords....Nothing comes to mind, not swords, anyway.

Staff of the Ancients turned out evil, obviously. The DireSpear. At high level, antipaladins manifest burning swords as a class attribute. I don't think the blades themselves are aligned, but I can check."

"Huh. Where would I start looking? Like, *Realms I*?"

"Oh, man...oh, man. I don't even know if you could. I don't know if even Simon and Darren had a copy, or one that would run, anyway. The thing was written in COBOL."

Black Arts had a game library of sorts, three gray metal bookshelves bolted to the wall between the *Realms* art pit and the kitchen. They were stacked unevenly with all the collected debris of four or five insular, feverish midadolescences. Rows and then boxes of fantasy and science fiction novels with doubles and triples of anything in the golden-age SFF canon — the Dune books took up their own shelf. Stacked, hand-labeled videocassettes of films someone considered essential reference (*Aliens, The Dark Crystal,* and *Ladyhawke* were visible on top), *Dungeons & Dragons* modules containing scribbled marginalia, Avalon Hill board games, stacks of comic books, an unused dictionary and thesaurus, a separate section for art books, histories of medieval architecture, and color plates of Vallejo and Frazetta and Whelan and Mead and Piranesi.

And of course stacks and stacks of computer games in no particular order. Most of them were in their original boxes, with worn corners and sprung seams after the long, rough trips from home to dorm room to apartment to apartment before arriving here.

Old consoles; the beetlelike curve of a SEGA Genesis; the triple-pronged Nintendo 64 controller.

I picked one up, already dusty and faded only a few years after being state of the art. *Quest of the White Eagle.* On the cover a blandly handsome teenage boy in a white T-shirt and jeans and an eighties feathered haircut hung in midair, frozen in the act of leaping eagerly from the sidewalk into a glowing doorway hanging a few inches off the ground.

He was grinning madly, obviously overjoyed to be getting the fuck out. Behind him, a dark-haired girl watched, lost in admiration.

The boy was already halfway through; his shoulder and arm emerged on the portal's far side wearing a medieval tunic and gripping a sword. There, the same teenage girl awaited, with an identical expression but wearing longer hair and dressed only in a few shreds of chain mail and a tiara. The back of the box showed an actual screenshot — blocky, pixelated stick figures.

All the Black Arts games were there, a few still shrink-wrapped, going back to 1988's *Clandestine,* the official first release under the label. *Realms I* was the kind of game that never had a commercial release. It was an underground classic that had been swapped over BBSes in the mid-1980s and been passed from hand to hand in the form of eight floppy disks bundled with rubber bands. I was sure a few dozen copies were out there lying in basements in cardboard boxes, filed away with cracked copies of *The Bilestoad* and *Lode Runner.*

I opened a few of the older boxes, shifted piles of loose graph paper, manila envelopes holding mostly 3.25-inch disks ("crispies"), even opened up and shook out a couple of the larger books in case a few floppies had been tucked inside and forgotten. There wasn't much from 1983 apart from an incomplete set of blue-and-white *Ultima III: Exodus* floppies.

It turned out there was a whole room in Black Arts that was just all of Simon's stuff. He had an apartment of sorts but he wasn't that invested in it. The rest of it was here at the office, where he'd slept most of the time anyway. Don and Darren had gone through Simon's notebooks page by page in search of the breakthrough they'd announced, and there was nothing, but I looked through their inventory list anyway.

Items included:

2 wooden stools
1 folding breakfast table

1 Dirt Devil vacuum cleaner
1 SEGA Genesis video game console, controllers missing
1 set of bed linens, soiled
numberless paperback books
countless graphic novels of the 1980s
1 colander, plastic
diverse pieces of silverware
1 bowl
1 plate
1 sword
5 desk lamps w/o lightbulb
1 dot matrix printer
4 reams printer paper
1 shoe hanger, shoeless
1 Marriott rewards card, expired
7 unlabeled VHS tapes, which all turned out to hold episodes of *My So-Called Life*
1 framed Boris Vallejo print, signed

I'd just given up and was looking through the manual of some old White Wolf game when a slip of notepad paper fell out. It was graph paper. Across the top it read REALMS OF GOLD: ADRIC'S TOMB. It held a few short paragraphs in what was definitely Simon's handwriting.

They'd always despised him. Called him a freak and a madman. But in the end he would save them all. Alone, grieving, he made his stand.

Adric would still be the last to pass through to safety. He rested with his back to the emerald portal half a mile under ground, in the depths of Chorn, his family's fortress.

All was silent and black save the light of the glowing portal, light that gleamed on Adric's alien features, the pale skin and high cheekbones. Beyond, in the darkness, he heard the padding of immense paws, the clack of bone against marble. He rested a hand on the hilt of the black runesword at his side.

A smile curled Adric's lips. He drew the ancient black blade from its jeweled sheath, felt its tainted energy flow into him. He thought of his father and brothers, all fled to safety; he thought of Arlani's beautiful face. He thought of Glendale, the home he would never see again.

He looked back at the portal, thinking of the woman he loved but would never marry, the children he would never see. He heard clawed feet on the marble floor and guttural speech. A split-hound had arrived, dragging itself forward, urged on by lesser wargs, mockingly bearing on its brow the Hyperborean Crown itself.

Adric welcomed it. He turned his face from the portal, an eerie light in his green eyes. With one last glance at Arlani's fallen form, he drew

The writing cut off. Sophomore year was ending. One day high school itself would end and the future would begin—long after the TRS-80 would be obsolete, after sixteen colors became 256 colors became millions of colors; long after sophomore year would be over, they'd have 3-D graphics like in *TRON* and computer games so real it would be like living in the world of *D&D*. I remembered believing that.

At the bottom of the page, at an angle, as if noted down casually at some later date, there was a phone number with a local area code.

PART II

THE FIRST AGE OF THE WORLD

Chapter Ten

The modem's tinny speaker gave out the touch-tone dialer's discombobulated melody. The phone rang once, twice, then a chunky click, like a car door opening. Silence and a staticky popping, and at last the two-tone digital shriek of a modem.

```
WELCOME TO THE NEWTON NORTH HIGH SCHOOL BBS
Tread carefully...
(1) Class Schedules and Locations
(2) Latest News!
(3) Contact Faculty and Staff
(4) Administrative Services (password only)
(5) Computer Center
(6) Fun Stuff!
(7) Forums (closed)
(8) Help
```

The words came up in a monospaced font in a white-bordered window; the letters were all white except for the words "Fun Stuff," each letter of which was a different color of the rainbow. It was almost comically dated, but it was also impossible to see it without remembering what it felt like to be on the cutting edge of 1983.

Another burst of shrieking produced another menu.

```
Fun Stuff!
(1) Canfield
(2) Word Wizard
(3) Hunt the Wumpus
(4) Mathstar
(5) Typing Tutor
(6) Adric's Tomb
(7) Snake
(8) Hangman
> 6
Welcome to Adric's Tomb!
v1. 8
press HJKL to move
Seek ye the Crown!
Copyright Black Arts Productions 1983
```

Adric's Tomb was a very primitive dungeon game, all glowing green dots and dashes, the old bones of the virtual realities of the nineties. Rows and columns of alphanumeric characters on a black screen were arranged in a simple maze that only to a very charitable imagination would stand in for the mossy stone walls and dank, silent corridors where Adric's body lay, no doubt in the form of a melancholy percentage sign. At the center of the maze there stood a single plus sign, +, and that was you. Whee. Hard to believe this thing shared a code base with the real-time 3-D world of fourteen years later.

It was easy to laugh at, like the first flying machines, with their pedals and stacks of redundant wings. But at the same time, the simulation had the eloquence of a cave painting. Once I'd touched it, I'd touched a program powered by the same imaginative electricity that powered every video game ever made, except this one was that much closer to the source. If the tech was primitive, the urge to make it shone through that much more strongly.

I waited for something to happen, then realized it was waiting for me. This was a turn-based world. I pressed *H* on the keyboard and the plus sign advanced one space to the left, then stopped. Time ground forward one turn, and then halted until I pressed the key again.

I had a sudden rush of sense memory—the smell of paint fumes, lingering school lunches, damp wool drying after late autumn rain. I really did know these people, once upon a time, it's just that I knew them when we were different people; when I was a different person, one that I'd tried for a long time to forget. When I saw them again we were all changed enough that I could feel safely at that remove—we were all older, fatter, clever enough that we could wink and say, well, at least we're much cleverer than the people we used to be, right? But *Adric's Tomb* hadn't changed.

We met in the fall, the four of us—Darren, Simon, Lisa, and me. We'd all signed up for the intro to programming elective as sophomores. It was taught by a slightly shabby thirtyish math teacher named Kovacs, an enthusiast who had a prominent mustache and published regularly in *Creative Computing* magazine. He was dismissed a few years afterward for smoking pot.

We sat at the back, not together but away from the in crowd, the clique of seniors in advanced integral calc who took all of Kovacs's classes, whatever they were. I knew them by sight: Simon and Darren, the mismatched friends, and Lisa Muckenhaupt, her long hair still wet from the dash across the quad. She was known for reading while walking the two miles to and from junior high, paperback science fiction held in front of her. She wore a lot of long, deeply unfashionable proto–Ren faire dresses, and had, as far as I knew, no friends whatsoever.

I would love to say I remember why I went, but probably it was just a résumé builder. I was already looking ahead to college applications. I never found out exactly why the others were there. Lisa was a math jock, so it made sense. For Darren and Simon it was one of those mysterious decisions that emanated out of their collective mind.

We split into groups of four, one group per computer. Kovacs shoved us together without thinking about it. We stood around the computer, shooting tentative glances at one another. I thought Lisa was going to step forward, but Darren smiled and pulled the chair out and gestured for Simon to sit. We started in on the canonical first assignment: write and compile a program to display the words *Hello, world*. After which Darren pushed us forward into: write and compile a program to display the words *ANARCHY RULES*.

Lisa, who evidently had a computer at home, leaned over in front of Simon, hair brushing the keyboard, and added a looping structure: write and compile a program to display the words *ANARCHY RULES* an infinite number of times. Mission accomplished.

At the end of class, Kovacs explained that each group would be responsible for a semester project, a long-form complete program of our own design.

Darren said, "We should do a game."

"Is that allowed?" asked Lisa.

"Why not?" Darren countered.

Simon nodded. "We should do it."

"What kind of game?" I asked.

"Like *D&D*," Simon and Darren said in unison.

"Just as long as it's not stupid. What do you think, Russell?" She looked at me.

"Fine, I guess," I said. I barely knew what *Dungeons & Dragons* was, and I didn't have any other ideas, so why not?

"Couldn't we do science fiction?" Lisa asked. "Did you guys read *Foundation*?" I'd learn later that Lisa had an incomprehensible bond with the long, dry, future-history sagas of Asimov and Olaf Stapledon.

In the end it came down to a coin flip, fantasy versus science fiction.

Fantasy won, and we wrote down our phone numbers for each other so we could meet later. In a year of firsts, it was the first time I received a girl's phone number in her own jagged handwriting. It was the second time Simon had touched a computer, and he left the classroom with Mr. Kovacs's copy of *Structured COBOL Programming,* second edition, by Nancy and Robert Stern, under his T-shirt.

Chapter Eleven

Could you make a computer imagine an entire world? How would you start? A generation of people would wrestle with this problem — they're still wrestling with it. At that point Simon had only seen or touched a computer twice in his life. He had played maybe two or three computer games at most. He came to the Thursday class with an actual computer program.

"Look look look," he said. "I've got it."

It wasn't clear whether Simon had slept since the last time we'd seen him. He had about nineteen pages of smudged, crossed-out writing on notebook paper, text bracketed and underlined, arrows connecting the segments across pages. He spent the first forty minutes of class just typing it in as we watched.

It was terrible code, as I now understand these things — no architecture, just one big glob of undigested, "uncommented" instructions looping back and forth.

I leaned forward, waiting to see what this odd, obsessive personality had brought us. Darren looked nervous for his friend; Lisa, skeptical. On the third try, Simon's program compiled and ran. We saw a grid of dots on the screen, thirty-two by thirty-two, except the dot in the top left corner was replaced by a plus sign, a +.

"I don't get it," I said.

"It's the world. There are a thousand and twenty-four places you can be in the world," he said. He showed us how the plus sign could move around from grid point to grid point. "And that's you."

I didn't know it, but what I was seeing was the equivalent of the first grainy black-and-white image of Mars sent from the Viking lander seven years before — it was our first glimpse of the primal Endorian landscape. We didn't have access to a graphics mode, so everything was drawn with alphanumeric characters. You could use the *H, J, K,* and *L* keys to go left, down, up, and right. (The *HJKL* movement scheme was copied from an antediluvian text editor called vi. Years later, at Black Arts, using vi as your principal text editor was one of a hundred things you could do to cultivate a hardcore image.)

And if there could be a "you" in the world, there had to be monsters, or it wasn't a fantasy world at all. The first species of monster was an ampersand, a &, and the first thing its AI ever knew was the rule that every time you moved, the & would move one space toward your previous position (and time was divided into turns; *Realms of Gold* wouldn't make the jump to real-time simulation until a decade later). And if the + moved on top of the &, the & was erased. So the first "human" inhabitant of *Realms of Gold* was the lone, all-conquering, invulnerable plus sign — Brennan's distant forebear — which roamed the primordial landscape and against which no ampersand could stand.

The world had to be made entirely of periods. This was going to be a dungeon maze, so there had to be walls. Rooms. So walls would be made of asterisks, *s, and open space would be periods, .s. We made a rule that you couldn't step on a *, and thus the grid of the world became a maze. And at the end of the maze, a prize, an exclamation point, !. When you stepped on it, the game ended — you had won!

We'd begun to answer that question — how to make a world. We still had no idea why one would, except that we needed to. We didn't know it, but thousands of people were trying to solve exactly this problem. Simon had no particular experience with the issues, nor did he

have a preconceived idea how to do it other than the way *Dungeons &*
Dragons did it—graph paper, numerical ratings for how good you
were at things, which determined your statistical likelihood of doing it,
and lots and lots of rules and numbers determining what weapons
there were in the world, what spells, what abilities, what monsters. A
generation of lawyers and statisticians cut their teeth on the to-hit and
damage tables of medieval fantasy. File it under yet another ridiculous
thing that probably saved somebody's life.

Chapter Twelve

We worked on it all through fall semester, in between my abortive acting career, Lisa's freeze-up on the debate team, and Darren's first ignominious fistfight. Three days a week, I'd park my bike by the garage, climb two or three concrete steps, and ring the doorbell. One of Darren's sisters would answer the door and almost in the same motion step aside while I wiped my sneakers and thudded down the carpeted stairs to the basement, where Simon would be. He'd wave me over to the C64 to look at a new game he'd found or a new feature he'd hacked into *Tomb*.

"I was thinking we could do flying creatures," I said once. "Birds or bats. Just the boringest version, just turn off terrain effects for that subtype."

Simon and Darren did their mind-meld glance to decide, then they both nodded.

"Sure, sure," Darren said. "Let's do it."

"Great," I said. In two hours I had created a subclass of monsters, FLYER, built out of hacked-together exceptions that let it ignore water, lava, acid pools, caltrops, and any floor-based traps and trip wires. Just birds and bats first, but later the category would encompass all dragonkind.

High school — no one wanted to say it — was terrifying. Every hour was like standing in a roaring blast furnace of excitement and terror and shame all at once. I'd come to Darren's house bruised and raw from the day, grateful it was over and grateful I had a place to go that wasn't home.

Simon or Darren would sit on folding chairs at Darren's dad's computer; I'd be in the leather recliner. Lisa claimed the plaid couch. If we had a milestone coming, we'd break at seven, when Darren's mom brought us all dinner on paper plates, with a two-liter bottle of Sprite or Diet Coke; then at nine thirty, when it was time for the big check-in and test, we talked over how the week's goals were going. One night I realized that Simon had started sleeping in Darren's basement.

A lot of things about Simon are obvious only in hindsight. I was far too sheltered and self-involved to notice that we never went to his house. His whole life, he mixed with the children of doctors and professors, professional couples who fought about spousal hires and what city the wife would do her residency in. He gave off a little feeling that maybe there was something wrong at home, but it wasn't the kind of thing you asked about.

Darren worked most weekends at the Baskin-Robbins, so Simon and I would ride our bikes four miles to Gordon's Hobby Shoppe, riffling through racks of role-playing game manuals, modules, magazines, and rules supplements. Gordon's was a hobby and crafts store that eked out an existence among the candle shops and lamp emporiums that populated the cul-de-sacs of suburban shopping malls, run by stoners with curious facial hair who did most of their business with model railroad builders and high-end doll collectors. They saw the market for gamers, and kept a magazine rack full of what we wanted.

We'd read all the manuals and pore over the maps, wander mentally from room to room. We'd wonder at the tantalizing histories behind the buildings, creatures, and odd artifacts, tracing the fragmentary links between Vecna and Saint Cuthbert and Mordenkainen, scraping the tiny bits of information out of each artifact's list of powers, its built-in curses.

We learned about other computer games from eighth-page ads in the margins of *Dragon* magazine, the ones adorned with Gothic fonts and fantasy clip art and inviting readers to send their orders to post office boxes in Madison or State College or midwestern college towns. I remember padded manila envelopes arriving, hand-addressed, containing the data on actual cassette tapes, which we slotted into Darren's cut-rate boom box, with its whining, wheezing gears, which we then plugged into Darren's computer, which then served as a disk drive. Simon played them avidly, solved every puzzle, ground through every dungeon from first room to last. But he felt they lacked ambition.

Simon's room had stacks of 5.25-inch disks in their white paper sleeves, all games, each one labeled in Magic Marker. Some of them had been copied over three or four times, the old game carefully crossed out and the new one added. Most of them had been double-sided manually.

He'd come to Darren's after school—fuck even stopping by home—with the latest one. Darren's mom might leave him a glass of milk, but mostly they left him alone; they considered him Darren's project. He'd put on music, something loud on his headphones, seventies classic or prog rock, and for an hour, two hours, three, he could disappear as long as Darren's dad would leave him alone, disappear the way he could in a fantasy novel, but differently.

Silly 2-D games, little guys jumping around on platforms—*Sammy Lightfoot, Hard Hat Mack,* cheap *Mario Bros* rip-offs. Adventures—*Escape from Rungistan, Mystery Mansion.* He didn't even know who made the things—were they teenagers? Professional software engineers?—but somewhere out there people were inventing his medium without him.

The world narrowed to the tiny realm where he was always pushing on to the next screen, the next castle, always in a private dream of concentration and hard reflex, like a stoner kid doing bar chords over and over until his fingers were cramped and the muscle memory was there even in his sleep, always on the verge of some conclusion on the next screen, the crucial revelation that never quite appeared, that he could spend his life chasing, unless he learned to make them, unless he got to set the rules himself, unless he could put what he wanted in that castle, lock it away and bury it in a dungeon for a thousand years. He'd come home at nine or ten, biking home even in winter, snow in his eyes and silting up in his collar.

The dungeon couldn't be just corridors. Simon had read his Tolkien a hundred times; this had to be Moria. There had to be great halls, chasms, locked rooms. That meant doors had to have multiple states — they could be open or closed, locked or unlocked. But if there were locks, that meant there had to be keys. And that meant there had to be objects you could pick up. So now there were things called objects, which could be displayed in the world, but could also be carried by your character — there was now inventory. And stairs. When you walked on stairs, you went to another map, notionally "up" or "down" from the map you were on. Just like that, the thirty-two-by-thirty-two world became an infinite series of levels extending upward and downward.

Darren added a level that was mostly empty space with two lines of pillars running through it. Then he added a level where the walls spelled DARREN RULES, followed by a pentagram level, then a stick-figure level, then a rough map of our high school, then an attempt to mimic a Nagel print, then a giant ampersand that the little ampersands (we started calling them ampers) ran around in, and finally a stylized picture of a penis. Simon added a class of command that printed more text beneath the map, to say things like "I don't recognize that key" or "You feel cold air moving" or "The walls here are covered with rotting tapestries," and invented without thinking about it the voice of the game, which skipped around between first and second and third person depending on what you were doing — the hidden narrator, the companion, the adjudicator behind the curtain. "You smell burning." "Suddenly you yearn for your distant homeland."

The maze didn't have a name, but eventually Simon added text that would appear when you ran the program, just so the start-up would feel less abrupt:

```
Welcome to the Tomb of Destiny.
Beware Adric!
HJKL to move.
```

Who was Adric? Why was he dead? Why was he interred in such an elaborate underground complex, and by whom? And what was a "tomb of destiny" — did destiny die and get buried? Never mind; it was the kind of thing one wrote. *Realms* didn't have a story. Not that it needed one to work. What's happening in *Space Invaders* is pretty clear by the time you're done reading the title. You live out your brief lonely heroic destiny in full understanding of the stakes, sliding an artillery piece back and forth while death creeps down from the sky in lateral sweeps. For the moment, no one needed to say anything more.

But eventually we couldn't help ourselves. We emptied out the school library's stock of fantasy and science fiction, from Poul Anderson to Roger Zelazny, taking notes, harvesting characters and story lines for later, irrespective of genre or period. It was all one contemporaneous fever dream. For underinformed fourteen-year-olds (or thirteen — Simon skipped fourth grade) it was a mass of curious ideas. Piers Anthony's *Blue Adept* first suggested the idea of dating a robot. Our consensus was that that was probably the best option for any of us, once it became possible.

"Robot, probably," was Simon's opinion. "If not, then alien. If not, then human." We all nodded.

"Or dragon," added Lisa.

I saw the way Lisa looked at Simon sometimes, usually when he was working on a problem, and I wondered why. I didn't know exactly why any girl thought anything. A girl's attention was like the mind of an alien in an

Arthur C. Clarke novel—shattering, sublime, unintelligible. I wasn't sure if "cool" was an idea that registered for Lisa. Did she have posters on her wall at home, a picture inside her locker—how did it work, exactly?

For the rest of us, cool was a deep fantasy, the stuff of *Heavy Metal* dreams, marble cities, adventure, fate, ancient curses, reaching its extreme limit in the lonesome, otherworldly hauteur of Elric of Melniboné. It wasn't possible to be cooler than Elric. I think there was a tacit agreement between them that Simon and Darren were in some way both Elric, which was as close as they could safely get, maybe, to saying they loved each other.

Darren was cool because he was tall and bitter and had learned how to smoke and was confident, and Simon was cool I guess because when he was thinking really really hard the air around him seemed to warp inward, as though there were a black hole behind his eyes. Or because he didn't give a shit about anything but what we were working on, and he had a way of making it seem like the problem that everything was staked on. He'd already found out what he really wanted—to carve something out behind the command line that answered his feeling that he was born in the wrong place in the wrong body. But this also made you wonder whether he gave a shit about any of us, and then you started trying to figure it out and couldn't stop. It made him a little bit like a dragon. But Lisa started dating a college freshman she met at Brandeis, where she had to take math, because I guess no one at our school was qualified to teach her. I learned that it was possible to hate reality as much as Simon did.

Which made me ask, late one evening, dizzy with caffeine and fatigue, what if you went up and up and up, climbing torch in hand, up the cramped spiral staircases, makeshift ladders, broad processional ramps, kicking aside bones and splashing through curtains of water dripping downward, up and up, until the orange torchlight or the blue-green glow of phosphorescent algae gave way to the pale gold of sunlight on the top few steps of the topmost staircase? Or until you smelled fresh air and looked up to see sky instead of stone blocks, and you were out in the world you started in? Where were you? What did you do then? The simplest answer, apart from just ending the game, was to make a metamap, a surface country, where you could walk overland between dungeons. There wasn't any new programming necessary to make this one; it was just a new map built on a larger scale. There were multiple stairways leading *down* to different dungeons, but none leading *up*. This map had a different character set — ~, ∧, and % for water, mountains, and forest spaces. And then the movement rules were altered so you couldn't move into mountain and river spaces. Just a hack, but it changed what Darren and Simon were doing. Now there was more than just the darkness of *Adric's Tomb,* there was a whole world to explore.

Realms map 1.0 was a big, blunt, teardrop-shaped landmass that Darren freehanded in the last fifteen minutes of a Friday study hall. It showed the continent of Endoria and its capital city, Kronus. Endoria sat in the middle of a nameless sea, and had two principal mountain ranges and then a couple of rivers sketched in after the first bell rang. Darren handed it around. Simon and his parents had gone on a summer trip to Israel, and Darren had been to Scotland, plus he'd lived in Iowa until he was eight. Between them they'd seen castles, farmlands, cliffs, ruined temples, and Roman fortresses, along with their own native terrain types — patchy, deciduous groves gradually being claimed by strips of pine tree, subsiding into streams and swamps, fronting onto asphalt. In art class Simon tore off one of a big three-by-four-foot sheet of paper, gray and pulpy, like newsprint, from a giant pad the teacher kept in the room and copied the blobby outline Darren had made.

Over the next week we passed the map around between us and it accrued tiny details. Each time it came back to me it had more tattered edges and creases from being folded and refolded. After a week it was almost illegible, having been written and rewritten. Kronus sat inland at the place where two rivers met, on the border between the southern grassland and the northern forest. Simon put Dwarven tunnels in the mountains, drew elf-haunted forests in the central valleys, and marked the pastoral west with tiny crenellated towers in blue ballpoint—the lands of men. Darren spent way too much time on the extremely detailed walled kingdom of Arrek, in the southeast, ringed by mountains he'd set up for that purpose. Simon aggressively marked out a swath of the northeast as the Plains of the Wind Riders, with no explanation other than a passable sketch of a horse and long-haired rider. The Shadow Marches, the Blackened Lands, Boralia (there was an Old Boralia as well, much larger), Skarg, the Perrenwood, the Bottomless Lake.

A line of dashes, never explained, wandered through the middle of the continent—A road? A tunnel? An ancient wall? Dungeon entrances were marked in black and were found in ruins, mountains, and the very center of the Duskwood. It took Simon and Darren months to translate the map into digital form, improvising ASCII notation as they went. When the continent of Endoria went live, there were fifty-six new dungeons to build and dozens of new monsters and terrain types to consider.

You had to really love computer games to get excited about a game this crappy, to really invest in this little shifting grid of letters as an alternate world, but Simon obviously did, believed in it to the point where the real world seemed like a gray shadow by comparison. I'd driven past his one-story house, at the shabbier end of our mostly affluent suburb. Simon slept on a pull-out couch in the living room.

When Darren's parents bought him a Commodore 64 Simon began sleeping over at Darren's at least three nights out of the week. When he wasn't there he was visibly fogged over. I'd see him eating lunch in the quad, blocking out code in a notebook. More than once I saw him in Radio Shack, standing up at a floor-model computer, typing furiously, trying out this or that idea, glancing over his shoulder at the salesperson hovering and waiting for the right moment to kick him off.

March and April passed, and Simon and Lisa mumbled through their bar and bat mitzvahs. The differences between Simon and the rest of us were getting more obvious. Simon probably wasn't going to college.

Over the next four months he and Darren wrote an enormous amount of code, mostly between the hours of midnight and four in the morning, sometimes individually, sometimes on the phone to each other.

When I was with them, I never before or since had the experience of concentrating so fluidly or intensely. There were nights when, midsession, one or another of us jerked up from a momentary sleep trance, still typing out dense functions with names like SPIRAL-BOUND, PROPHET, and CORINTHIAN, the purpose of which we would know fleetingly once and then never again. What came out of it was a shockingly flexible simulation and procedural content-generation engine, elements of which survive today. It generates random encounters, manages some of the large-scale flow of the game world, and controls interactions between objects, character attributes, and what players can and can't do. Countless Black Arts programmers have thrown APIs and GUIs on top of it, added functions that search and query and parse output; they've added graphics, physics, and sound engines to display the world WAFFLE imagines. But nobody knows what makes WAFFLE quite so fast, and eerily acute in its heuristic take on large-scale simulation problems.

There is a core there—so compressed as to be molten and illegible, forged by a now-alien cognitive self, a mix of hubris and anger and innocence and catalyzing hormonal change—that simply can no longer be understood.

Chapter Thirteen

It was the first time I walked through the empty halls of the high school at five in the afternoon, the silence almost ringing in my ears, the place seeming for the first time like it belonged to me, belonged to me only.

It was the first time I stayed out past midnight, feasting on Sprite and M&M's, playing Styx on repeat, the cassette tape clacking and reversing itself each time "Too Much Time on My Hands" came to an end. Our communal sound track was anchored by Led Zeppelin and a great deal of Pink Floyd, and by artists whose ponderous sense of grandeur made its way into the game's thematics. Jethro Tull showed up on mix tapes, and, let's face it, a certain amount of Styx. Punk was never more than a distant rumor.

The first time I was alone with a girl in a car was when Lisa gave me a lift home from Darren's at one in the morning. His parents were sleeping, so we whispered our good-byes to Darren, then walked in cold starlight to her car, giddy and pale with sleeplessness. I was wrapped in my parka; she was wearing a black overcoat on top of a flowery dress. I didn't know cars, but hers seemed huge and comfortable and expensive.

She ran the engine a few moments to warm it up. I told her the lefts and rights, but she didn't say anything — it seemed she didn't talk when she didn't have to. She looked tiny at the steering wheel. She rolled to a full, exacting halt at every intersection, crunching on yesterday's snow.

It was the first time, also, that I had to get out of a car when I wanted to stay sitting there forever, the first time I looked up at the black sky while the car pulled away, and the first time I hung around outside my house at one fifteen in the morning, freezing and wanting to stay out there so the moment held and so that I stayed the same new person who'd just ridden in a car with a girl, because I knew when I stepped through the doorway into my house I'd go back to being the old person. I stayed out for another half an hour, walking in circles like a lost polar explorer, waiting for dawn.

What I remembered, for some reason, was a high school party, late May of sophomore year, a Friday night, one of the first nights of almost-summer. It was a house party that only Darren was invited to because he ran track that one semester and hadn't disgraced himself, and that still counted. But Simon and I tagged along because there wasn't anything else to do, and Darren had the gift of making wherever he went into the place we all wanted to be.

It was a big party, big enough so we didn't have to ring the doorbell, big enough to get lost in, and we did. Darren went off to get a beer and say hi to his cooler friends, and Simon and I split up by tacit agreement, figuring we would actually look less dorky apart than together. But I kept track of him. I think that if nothing else, you could say in my defense that I noticed Simon in ways that none of the others did. I noticed what he did, what he was like, and what he thought.

Simon didn't know what to do, so he stood in the first-floor hallway next to the stairs, so people would pass him on the way up or down and not stop to notice that no one was talking to him and he wasn't talking to anyone else. He pretended to sip his beer, and all he could do was notice what the house was like and make a map of it in his mind — where the rooms and corridors branched out, where the monsters and the treasure would go. Where the jocks and the Goths and the nondescript middle-range types were standing. Where the girls congregated. He tried to imagine that it was a dungeon he could explore, or at least that there was a treasure chest involved. He tried to imagine it was made of asterisks and dots and ampersands, and in his mind he was the plus sign. He breathed in the concentrated smells of beer and sweat that accumulated. He watched the other students arriving, meeting their friends, going upstairs, or spilling out onto the lawn behind the house to trample the pachysandra and decapitate the agapanthus blossoms.

If the house were a dungeon then it was upside down, and the treasure and the mad wizard would be on the top floor. He climbed the stairs, stepping between and over two girls having a conversation about field hockey.

By eleven thirty Simon was in a curious state, not sleepy but hazy from the heat and damp air and mist of alcohol that surrounded the house. He wandered down the hall, straying vaguely toward quiet and cool air. The truth was, high school was almost more than he could stand, and he was not a wimp except in the most strict and physically literal sense of the term. He had never been to a party like this and it struck him as a little bizarre, like a feverish nightmare version of school. It was the exact same mass of people, but they had all shown up in the middle of the night, and now there were no teachers and everyone stood in the hallways talking as loudly as possible, and there were no classes except lunch, or else the classes were all different and he hadn't ever studied for any of them. The house was a new one, a huge three-story box on a low hill. Until a few years ago there was a small one-story house on the site, a dirty pale blue with a permanent accumulation of newspapers out front, whose owners were somewhat mysterious. They'd disappeared, and the whole lot was bulldozed, and the new house was canary yellow, maybe four times the size of the old one, with curious classical touches — columns and broad steps out front, a temple to a pagan god remembered only for its class connotations. On the way in, Simon had rapped on one of the columns with his knuckles — hollow.

The third floor seemed to be all guest rooms and half baths, like a dormitory.

He crept into one of them, wary of disturbing a couple, but it was empty. He went to the window. His own parents owned a liquor store and lived across town in a house not unlike the one this one had replaced. It was near the end of the school year. He looked down across a wide green lawn scattered with stray revelers, and out over the maze of old trees and amber-lit streets of Newton that he'd biked through to get here, a great, tangled, supremely lazy serpent that had fallen asleep and would never rise again. He could see the stars. He was probably, literally, farther off the ground than he had ever been in his life. At the back of that labyrinth was his future, the college he'd go to if he could afford to, the faces of the friends he'd make, a made-up world where people would be glad to see him every day—everything that would happen to him when he left Newton. He tried to picture it and couldn't. Something would come along—he'd take up smoking or learn a foreign language—and it would make him a new person. Or would it? All he could see from here was a kind of tunneling into himself, an excavation of more and more chambers full of skeletons and gold and magic, lands of kings and queens and monsters. It was the thing he was good at, and what was to stop him doing it the rest of his life?

He was less popular than ever, but he'd also discovered a fact even Darren hadn't, which was that they were not the only ones playing *Realms*. There were about thirty players now from around the school, and together they'd played more than a thousand times. They weren't just making *Realms* for themselves now; other people believed and other people cared. That was going to matter.

I saw Simon, leaving, which I remember distinctly, even though it was the first night I ever drank enough to throw up, and it may have been the night of my first kiss—I never quite got it straight. But I remember that Simon walked off and got on his bike without talking to any of us, seemingly immune to the lure of alcohol and the glamour of a Friday night party. He biked home in the warm air with his Walkman on, listening to the Violent Femmes on cassette, which he listened to every single day.

In the dawn of time, way back in what Simon called the Prime Age, the great Powers of the World came together and created Endoria. They were a multitude—the Power of Fire and the Power of Earth, the Power of Lightning, the Powers of Mercy, of Calculus, and Last Resorts. They made the world and its many wonders and riches, working alone or in combination. Just before they left they made the Firstcomers, a mighty race of humans whose wondrous works fell scarcely short of the deeds of the Powers themselves. So began the First Age, with generosity and measureless hope, but that's not how it ended.

It ended with a little boy. This little boy lived in the great palace Chorn, at the heart of the nation of Hyperborea, built on a mountain atop the remnants of an old palace, where they say the twin Powers of Memory and of Change once lived.

The boy's father was dead, but the boy was too young to take the throne. His mother ruled as regent, so in the afternoons the prince played idly in a walled garden at the heart of the palace with Zara, daughter of the castle blacksmith. His mother soon married again, to a much younger man who despised the young prince. To be fair, he didn't look like much of a prince, just a boy dressed in a set of cut-down royal robes.

One day his mother came to him and explained that he would have to leave. His stepfather could no longer stand the sight of him, and wished to put his own son in his place. The following day he was to be sent away to a castle on a far coast.

But that night, in the single bravest act of his life up to that point, Adric ran away. He found his way by moonlight down the mountain and rested among the rocks by the side of the road while his stepfather's men searched.

Where Adric went next no one knew. Some say he became a bandit and assassin; some say a wizard; some say a simple fisherman who married and had many children.

Adric's stepfather was the one who stole the Hyperborean Crown, a simple silver circlet with a huge emerald set in it, and sold it to a dark Power who lived under the mountain. The crown dated from the time of the first Powers, and no one knew what its significance might be.

Not long afterward the Dreadwargs began to emerge from the deep places under the mountains and the Shatterwar began, a war that nearly destroyed the world.

It is recorded that two decades later, in the final siege of Chorn, Adric returned, but much changed. The boy had become a lean, bronzed man, and he carried Mournblade with him, the sword he himself had forged. He took his place among the defenders of Chorn, and sometime in the hours after the castle fell, he drew Mournblade and held the enemy back for a time while the castle's survivors made their way out through a magic portal. Adric didn't follow — he dueled with the mightiest of the Dreadwargs, the one to whom the crown had been sold, and fell.

The castle was laid waste, ice flowed over it, the Hyperborean Empire fell, and its name was all but forgotten. But somewhere amid the vaulted halls and the underground lakes and the city beneath, down in its secret heart, the crown waits, there to remain until the end of Ages and perhaps beyond.

In the cataclysm that followed, the Dreadwargs perished, the Firstcomers were divided, and their descendants became elves and dwarves and humans and lizards. And little was left of the Powers and their great works except the strange places, poisoned mountains, odd forests, and deep tunnels, with their curious denizens. Lesser nations rose, and the great empire of Hyperborea, which seemed poised to restore the world, was never heard from again. But Mournblade was not lost to the world, not at all.

Chapter Fourteen

I played *Tomb of Destiny* for a solid week, at night, while trying to suck up modern-day *Realms* knowledge during the day.

Once, very late at night, I walked onto a random-level teleporter and found myself in a strange place. The population was nearly all dwarves and gnomes, creatures who didn't normally live aboveground and usually hated each other. There were long rows of stalls, with dwarves and gnomes running indiscriminately between them. The stalls radiated out from a central circular plaza, where there was a pedestal on which I read the word HOUSTON. On top of the pedestal, immobile, was a figure I did recognize—Algul the Nefarious. I clicked on him but nobody had written conversation for him, so he ignored me.

A dwarf came up to me and offered to sell me some oil futures. I clicked on Appraise. YOU THINK YOU ARE GETTING A TERRIBLE DEAL.

The next day I asked Don, who just laughed.

"You saw that," he said. "Okay, that was how we got money for the art on *Realms III*. Darren hooked it up for a bunch of rich frat kids.

"This was freshman year of college, and there was a rumor that Simon was, like, a magic computer genius, and these guys came and told us what they wanted—a stock market robot, they called it—and they were going to build a little company around it called AstroTrade. Darren played into it, I swear, had this whole act going, this high voice, like a movie idea of a nerd. Whatever they said, he'd give this jerky nod and then push his glasses up his nose, and they'd smirk and nudge each other. I thought I was going to start laughing and blow the whole thing. We did the deal for a lump sum, then Simon went off and did it in a weekend."

"But what exactly was it?" I asked.

"I mean, it wasn't a con or anything. They were just so stupid! He took the Endorian economy and made it stand in for America's. Of course we did a lot of tweaking on the world. I mean, more dwarves. Way more dwarves, quite a lot of dwarves, they stood in for the oil industry, everything heavy industry. Then the high tech and software were modeled as elves—you know the way they live off in forests and spin stuff out of nothing? Agricultural sector, humans. We suppressed all combat in the marketplace. Feed it the right parameters, it's a little toy industry.

"And there were no graphics, just spreadsheets on what the market was doing, price fluctuations, and...you know. And then we just let the sim run.

"We gave it a title screen like GLOBAL FUTURES MARKET ALGORITHM GENERATOR. But if you open up the code, it's all elves and dwarves, a couple of good and evil wizards playing the federal agencies, who stepped in if things skewed too far. The actual thing that made the calls for them? A modded version of the semidivine necromancer Boris, wearing a plus-four Ring of Cunning and a Mild Prescience Aura. Brutal, brutal hack.

"And you know what? It wasn't the worst thing in the world. It basically did rational things. It was like everything Simon did on that engine. God, he was smart."

"Did they make money?" I asked.

"I have no idea. They talked about using it in the Hong Kong market, but this was right in October of eighty-seven—Black Monday, remember?"

I did, the same way I remembered Walter Mondale running for president.

"A stock market crash."

"A pretty big one. They lost their money, or so we assumed. We didn't care — they were laughing at us the whole time anyway. It was like doing business with Biff from *Back to the Future*. We never heard from them again."

"So you never found out if it worked?"

"It was a nice little system, and it had a logic to it, just the way the game does, but who knows if it worked in reality? Darren walked away with ten thousand dollars and put it all into revamping *Realms III* for the commercial version. That's how we seeded Black Arts."

In the final reckoning, *Tomb of Destiny* got a C plus because it was buggy and, as a piece of code, it didn't solve even its reasonably simple problems elegantly, but it was not a terrible game when you got used to the lack of graphics. More than once, I played until two in the morning, and after a while the &s and +s and all the letters and numbers fell away and it was all the same to me, like looking through the black screen and glowing letters to a darker, hidden place — daemons and sepulchral stone chambers and stairways and landings corkscrewing down into the earth. Maybe the story wasn't complicated, but maybe "downward" was all the story I needed just then, simple and elementally real. I tapped forward grid point by grid point, braced for the next horror to spring out at me in the form of some friend or foe. All you know is to go downward from stair to stair, down into the unknown, in spite of the dangers, keystroke by keystroke, further into the data. I delved into the substanceless phosphorescent earth for that priceless treasure, always elusive, the transcendent loot of memory.

Chapter Fifteen

On April 14, Darren Ackerman, lead designer and legitimate game-industry legend, quit. He came in at eleven and spent maybe twenty minutes in Don's office, and then walked through the empty office, ponytail bouncing briskly, past the Excellence in Game Design awards, past the cubicle maze, past the testers playing split-screen *Mario Kart* in the conference room, past the life-size cutout of a man wielding an ergonomically impractical sword, and out of the building forever, past the two shaggy guys still porting *Solar Empires III* to Mac.

I watched him Frisbee his security card far out into the weeds, get in his signature Rolls-Royce, and drive away. About twenty minutes later, Don sent a company-wide e-mail explaining that over the weekend Darren had "chosen not to continue his journey with us."

Twenty minutes after that, another e-mail came with a list of fourteen other employees who were also not making said journey. Most of them I didn't know, but the employee directory put them as nearly all the senior design and programming staff. It seemed that Darren had taken his pick of the developers before he left. He must have been arranging it for weeks. He didn't take Lisa.

A few minutes later I got a private e-mail from Don asking me to come talk to him in his office.

His door was ajar, but I knocked anyway. No one at Black Arts would wear a tie, but Don wore the nearest equivalent, the scaled-back management uniform of blue button-down shirt with khakis, the shirt bulging in the middle a little and giving him the overall look and feel of a Best Buy employee. He looked uncomfortable, as if I were trying to return a copy of *Quake II* after the ninety-day deadline without a receipt.

He owned part of the company, but I couldn't tell if that made him rich or not. I was starting to realize how little I knew about how Black Arts worked.

"Hi, Don."

"Hey, Russell."

Everything at Black Arts was so purposely informal that when actual business conversations had to happen they became ten times as uncomfortable. Or else maybe people came to Black Arts because they were innately terrible at this kind of thing.

"How are you liking it here so far?" he asked. Uh-oh.

"It's — it's really great," I said. "I'm pretty much trained up on existing tools, just waiting for the new engine to happen."

"Okay, good, great." Don sighed — not like I'd passed a test; more like I'd left him no way out.

"So, this weekend…" he began. Was I really being fired? I had never been fired, not even from a job taking tickets at the box office of a summer-stock theater over an exquisitely lonely summer on Cape Cod — not even after drunkenly losing half a night's receipts.

"This weekend the company was sold to Focus Capital. It was a decision between Darren and myself. Darren holds — held — a majority stake, which he no longer does. This is confidential, for now."

"Okay," I said. Did Don think I knew about things like this? Did he want advice? It looked like he hadn't slept much. Also like one of his oldest friends had betrayed him.

"But this turned out to be part of a — maneuver — Darren had been planning, I think for some time," Don went on. There might have been a slight quaver in his voice. "He left and took a lot of senior developers with him to a new start-up. It was perfectly legal. No one ever signed a noncompete agreement.

"I know you're wondering where this is going. The partners at Focus are...well, they're not too happy. They thought they were buying up the talent that was Black Arts' principal asset, but that's not what they got. What they have in Black Arts is a slightly rickety code base, a whole bunch of intellectual property, and game franchises. And a bunch of desks and computers and a pretty high burn rate. I'm being candid here.

"So I guess what I'm getting to is, there's been a restructuring. The partners reviewed a lot of the personnel files and they've decided to ask you to take on a bigger role here. We'd like you to be design lead on *Realms* RPG."

"Oh. Oh, wow. Okay. I mean, thanks," I said. There was more, about compensation and stock options; I keep saying thanks and nodding and waiting for the meeting to be over.

"Look, can I—" he began. It's funny that I was thinking of him as much older than I was, but it came to me that he wasn't out of his late twenties; he was Darren's contemporary.

"Sure. Sure. I know it doesn't make sense. Making me that," I told him.

"If I can be honest, design got hit a lot harder than programming. Focus doesn't know that much about games, and I think your chess background weighed pretty heavily. I said we would do it, but to some degree it's going to be in name only, at least until we see how you're doing."

"Of course! Of course," I said. Maybe he'd hoped I was going to refuse the position, which might have been sensible.

"I'll see you at the leads meeting Tuesday morning," he said. "I'm looking forward to working with you."

He leaned forward and put out his hand and I shook it by reflex, and that was our good-bye. All I could think was the profoundly unprofessional thought: Thank God. I'm in the club now.

I left and went to the kitchen and shouldered through the fire door to the loading dock. I didn't have an office so there was nowhere else for me to go if I needed to be alone for a moment. It was raining but not for real, just enough to speckle the warm sidewalk.

I walked a little ways across the parking lot, feeling the unfamiliar midday brightness through the clouds, the warmth and smell after half a day indoors. It was just after one o'clock on a Monday, and Arlington Avenue was jammed. The land around Cambridge and Somerville gave off a peculiarly exhausted feeling, feeble wetlands mingled with land that had been built on and paved and rebuilt on since colonial times.

I shook my head and walked down to the Mobil station. I went there a lot for Skittles and raspberry Snapple, both of which I could perfectly well get from the office kitchen but I liked the walk, and I liked the smell of gasoline.

I went to badge back in but I'd left my security card on my desk, so I just stood there until one of the workers from one of the other offices — blue shirt, tie, ex-jock demeanor — opened the door for me. Everyone recognized the Black Arts guys; we're the middle-class adults wearing T-shirts. Sometimes I felt superior to the people in the other offices — I make dragons, what the hell do you make? — and sometimes I felt like a loser.

Inside, everyone was recovering from the news and there was a feeling of mixed panic and relief fizzing on top of the usual post-shipping daze. It looked like nobody knew about my promotion yet. Don sent out a "don't panic" e-mail to say things were being handled, then a private one to me saying he was holding off on a formal announcement until Tuesday morning.

Darren was the lead writer and designer, the force that had held several successive Black Arts products together, the animating creative voice of the product line. Darren was Black Arts. From what I understood, he also held regular temper tantrums and blamed anything and everything possible on the programming staff. He was a relentless micromanager, mitigated only slightly by the fact that he was right 98 percent of the time. He and Simon had been the rock stars of Black Arts Studios, and after that Darren held that post alone. Depending on how you looked at it, Darren was our Mick Jagger (designated swaggering extrovert) to Simon's Keith Richards (quietly virtuosic, blatantly self-destructive). Or else Darren had been Paul McCartney (chirpily commercial) and Simon had been John Lennon (moody, introspective, possessed of quasi-mystical insights).

Darren/Paul/Mick had left, and Simon/Keith/John was long gone, and I, hypothetically a backup singer or maybe just the guy who shakes a tambourine at the side of the stage, was in his place. A few other designers were in a huddle around one of their desks—including Peter and Jared, who graduated from Harvard together three or four years ago. I could tell they were talking about who would step up as lead designer. It made sense that it would be one of them, especially Jared, who had taken point on revamping the combat system and tools chain in the last cycle.

They were going to be surprised on Tuesday. Well, let Don explain it to them. Nothing else was going to happen today. I wondered why I wasn't more panicked, but also I knew I had a right to this.

I had been handed it back on a platter, a second chance to be Simon. I thought of Brennan and his lost inheritance, and the crown of the true king lying at the bottom of a cave somewhere in the world, just waiting to be picked up.

A great deal of *Realms of Gold* RPG was going to come from me. This was so terrifying as to make it almost impossible to sit in my own chair. I wrote in my notebook the things I knew so far:

Place: Endoria.

I was slowly finding out more about that.

Time: The end of the Third Age.
Genre: Fantasy Role-Playing Game.

That was the hard part. It was going to be told in the weird format known as the computer fantasy role-playing game, a literary form that did not exist until about 1970 but had already become as strictly formalized as Kabuki.

I didn't know the genre especially well, but I did know enough to realize that it was an almost unbearably dorky storytelling form that was, roughly, a series of jury-rigged, slowly evolving attempts to marry the feeling of storytelling to the feeling of controlling a character.

I understood what its creators were trying to do, but their games didn't do it for me, at least not that way. The computer wasn't a human storyteller; it couldn't respond if I talked back to it. Little Red Riding Hood was a good story, but it wasn't interactive. Sooner or later I wanted to say "no, I may be Red Riding Hood but I don't care about my grandmother; what I want is heroin and only heroin," whereas the game had only "over the river and through the woods" to offer me. Which was a good story, it just might not be mine.

I still wanted adventure. I wanted to see places untouched by human hands. I wanted to make mistakes and learn from them; I wanted to fight battles I knew weren't rigged. The longer I worked at Black Arts the more I felt like it had to be possible.

I was going to bump up against the same problems Simon and Darren had. I was going to go to war against the same forces they had. I had to learn their tricks. And I had to see their mistakes.

I hadn't seen the Heroes for a while, so it was a surprise when Brennan showed up on his own that night. It made sense that it would be Brennan, as he was always the default character choice. He had the distinction of being, typologically, the hero.

Brennan, of the House of Aerion
Strength: High
Reflexes: Medium
Intelligence: Medium
Endurance: High
Special ability: Can wield dual weapons at no penalty
Goal: Restore the true king

"Hey there, Brennan."

"Forward against the dark!" he said. This was one of the recorded phrases he'd say when anything interesting happened during games. His utterances were written to be vague enough to fit various situations, which meant in any given specific situation they sounded slightly nonsensical.

"Uh-huh."

"By the honor of my house!" he cried.

"Yup."

In person he was a little more funny-looking than handsome. He had plump cheeks, and his head seemed slightly small for his enormous, muscled body. He was big and round-shouldered rather than classically proportioned. He had a battered wooden shield, spattered with flecks of red paint and adorned with a faded yellow griffin crest, strapped to his back.

"Forward against the dark!"

There must have been someplace else to take this conversation, but I couldn't think of it.

"For the quest!" he said. It came out with a slightly interrogative lilt.

"I don't have a quest, exactly. I'm trying to figure out how to make better video games."

"Aye. Seek the prize that was stolen!"

"It wasn't really stolen, though. More like it's been left lying around, and if I'm lucky I might find it."

"Aye." He sounded a little less certain.

"Why, what do you do all day?"

"Forward against the dark! For the quest! That sort of thing, you know. I pick up gold pieces that I find in chests."

"And that makes you feel satisfied?"

"Long ago I had a backstory. It's written in the manual but nobody reads it. My father stood against the false king, but we were beaten. If only we had found the king's crown — the crown of the true king. The Crown of Winter! Simon knew about this." He sighed. He seemed as disappointed as his inflexible features would allow. He wasn't designed to look very sad.

"Yeah, so I'm going to bed, Brennan. I have to work tomorrow. I can't just ride around looking for loose gold, like you. I have to go to work every day."

"In sooth, thy life sounds passing strange and shitty."

"Yeah, it sucks," I said, climbing the stairs to my apartment. "I'd rather be you."

"In sooth, my life is kind of better than yours. Maybe you should play more video games."

"Aye," I said.

Chapter Sixteen

made sure to be in the office by nine fifteen on Tuesday morning for the ten o'clock leads meeting. On my way in, Holly, the receptionist, smiled and congratulated me, then Roger in QA waved to me in a low-key but cheery way. I sat down at my computer and there it was, a company-wide e-mail about the restructuring:

> We are happy to announce that Russell will be stepping up for us as lead designer for *Realms of Gold VII*. Gabby will stay on as art lead. Lisa will fill in as lead programmer.

Peter and Jared came in together around nine forty-five—they were roommates—and my skin prickled as I sat rigid in my chair and waited for them to sit down and get the news. Should I have met them as they came in and greeted them with the news? I'd hoped they would come in later—I wanted to meet them coming out of that meeting, after they'd had time to adjust to the news.

I strained to hear a reaction. I think I caught a whispered "No way!" I knew I was going to look weirder and weirder just sitting there and not saying anything, so I went around for a low-key hello. Jared and Peter shared a table side by side, among a tangle of cables and action figures (ironic? I never knew) and Jared's trackball, which he brought from home and insisted on using instead of a mouse. I hate going to see people at their desks, because they're always facing away from you and you have to figure out how to get their attention, but this time Peter was perched on one of the desks and could say "Hey" to get things started. They were—how did this happen without me?—cool. They had actually competed to get into the industry instead of retreating there because no place else would take them.

They went out and (I assumed) hooked up with girls. For them, a video game job was a little like a job in film. It was actually, sincerely, cool. "So you got the e-mail?" I said. It was, in fact, up on Jared's screen. "Yeah, congratulations, man," Jared said, while Peter came up with some combination of "Totally cool!" and "Yeah!"

"So we'll meet, like, eleven thirty after leads and go through some stuff," I said abruptly. I didn't know why eleven thirty.

Nobody had anything to do that day, and I had my first realization about management, which was that a big part of the responsibility is making sure everyone under you has something to do every second of the day.

"Right, right."

I added, "Okay, cool. See you then." I left them with this sparkling witticism. Troops rallied.

The leads meetings were a daily status update where the heads of different disciplines reported on progress and exchanged information. For the most part, Black Arts had a non- or antihierarchical ethos, but there were limits. The conference room was always freezing for some reason. I had only been in there for company-wide meetings, where we all crammed in and stood against the walls, or for the occasional office party, or because it was the only place to make a private phone call.

We were a revised and reconstituted Black Arts, headed by me and Lisa and Don, the old second-string players. Genius had left the building. There had been a couple of summary resignations since Darren's announcement, and the vacant tracts of third-floor land encroached still further on our cubicle village. Lisa was the only person there.

"Hi," she said. She looked tired.

"Hey. Congratulations."

"It's not that much of an honor," she said. "Just seniority. Everyone here now is leftovers. Producers, a couple of level designers, journeyman programmers."

"So, ah, how come you didn't go with them?"

"Nobody asked. I'm a tools programmer; it's not sexy. Plus, Darren's guys, they're kind of…assholes. I'm not sure I would have gone even if they asked me. I know them pretty well."

"So…what exactly do you do here now?" I asked.

"Rendering and lead," she said. She was doing her best to hide it, but for the first time since I could remember she may actually have looked pleased. "Our deal with NVIDIA is toast, obviously. I have a *Quake*-style renderer I've been doing in my spare time. We shouldn't have to change the data scheme radically from what we had, so we're going to see what it can do."

"Did you write the renderer for the last one?" I asked, wondering what the words *spare time* meant to her.

"Some asshole in Ukraine did it. We bought it through the mail. Women don't write renderers, not on Darren's team, anyway," she said, and underneath the blanked-out affect I felt just a hint of her bitterness. "Not anywhere, really. This one's going to be first on a triple-A game."

Black Arts was already starting to look different to me now that I was a leading player. It had its own rules and character classes that I needed to know. I realized it as Gabby, the lead artist, came in — I still didn't know anything about her other than that she was tall and bony with frizzed red hair, and that she was supercompetent. She wore jeans and a tank top and generally had more color than the average BA drone. Artists in a game studio are their own species. They produce the showy graphics that are the only things game publishers care about. They are all, on average, cooler and sexier than the usual employee, which is also a mystery, since the last time this class of people were seen they were drawing dragons on the backs of their notebooks in biology class. Four years later, they would come back from art school with different clothes and an attitude that told you they were only here because they had to be, which was probably true.

Gabby ran the art department as a fairly closed shop; which was okay with Don because it was also the only department that was reliably on schedule. I could see it was going to be embarrassing to have to go stand over her at her desk and explain why the green dragon couldn't be breathing fire on the cover of the manual because, "Um in *Realms* um green dragons only breathe poison gas um it would have to be red it's just what the rules say."

And then, Lisa. I didn't understand all of what programmers did, but as a game designer I knew I would have to talk to them. I was starting to divide programmers into two categories according to the two basic ways they accommodated their personalities to the weirdness of having to invest a massive cognitive load into an invisible, inhumanly intricate rule-based system that functioned on many, many levels of abstraction. To appear normal even though they spent their lives in a dark empire of strict and arbitrary rulings.

First, there are the ones who try to normalize it. They make an effort to show that this is just a regular job to them; they have pictures of basketball players and racing cars, and whatever else normative adults post, in their cubicle. They go home at five thirty in the afternoon; they're good at scheduling, and always deliver product to spec and on time. They are typically very average programmers and mediocre-to-poor conversationalists. They simply choose not to look into the dark cognitive mirror of the machine.

Then there are the ones who in some way let themselves invest in what they've taken on, give a core part of their personalities to it, and embrace the damage that results. It comes with an inward depressive streak. The world of the compiler is an extension of the cursed, Chekhovian world they already live in, with the same mocking sense of humor and dour Slavic fatedness. When the world goes right, when the code compiles, it's a brief, anomalous suspension of the rules.

They work irregular hours and make a fetish of using the slowest computer in the building. Don would send an IT guy in after hours to install upgrades without their permission, just for everybody's sanity. I got the sense that Simon had been one of these compilers. It was a tribute to his brilliance as a coder and manager that no one ever tried to interfere with his nakedly pathological jaunts into the abyss. I was starting to suspect Lisa fit the pattern, too.

And there was me, acutely conscious that if called on to define the term *game designer* I would be at a loss. Designers straggle in from other fields, English or architecture or political science or creative writing. They work on a cluster of tasks no one else has hold of: they do interface design, story, game mechanics, map layout. How many hits it takes to kill an orc, and what's behind the next door, and what kinds of spells you can cast. It's not a solid science, and up to this point I'd muddled through on a knack for not offending people and an ability to imagine far-off places. I knew what a Great Designer looked like, and that was Darren — loud, brash, inventive, charismatic, never at a loss for a bigger, better, crazier idea.

"Our ship date is twenty months from now. Focus has looked at what we're costing them monthly and they're hoping to get one good hit out of the next-gen technology," Don was saying. "Otherwise they're going to sell that off and dissolve the company and recoup whatever they can. They may not even wait if it looks like we're not getting anything done."

"I take it they've never worked with a game developer before?" Gabby asked.

"Dead-on. They have no idea what they're in for, or what games look like halfway through, or why delays happen or schedules change. That, I'm afraid, is going to be my job." Don had three jobs, which were: first, pitch our games to publishers and retailers. Second, stay on schedule. Third, keep everyone happy. Much of Don's job had been managing Darren, who took care of the creative and technology leadership, the vision—whatever that meant. Now that would be Lisa and me.

Don and Lisa started wrangling about technology questions and Gabby joined them. She turned out to have a lot of technical knowledge I had no grasp of—texture sizes and resolutions, animation data structures, content pipelines. It seemed there was a lot of work that goes into taking a piece of art from an artist and getting it to show up in the game. I stayed quiet and acted like I understood.

Really I was thinking about mammoths and wolves, and snow falling into Brennan's face as he hurries through a forest hoping to make it to a village before nightfall. I pictured him bursting into an inn and shaking snow off his cloak, drinking a whiskey by the fire, falling asleep on a straw mattress, and lying wrapped in furs picturing the miles and miles of snow-covered forest around him in every direction. I was thinking about a dragon made entirely of ice that lives for a thousand years.

Chapter Seventeen

Ten o'clock, story brainstorming meeting.

Place:

Conference room.

Dramatis Personae:

Don
Gabby
Russell
Matt
Lisa

Excerpts follow:

Don: We're going to start from story with this. Games are never going to grow up until they tell a proper story, can we agree?

(Everyone nods. It seems true. Movies have story, and characters and emotion. And our whole goal is to make a game that's like living in a movie. And then movies will go away, and we will reign supreme.)

Don: Russell's going to be the one executing the story, but I want to come up with the main idea together. Let's brainstorm a little about the scenario.

(Don looks up expectantly at our silent, reluctant faces. It feels like somebody else should be doing this, but this was it.)

Lisa: Is there a starting point? What do we already know for sure?

Me: Well, we know it's the Third Age. And we're dealing with Brennan and he's on a quest. For the Hyperborean Crown.

Don: What is the crown, exactly?

Matt: Well, it's a First Age artifact, so not that much has been said about it. It belonged to a prince named Adric, but it was in play long before that. Crown of an elder civilization. Like the Númenóreans.

Don: [Feigned comprehension]

Me: It was the big prize in *Realms of Gold I.* Sort of cool for the fans to see it again.

Don: Okay.

Lisa: What's Hyperborean?

Me [primly]: Hyperborean means "from the north."

Don: That's going to look like shit on the back of the box. No one wants to find that thing.

Lisa: We could say "Crown of the North."

Don: That works.

Me and Matt [simultaneously]: It's not canon.

Don: Canon can be flexible, though, right? Darren modified a lot of things over the years.

(Matt and I nod, telepathically agreeing to use "Hyperborean" anyway; if they catch us and make us take it out, so be it.)

Don: So a long time ago — what?

(*Matt has cleared his throat.*)

Matt: There's some argument that *Realms* is set in the far future —
Lisa [hastily]: Who exactly is Brennan?
Me: Your basic RPG hero, handsome, muscular. Younger son of the House of Aerion, which was defeated in the Fool's Gold War. That's where we start. So...
Don: The House of Aerion's in danger?
Me: It already got its ass kicked.
Matt: Leira's in danger?
Lisa: It's out of character. Plus enough with the princess thing. Prendar's in danger?
Me: I think that would be weird.
Lisa: I don't really know why I'm here. I don't really do fantasy.
Don: Woman's perspective.
Me: Brennan's just starting out in this one; he doesn't know these guys yet. He's just left home.
Don: So Brennan's an exile, he wants to get his throne back. He wants to go home, right? So what's stopping him?
Me: Uh, accused of a crime he never committed? Every man's hand is against him, he must clear his name with the help of his friends, find the crown, and set the kingdom to rights.
Don: [Nods. What more need be said?] So where does the crown end up being?
Lisa: "Crown of the North."
Matt: The end of the Third Age is when Soroth the ice dragon descends from the Pole and brings winter to the Perrenwood and the Tomb opens.
Don: Wasn't Soroth dead?

Matt: Well, in the War of All Souls he flies to the Lich King's aid in battle. He was driven off, but no one says if he died. In fact, he's glimpsed by Leira Prime about two hundred years later in the skies, heralding the end of the age.

Don: Leira Prime is...

Matt: In some versions of history Leira gets to the end of the Third Age but goes back in time to marry Prendar and has their son, who later becomes the Lich King, following the corruption of the Circle of Seven per Second Age prophecy...

(Omitted due to period of inattention spent staring at Fallout *poster...if only the bombs would fall...)*

...which is why Lorac turns dark in the first place.

(Pause)

Lisa: But—last question—what exactly is the crown? Like, what are its powers? Why do they want it so much, anyway?

Matt: To start with, I think a substantial to-hit and damage bonus.

Don: Okay, well, what we have is, Brennan's exiled, looking for this crown, meets his friends, they go up against the ice dragon. Working title?

Matt: *Realms of Gold: Dark Lorac.*

Lisa: *Realms of Gold: Ice Dragon.*

Matt: Soroth Strikes.

Lisa: Dragon of Ice.

Don: There's a winter theme.

Gabby: He's, like, ending the winter.

Matt: Winter's End.

Lisa: Not-winter-anymore. Or maybe just "Spring."

Don: Let's think about the goal here.

Me: King of the North.

Matt: Crown of the North.

Me: Arctic Ascension.

Lisa: Behold the Northcrown.

Matt: Crown of Ice.

Lisa: Seek Ye the Northcrown.

Don: We get it.

Matt: Crown of Frost!

Lisa: Crown of Winter!

Me: Winter's Crown!

Fin.

Chapter Eighteen

Sometimes I'd get to the end of work and realize I just didn't feel like going home. There were people at Black Arts, and snack food, and infinite soda, and a lounge stocked with games.

When Lisa walked by, the Heroes from Across Time were hurtling over a rocky chasm and through a tunnel, jostling for the lead in 100-cc engine-powered go-karts.

I called after her, "Hey. You know, you could play an actual video game sometime."

She sighed audibly, but stopped, and I already regretted having spoken. "Okay, so what's happening in this one?"

"Wellll, this is *Black Karts Racing.* So plainly, I am Lorac, and today I am racing against my friends."

"Uh-huh. Where did you guys get those go-karts? Did you invent internal combustion?"

"Found 'em. And I'm crossing this bridge," I said. "Aaaand . . . now I am dead."

"And now you're alive again," she said.

"Right. So now I'm jumping over the lake of fire. And now I'm on fire. But I'm jumping in the water, and I'm not on fire anymore."

"Nope." She sighed, but she didn't leave. With the audio off, the only sound was the creaking and clacking of the controller itself. "Why is there another Lorac up ahead?"

"That's Lorac from the future. Space-Lorac."

"And the Lorac you just passed?"

"That's Dark Lorac, my evil self. And now I'm being eaten by piranhas. Aaaand I'm dead again. Not really, but I lose ten seconds."

"I can see why this is so meaningful to you."

"Check this out," I said. I veered through what looked like a vine-covered rock wall and through a portal into a sparkly, purple-and-white abstract space, a bonus area, until another wormhole spat me out again at the head of the pack. "I am so getting the Paris 1938 trophy and the points bonus."

"Awesome. Where are you going to spend all those points?" she said. She sat down on the arm of the couch.

"At the Motor Shop. Duh. Do you want to try?"

"No. I find this disrespectful."

"Fine. You'll never marry the princess, though." I started another race, this time through a gleaming city in the far future. Alien constellations glittered coldly overhead.

"Where's the princess? Princess of what? When the fuck is this happening?"

"She is waiting in her diamond castle outside of time, for one thing," I said, trying to make it sound obvious. "Matt and I decided there's a thing called the Ludic Age, where all these things happen. It's not a part of history, and the characters were all summoned here by mystic forces. Or I think by an experimental drug, if you're in *Clandestine*. Or a temporal-spatial anomaly for *Solar Empires* characters. And so then all the characters come here and you're stock-car racing or in a giant pinball machine, depending, then you're back to your lives."

"But did it happen or did it not happen?"

"I think we all saw what we all saw."

"And so now why are you child versions of yourselves with giant heads?"

"No more questions."

"I mean, it's not good parenting."

"Don't be jealous."

"Well, you're right—obviously I need to be doing this more. God, I've wasted my life," she said. She went to get coffee.

Later, around midnight, I glimpsed her at her desk, crouched forward, her face held six inches from the monitor. Coding, she lost her nervous smile, and her rounded features took on an expression of calm, searching intensity, like that of a hawk circling above the keyboard, waiting for its prey to make its fatal error.

Chapter Nineteen

Vorpal Games announces
Clandestine: World's End

Following his departure from Black Arts Studios, Darren Ackerman announced today that his startup, Vorpal Games, will debut with a new game in the award-winning *Clandestine* franchise. Late last week Ackerman closed a deal with Focus Capital to license the rights to *Clandestine* from his old company.

Matt read the press release aloud to me and Lisa. For some reason Black Arts had about 50 percent more desk chairs than it had desks, and the Brownian motion that governed the progress of these chairs seemed to deposit them all in my area. This, combined with the fact that my desk was on the way to the kitchen, and the fact that Lisa and Matt both liked to complain a lot, led to some impromptu meetings.

"Clandestine: World's End will give us a whole new Nick Prendergast," vows Darren Ackerman. "He's the ass-kicking machine we always knew he could be. He's not here to play. I look forward to carrying on the level of design excellence I established at Black Arts. Expect to see Nick's new incarnation this summer at E3."

"He's not here to play?" said Lisa. "Is that really their catchphrase?"
"Fucker. It's going to be just a next-gen *Doom* clone with a bunch of

Clandestine stuff painted on top. They're stripping all the character and storytelling stuff out of the engine," Matt said. In his view, franchise integrity rose to the level of a moral issue.

"So isn't that our advantage?" I asked. "That's how we win. They don't have story. We have actual plots. They make games, we make, you know—"

"If you say 'interactive movies' I'm going to hit you in the face," Lisa said.

"But it matters, though," I said. "Without a story you're just jumping around on polygons." I was getting a little heated. Why did I have to justify my own job? Lisa had an engineer's way of shrugging off the entire field of the humanities, all three thousand years of it, as self-indulgent fuzzy thinking.

"Well, let's think about that," she said. "Let's contemplate the profound wonder that is plot, and then think about how many Ferraris John Carmack owns, which is four. Whereas between us we have zero Ferraris, unless I miscounted."

Carmack was a cofounder of id Software, creator of *Wolfenstein 3D* and *Doom* and *Quake,* which invented, fairly single-handedly, the first-person shooter genre. He also led the field in real-time graphics; plenty of other programmers just waited for his next game and then cloned it. Designers, too.

"Darren has a Rolls," Matt put in.

"Well, we play to a different market," I began.

"That's one interpretation. The other is this: story sucks."

"Well, I mean, yeah, our stuff is pretty derivative sometimes, but—"

"No, it's not even that the stories we're doing suck, although they do," Lisa went on. "What if story *itself* sucks? Or it sucks for games? I mean, imagine you're twelve years old, and you want to play a video game. Can I—" She gestured to my computer. I rolled my chair away, she rolled hers in.

Her hands crawled over the keyboard.

```
cd doom
doom.exe
```

A spray of system messages, then the familiar splash screen — towering blue-and-gold letters on a hellish red background; in the foreground, a freaked-out space marine in green armor. She whacked the Return key a few times, blasting through starting options, and the game started instantly. "Look, I'm running around moving and shooting and that's fun because I'm twelve. Seven seconds and I'm on Mars."

"Phobos."

"Phobos. Now let's do ours. *Realms of Gold VI: Far Latitudes.*"

```
cd
cd rogvi
rogvi.exe
```

We watched the loading screen for about ten seconds, then intro animation. Splash screen. Character selection. Another animation introducing the story, this one forty seconds' worth. Then we were in the game, walking around.

"You still don't have a weapon. Barely know what you're doing. No gameplay. All you've done is watch some animations and waded through a ton of exposition in fake medieval. Haven't even done the tutorial."

It took, maybe, thirty more seconds to get to the first character, a woodsman who starts to explain that while you were away, something terrible has happened in the capital. She folded her arms.

"Still no weapon. So, yeah, I'm twelve years old, I left five minutes ago. I'm riding bikes now. You see why people like *Doom* more?"

I remembered the IT company across the lobby. I could see into their classroom from our floor. It was just a room with rows of computers on long tables. I knew when the *Doom* demo came out because I could see just from standing there that a third of those machines were running *Doom*.

"And it even gets worse. I'm playing Brennan, but as a player I don't know anything about him, so it's like I have amnesia and for the first hour everybody who talks to me has to explain things like where I live."

"Okay, okay."

"And they're telling me what to do, which is — here — helping these villagers, who I don't give the tiniest fuck about. And this guy has a horse, and what if I want to just take his horse — oh, no — I can't! I can't do anything except what I'm supposed to do. None of these people are real and they're all telling me — THE PERSON WHO OWNS THE GAME — what to do."

"Okay!"

"And then when I've gathered twenty sticks or killed twenty rats I get a tiny bit more powerful. And then at the end of it all they tell me I've saved the king, the same asshole who's been telling me what to do in the first place. It's the opposite of play. It's work."

"Okay, but wait," I put in. "*Doom* has a story. You're, like, a marine. You went to Mars to figure out what's happened to the Union Aerospace Corporation."

"Nobody knows that but you!"

"And me," said Matt quietly.

"And Matt! The only two people in the world who read the *Doom* manual! It's *Doom*! You're just on Mars and daemons are trying to mess with you and you fucking kill them. Why? Maybe at some point you feel a tiny stirring of curiosity about the proceedings. Might be cool to look into at some point! But you don't have to read a page of text, you don't have to stand around having pretend conversations that feel more like creating a macro in Microsoft Word. Story. Sucks!"

"Okay, wait, but this is exactly why people hate video games!" I had to stop her. I knew on some level I was right. At least I thought I was.

"Why?"

"Because they don't mean anything. You just run around murdering things! *Moby-Dick*, on the other hand, has story. *Citizen Kane* does. *Star Wars* does. Until we have proper stories and characters we're not going to be anything. We're not going to be art."

"Did you ever think maybe we shouldn't try?" she said.

"And just be about shooting things?"

"Yes! If I absolutely have to play one of our video games, the first—the first—thing I do is kill everybody I possibly can—"

"But w—"

"Let me finish! Not because I'm psychotic but because these fake people creep me out, and because it's a game, it's supposed to be my story, and that"—she pointed at *Realms of Gold*—"isn't my story."

"I thought you didn't care about games."

"I said I didn't play them. I'm not going to play an art form—excuse me—that says it's about me, and then it's about some patronizing, do-gooder asshole and the shiftless fuckwits who asked him for help. Who's that asshole? Is that your story? Darren's?"

"So what 'your story' do you want?"

"She killed every fucking person in the world and threw their goddamn key in the lava."

I left work early that night, around eight, and walked to Alewife station and rode the escalator down to the platform. I tried to work the question out.

Let's admit some things about video games. They are boring. They induce a state of focus that is totally absorbing but useless—like the ghost of work or creative play, but without engaging the world in any way. They are designed to focus attention but don't train you to overcome the obstacles to being focused.

They are fun but don't tend to make a person more interesting.

The rewards are false coin—they are rarely satisfying or moving. More often, they offer something like a hunger for the next game, promising a revelation or catharsis that they never quite fulfill, that they don't even know how to fulfill. They work in a single small corner of the emotional world, stirring feelings of anger or fear or a sense of accomplishment; they don't reach for any kind of fuller experience of humanity.

But when I thought about story, I felt I couldn't really be wrong. Because when I lay awake at night I wanted to be in a story; I wanted it so badly it was an ache in my bones. Anything story but the story I was in, of early disappointment and premature world-weariness. I wanted to feel like I was at the start of a story worth being in, instead of being twenty-eight and feeling like my story was already over, like it was the most boring, botched story imaginable.

I used to love books in which somebody from our reality got to go to another world. The Narnia books, the Fionavar books. Isn't that what we could do, take people into another world? If not, why not? Why couldn't that be what we did?

The next evening Lisa came by my desk while I was playing *Realms of Gold: Prendar's Folly.* It had a Gothic feel, one of those impossibly beautiful CD-ROM puzzle games. I was searching around in a graveyard, at night, naturally. The tall, grotesquely carved headstones cast wild shadows, a flashy bit of graphics tech.

"God, what an ugly hack that was," said Lisa.

"Looks nice, though."

"Thanks," she said.

I cleared my throat. "So. If you could make any game at all for yourself, what would it be? I'm asking everyone."

"I'm not really a gamer, you know? It would be just like programming, I guess. Mostly games are about taking the computer and shutting down all the interesting things about it. All I can see in this thing"—she pointed at the screen—"is, like, a dumb kind of story pasted onto the computer, which is much less interesting than the computer itself." I had the silver skull in a bag now. They knew Prendar had turned werewolf. I was on the path that would lead to recovering the NightShard—the price of Leira's love and the thing that would divide the heroes for the rest of the age.

"Yes, yes, honor is satisfied, thanks. But if you had to try and make an actual game that you would like."

She thought for a long while. "Talking horse, I guess."

"Really?"

"You could ride it around and it would be your friend. Why? What superamazing game would you play? Honestly," she said.

"I don't know." I thought for a long time, too, before answering. What did I want? "Probably I'd have a gun and go into Harvard Square and murder people."

"This is why they hate us."

Chapter Twenty

Okay, so just a clean sheet of paper.

I tried to think it through. Was it possible to tell the story without all the baggage Lisa talked about? No conversations, no cutscenes. Just gameplay. No interruptions, no one telling you what to do.

I thought about *Doom*. I thought about what it's like to grow up in Endoria at the end of the Third Age, about the forest and the castle. What does the start of a story look like?

Once upon a time...

Like a path leading into the great forest at the edge of your father's land. You can only see a short way down, then it curves out of sight, darkly shaded by the old growth above.

There's a field behind you, and a low castle in the distance, smoke trailing up into the chilly autumn air. Sigh. There's something expansive and melancholy at the same time. The sun is well into the afternoon. It's almost too late to set out.

You can walk back to the castle if you like and see sunburned men and women bringing in the harvest. The castle feels like home, but they don't need you there. Sooner or later you may want to leave and start your life in earnest.

Maybe it's not that hard to begin a story. You can walk into that forest anytime. Break off a branch and walk as long as you like. Farther on, the pathway forks at an old stone milepost dating from the last empire. In one direction you hear the sound of a stream. In the other, silence. The start of a story.

There are brigands moving around in the forest. You might meet one and kill your first man in a breathless scuffle. A carriage might pass through, carrying a noble lady of House Gereint, which your father warned you against. There's a hole in the ground where the people of that last empire mined the stone for their mileposts, but it's been long ages since they ceased work there. Their tools lie abandoned in their places, as if they left in haste.

But what does the start of your story look like? Maybe you don't feel like taking that path. You can see there's also a road leading from the city out through the fields and through a mountain pass and into the town, which sits on the border between the House of Aerion's land and the Gereints'. Caravans run through it and halt outside town at camps, where the caravan drivers tell tales by the firelight. There's a tale that mentions your great-grandfather's great-grandfather, and the war he fought in a frozen land, where he lost a crown. The next day there's a brawl in the marketplace. There are rumors of war. There's an old woman who can teach you how to find due north by starlight.

I sketched the map freehand, using a contour map of Cambridge as a guide. The mines went in at Porter Square, the deepest station in the Boston subway system. I let the Mass Pike heading east lead off toward other kingdoms, and the train lines running south became a deeply rutted cart trail.

I looked at the result. Seen this way, Cambridge almost seemed like a cool place to be.

That night I thought about the game again as I was falling asleep.

Project Proposal: The Hyperborean Crown

It hovers like a cartoon logo in your head as you lie under the glossy, striped sheets you chose at the store and the heavy sleigh bed you assembled a few weeks after you moved in. But you wake remembering it, as you listen to students talking underneath your window and skater kids rolling past at all hours. You live in a college town, though you're no longer a student yourself, and haven't been for a long time.

It's raining outside. How did you get here? And how did you get to be twenty-eight?

Picture the road north to the country, where the crown is. It starts with getting out of this bed. You would get up right now, stand in your boxers and complimentary T-shirt from a theater conference two summers ago, go down the stairs, the carpets no longer showroom quality, down through the black rooms of dinner smells to the sliding door out into the backyard, the air still warm from the late summer heat. The stars are desert-clear.

You're in one of your quiet panics that get worse at night. Around the side of the house and into the quiet street, asphalt even and warm. Where the block ends, there's only scrubby grass and dry soil and wild-flowers, now just dried-up seedpods ready for fall. You walk into the middle of the road and sit down. The street is so quiet you could linger for hours. The moon is desert-clear as well. There's a path leading off down the hill, marked with pale amber lights mounted at ankle height, leading down through the park.

You think about your sister, Margaret. She just turned thirty-four. She's moved into a trailer she bought and parked on your father's land, by the house he bought in upstate New York a few years ago. She seems happier than she was. She has a small dog. She's dating a guy ten years younger, an undergrad at SUNY Buffalo. You worry about how the trailer will do this winter.

In the middle of your life you find yourself in a suburban housing development. You're sure as hell not going to law school, so what's going to happen to you? I mean, seriously, what happens at the end of the Third Age? To any of us?

Chapter Twenty-One

For the last week of preproduction my section of the schedule read WRITE TDR DOCUMENT. It turned out this meant "technical design review," and I tracked down the one Darren wrote for *Realms of Gold VI* and set it to print, which resulted in a stack of printouts four inches high. The TDR was the universal blueprint for the entire game, the almighty spreadsheet of creation.

It listed every object, every feature, every level, every scene, every character—everything from the Save/Load screen to the closing screen. When I was done with it, the other teams would take it for holy writ. Gabby would take it and break down every texture they had to draw, every 3-D model they had to build, every animation they had to script, and assign it all to somebody, and estimate how much time it would take and put that in the schedule. Don would take the schedule information and track everybody's progress and figure how many people we'd need and how much money all this would cost.

Lisa would do the same thing—break down all the functionality, systems, and subsystems for the programming team, including all the process-oriented stuff—tools for the designers, the mechanics of taking raw graphics files and importing them into the game engine, etc., etc., etc.

I would do the same for the designers, who would then build the levels, spec the interfaces, write the dialogue, and place the objects, traps, and monsters.

It occurred to me to read through Darren's TDR in case he'd listed "crazy black sword of insanity" anywhere. He hadn't, which only added to the mystery. If you didn't put that on a list, how did it get in the game?

At the top of a fresh legal pad I wrote:

Technical Design Review: *Realms of Gold VII: Winter's Crown*
"The World Is Everything That Is the Case"

For example: What is every possible action you can ever possibly take? For example: Walk, run, jump, crouch, pick up, drop, throw, stab, chop, slash, parry, shoot, cast a spell. Talk. Sneak. Get on a horse, get off a horse, open a door, close a door. Lock a door, unlock a door. Light a torch, snuff out a torch. Fall over. Die. Was that everything?

Next there was, oh, God, every single object in the entire world.

    door
    horseshoe
    catapult
    tiara
    bucket
    stone, large (4')
    stone, medium (2')
    Stone, small (1')
    Stone, tiny (1")

Oh, God. Maybe if I worked by categories. I started with foodstuffs.
Turkey leg; pint of milk; seedcake (the contents of Black Arts' refrigerator).
What next?
Weapons? Light Sources?
What about Light Sources That Are Also Weapons? A glowing sword? A wooden club that has caught on fire? Oh God. Could you

even contemplate an ultimate game unless you had an infinite list of possible objects? And were there by any chance foodstuffs that were also light-emitting weapons?

The sun was long down by the time I was done with every inanimate object I could imagine us needing in a fantasy universe. By then I was starting to realize I couldn't just list nouns and verbs. I was making a system; the world was a space to play in. The objects related to each other and to the game system that ran the world; they were more like clusters of adjectives, properties. I would need to specify how much everything weighed, cost, how durable it was, whether it damaged an enemy, what it was made out of, whether it burned, floated, emitted light, harmed werewolves, drained levels, or damaged the undead.

And how much it cost! At the start of the fourth century, the Roman Empire was having a lot of trouble with inflation. Nobody understood economics back then, so Emperor Diocletian simply issued the Edict on Maximum Prices. He made a list of the prices of every possible thing you could buy in the empire and how much it could cost. An egg cost one denarius, no more. The two most expensive things in the empire could cost, at most, 150,000 denarii each. With that much money you could either buy a pound of purple-dyed silk, which no one ever needed except Diocletian himself, since the emperor was the only one who wore purple. Or you could buy a lion. Up to you. But game designers had as much luck controlling prices as a Roman emperor did. WAFFLE had its own ideal about economics and adjusted prices by the whims of its scheming elves and greedy dwarves. We had to built an "appraise" skill just so players could keep up with them.

Later that night I wandered the office trying to think of reasons to leave, to go home and get some sleep. I saw that Lisa's desk light was on. She was playing the last *Realms of Gold* game. I'd never actually seen her or anyone else playing it in the office. I stopped to follow the action. The game was in isometric view — not true 3-D, but as if the player is looking down at the world from above, at an angle. The characters looked like colorful, delicate paper dolls. I watched while Lisa carefully, patiently murdered everyone in the entire world.

Chapter Twenty-Two

Every day, I had in the neighborhood of twenty or thirty questions for Lisa.

Q: Hey, Lisa, can we have a pet wolf that follows you around and fights for you?
A: No.

Q: Why not?
A: Pathfinding. The wolf has to follow you around all the time, but there are cases when that's too hard to work out.

Q: Can we have Dark Lorac cast a spell to make himself a hundred feet tall?
A: No. Wait, does Lorac have to move around? We maybe do him as terrain.

Q: Never mind. Can the player dig a hole in the ground and wait for the monster to come by?
A: No.

Q: Why not?
A: Because what if they decided to keep digging and dig away the entire continent? Plus, changing terrain creates bad pathfinding cases. Next version we'll do it differently.

Q: Can the player cut down a tree?

A: No.

Q: Why not?

A: What if they dedicated their life to cutting down all the trees in the whole game?

Q: Exactly what kind of an asshole is this person?

SMALL HUMANOID CREATURES

goblin, warrior

goblin, chieftain

goblin, warrior, dead

goblin, chieftain, dead

orc, warrior

orc, chieftain

orc, warrior, dead

orc, chieftain, dead

human, farmer, male

human, farmer, female

human, town dweller, male

human, town dweller, female

human, merchant, male

human, merchant, female

human, nobleman

human, noblewoman

human, king

human, queen

human, warrior, male

human, warrior, female

human, magician, male

human, magician, female

human, rogue, male

human, rogue, female
human, farmer, male, dead

JESUS FUCKING CHRIST.

Friday was my first morning waking up underneath my own desk. My sleeping mind had decided that my sneakers were a good idea for a pillow. It was, let's see, ten forty-eight. I'd been up until five doing terrain types. I sat up, but left my eyes closed for a moment and listened to somebody typing. Jared, I realized.

"Yo," he said.

"Hey," I said.

I took a moment to think about what I might look like, then had what seemed to my tired brain to be a profound epiphany: given that I had all my clothes on, and I knew where my shoes were, things were probably okay.

"Hey, Russell," Jared said. "Are we doing mounts at all? Gabby says the art's not hard."

"Why not? Ask Lisa if we can."

I levered to my feet and padded to the kitchen in my socks. I made coffee slowly, leaning against the counter. I'm already at work, I thought. Timewise, I am way ahead on my day.

I took the coffee to my desk. It didn't actually feel that weird. Really okay, actually. Fuck parents, fuck having a real job. Maybe this is what we do.

Magic Items

Some items in Endoria were enchanted. People knew how to do these things. I started the list. Magic swords I knew how to do. Rings could be magic, duh. Wands and potions. But then couldn't other things be magic? Decks of cards, rocks with holes in them, masks?

What caught my attention was the artifacts category. Singular items, storied, created by gods, legendary craftsmen, or powerful historical forces. On the very, very rare occasion the game generated one of them, it was taken off the list and couldn't be generated again.

Brass Head: A male head of noble appearance, fashioned of brass. When heated to body temperature, its eyes move in sockets and it gains the power of speech. If damaged or opened, it is revealed to contain a small amount of sand. Can recite a character's name and details of his or her history; clairvoyant. *Glaurus VI was so taken with the Head's abilities that he gave it a dukedom and an infantry command. History does not mention a Glaurus VII.*

Dragon-Turtle Armor: A suit of plate armor evidently made of bone or shell, densely inscribed. Any damage it sustains will be distributed equally among nearby allied characters. *Share my glory, friends. Share my doom.*

Hyperborean Crown: What the fuck is the Hyperborean Crown? Why does anyone want it? Even Matt didn't have an answer to this one. It was just the ur-quest Item. Finding it means the game's over and you won, which makes sense in a little ASCII dungeon game that doesn't have to explain itself. But we were gaming in a realistic world at this point, and everything needed a reason.

Idol of Arn: A small jade figurine of a grinning, Buddha-like man, quite ordinary except that it is always warm to the touch. There used to be two of them. The other one disappeared in the Second Age, around the same time the Inland Sea appeared . . .

Mirror of Becoming: User polymorphs into one of the following: 40% chance, dragon of random color and size; 25% chance, giant rat; 25% chance, minor daemon; 9% major daemon; 1% chance, minor demigod. Transformation lasts anywhere between one and twenty-four hours. *"Who's the fairest now, dearies?" she hissed.*

The Soul Gem: A faceted black jewel two inches across, ageless and imperishable. It has appeared in a variety of settings over the ages — pendants, crowns, breastplates, skulls. At the end of the Third Age it returns to the beginning of that Age, along with whoever possesses it. *"Take it,"* the old man said. *"Make a better world."*

Staff of the Sorcerous Gentleman: All spells cast by the wielder have quadruple effect and duration. Intelligence increases. Staff cannot be discarded. After 3–4 hours, wielder will involuntarily begin moving toward the nearest body of salt water and immerse him- or herself, there to die unless sustained by artificial means. *"Do you know extended underwater breathing? How fast can you teach it?"*

Unique Monsters: Liches, Daemons, Demigods

Arch-lich: mightiest of the undead; the animate corpses of mortals too proactive to die. Being a sixteenth-level spell caster with genius intelligence was merely the price of entry. You'd need a 120,000-gp soul repository, a dream quest to the Negative Material Plane, the sacrifice of a true innocent, and the iron will to die bodily but just keep on trucking. Whenever you saw an arch-lich walking around, you saw the remains of somebody who didn't mind having a skull for a head, if that was what it took. You may as well use its name.

Daemon Prince. Did this mean the Devil? This is where my fantasy theology got muddled. Who were these guys, again? Did they live in hell? If so, why was there a hell in Endoria, if the Christian God wasn't there?

I had to be one of only a few English majors to find *Paradise Lost* of practical, on-the-job utility. But how did "the unconquerable Will, / And study of revenge, immortal hate, / And courage never to submit or yield" translate into to-hit and damage values?

Chapter Twenty-Three

The black sword came back. This time it was in a test level I built in the old game to look at all the different terrain types—just a big room divided into strips of grass, marble, ice, dirt, and cobblestone. I looked away and looked back, and there was a goblin with an outsize black sword in its hand. It was a standard broadsword, but it was a flat black and had markings on it.

It was charging straight toward me and I watched it come. It had spawned from nothing. Just before it closed to combat distance, I took my hands off the keyboard and mouse, as if the sword held a mysterious charge that might have come up through my own character and into me. My stats cratered at its touch and I watched from the remains of my default first-level fighter as it collapsed in a heap. The sword vanished. I checked; invulnerability was set to ON.

But I knew, now, what it made me think of.

"Hey, Matt, what happens in the Second Age?"

Matt was in the kitchen, planted before the snack machine with the solemnity of a pagan idol.

I no longer felt bad about interrogating Matt about the Black Arts canon. I needed to know these things if I was going to be in charge of the story, and if Matt was shocked at my complete ignorance of a large section of my job he never showed it. In fact, I gradually realized that his fundamental good nature was one of those intangibles that made it possible for the office to function. That and I was pretty sure these conversations were the best part of his day.

"The Second Age? Well, of course, there are conflicting accounts." He paused, maintaining a sleepy professorial air as he considered the uppermost tier of treats, the chips and trail mix.

"But there've been actual games set there, right?"

"Well, supposedly *RoGII: War in the Realms,* as you know. But it's precanon, right? More what I'd call a narrative possibility space bounded by the strategic parameters of the game." He broke off, shyly. He'd thought about these things a lot.

"Do we have a copy?" I asked hopefully.

He shook his head. "Probably not. I used to play it on the C64 way back, but I don't think it ever got ported. I think it was a high school thing, in fact. Darren had a copy, but he probably just took it with him."

"Thanks."

The sun outside was just touching the line of trees at the back of the parking lot, so I went back to my desk and spent a little while puzzling through sample code for the scripting language I was going to be using. It was the moment, around six thirty, when the music was turned up, when anyone intent on keeping to a regular work schedule had already left the building, and anyone else still there was slacking and playing games, or else crunching on a serious deadline, or simply keeping a nontraditional schedule. People arrived as late as one in the afternoon and stayed at work until midnight or one.

By midnight the population of Black Arts had dwindled to a couple of programmers typing in the semidark *Realms* pit, headphones on, and a QA guy snoring in an oversize beanbag chair. No one was watching as I stepped into Darren's office and closed the door behind me. I pictured Adric at the unholy forge, hammering and binding the secrets of the world into the glowing black broadsword engraved in the runes of a language so obscene that the Powers themselves recoiled to hear it spoken.

It looked like no one had cleaned up the office since he left. There wasn't much reason to: it was furnished with just a standard gray Black Arts office desk facing the door, plus a whiteboard on the wall and a low metal bookshelf. When he walked out, he had taken his desktop computer. His power supply, monitor, keyboard, and mouse were all still there, as well as posters of *Duke Nukem, Sonic the Hedgehog,* and *Johnny Lightning,* plus a beach-ball-size inflatable icosahedron. He hadn't even taken any of his game design awards. A pile of three-ring binders had been emptied and dumped on the floor, along with what proved to be a sheath for a katana. There were a few more binders on the low bookshelf, an employee manual, and a couple of manila folders. There was no desk chair. Probably it had been a nice one, and an alert coworker had made off with it.

Darren had cofounded the company, and his designs were, to use the term, legendary. What did he think about at his desk? Both his desk drawers were locked — maybe he hadn't emptied them. The venetian blinds looking out on the office were closed. There was no reason not to poke around. Black Arts' Ikea-grade office furniture locks weren't exactly bank vaults. I looked around for a paper clip. There were plenty.

After a few minutes I decided that office furniture locks are pretty underrated as a first-line defense. I looked around for anything else clever to jab into the metal lock. Maybe that was why Darren took his sword with him. I was starting to think about how it would look if somebody came in. I looked at the shoddy little desk again. Real game designers knew how to pick locks, I was sure.

I sat down where the office chair used to be. The desk was just too cheap an object to stand between me and whatever was locked inside. It was a crappy grade of chipboard, the kind most movers won't even consent to put on a truck, even if you ask nicely. There was just about a finger's width of space between the face of the desk drawer and the face of the desk itself. I made a mental assessment of how desperate I thought I might actually be, then I scooted in, put a foot against one of the desk's feet, got a two-handed grip on the front of the drawer, and pulled.

It creaked a little, then ripped out by half an inch. I could see it was just stuck together with metal pins. I pulled it farther and it crackled and bent outward. I shifted grips, pulled it out farther, and looked in. It was empty inside. I should have started with the upper drawer, I realized. I got a grip on the edge and pulled. Inside were foam rubber nunchakus, knitting needles, an unopened packet of yarn, and an old manila envelope labeled TRS-80. It held a lot of 5.25-inch floppy disks, mismatched Maxells and 3Ms, unevenly hand-labeled in ballpoint. They comprised a library of old Apple II and TRS-80 games, some I recognized and some I didn't, but the set of eight was all jammed into the same paper sleeve together. A few had been notched on the left side by a hole punch. The top disk on the stack had been used and reused. The label read WORDSTAR (crossed out), then M.U.L.E. (crossed out), then ROG2 DISK 4. And underneath, a notation. LANESBOROUGH, AUGUST 83.

There was something else left in the envelope. I tipped it out, a glossy brochure whose cover showed a photograph of a lake ringed with pine trees, a boy in his late teens just in the act of diving from a dock while a lifeguard or instructor looked on, smiling. Underneath it were the words KIDBITS: A CAMPING AND COMPUTER EXPERIENCE FOR TEENS 13–17. SUMMER 1983. LANESBOROUGH, MA.

PART III

THE SECOND AGE OF THE WORLD

Chapter Twenty-Four

The cafeteria was thick with tension and nerd sweat. The walls were hung with long streamers of printout—code samples, ASCII art, player rankings, daily schedules, tournament rules—in the gray, uniform characters of the camp's two dot matrix printers. It was just after midnight, the last Saturday in August, the last night of computer camp, and the *Realms II* tournament was down to its last two players. It had been a long summer.

A small contingent of light infantry, literally just eight units, charged Darren's shield wall, maintained by ogre irregulars with dark-elven support, all with the Discipline upgrade. Nothing short of heavy cavalry should even have distracted the line, and Darren wrote it off as a tactical oversight. Three turns later he looked again and saw the break in the shield wall. The whole flank was collapsing. And the small band of fighters was still on the move, eating up elite guard units right and left. It was the arrival of Mournblade, the Sword that Ruined Computer Camp; it was the end of summertime.

Summer arrived early, the rainy, overheated summer of 1983, the summer that changed things. The movie *WarGames* came out in June and we went to see it four times in the first week. Simon was entranced; I think it was the first time in his life he saw a smart person who kicked real-world ass.

For another, Darren found the brochure from KidBits in a pile of magazines and mimeographed handouts in a classroom drawer when he was looking maybe for a scrap of paper with an admin password, as Matthew Broderick would have done, or evidence of Mr. Kovacs's drug habit.

Darren pitched it to us during one of those aimless car rides, the key point being that each of our parents would contribute a little to help pay Simon's way. Even if no one talked about it, it was clear Simon had fewer options than the rest of us. There was no hope of getting a computer of his own; even if he could afford one, his mother wouldn't allow it. She'd seen his grades drop, and she worried about him. No computers in the house, no computers anywhere.

The brochure from KidBits cannily anticipated this line of thinking and promised a "balance of computer activity and outdoor recreation." We'd meet people our own age, get out of the house. The brochure promised five hours of classes a day, sports, hiking, and "a fun and instructional atmosphere."

What clinched it was a letter from UMass Amherst that came almost the next day. Whatever had happened to Simon's grades, he could still destroy a standardized test when he wanted to, and UMass decided to overlook his record and treat him as a diamond in the rough. Simon had applied early and been offered a full scholarship. From what I understood it was the only way he was going to college at all.

Even then, I thought there was a little more to the summer-camp plan. For one thing, on the last day of school I saw Simon by himself in the computer lab. The air-conditioning had shut off for some reason and school was stifling hot. He was typing, banging the keys on one of those huge old single-piece terminals. The printer started up, an old chattering dot matrix that took in a single long stream of paper, perforated on either side for the blunt teeth of the plastic gears that would catch it and pull it through. The printer head jolted back and forth and the machine rocked with the effort of churning out 148 pages of source code for *Realms of Gold I: Tomb of Destiny.*

Simon fit the entire slab into a three-ring binder — the largest kind, with rings that could have fit around his upper arm. He snapped them shut with the nervous gravity of a man carrying nuclear authorization codes. It was the Codex of the Realms, and it felt weighty and danger-ous, less like code and more like the warhead itself.

Darren's father drove the four of us up to computer camp on the last Monday of June. The station wagon pulled up in front of the Bertuccis' and Simon came out, waving good-bye to his mother inside and run-ning to the curb. We pulled out and onto I-90 for the long quiet drive west, the road bordered with pine forest and fast-growing high-tech office parks, buildings with shiny black glass and no signage, computer start-ups and defense contractors. Darren's dad worked at one of those contractors, doing he couldn't say what sort of work on Cold War ini-tiatives. He was tall, red-faced, an aging athlete who didn't pretend to understand what the four of us were up to. He made awkward small talk with Simon, asking after his parents, his grades, before falling silent.

It was almost noon by the time we turned off onto a single-lane road that wound for miles with no houses on either side, just pine trees. Mr. Ackerman missed the turn and doubled back to turn in at a dirt road with a pink construction-paper sign stapled to a tree, just KIDBITS in black Sharpie and an arrow. The road gave out at a circular drive before a two-story brick building with slightly dirty white trim. The main building (called Main) was a boarding school most of the year, rented out for the summer.

About forty boys and eighteen girls were collecting in and around the building, each orbited by one or two parents, unglamorous fortysome-things who had an air of competitiveness and also a shared, head-shaking embarrassment. They were the parents of computer geeks without knowing what that meant.

Neither did any one of us, quite. It was a deeply peculiar moment, the teenage geeks of the personal computer era emerging from CRT-lit curtained bedrooms to behold each other for the first time. To see ourselves as a strange, incipiently powerful cohort. And it wasn't so much the way we looked—there were plenty of soft bodies, T-shirts, and bowl-cut hair, but there were also more than a few would-be tough kids. The girls were alert and conservatively dressed, most of them used to passing unnoticed at the back of the class. A few of them towered over the tinier late-blooming boys. There were angry nerds, frightened nerds, nerds that didn't know yet they were nerds.

It might have been the eyes; quick eyes, with a way of focusing then looking away. We'd all discovered the same things privately and were meeting for the first time, like a meeting of UFO abductees. Moments of eye contact seemed to have a stealthy tentative question there, something like, "Do you think this is as important as I think it is?" Which at some point changed to "Can you believe they're really letting us do this?" and "When do you think our parents are going to leave?" It wasn't the first time in history that nerd was meeting nerd, but it was the first time for us, our cohort—the first nerds of the modem age, floppy-disk drives, game consoles, Apple IIs, and C64s—and we were different.

A cheerful, overweight man sweating in the heat handed out thick orientation packets, a manila folder with a name handwritten on the front. "Welcome to KidBits," he said. The folder held a medical release form; a personal information sheet to check. A room key, taped to a map of the dorm with a room circled. A map of the area. There were a few stapled pages of orientation information; curfew and lights-out times. We'd be doing swimming lessons and outdoor sports, the camp regimen from time immemorial — hiking, tennis, soccer. And computers.

After dinner, most of the campers sat on the front steps below the entrance to the dorm long after quiet hour, a few boldly smoking cigarettes. I looked out through the screen door, breathing the warm air. I couldn't see out past the circle of orange-yellow lights that shone down on the granite steps and a few yards out along the asphalt, just to the edge of the grass. Beyond that there was only blackness out to where the quad ended and the trees began. I heard a car pass on the main road, too far off to see.

I wasn't ready to sleep. It would be the first time I had ever slept away from home. I slipped out a side door and circled the building, trailing one hand along the rough brick. I heard Darren's voice mingled with the others, but I wasn't ready to join them. I walked straight out onto the quad, into the darkness. The stars got visible really fast out there. I couldn't see my own body and it made me dizzy. I ran a little ways. I was the only one out there — was that strange? Why was I different? I spun around, the stars whirling above me, then lay on my back in the grass. I'd forgotten what it felt like to be comfortable. Nobody knew me here except the *Realms* gang, and they didn't care who I was. I was starting to feel, maybe for the first time in my life, that I had arrived where I was supposed to be.

I listened to the others back in the circle of light behind me. "What group are you in?" they called out to each newcomer. "B Group," a male voice answered, followed by two or three cheers. Introductions. There were already rumors of a hookup but nobody knew exactly who; and they said a few people had broken into Main and hacked the phone switchboard to call — depending on the version told — Anchorage, the camp office, Hong Kong, and/or NORAD. Tomorrow, classes would start, and the whole summer's saga, but this is what I would remember. The crickets were incredibly loud. It was summer; there would be weeks of this before I had to go back. Oceans of time. I'd be a different person. I couldn't wait.

All the next day, we were trying to figure out who exactly everybody was, who we were, who showed up to this. Who exactly likes computers? We picked our way barefoot along the dirt and pine-needled track to the lake, where, two at a time, we lowered ourselves off the dock and swam the length of the roped-off section of chill dark water and then back. A full dozen of us mustered signed medical exemptions and stood off to the side, arms folded against the cold, watching the spectacle. The others floundered, heaving, to the finish line or turned in smoothly athletic performances.

Who likes computers? The skinny mantislike kid with the bowl-cut hair; the one girl out of twenty who wore a bikini instead of a one-piece bathing suit; the seventeen-year-old boy with noticeable abdominal muscles and an almost-mustache; the kid who just froze at the end of the dock for a full minute before being let off the hook by the bewildered swimming counselor.

The programming classes were no less brutal. Most of the campers were self-educated in different languages, BASIC and FORTRAN and LISP and C, and now they were all expected to pick up and use Pascal whether or not they'd seen it before. Kids talked over each other, and insufficiently brilliant questions could be punished with an eye roll and an audible "Tch!" from the back row. Nerds could be bullies, too, and the usual targets were poorer kids who hadn't had much computer access and, unfortunately, girls. Maybe this was part of why *Realms II* took hold. It was both an arena for people to prove themselves and a collective goal bigger than any one person's test scores.

It was the first time Simon had been thrown into the larger population of kids who programmed, up against kids whose parents had money and bought them Sinclair ZX81s the moment they started to be available. This was how he must have learned he was good at programming. As the summer went on he fidgeted more often in class, or asked questions that jumped ahead of the curriculum or out of it altogether.

There were two or three kids marked out that way, and a dozen others who pretended they were, but for some reason genius is terribly conspicuous in computer programming. As is mediocrity—I knew that no matter how hard I worked I wasn't one of them. I wrote code that merely did what it was supposed to do. Simon's solutions were rapid and weird—convoluted, sometimes in a pointless way, often in a way that looked pointless until you saw how elegant it was.

On the third night of camp, Simon and Darren and Lisa and I, with two recruits from among the campers, stayed up until one in the morning entering the entire *Realms* code base onto the local network, all four of us sweating, typing in silence as crickets buzzed and chirped outside. There was no air-conditioning and only dim fluorescent lighting from overhead panels dappled with the bodies of trapped insects. It took two more frustrating hours of compiling and recompiling to weed out the typos and the little glitches from the slightly different flavor of the local COBOL variant, but at three twelve we had a local executable version of *Realms 0.8*. Before he went to bed Darren handwrote a note giving its location on the Net and tacked it to an inconspicuous corner of the computer lab's bulletin board.

At lunchtime the following day Simon discovered three sheets of notebook paper tacked up in the same spot, written in blue ballpoint in an unfamiliar hand. He took it down. It was code. The style was alien to him, but reading and rereading it he gradually understood that it was a program that, added to the game, would set up an AI pet that followed the player around, fetching useful items and nipping at enemies. The pet could be a dog, cat, hawk, or iguana, each with different behaviors and special abilities.

That evening there were two more code samples in two new sets of handwriting. There was a primitive lighting model that found lines of sight and the strength of different light sources, and could reveal or conceal the world accordingly. There was also a rewrite of the wind direction code that incorporated the basic idea of moving hot and cold air masses and the position of mountains and oceans in the landscape. A day later Darren came back to the lab to find that someone had printed the source code and annotated the entire length of it with scribbled taunts in the margins alongside code optimizations and fairly witty critiques of Simon's amateurish code architecture. On the fourth night Darren called a full-scale camp meeting in a note tacked up in the same spot. We'd meet at eleven thirty in the dining commons. Bring a pen and a flashlight.

It's a moment I think back on, a moment Darren instinctively grasped and owned. The product pitch was its own minor performance-art form, and Darren was born a master of it. Standing on a bench in the dining commons, lit by a few flashlights, Darren already had the bobbing walk and mischievous almost-grin that would be so devastatingly charismatic on the stage at CES and Macworld, and he never really needed the stagecraft of a fifty-foot-high projection to make you want what he was selling. He had his own hyperdorky magnetism, a controlled contagious excitement crossed with adolescent cool. He gave you the sense that he really, really hated to show you what he was working on, but he couldn't resist because it was so cool he couldn't hold it back any longer. A bit like the mean but terribly charismatic older brother who was busy all the time, whom you couldn't help longing to hang out with, who just once was going to let you into the clubhouse.

He talked about the game we'd make, its ambition, its potential. He sketched the outlines, and then he opened a copy of that month's issue of *Creative Computing* magazine. *WarGames* wasn't the most important gamer-related media event of June 1983. That was also the month when the most important advertisement in the history of computer games came out. It ran in *Creative Computing* magazine and took up two full pages. On the left-hand page, two columns of text were spanned at the top with the sentence CAN A COMPUTER MAKE YOU CRY? The right kind of person understood the question intuitively as a challenge. The text underneath began:

> *Right now, no one knows. This is partly because many would consider the very idea frivolous. But it's also because whoever successfully answers this question must first have answered several others.*
>
> *Why do we cry? Why do we laugh, or love, or smile? What are the touchstones of our emotions?*
>
> *Until now, the people who asked such questions tended not to be the same people who ran software companies. Instead, they were writers, filmmakers, painters, musicians. They were, in the traditional sense, artists.*
>
> *We're about to change that tradition. The name of our company is Electronic Arts.*

Darren read it aloud: "In short, we are finding that the computer can be more than just a processor of data.

"It is a communications medium: an interactive tool that can bring people's thoughts and feelings closer together, perhaps closer than ever before. And while fifty years from now, its creation may seem no more important than the advent of motion pictures or television, there is a chance it will mean something more.

"Something along the lines of a universal language of ideas and emotions."

He broke off and looked up at the crowd, letting them all get it, feel the hubris of it, the vision and the sheer swagger. Everyone felt like summer camp just began for real.

For me it was the photograph that ran on the right-hand page that almost rendered the text superfluous. It said anything anyone needed to know. Seven men and one woman, all wearing black, shadowed dramatically, few of them smiling, all looking into the camera. Bill Budge of *Pinball Construction Set* fame wore what looked like a leather glove with metal studs; John Field, creator of *Axis Assassin,* held the center with folded arms and an arrogant sprawl. They were setting these unglamorous software developers up as icons, self-consciously, a bit of theater that sent a message. It said, "We're making ourselves look like rock stars or movie stars just to show you what it would be like if our work meant as much as theirs does, and to make you imagine for a second that it can." And once you've imagined it, you know it's possible. For certain people in a certain generation it was that first moment when someone looked us in the eye and challenged *US* to take ourselves seriously.

"So who wants to do this?" he said. "Who wants to make spreadsheets and plot data points and whatever bullshit the counselors want to hand us? And who wants to make something the world has never seen before? Who wants to make the language of dreams?"

Chapter Twenty-Five

We'd already talked it over and set the outlines of the new project. The new game wouldn't be about dungeon levels; it would be set aboveground, in the world of Endoria. And the scale would be epic. You wouldn't be a tiny + sign at the mercy of &s; you would be a king, directing peasants and ships and whole armies of +s. You wouldn't fight to stay alive; you would make war for a place in history, for the survival of the Elven lands or Dwarfholm. *Realms II* was about the grand strategy.

We had sign-up sheets ready, broken down by general areas of interest. The ad hoc Realms Committee would oversee code architecture and control what features would and wouldn't go in. It would also, collaterally, codify the camp's nerd hierarchy.

It still might never have happened if it weren't for 1983's rainy summer, which unleashed a downpour for five days of the second week. KidBits had laid in jigsaw puzzles, two Ping-Pong tables, board games, and a small library of worn paperback fantasy, science fiction, Mark Twain, and Faulkner, leavings from one of the counselors' freshman American lit classes.

Because we were trapped indoors, there was a kind of imaginative fermentation that took place in the common rooms and computer lab. Campers broke off in twos and threes, tasked with bits and pieces of the world, rules for siege warfare or cavalry charges or the interface for diplomacy or troop psychology and morale or the rules governing succession in the rare case of a royal's death on the battlefield. They sat in circles and perched on tables or huddled at computers, each of the fastest typists and thinkers surrounded by onlookers, all rapidly conversing. Kim, a high school freshman who had revealed himself as the phantom coder, recruited a steely-eyed brother and sister to port the entire original code base into C. Hours would pass uninterrupted with only the sounds of low voices, the hollow clattering of keyboards, the occasional roll of thunder, and the steady ticktack of the Ping-Pong tables.

On the fourteenth day of camp, the first full beta of *Realms II: The Second Age* debuted at KidBits. Open computer lab started at seven that evening. I drew the short straw, so it was Darren, Kim, Lisa, and Simon who solemnly took their places at the keyboards. Someone at the back of the room dimmed the lights, and the first *Realms II* tournament began. It would conclude, interrupted by three restarts and two full recompiles, six hours and 872 Endorian years later.

Realms II was still unmistakably the direct descendant of *Realms I,* just enormously enhanced and reworked in certain directions — world simulation, multiplayer control, different viewing scales, simultaneous combats resolved en masse.

The alphanumeric characters were replaced by minuscule tiles, twenty-four pixels by twenty-four, each one a tiny miracle of miniaturization. Like the mosaic tiles in a Byzantine church, they made a virtue of simplicity. A tiny tree stood for a forest; a tuft of grass stood for a plain. A tiny cave mouth. A knight with sword upraised. A castle with a flag bravely flying. A horse, a three-masted sailing ship, a peasant clutching a spear. (Stacks of photocopied paper, a combined bestiary, almanac, and gazetteer, identified each feature with numbing precision, detailing its capabilities, strengths, and weaknesses.)

The tiles stood together in insane profusion — districts, duchies, city-states, nations, and continents, the Lewis Carroll chessboard landscape come to life. Years later they would remember it in color, as it was in subsequent editions, but in the summer of '83 it was all black-and-white.

The geography was recognizably the layout of KidBits spread to continent size, the hills become mountains, the pond an inland sea, the whole thing a quilt of small nation-states, forests, mountains, badlands, and mysterious blank areas. Players zoomed and tracked across multiple screens to encompass it.

It was a crazy, kitchen-sink work of simulation and strategy, with a profusion of subsystems running diplomacy and AI management and a dozen other tiny disciplines.

The effect, which might have been sterility or confusion, was one of richness, of possibility. This was a world, or an outline of a world, in which you could do anything. The tiles themselves were static but evocative; the numerical blood of the simulation engine flowed through them, giving each one life, choice, consequence, a tiny destiny. A story was going to unfold, tonight.

The foursome had played before, of course, even sped through a game, but never in earnest, never for blood. Everyone knew the rules of the game, but they were learning at the same time what strategies would and wouldn't work, and what exactly was going to happen when players were at each other's throats.

They took turns moving. By house rules, the game played silently. People in the crowd shifted once in a while; the ceiling fans rotated. Someone got a soda from the machine. Every few turns a new feature would come to light, rules for mining or applying wind direction as a modifier to naval movement, and its author would lean over his or her neighbor or camp best friend and say, "That's mine," or, more often, "There's ours. I can't believe it's working!" The four monitors were the brightest things in the room, but from time to time the players would glance up and see the crowd perched on chairs and bookcases and desks, occasionally shifting to another side of the room to follow the action from another perspective.

I watched from the sidelines. It was interesting to see Simon as a player and not a programmer. Whereas Lisa held a decidedly ironic distance from the action — playing the game was a systems test to her, merely an artifact of the coding process, and I was surprised she turned up for it at all — Simon played as if it mattered, and seemed always slightly surprised, as if he'd written the code but never in a million years expected it to work.

Simon and Lisa had the fortune or misfortune of starting out relatively close together, which might have made for a preemptive death struggle, but they lost no time in establishing embassies and trade relations through the diplomatic interface. The Second Age was founded on a human-elven alliance.

After a few turns a rider appeared from the southeast, announcing peaceful intentions from a wizard king, and Kim's capital appeared on the map, sequestered in a forested bowl between two mountain ranges. A good portion of the world was still in darkness. In the corner by the soda machine, Darren was working alone, four or five campers clustered behind him.

Years flashed by. Nations grew and changed. It became apparent that the players were working in vastly different styles. Simon's territory was expanding in steady, regular blocks of farmland, harmonious and efficient, sprouting feudal castles as it went.

Lisa, in decidedly unelven fashion, was rapidly stripping her forests of timber, the purpose of which was revealed twelve years into the game, when a large cluster of catapults, siege towers, and elven foot soldiers appeared outside the walled city of Carn. The elf queen had brought overwhelming force, and the elves breached and overran the walls simultaneously after only a few turns of action. They pillaged, garrisoned, and trundled on.

Kim wasn't visibly expanding at all. Only a set of mine shafts ring-ing his capital—and a rapidly growing surplus in precious metals—showed what he was doing. Everyone knew there were other resources underground, though, if Kim managed to hit one.

Darren's people finally came into view in a series of raids on Simon's coastal settlements. He had opted not to have a capital city at all, only a moving fleet of pirates and a rogue band of horsemen who poached caravans here and there. When Simon mustered a well-armed citizen militia, the first player-on-player battle occurred.

The action stopped while a battle screen replaced the world map on Simon's and Darren's screens. The view shifted from displaying a con-tinent to an expanded view showing a ring of seven hexagonal tiles. From viewing the world from ten miles up, we went to seeing it from five hundred feet, as though we were in a Goodyear blimp hovering over a football game.

The terrain in each hex was randomly generated depending on its type. When viewed from up close, a plains hex was mostly level grass with a few trees and boulders. A forest hex was trees with a few paths and clearings, and so on. The troops fought it out until the battle was resolved, then zoomed back out.

The icons representing platoons and cavalry detachments were laid out on a field of speckled tiles evoking grass. Darren's nomadic cavalry was a collection of fearsome riders armed with spears and wicked scimitars, but Simon had prepared well for the encounter and his pike-men were formed up in neat squares. Darren's horsemen charged the line, but the pikemen were revealed to have sky-high discipline scores. They refused to break formation, and in the end only a few bloodied horses managed to escape the encounter.

The pattern of border conflicts continued until roughly halfway through the game, when Lisa was revealed to be holding almost three-fifths of the map and the other three players agreed to a five-year alliance. Her rapid expansion had left weak points in the frontier, and her faerie empire was broken into two sections before the former allies turned on one another.

From then on peace never resumed. Simon poured resources into a regular navy and swept the seas clear, but even as he did so his fields were burning. Kim had poured his treasury into a motley mercenary army—northern axmen and southern archers, even a small dragon.

Then, at eleven forty-eight, in a single turn, an enormous swath of Lisa's and Simon's territories converted to a scrambled, blinking wasteland of desert and lava hexes, a brushstroke of annihilation smeared through the center of the map. Hundreds of miles of fertile farmland, teeming cities, and unbreachable fortifications—not to mention tens of thousands of elves and men—were gone in a single update of the board.

The room froze as Simon and Lisa broke the silence rule with, simultaneously, "Holy shit" and a whisper-sung "What the fuuuck..." Noise began bubbling up from the room.

Kim cleared his throat. "It's not a bug," he announced distinctly. He'd found what he was looking for under the mountains, a daemon or artifact or spell. After a few moments, the room quieted and Simon and Lisa began entering their moves. The strategic landscape had been turned on its head: Darren's horde was soon reduced to irrelevance. He formally resigned and his remaining units flipped to Simon's control. But Simon's economic base had turned to ash and sand in the cataclysm together with much of his royal family. A half dozen turns later, he bowed out. Lisa survived at the edges of the blighted lands, coldly rebuilding.

It was one of the few times I saw Lisa suspended at the center of a frozen, attentive room. I knew she was nervous, because she kept looking down to check where her hands were on the keyboard. But after a few minutes I decided it wasn't stage fright, it was something more surprising. It took a little while to grasp it — Lisa was playing. I was more and more sure that if she hadn't before, she now wanted to win.

Lisa pursued a Fabian strategy, ducking and dissolving her army whenever Kim's massed dwarves appeared until she had managed to back them up to the desert's edge, and then she revealed her hidden card. At the head of Lisa's army stood a tiny stick figure of a man with a conical hat and a staff. A #info command revealed it to be the Archmagus Lorac. This final touch had been added by Darren and Simon. Four Heroes, powerful and nearly immortal, roamed the map: the wizard Lorac, Prendar the thief, the warrior Brennan, and the princess Leira. If a player's conduct had appealed to them, they would lend their talents to that nation. Lorac had been called to the elf queen's banners. This was their first appearance, the Four Heroes of the Realms. They started as essentially a couple of power-ups for lucky players, a little bonus to combat or magic or scouting that might tip a battle or two.

(A note on naming: Lorac was Carol spelled backwards; she did the initial pass on the special-unit code; when last heard from she was doing her residency at Johns Hopkins medical school. Brennan was Simon's old *D&D* character. Leira because Darren had a crush on a girl named Ariel at computer camp. They made out twice and nothing else happened, but by then the name was already canon. No one knows where Prendar comes from.)

When Lorac, a stick figure with a grinning skull, a crown, and a wizard's staff, took the field, his magical protection became the vital counterweight to Kim's undead sorcerous monarch. Kim's wizard king had died a century into the game, but his magic sustained him beyond the grave — all hail the Lich King! — and until then he had had no match on the battlefield.

The two battle lines met, and the elves won out over a mixed force of living and dead in a grinding battle of attrition. The power of Ahr was broken. At one forty in the morning, all four screens cleared at once, then displayed the same message in block capitals:

THE ELF QUEEN REIGNS SUPREME
AND THUS
THE SECOND AGE IS CONCLUDED

The room was silent except for the two ceiling fans. No one seemed to know when to break the six-hour hush until Darren pushed his chair back to stand and it toppled over. The brazen clanging seemed to unlock something in the crowd, because they realized they could cheer what we were doing, and that we had figured out how to be awesome, together. The sound that followed sounded just like what it was, history being made. Simon and Darren looked at each other, and Simon was grinning his face off.

Chapter Twenty-Six

There were sixty-three participating campers, and it would take a punishingly intense schedule to run sixteen official first-round matches, and four official second-round matches in eleven days (with one three-player match). The second round would produce a final four, with a twenty-first and final match on the final night to produce an ultimate winner. A grueling but unmistakable necessity. A moral imperative, in fact.

There was no prize for winning, at least nothing tangible. But there was a slightly sleazy unspoken question that hovered everywhere at camp, which was, who was the smartest. Who wrote the tightest search function; who could find the optimal shortest path between cabin, lake, and dining hall. There were people who wrote brilliant code and people who wrote workmanlike functional code, but there was no scoring system. *Realms II* was a contest you could win, though. Seen in this light, Darren's easy assurance that he'd make the finals was a stark provocation, and Simon's mouth-breathing gamer stare became a challenge. Mind to mind, who was smarter?

You couldn't set the question aside, because for a lot of these people it was the arena of last resort. They thought they were ugly; they thought they were losers; but they knew they were smart and it kept them afloat, and, in some cases, it kept them alive.

I hadn't fought for rank on *Realms I*; I'd ceded that fight without thinking of it. But one of us was going to win this. *Realms II* made me ask myself: Was it possible that I could be the best? And I was a little surprised to find myself answering, "Let's see." I suspected Lisa felt the same way, that a lot of us did.

Watching the first round of sixteen four-player matches was like watching sixty-four fantasy novels in a fast-forward tabletop brawl. Nobody played the same, maybe because everyone felt that the feature they authored held the mystical key to victory — they could game the way weather patterns influenced land and sea battles or price-control laws or weapons-forging expertise or the breeding of magical creatures. A few were proven right, such as the kid who attained a first-round victory by cloaking a capital's location until the final three turns. Darren's highly focused assassin's guild planted moles inside its three opponents' ruling bodies and won the game on a single invisible signal at the two-century mark, resulting in the shortest game on record and the first flash of his pro gamer talent at work. (The longest-lasting game featured a diplomatic alliance that spanned 312 years and ended in a brutal twelve-year siege with a Masada-style finish. The traumatized victor had to be talked out of conceding.) But just as often, these strategies failed spectacularly. The game world was just way too complicated for a single strategy to rule. Lisa's game saw a fluke roll on the wandering monster table produce a huge ancient white dragon, a great three-tile monstrosity that sent sovereigns scurrying for the corners; the remainder of the match depended on relocating forces out of its way.

The wandering AI heroes were decidedly a factor. Brennan reinforced troop discipline and morale; Leira, movement rate and aggressiveness. Prendar could scout and reveal troop movements, or conceal one's own, and one time performed an assassination. Lorac's abilities ranged from defensive magic to illusion to terrain alteration to explosions. The AIs weren't under direct player control. They chose what battles to show up to and which abilities to use, and it was up to players to woo them however they could.

At the conclusion of the first round, five girls and eleven boys emerged from sixteen matches (one of them three-handed). Five of six RealmsCom members had pulled out first-round victories, except for Don, whose good nature had been a little bit preyed upon by a Yale-bound Hotchkiss junior. We met formally to discuss bug fixes, rules changes, features, and tweaks to game balance. The white dragon was duly adjusted. Play was suspended for a day as everyone collectively relaxed. Broken friendships were patched up, homework was done, and the camp, generally speaking, realigned itself around a new class hierarchy — the audience and the sixteen players.

I could reconstruct every single game of that tournament, and years later, when I had trouble falling asleep, I would try. But I could remember other things. We were all wobbling, sleep-deprived, and night-blind through a summer of early adolescence, some of us more functional than others. At night, we would sit up late on the porch of Senior Cabin, Simon and Darren and Gabby — the tall, world-weary Long Islander with a terrible case of acne whose parents were divorced ("Stepmom's a bitch. It's no biggie") — and Lisa and me, and one night the five of us made a dash out past the floodlights to the fence and then walked a long two and a half miles in the dark down the main highway with no streetlights. I remember the brilliant stars and black, creaking pines, and screaming with laughter and dashing into the trees at any flash of far-off headlights until we hit Lanesborough's bare quarter-mile downtown. We all watched while Gabby, four inches taller than anyone else in the group, crossed the parking lot to the pale buzzing circle of light surrounding the Quick-Stop: Food and Liquor, strutting like a gunfighter at ten minutes to noon, waiting until the very last moment to flick her cigarette into the shadows before yanking the jingling door open. We waited, hushed with the audacity of it, four and a half minutes while she stood in line, until she came out, unsmiling but radiating triumph, carrying a six-pack of Rolling Rock and a small paper sack with the mouth of a brown bottle projecting out of it, and I felt a peculiar joy, the indelible cognitive rush of living a moment for the first time, and knowing it and feeling every part of it.

And we half ran back into the darkness and huddled in a natural clearing a short ways back from the road, where moonlight showed our faces just a little, and Gabby parceled out the glass bottles, which Simon opened neatly with a Swiss army knife. We toasted and Simon had only a few sips of his. I gulped as much as I could.

We passed around the other bottle, Maker's Mark, and he made himself take a long swig. The walk back passed in a blur of hilarity and at least one genuinely drunken face-plant over the curb and into the grass, and it was only when we were maybe a hundred yards short of the cabin that Simon and I took in, with a kind of cresting heartbreak and what must have been pride, that we were now three, that Darren and Gabby had disappeared during the walk back without our even noticing. Simon waved a kind of stunned good night to me and Lisa and waited a moment on the porch before turning in. We were still the coolest kids in camp that night, and he could hold on to that as long as he needed to. I think he knew there were things Darren was always going to learn faster than he could. That he'd always be running to catch up, if not falling farther and farther back. That in the end he'd be left behind.

Chapter Twenty-Seven

Four second-round games for the winners; killers and survivors only. In the opener I got pulled into the game's first player-on-player aerial battle, my giant eagles to the Hotchkiss kid's dragonets. With the aid of graph paper and a few trig functions, I was the first to spot a small inequity in the turn radius. A hungover Darren surprised everyone with a rather elegant and economic victory over Lisa, steamrolling two other hapless campers in the process. The third match got replayed because an Italian camper, Val, had exploited a bug in the river-travel rules that enabled her to effectively teleport masses of troops. She won the replay as well, on a truly grisly display of high-level necromancy.

Simon's match deadlocked in the medieval fantasy equivalent of trench warfare. The war turned on productivity, all four sides straining to squeeze more gold pieces out of hyperoptimized economies as play ground on for a full millennium. But Simon always played dwarves—eldritch miners with iron in their blood—and as dawn came the lines finally cracked, and the last slot in the final four was his.

The summer was peaking in the third week of July, the smell of wet trees after rain, the slow fade to darkness during evening rec period—it all seemed to have come to its fullest, long days we hadn't been counting until now. We had the second-to-last Thursday night booze run, the last hot-fudge-sundae night in the dining hall. Most of all, it was the tournament that was measuring out the days to the end of summer friendships, the rare (three, by my count) summer flings, the whole prolonged sweet moment of it. I felt how much Simon wanted to stay in it, to drink in everything he could.

Darren was busier and busier, and more and more popular, and Simon and I fell into the habit, I guess, of being close friends. We'd go for walks sometimes, or have long confessional talks in the darkness of our shared room. Most of what I know about Simon firsthand I know from this period and a few long phone calls he made to my college dorm room.

The calls came once every two or three months. I'd go that long without even thinking of Simon, and then when the phone rang I'd know it was him. He'd want to reminisce and go through old inside jokes together, or talk about games he'd played. Mostly I was humoring him. Occasionally he'd talk about an idea for the Ultimate Game based on this or that new intellectual passion of his, Chomskian linguistics or psychological profiling or Propp's *Morphology of the Folktale.* Or there would be a new way of arranging menued conversations or new ways of measuring player behavior that opened and closed new branches in the story in ways guaranteed to be meaningful. And it was always the same result—a frantic brittle enthusiasm, and then he would never mention it again. In the last call he said he'd found it, yet again, but he was uncharacteristically evasive. His own idea, this time. And not to tell Darren he'd found it. I honestly didn't feel like following up, and I didn't. I was in college, and I'd be a different person now. It was all exactly what I was trying to get away from.

Simon's dad left a long time ago; his mom seemed to be a step behind, working at a tragic little crafts store. He was smart, but in a way he didn't ever quite value in himself. He was short and unpopular and had no visible means of support in the world other than that he genuinely loved computers and computer games, probably more than I loved anything.

In a certain way Simon…shamed me, I'm forced to say; something about him gave the lie to what I was then. I wanted to be popular, I wanted to be very conventionally well thought of. I wanted a girlfriend and a car and a good college. I would have traded places with a lot of people. I was his friend, but I transparently didn't want to be like him. I could never have stood it, being him. I was, I think, a contemptible little climber, waiting for something better to come along. If I could have, I would have been a lot more like Darren, charismatic and loud, always at the center. It's fair to say that I was more a failed Darren than I was anything else.

Simon told me later about the walks he'd go on, through the baseball field to the trees bordering the ratty "Nature Woods." He found himself on the shore of what they stupidly called the Lake, really just a large pond.

He stood on the beach, just a thin strip of sand and pine needles, letting the water lap at his sandals.

He needed *Realms* to save him, I think, more than the rest of us did. This was his summer, the summer of his life. For most of us — me, certainly — computer camp was a logical stopover, a little bit of college prep; a résumé builder; for Simon it was a last resort.

The day Simon lost it, at first I didn't understand what I was seeing. Fights weren't a part of KidBits; there wasn't even much roughhousing. People were laughing. Simon self-evidently wasn't a boxer — he clawed — and Darren's advantage in reach only increased the farcical look of the contest.

Darren's expression was somewhere between angry and amused, part of him still hoping to pass it off as a play fight, to bring Simon in and wrestle him out of it. But Simon was serious; there was blood on Darren's forearms, and at some point he got a fingernail into Darren's cheekbone that left a scar I could see fifteen years later. In the end Darren was left holding his oldest friend at arm's length until four counselors could pull him away. Simon was panting, his pudgy face red and smeared, his shirt hanging half off. He'd torn it trying to get at Darren. Simon was escorted from the camp and put on a bus.

But the fight itself was forgotten an hour later, when word got out of something a lot more serious. Simon had managed to release a computer virus onto the KidBits servers; it erased a fair amount of data, mostly personal e-mail, as well as the grades database. A lot of people ended up getting free As because of it. But it wasn't terribly sophisticated—in fact, it was an uncharacteristically clumsy piece of execution. There was no doubt as to where it came from.

It wasn't anything more than juvenile mischief, but this was the heyday of teen hacker paranoia, of experts testifying soberly that one unsupervised kid could set off a nuclear war, and of federal agents breaking down the doors of unsocialized fourteen-year-olds. Once Simon was tagged as a computer criminal there was nothing even Darren could do to keep him from being prosecuted. He ended up with a hundred hours of community service and was lucky to get it; but his scholarship was revoked. Simon wouldn't be going to college, then or ever.

It was a deep unsolved mystery, one Darren would never shed any light on. Was it about a girl? Was there a love triangle? That was the most popular theory, one with endless variants. Or was it creative differences, or just old business from the antediluvian past? All I could think of was how Simon could have explained it to his mother, whose vague ideas about the dangers of hacking, of computers as the gateway to cloudily imagined supercrime, would only be confirmed.

And the more I thought about it, the more serious it seemed, and I couldn't help thinking Simon knew it. Simon and his mother had had early experience of downward mobility when his father left. Some part of him knew that his sullen refusal to engage in school was turning into more than just an adolescent funk, that it was self-dooming. But this was it for him, a clean break with the future. What was Simon thinking, on the long bus ride home? How would he save her now?

Five days afterward, at ten thirty on the last night of computer camp, Darren, Val, and I entered the computer lab for the first and last ever official *Realms II* world championship. After some debate, we'd left the final slot open in honor of our fallen comrade rather than replace him with the second-place finisher from his bracket.

We sat down with the charged solemnity of a world-renowned string trio and a nameless feeling, something between pride and anticipatory bloodlust, that verged over into a round of pregame applause — for the finalists but mostly for ourselves, for the game, for the whole summer, for what it had all been for us. But when the applause was over there was still something left to be decided.

I'd always credited Darren with a showman's instinct, but when the door slammed open every camper in the room turned and then froze. I didn't want to meet Simon's eyes. Ten long seconds passed, and then Darren stood and pulled the empty metal folding chair out from the table and gestured for Simon to take a seat. We went through the now-familiar routine of setting keyboard macros and setting starting parameters, the *Realms II* equivalent of rosining and tuning our instruments. The evening now promised carnage unparalleled. Each of the four of us was the sole survivor of two previous four-person matches averaging six hours apiece, and had watched half a dozen others.

I specced out a bandit kingdom made up of a mixture of humans, elves, and the odd faerie. I planned to lurk in the forest and prey on stragglers while the others slugged it out in the field. Whatever he was doing, Simon took the longest. In the long interval Darren held up two quarters to signal for a Mountain Dew. Val sipped her black coffee. When Simon slapped the return key, all choices had been entered, the lights were dimmed, and war in the realms commenced.

My scouts quickly sussed out the terms of the conflict. Darren's forces looked like tenth-century Normandy, a tightly controlled balance of aggression and monetary craftiness along with a good deal of careful castle-building.

Val was lucky enough to spawn in a mountainous corner of the map. My scouts reported her walling off a passage in and out, then they stopped reporting at all. My people vanished into the Perrenwood and started swallowing caravans whole. Nice, but I'd be noticed before long.

And Simon's choices were…eccentric. His entire nation was made up of tiny bands of humans wandering the map. I saw a few of them hack down trees and build a galleon that sailed away before I could catch it. What was he doing? He seemed to have opted out entirely. Maybe Simon really wasn't a fighter.

I harassed Darren's militia while he huddled safely behind walls, playing Sheriff of Nottingham to my Robin Hood. I could bleed him, but once his castles were up they were proving impossible to dislodge. He took land and held it. He had just begun to get cocky again when the gates of Val's enclave opened and (there is no other word for it) disgorged a horrifying army of daemons that ravaged and blackened the countryside as only the sons of a nation built on profane sorcery and purest evil can. We could practically hear the crackling flames and panicked horses. Castles that a few turns ago looked like permanent chunks of landscape were being reduced to sad little rubble icons, which after a few years blinked into peaceful little grassy icons. One hour in, Darren signaled for another Mountain Dew. I spotted him the fifty cents.

I waited for him to crack, for the weakness to show under his cocky exterior, but two things saved him. He put his king into the field. It was a grave risk, but it was the only thing that would put heart into feudal lordlings who were almost visibly shitting themselves. And on the next turn, the familiar icon of a man with an oversize sword presented itself at Darren's capital. Legendary Brennan the warrior had joined Darren's cause.

Gradually, desperately, Darren slowed, stopped, and reversed Val's advance. But Val had another card to play: Lorac the wizard. Further, it was the rare Inverse Lorac, the tiny wizard drawn in white on a black tile to indicate that this was the sorcerer's evil incarnation. This was the first game to put three Heroes on the board. I watched from the safety of the forests as a last great war of light against dark was contested.

But when the turn counter reached 446 of the Third Age, my screen blanked itself and the map was simply replaced by a tally of personnel, wealth, and territory. I'd never seen the Game Over screen before; I didn't realize what it was until I saw the entire room looking at me. Darren stood and led a brief, respectful round of applause. The bandit king was dead, and I didn't even see it happen. I was too shell-shocked to feel the sting of it yet.

It wasn't either Darren or Val; they were obviously dumbfounded, and Simon didn't even look up. Spooked, they nonetheless rushed to claim the eastern forestland I'd been stalking since year one. Ultimately, Darren was simply better placed for it. Inside two turns he was cutting timber, building siege engines, and ridding the world of evil at an admirable rate. Val fell back to the mountains, still contesting the field but already looking done. Simon was still technically in the game, which meant that attrition hadn't claimed all his wanderers yet. But short of a miracle, Darren was going to be the *Realms II* champion of KidBits, Western Massachusetts, and Planet Earth. I felt unexpectedly disappointed. He already acted like this belonged to him and had for weeks; he shouldn't have it. I wanted it to be Simon, but his game looked like a preemptive concession.

The bitter fighting in the mountains was all but over, and on the very same turn that the spider queen fell, the tattered sons of Simon's horde came into view of Darren's rear guard. I think we all assumed that Simon was now sportingly presenting himself for termination so as to let the game end.

Darren's forces met him on the field, the king personally commanding. Simon's people had stats as individual fighters, but the king's escorts were all elite heavies of their type, and they outnumbered Simon's entire country.

The sides touched and bodies began piling up, and then Darren's left flank began falling in on itself, its numbers swallowed as if a black hole had formed in its ranks, centered on a single fighter. Darren ID'd it. A star indicated that it was Simon's sovereign unit, his king, inexplicably placed at the front lines.

Simon's king was an apparent nobody, a midlevel fighter in a half helm, wooden shield, and chain mail. But listed in the weapon slot was a piece of inventory called Mournblade.

The room was on its feet in a babble of voices. Out of sixty-three campers, no one failed to grasp the grave provenance of that eloquent portmanteau.

Mournblade. The author Michael Moorcock wrote a series of novels starring the antiheroic Elric of Melniboné, the last king of a doomed race, a tall albino with long hair and amazing cheekbones and a hereditary frailty owing to his weak, rarefied, inexpressibly noble blood. Isolated by his gloomy destiny, he wanders through a world torn by an endless war between Law and Chaos. He also carries a huge, extremely handy black sword carved with eldritch runes called Stormbringer, a sword that absorbs the soul of anyone it kills and gives Elric the strength to get through the day. It's horrendously cursed, of course; in fact, it's really a daemon that will one day devour him. (In the plus column, in the far, far future, as the solar system goes into decline, Stormbringer will have absorbed so many souls that its energy will be used to reignite the dying sun and save humanity.)

I was extremely murky on the rest of it, but I did remember that Stormbringer had a duplicate named Mournblade, an equally powerful but apparently less ambitious cousin that wandered in and out of the various books on its own business, which was rarely explained.

Why shouldn't Simon use it? He probably had Excalibur, Glamdring, Durendal, and the Sword of Shannara wandering around in there, too. But the one he wielded had to be Mournblade — it was black and uncanny and runic — but more than that, it fit Simon. I could just see him lying in bed staring up at the ceiling and thinking "God, I am so Elric," having the inner certainty that on some level he was the lonely king of a lost people and a land that was no more.

* * *

Loose in the world, it was just a tiny icon of a standard broadsword, with a black border and a tiny squiggle or two on the blade denoting the fact that it was deeply incised with obscene carvings and cryptic runes. It was Endoria's first artifact-class item: unique, overwhelmingly powerful, storied, and cursed. Darren simply stopped play and brought up the Help file, in which Mournblade had been duly entered, if anyone had thought to look for it. It wasn't a complex bit of code, just a simple piece of algorithmic hatred:

a) Any attack by a unit wielding Mournblade would kill automatically.
b) Anyone holding the sword would slowly lose hit points, one per two rounds. Not immediately lethal, but a ticking clock nonetheless.
c) Any time you killed a unit it restored two hit points, which meant that as long as you had enemies to kill you had nothing to worry about; in fact, it would prove terribly difficult to bring you down.
d) Once you picked up Mournblade you couldn't drop it, ever.

There were a few more details to fill in. Mournblade could destroy objects such as siege works, but that wouldn't restore life to the wielder. And there was a 10 percent chance that it would attack an adjacent friendly unit, even if you didn't want it to.

Anyone foolish enough to pick up the cursed thing could be an unbeatable champion in war, but thereafter the logic of the item turned grim. You'd end up wandering Endoria in search of victims, ultimately turning on the few friends you had left. It was a tiny encoded curse, a few simple rules that, combined in a single item, gave rise to a lonely, haunted destiny.

It certainly hadn't been in Simon's manifest when the game began. It was there, it was in-fiction, it was surprising but hard to call illegal. Endoria was still Endoria, but nobody had bothered to delete Adric's Tomb. All Simon did was find it again, navigating the twenty levels down, past the fearsome &s and putting Mournblade in one of his wanderer's hands. Then he walked the chosen bearer back up and outside and Mournblade had returned to the world. Then the carrier made the long trek, a hundred hexes cross-country, to Darren's encampment, murdering lesser units as he went to keep the wielder from expiring as a result of the curse.

Nothing was going to stop the accursed broadsword from reaching its target. The room fell silent, and Simon rested like a virtuoso violinist, letting the final notes of a plaintive, triumphant melody ring into silence. Darren looked as devastated as I'd ever seen him, but managed to shake Simon's hand nonetheless. The victory stood; the game, and the long summer, were over.

The friendship never officially ended, but Simon and Darren didn't talk much for a while. They nodded in the hallways, sure, but their collaboration had gone slack and awkward. Darren gravitated back to the tall, buzz-cut kids from the track team, to roughhousing and weekend parties, and Simon gravitated back to himself. But Darren's father took pity on him, maybe, and set up an office for Simon in the garage, and bought him his own used C64. He sat up late that first Indian-summer night with the crickets buzzing. By November he was there every night, with the door closed and a space heater on, learning to code C properly and beginning what would become his imaginative lifework — the hundreds, maybe thousands of pages outlining the past and future histories of the *Realms* worlds. Time lines, city maps, histories, sagas, encyclopedic descriptions of imagined countries and planets, floor plans, character sketches. He developed a mild addiction to clove cigarettes. He once alluded to those months as the happiest in his life.

PART IV

THE THIRD AGE OF THE WORLD

Chapter Twenty-Eight

The mild summer stretched on into September. Each day the clouds piled up and rolled over Cambridge like a slow, soundless wave, but there was no rain, only a faint haze that made objects and buildings seem to be enormous distances away.

The first alpha phase began on September 1, 1997, and was expected to run three or four months. Programmers would try to hack new features into the old engine under Lisa's direction, while she got together the rendering module that would give *Realms* its bright, next-gen new look. Meanwhile, I would shepherd the other designers through building the first areas of the game to try to get something decently playable together — early versions of the game maps that we could run around in, testing puzzles and combat. By the end, we'd hope to have the first third of the game built.

Usually I would walk the two miles to work, letting cars whoosh past me. I thought ahead, mentally setting up an agenda for the morning leads meeting. It was an unfamiliar feeling, waking up with a place to go, a place I was actually beginning to comprehend and face without a sense of terror.

More than that, I was even questioning the assumption that I was, in my bones, a scared and anxious and miserable person. It felt like the days were almost supernaturally good, that I could wake up without the usual wave of terror, that the days were admixed with some foreign substance dripping into them, some animating essence, like the dragonborn races of Endoria, dragonborn days. I felt like I'd stumbled on one of the open secrets of the world. Why hadn't I realized before that being a grown-up could be anything you wanted it to be?

We had our maps ready, neatly sketched out on graph paper. I'd done the forest area; Jared did the mines underneath, and Peter handled the nearby town. WAFFLE would generate low-level detail for us: it could do even more than that, but we wanted handcrafted content for this earliest section of the game. I'd printed out maps of Central Park and Disneyland; we'd try to imitate that ineffable quality of promise each pathway seemed to hold, curving out of sight in a deliciously inviting manner. Every grove, every crossroads needed to contain the potential seed for a decision or an adventure, or a way to decide something about yourself.

In my mind, it was all perfect. This would be the very last gasp of the Third Age, an age gone wrong, the quest for Mournblade all but abandoned.

The world of *Realms* would have become an old world by then, rich in history and magic, but the bright shine of the early Second Age would live on in half-forgotten stories. Now, the Heroes the world once revered would be seen only rarely. The humanoid races snap and squabble, and the great secrets seem to have been lost forever.

You're given sparse clues about who you are and what you're doing. You're the youngest child of a minor house that has been losing power and influence for centuries. Its scattered descendants live in a forgotten backwater. The rare traveler that passes through brings news of a world going downhill.

You're just this close to being nobody, a punk. Your family's keep is not even a real castle, just a rough curtain wall of stone enclosing a stout four-story tower and a few wooden buildings — kitchen, pantry, eating hall. There's a chapel for one of the *Realms* deities, I'd have to decide which — the harvest god, let's say. At midwinter the villagers burn corn-husk effigies of the dark winter god, and in spring they carry offerings of the first fruits to the keep. You spend a lot of evenings just sitting by the fire in the bottom room of the square tower, listening to stories or some traveling joker on a lute, before climbing the rough stairs to lie shivering on a bed of rough matting.

You sigh through endless freezing winter services, painstakingly learning the runes of a prior culture out of a damp, ruined tome in preparation for your manhood ceremony, even though you're not even the heir. Your three older brothers come first, but the eldest has taken an unlucky arrow through the eye at the Battle of Atrium, fighting for your third cousin Vellan in a political struggle you didn't and don't understand.

They come trooping home to tell you the fighting's over and your people lost, and from then on everything gets worse. Your father drinks more, the House of Aerion demands a punishing tribute from those who rose against it, and brother number two (your favorite) has to ride two hundred miles to present himself as a squire-hostage at court.

You grow up riding in the forest in summer, shaking hands with village elders, and helping out at harvest time for lack of anything better to do. But more and more often you climb the stairs to the top of the tower and look out over the forest stretching out forever under a cloudless sky in summer, or into the misty rains in spring, dark green leaves out to where the hills meet gray sky. These times, when you're alone, are the most perfect moments available to you. You wonder how brother number two is doing. You've never even heard of the Hyperborean Crown, or maybe you've seen one or two mentions of it in that old book, which has its own pedestal in the chapel. Once you had your coming-of-age moment, you never touched the thing again. It will probably sit unopened until your older brothers' children have grown.

You get to know the land around where you live, but when you leave town it's not going to matter much to anybody. One day you set out, son of almost no one, prince of fuck-all, but you have your own secrets and you take them with you—a tarnished old locket you found in the abandoned mine in the forest, a sword you swiped from a forgotten storeroom, a kiss from a girl you met when her parents' carriage broke an axle and she wandered off. Her parents came and got her before you even learned her name.

Someplace out there, you think there might be a crown, and maybe you deserve that crown. It's north, that's what everyone says, the crown Adric lost, but it's under the mountains now, under a hundred tons of snow and ice. Lost a thousand years, frozen and buried, but not destroyed, not quite.

Chapter Twenty-Nine

That night, gathered around my desk, the Heroes were noticeably shabbier than when I'd first met them. Brennan had run to fat; Leira's face was windburned. Her hair was dry and frizzy, not the lustrous silk of a princess's. Lorac's hem was frayed and dirty, and Prendar kept glancing into the corners of the room with a jittery meth-head intensity. We're your Heroes now, they seemed to say, like it or not.

"We told you the realm was in peril," Prendar said. "Didst thou not believe us?"

"Okay, okay. But what are we going to do?" I asked.

"Lorac has a few things to say," Brennan said quietly.

"Run the game," Lorac said, and scooted himself forward. At character selection I chose Leira, who blushed a little.

REALMS OF GOLD III: Restoration (1987)

The screen showed what seemed to be a child's drawing of a dirt road by a field of wheat. Sixteen-bit crayon colors, green grass, brown dirt, gray rocks. It was the cutting edge of mideighties graphics tech, the first graphical portrayal of the world of Endoria — whereas *Realms II* had been a chessboard map of the otherworld, *Realms III* was a blurry window into it. I was seeing Endoria — through a shitty sixteen-color graphics mode, but I was seeing it.

There was a figure at the left side of the screen, a forty-pixel-high woman with brown hair pulled back in a ponytail, blue eyes, and a button nose. She wore a leather jerkin and a dagger at her hip. The Heroes had just started the process of evolving from game pieces into people. It was (although Simon and Darren didn't know it) the same way *Dungeons & Dragons* had started, the first role-playing game, when tabletop strategy-game rules had been modded to include individualized heroes with their own traits. In 1987 Leira, Brennan, Lorac, and Prendar were like late-Devonian fish struggling up past the high-tide mark on stubby, finny legs.

To me, as I huddled in front of the computer screen, the Four Heroes and I looked just like an old C64 magazine ad I remembered, a photograph of a kid and his computer and a bunch of dressed-up, sheepish-looking actors, there to show the grand worlds of imagination the game would unlock. Except, of course, that I was twenty-eight.

As Leira walked, pieces of the background scrolled past at different rates, giving a cute, crude sense of depth, another of Simon's tricks. In the foreground, a muddy road. Then wet fields of stubble and orchards bounded by old stone walls. You passed the slowly dissolving outline of a house's foundation, a broken catapult, and the shrine of a nameless deity, its features worn away but fresh flowers at its feet. Farther off, a shallow river; mountains; clouds.

After the final battle, an exhausted peace descended. Mournblade had disappeared. Perhaps carried off as a prize by a soldier. Perhaps buried under a mound of bodies slain by its wielder before the wielder himself was consumed. It was the closing of an era, and the gods had withdrawn even further from the world.

"I notice you haven't been playing as me," Prendar said as we walked, tapping the pointed toe of his shoe against my desk.

"I don't really get you, to be honest. Aren't thieves kind of…useless as a class? You're like Brennan, but with weaker stats."

"That's why I have backstab. And poison. And I have infravision from my parents' screwed-up marriage."

"Cut him a little slack, Russell," Leira said. "It's not his fault he's not game-balanced." Ouch.

It starts to rain, and Leira dons a gray wool cloak with a hood. You could imagine her on that road since dawn, a whole day just walking through the fields and forests of the Long Marches in a cold rain that came and went. She probably slept in that cloak last night. She doesn't mind the rain; you feel she could walk forever.

After a few hours she starts to pass farmers with carts full of produce and traders with covered wagons. A man stares at her from the back of a wagon, holding a crossbow inside, out of the rain. She can see the worn-down stock and the five mismatched quarrels in the quiver slung from the man's shoulder.

You walk through the concentric walls of the old city, crumbling like smoke rings in the air, and into cobblestone streets. The sunset is banded with red, orange, and yellow, as elegant as it can be in the sixteen-color palette. The parallax effect is soothing and hypnotic. There is an armorer's stall and I buy Leira a shield striped in blue and white.

"Stop," said Lorac. "I will show you things few mortals ken. For this is WAFFLE, and mine is a dark knowledge."

The renderer showed us what the world looked like, but Simon's world engine WAFFLE pulled its strings. No one knew everything about how it worked. All they had was the API, the application programming interface (as laboriously explained to me by the guy sitting next to me that day, whose name I never successfully learned)—it fed parameters in and got data out, but it didn't mess with what was inside. Simon built WAFFLE and he died, and left a black box at the heart of Black Arts.

Lorac led me through the rules.

a) It was a simulation, and it was pretty bossy. Designers didn't run the economy, it did. If you wanted to say that a suit of leather armor cost ten gold pieces, you couldn't tell it that. You might be able to jiggle a dozen other variables into place so that leather armor logically *had* to cost ten gold pieces. Or you could just let WAFFLE charge what it wanted to charge.

b) Objects and creatures acted the same way over a great many different contexts. A dagger was a dagger — as a character, you could pick up the dagger and use it. Any creature in the world, player-controlled or not, could also use it (provided the creature had hands, or a sufficiently prehensile tail).

c) Objects had a set of properties that made the same sense everywhere. An iron dagger was a weapon that could damage creatures; it could also damage certain objects (such as a length of rope). An iron dagger was magnetic; stone and bronze daggers were not. Flint struck against it would make a spark, and so forth.

d) Characters and creatures in the game had a decent amount of native artificial intelligence; in danger they would flee. They would pick up desirable loose objects, which was why that skeleton had looted my body the night I had played the game and discovered the bug. Later programmers had extended and added on to these behaviors, but the core remained. Like the simulator itself, character behavior wasn't always easy to control.

e) Lastly, the engine (which is to say, Simon) was a complete bastard about saving your game. For a given character, it would save a record of your game when you quit; it would load that record when you started again. You couldn't save during a game and keep playing, which meant that you couldn't, for instance, save the game and then try something stupid or risky and then just reload your game if it didn't work. The effect was that you played through as a single continuous narrative.

This last piece of code was one of a number of features that reflected deeply held ideas about video games that Simon had encoded into the system. Apparently he thought it helped players invest in the game as real; real risk, real consequences.

Its real effect, ultimately, was to limit the extent of the Black Arts audience—not everyone wanted to take these games that seriously. Sometimes they just wanted to goof around and try things. On the other hand, it also created a hardened core of Black Arts loyalists who would buy every game and who at parties would get into long philosophical arguments about the use of the Save command in games.

And no one, anywhere, knew what the letters in WAFFLE stood for.

"Okay, now what?"

"Play the damn game," said Prendar.

A small plaza well back in the merchants' quarter. A modest cobblestone circular plaza and, in the center, a worn-down statue of a bear on its hind legs silhouetted black against the purpling sky.

It's almost nightfall when Leira sees the tavern's light ahead, the Duke and Dancer. A shield hangs on the wall outside, the griffin sigil of Darren's old kingdom. She ducks under the low door frame and steps inside. Self-conscious, she keeps a hand on the hilt of one long blade just to make sure it's still there. There are two lanterns hanging from a thick wooden beam overhead, a beam that must have been cut from a hundred-year-old tree, a tree that probably never heard a word of Common spoken in its lifetime. A fire is going at the far end of the room, and everything smells like wood smoke and beer and sweaty people. It's warm after a day of walking in the rain, and her cloak steams a little. The stew is salty and the dark ale is bitter and incredibly good.

The tavern is full of two dozen men, and Leira is comfortable being lost in the din. She's small and used to not being noticed; it's a talent. Most of the men are farmers and craftsmen, there every night of their lives, but the inn hosts a few travelers, too.

She thinks back over the day's walk. Video game characters are only half there except when you're involved. But the whole saga is built around their roles in the world, half you, half them, a grand-scale millennial puppet theater.

You know from writing the TDR that as a playable character Leira has a high movement rate and great bonuses on ranged attacks. But you know so much more about her, even more than the computer does, because inside the outlines there is what you put into them, so much more memory and awareness and feeling, a whole country of it. And as the evening wears on, she thinks, or perhaps you think, about a summer night in a storybook castle long ago, before the wars began.

You had skin under your fingernails. The prince crouched, cursing, and spat on the floor. You scanned the gallery. It was empty. The mirrored walls showed only candlelight, paneling, your strange, ashen face.

The ball was still at its height. It was the day you'd been looking forward to since you turned thirteen, the thing you'd lorded over your younger sisters. You were going to have a ball. You were wearing the pale green dress you'd forgone a horse for, and saw for the first time how poorly it suited you. You heard your father's too-loud laugh over the music and the crowd. You tried to imagine how you would explain this to him. It seemed so implausible. You had always been the proper lady to your sister's tomboy. You were the one they expected to marry off early. Nothing was going to prevent that—or was it?

Flustered, you cast around and settled on a silver candlestick. You held on to your skirt with one hand to keep from tripping over it as you swung the other hand in a broad, hearty sidearm motion that brought the candlestick's thick, square base into contact with the prince's kneecap. It must be midnight by now, you thought, and there were an enormous number of decisions to be made in a short time.

Enter Lorac. He has low hit points and armor but above-average foot speed. He has high intelligence, a wisdom bonus, three extra languages. Metal armor is forbidden; metal weapons are used at a major penalty.

The spell caster allows four specialties. All magic items operate with a bonus. There is a 20 percent chance that he will be able to evade the effects of cursed items.

In *Realms III* Lorac has a range of powers that get him through his obstacles. A gesture that lets him drift slowly through the air instead of falling; a word that shatters nearby objects. For all his age, he looks unruffled by the obstacles. When the rain comes he adjusts his hat, but that's all. In town he gets to choose new robes. When he enters the tavern he gives Leira a sidelong look but doesn't speak to her. In the firelight he looks a little like one of the three kings of the Nativity scene.

He wasn't a king but he might have been a king's vizier, a cunning man and master of many subtle arts. One of the ones who secretly lusts for power, and one day he betrays the king.

Why? It's hard to remember, just that every step seemed at the time like the logical and smart and easy way to play it. Maybe it wasn't before, but now it's what you do. It's your story.

You saw your moment. The king wasn't watching, and you stole the key to the royal aviary, in which there was a magic bird whose magic songs foretold the future. Of course it went wrong. You're not royalty and you're not the hero of the story. You're just a civil servant with a prelaw degree and a flair for languages. What made you think you could hang with the royals? Princes and kings have this kind of story in their blood.

When the king came back you panicked like a fool. Your sorcery lit the tower, but he tossed you into the moat anyway. It was the birdseed you bought, in the marketplace, the day you were wearing that disguise. It wasn't that good a disguise, was it? Who knew a king would have those kinds of connections on the street? If they'd enacted the educational reforms you'd asked for, those fucking urchins would have been in school, where they belong.

The townsfolk threw vegetables as you limped, dripping and sobbing, through town. The worst of it is, that king really liked you. He was a genuinely nice guy, never made you feel bad about the money thing from the first day you roomed together. As vizier you lived at the palace, ate with his family, played with his children, showed everybody magic tricks, and told stories from your early life, before the days of jewelry and fancy hats.

You pawned your scepter of office for enough money to book passage out of the kingdom. No more dining on pheasant, no more carpets, no more starlit desert nights. You never wanted to see that place again. There are other lands, other kingdoms. You walked north until no one had heard of your crimes. You'll go as far as your movement points will take you.

You rode on barges, slept out on deck under the stars, bargained with men in their own tongues. At first your academic diction marked you as a stranger, but gradually you picked up their vernacular rhythms, dropped the subject and your fancy tenses. You crossed the continent's central desert in the company of a caravan, entertained their children with fire tricks from a first-year alchemy class you dug out of your memory. In return, a wiry, tan man taught you the basics of fighting with a short blade by grabbing your arms and yanking them into position. You left the caravan at the foot of a mountain range, and you kept going.

In the mountains you learned another form of magic, whatever's fast and cheap. There was no time for a three-hour warm-up, and there was no place to get powdered peacock bone; there was only time to shout or make a rapid sketch in the dirt. You lay by your fire, looking up at the stars, and your days at the academy, your days in the king's court, all of it seemed far off, which is what you'd like, really. Farther, if you could possibly get it.

On the far side of the mountain, the country was different. You met your first dwarves. They'd heard of your country, but maybe one in four could name the king, and none could speak the language.

You moved north through the forest lands while the long summer lasted, following the track of a lazy green river. At night you heard bats hunting in the warm air. You crossed a low stone wall that once marked the border of a farm. No one had lived there for centuries. You had never felt that alone, or that free. After weeks of travel you reached the northern ocean, and walked east.

Caracalla is a city you didn't know, a northern city that trades with the hunting and mining tribes. No one you knew, no one from your family, had ever been there. At first, tradesmen looked askance at your currency. You decided to wait a few days before booking passage north.

You slept alone at an inn that first night, lying awake long into the dark. The city was never quite silent. You heard bells, here and there a shout, the yowl of a cat, or hooves. You smelled horses, dirt, the ocean.

In the darkness you thought again about who you were before this, a life you remember less and less well, but what you remember doesn't flatter you. You remembered lying to people about what you were thinking and feeling. You remembered constantly thinking about how unhappy you were. It was very different from the way you are now, before you wore a dagger and slept in forests.

You fell asleep trying to count days, trying to guess how many weeks are left before the snow will cut off the mountain passes. In the morning you learned how to negotiate with a sailor. You're not sure if you're here for forgetfulness or redemption, but you notice they're not calling you a vizier anymore. They call you a wizard.

Brennan has an easy time on the road. High strength, endurance, hit points, medium speed. All weapons usable, bonus with long sword or dagger. When the rain comes he lets it fall on his broad bare shoulders, but ties his long hair up in a bun over his round, boyish face. Bandits are nothing to him, he's — God, twelfth level or something. He faced down the spider queen herself in her mountain lair. He can let his mind wander.

There was a yellow patch in the snow by the side of the roadway. They stood around it, eight of them, mildly puzzled. There was a faint smell of wood smoke, but otherwise the mountains were silent.

Your two cousins exchanged glances behind your back. They were each fifteen years older, almost twice your age, but a few inches shorter. You outranked them by birth, but they'd ridden this way a dozen times before, and the bearers had long since stopped looking at you for confirmation of your orders.

Your father was getting older, and your brother was spending more and more time running the place, so it was your turn to ride out with the annual tribute caravan, through the pass and over the mountains you'd heard of but never seen, carrying your family's third-best sword to the stronghold of the House of Aerion.

"Bandits, maybe. We'll go have a look," Eran said, the dark one. The two older men set off through the trees, up a short ridge and out of sight, one looking back to make sure you and the others stayed put. But the snow was half a foot deep and it was getting on to sunset, and the other men got cold fast. The wait was awkward; the party had run out of things to chat about an hour into the first day.

What if your cousins weren't coming back? What was happening? Sound didn't carry well in the snow. After ten minutes of looking at the other men and the darkening sky, you cleared your throat and said, "I'll just look. To see what's happening."

You climbed the ridge and looked off into empty pine forest. Your cousins' trail was clear. You walked quickly, breaking through the snow at each step, already feeling too hot in your chain mail. Up ahead you heard what might be a man's grunt—how far off? You started to jog, then ran to a cleared space, where your cousins were fighting four men.

They stood, swords drawn, with their backs to a tree. Berik, the fair one, was on one knee, with no wound showing but drops of blood in the snow around him. Four men were fanned out in front of them. They were dark-skinned, wearing embroidered cloaks. Southerners? Two held spears with bronze heads; one had a broad, short sword of old and discolored metal. One had a proper heavy longsword. It seemed silly, four against two, the kind of fight you'd fall into while goofing around at the end of arms practice. You weren't supposed to win, just have fun battling the odds.

No one looked at you. Eran rushed the swordsman on his extreme left, trying to push him away from the others. Berik turned to watch, and a man put a spear into him, soundlessly, once and then twice to be sure. Metal was banging against metal. You stepped forward and lunged at the spearman's neck with your sword. It went right in and stuck there. It was like a trick, a sword through a man's neck, made more absurd by the way the man stuck out his arms and looked around. You wanted to laugh, but another man with a sword ran at you and tackled you. You landed on your back, then twisted to the top, the way you used to wrestle your brothers, except this was a stranger, heavy and stinking of sweat and smoke and thrashing under you, biting unfairly as your brothers never would, and that was the enraging thing. You shifted your weight and pinned the man's sword arm with your left hand and got your right forearm stuck under the man's chin and pushed with all your strength for long, long seconds, long after you would have let up in a play fight. You held it there until your opponent stopped moving and someone jabbed you rudely in the small of your armored back.

You rolled to your feet with the attacker's tarnished short sword in your hand. How had it gotten dark so fast? You remembered now how Eran had been calling your name for some time, then he'd stopped and turned into one of the black shapes on the ground.

Now you felt warm, like you could make the world go in slow motion. The last man was small, thick under his cloak, with wide-set eyes. He was castle-trained but fatally tired, and he knew it. It was almost too easy to knock his blade out of the centerline, slip his guard, and strike him in the temple with the hilt. The thought, involuntary, was that you were killing the third man of your life and no one was watching. You never knew who they were or what started the fight.

Your father's men had gone, in which direction you couldn't tell. It was starting to snow. You sobbed a few times with shock and exhaustion. The strangers' camp wasn't that far. You sat in the dark under the firs and watched snow fall, hissing into the coals. Your cousins were freezing solid a hundred yards away. Your mind jumped from one image to the next, Berik dying, the swordsman's blue eyes, climbing the stairs of the roundhouse in summer,

*your cousins talking about a peasant girl they'd shared, a girl you'd grown
up with.*

*You woke up three or four times in the night, terrified, thinking you
heard voices, and that was when you realized that what you dreaded most
now was your father's men coming back to find you and take you back to
your old life, your coward of a father, and the name of a house that would
never rise again. In two weeks, you thought, you could be anywhere.*

I bought Brennan a shield with a griffin on it, crimson on a field of gold.

Prendar is the only one left. Quick and stealthy, with devastating surprise attacks. Forbidden from wearing metal armor, but bow, dagger,
and sword are all permitted.

You can imagine Prendar's home as clearly as you can your own. It was
a muddy village of three hundred at most. Everyone knew him, everyone
knew his mother was gone, and everyone knew his father worked his field
during the day and at night sat in his home in the dark like a fucking
ghost. He learned his letters from a priest who came through once every
two weeks and taught whoever would listen. He knew the long chants
that told the history of the world, and he could draw the shape of the entire
continent in the dirt, with a dot for where the village was.

Prendar wore his hair long but the truth was obvious. Elven blood
shows, even in a half-blood. It took a stranger to point it out, a traveler,
drunk and hateful, who seized him by the hair and dragged him into
the street. Prendar jerked away, and was out of the village before anyone had a chance to follow, over a low fence and through an overgrown
field to the forest. He wasn't hurt that badly, just bruises and a bloody
nose. He stopped and washed his face. At least he was wearing shoes.

He had nowhere to go, so he waited in the woods for the priest to
pass on his way to the village. The priest had already heard what happened. They talked a long time as they walked together from one
league marker to the next. The priest gave Prendar his hat and a bronze
coin stamped with a crown on one side and a coiled sea monster on the

other. He explained how to find due north using the stars, and made Prendar repeat it back. Prendar thanked the priest and, with no more ceremony than that, he set off walking.

(None of this has any relation to you, a person with normal-looking ears who went to high school and college in good order, who had normal parents and suffered no beatings to speak of. You would not, frankly, have had the guts in a million years to run away, no matter what you told yourself as you lay awake.)

The intervening years have given Prendar five inches in height and a cloak he can travel in, as well as matching long daggers he's learned how to use. It's late in the autumn season, and that long-ago quest was forgotten the first night he spent in a city.

He was paid prodigiously, but it was his last night in the city-state of Arn. The wars of the Second Age brought him better fortunes. But those wars ended some time ago. He wondered if his mother had survived them or lay dead in an unmarked field. He'd find her one day. Elves lived forever, didn't they? Maybe he would, too.

The scarred, muscular man with long hair tied back in a bun and a hunted look around the eyes, a weathered, cord-wrapped sword hilt projecting above one shoulder. An older man, bearded, his cloak stiff with whorls of gold thread. A tall, pale half elf dressed in gray with sandy red hair and a beak of a nose. Like the older man, he wears clothes that were expensive a long time ago.

I'd never thought of them except as game pieces, as tiles on a map: sword, staff, arrow, dagger. In the new engine, they're people. Each one stops in the doorway, hesitates, then slowly takes a seat in an unoccupied corner. They've seen each other across many battlefields but never before in peacetime, across the scarred wood of a tavern.

What now? There's no reason to fight; all those reasons died with the Second Age. The great Four Heroes of the Second Age are now stateless wanderers.

They're aware of each other. Lorac, who sits with his bitter ale half drunk, nervously ghosting through ritual gestures with limber hands. Prendar, who fidgets in his seat, well into his second tankard. He flirts with a bar maid, and plucks a white flower from her hair. Brennan, who sits completely still, staring straight ahead, one finger resting on the hilt of the sword leaning against the bench.

Only one corner remains free. The moment you, Leira, take a seat there, time accelerates. In the space of a few seconds the sky outside dims to blue-black, a yellow crescent moon surges into view, and twinkling stars appear. It's approaching midnight, and most of the regulars have left. The fire burns low, but the four travelers haven't moved from their corners yet.

The image fades out with the words,

```
AND SO THE FOUR TRAVELERS MADE A SACRED VOW,
   TO  FIND  AND  DESTROY  MOURNBLADE,  AND  TO
   RECOVER THE HYPERBOREAN CROWN OF THE KINGS
   OF OLD.
THIS WAS THE DAWN OF THE THIRD AGE, THE QUEST
   FOR THE RESTORATION OF THE WORLD.
```

It's only when you finish the entire damned *Realms of Gold III* and start on the next one that you see one of the deep truths of the WAF-FLE engine. Because when you type rogiv.exe, you get the prompt Import rogiii.dat?

Lorac reached in and depressed the Y key with one long, stained fingernail, then gave me a long look, as if to say, "On this everything depends."

When played in order, each game imports the previous game's end state. Which is to say, if a character found a unique item or a highly developed skill in add-on packs like the *House of the Unborn Duke,* that item or skill will be present in his or her character sheet at the beginning of *Forbidden Tales*. It was an odd idea but not unheard of, and it lent the game the quality of an Icelandic saga or a long-running soap opera. It even seemed as if the Heroes' AI files noted certain experiences. As a player you never controlled more than one Hero at a time, and the Heroes you weren't using were programmed to act reasonably autonomously while following you around—to fight when attacked, collect useful valuable items, and (usually) avoid walking off cliffs. After Prendar and Brennan were tricked into fighting each other in *Elven Intrigue,* Prendar never again healed Brennan in battle or even walked near him in the lineup.

I thought about how that was supposed to play out. They were video game characters. They'd been sentenced to run and jump for their entire lives, to quest and fight in causes not their own. Longer than their whole lives, because they're going to die and be resurrected forever. They're pieces in a cosmic game, and they know it. They can only do what you tell them.

In the tavern, they fall into conversation, haltingly at first. War stories, mostly. They've all heard the same story, told around the campfires of an army that marched west to the Elder Wars and the lost crown. The story of the king who fled south from Shipsmount when the dragons first came, who journeyed to the White Mountains and never returned, leaving his crown there. That crown was worn by the kings who built the walls that once surrounded this city, the kings who ruled before the great crash at the end of the Second Age.

And what brought that on? Brennan describes the aftermath of the battle, to which he arrived too late. Bodies piled high around a king, who died afraid. Mournblade, the cursed blade that is a cancer, the black sword, the black temptation that makes any wielder an immortal killer while slowly eating him or her alive.

Already the necromancer in the east and the merchants' convocation, as well as any number of petty nations and warlords, were at work tracing it. Mournblade had proven itself a weapon to devastate armies and murder sovereigns on the battlefield. And who would stop it from ravaging the world forever, for all the ages to come?

The fire dies and you, Leira, stumble to bed, still thinking of the feast days, which matter less than they used to, and the mean look in merchants' eyes, and cheap, ill-made goods, and the feeling that one man cannot trust another, and what force, if any, can repair the broken world.

But it's awkward in the morning. The four of you are in the tavern common room, the two southerners sitting together silently, Prendar and the wizard off in separate corners eating the gray oat mush the tavern offers. Without the firelight's warm tones and flickering shadows, the room seems smaller. The stone floor is filthy, and the smell of urine cuts through the smoke.

The spell of last night is gone, and the remembered intimacy is embarrassing now. It would be easy to nod and step outside and keep walking, all the way up to Shipsmount in a day and a half, but somehow nobody does. You don't want to forget about how it felt to talk about the crown. Everyone is waiting for everyone else.

The bearded man stands to go. You clear your throat. You're lousy at breaking the ice.

"Where are you bound, mageborn?"

"West, perhaps, across the mountains, maybe. If it matters to you."

"I might be going that way," you reply. You sound younger than you mean to, and you hope he doesn't notice. The last thing you need is another father figure.

The scarred man stands up and says, a little too eagerly, "We're walking that way ourselves. To Orenar, perhaps, before the winter closes the pass." He wears chain mail, and the hilt of his longsword is wrapped closely with fine wire, a journeyman's sword.

"A strange chance, but mayhap a fortunate one," you add.

"I'm Brennan," says the swordsman to the room, pausing briefly, as if we might have heard the name.

"Leira," you say.

"Lorac."

"Prendar."

I can feel them even though they're not real, they're not even fictional characters. They're simultaneously less and more than real characters. Less because they don't have real selves. They don't have dialogue, or full backstories. They're just a bunch of numbers. They're vehicles or tools players use. They're masks.

But more because part of them isn't fiction at all, it's human — it's their player half. It's you. Or Simon, or Darren, or Lisa, or Matt. And I wonder what that moment is like for them, when they become playable. It must be like possession, like a person succumbing to the presence of a god or daemon. A trance, then a shuddering, as of flesh rebelling against the new presence. Then the eyes open and they're a stranger's. The new body is clumsy; it stumbles around, pushes drunkenly against walls and objects, tumbles off cliffs.

But what's it like for the god that possesses them? There's a little bit that goes the other way. The fleeting impression of living in their world, playing by their rules.

The Heroes swore to find Mournblade themselves and destroy it — swore by the great secrets, by the fifty-six opcodes, by the sixteen colors and three channels and four waveforms, by KERNAL, whose stronghold is $E000-$FFFF, by the secret commander of the world, whose number is 6,502.

They didn't know the vow would follow them through a hundred lifetimes, through the end of the Third Age and beyond. Through seven generations of console, through the CD-ROM and real-time 3-D and graphics accelerator revolutions. For that matter, they didn't know they were characters in a series of video games.

It was one thing to destroy Mournblade, but it didn't have to happen right away, did it? It was hard not to think of what you could do with Mournblade's long, black, soul-devouring weight in your hand.

It could have all kinds of uses, Lorac thought, calculating the to-hit and damage penalties he'd suffer using a class-inappropriate melee weapon. It could be a tool for redemption, or maybe for finishing the job he'd started. He could always decide when he got there.

Why not bring it back home to the folks, why not teach people a lesson, teach a lot of people lessons? Leira thought.

Brennan was in fact reasonably clear with himself that he'd think about destroying Mournblade only after he pulled it from the heart of the last son of Aerion. He thought about his sad father's humiliation. That wouldn't happen to him. Prendar had already thought out how many people he'd have to kill per annum to keep the thing going indefinitely — if there was one thing a game character understood, it was mechanics.

Brennan, Leira, Prendar, and Lorac were the characters, but you were the one who would decide what to do. You would come into their world, and your decisions would be the only ones that mattered. Why not take the sword, if that was allowed? Why not smash all the rules there ever were, and live forever if you could?

Chapter Thirty

A few weeks in, I sat down with the level designers to debug mission logic in the first third of the game. The question was, how do we keep the player involved in the story, and how do we make the story seem to unfold naturally around the player? As the players travel through the world, new plot developments must spring up seamlessly; nonplayer characters (NPCs) must react naturally to whatever players choose to do. A fiendishly complicated set of triggers, metrics, and trip-wires would set the bits necessary to move all the scenery and cue all the NPCs in exactly the right way. Collectively, this apparatus was referred to as the plot clock.

Most of all, we focused on keeping the player from breaking the illusion of reality we were projecting. There were players out there who thought of nothing else, who took every game as a challenge to outsmart the designers and do exactly that—break our game. It didn't take long before we developed a siege mentality. Everything became about containing players in their all-out assault on the bones of our alternate reality. They wanted, deeply and viscerally, to break our world, and we needed to make it bulletproof.

What if the player walks by and doesn't talk to the old man? No one opens the gate until the talking takes place.

What if the player collects all the boulders in the world and makes a giant pile and climbs over the wall? Ask Lisa.

What if the player decides they don't like the princess? Make the princess really nice so this doesn't happen.

What if the player finds all the gloves in the world and takes them back to the store and sells them and the income is enough to buy a Sword of Nullification? A large supply of gloves depresses the local glove market, so the glove sale yields diminishing returns. Also, let's reconsider the Sword of Nullification.

What if the player sets the store on fire, then takes everything when the owner is going into the "I'm near fire" AI behavior? The player can take the stuff, but city guards are set to hostile.

What if the player casts Genocide on all shopkeepers? Genociding any human type results in player death.

What if the player uses a wand of cold to freeze the sacred pool? Note: Sacred pool immune to cold.

What if the player casts Fireproof and walks through the flame barrier? Note: Change flame shield to force barrier.

What if the player teleports back past the doorway once it's sealed? Teleportation requires line-of-sight.

What if the player drops the chalice into the lava? Chalice disappears, but we spawn another chalice at the altar.

What if the player does it again? There are infinite chalices.

What if the player jumps off the cliff and has so many hit points that they survive, and then they bypass the entire scene with the princess and they go on to the castle and don't know what they're supposed to do there, and the AI doesn't have any kind of scripting for that? Put an automatic-death trap at the bottom of the cliff.

What if the player puts on a ring of fire resistance, casts Fireball, and the explosion hurls them over the wall, so they don't need the key? Good for them.

What if the player summons a genie, stands on its head, wishes for another genie from a bottle, steps onto that genie's head, and thus builds a staircase out of the level? Add genie bottle to the list of things you can't wish for.

So he tells you to meet him in the cellar. Can't he just walk to the cellar? Pathfinding.

So then when you leave the room we just teleport him to the cellar, and it's like he walked there? When you pass a certain radius, yeah.

What if you double back? He's already gone to the cellar.

But there's no other exit. He should have passed you, but he hasn't. Shut up.

What if the player kills the princess? We make her immortal.

What if the player kills the lady-in-waiting? We make her immortal.

Why doesn't the player stay home and let the immortal princess and lady-in-waiting kill every single monster in the dungeon? Because the artists didn't make any combat animations for them.

What if the player puts a bag of holding inside a bag of holding? What if he turns it inside out? Cuts it open? Sets it on fire? Quit fucking around.

What if the EXACTLY WHAT KIND OF ASSHOLE ARE WE DEALING WITH HERE?

Chapter Thirty-One

It was becoming clear that high-end game development had a bizarrely sadistic chicken-and-egg quality. During preproduction we'd all sat around and designed a game as we'd imagined it, inventing features and game mechanics and systems and telling ourselves how much fun they were going to be. And so we'd begin building levels months before the game was actually playable. When we actually began playing the game we'd discover that everything worked entirely differently from the way we thought it would, and the things we thought would be fun weren't; the things that were fun, on the other hand, would be things we'd never even thought about. But by then the game would mostly be built and we'd have to scramble to change everything and resign ourselves to all the missed opportunities and promise to do everything correctly in the sequel, which would take another two years to build and would have an identical set of problems. The exact same thing was true for the look of the game; half the art would be built before we had a solid idea what the renderer really looked like. Not just technical specs, such as frame rate and resolution, but the intangibles — how the light fell, how solid the shadows felt, what exact register of realism or stylization it seemed to occupy. Don said it was like we had all the problems of shooting a movie while simultaneously inventing a completely new kind of movie camera and writing the story for a bunch of actors who weren't even going to follow the script.

* * *

There was an arcade-style cabinet that sat in the corridor that ran between the library and the kitchen. It wasn't a real arcade machine, but a PC running an emulator that let you choose from an encyclopedic menu of vintage arcade games, from *Space Invaders* to Japanese-only knockoffs of *NBA Jam* titles. It was the type of device I would have sold either of my parents for when I was nine. I was pretty sure it was illegal.

Lisa was playing an old-style vector graphics game, a world sketched in plumb-straight green and red lines. It looked like *Asteroids* but was more complicated; there was gravity and terrain. In fact, it was a distant descendant of *Lunar Lander.* She scowled as she piloted a triangular ship above a hostile landscape, dodging flak, managing the fuel supply. As I watched, she picked her way through a cave system on precisely gauged spurts of acceleration. As I watched, she bombed an enemy fuel tank and her fuel meter jumped up.

"Why would shooting their fuel give you more fuel?" I asked.

"Do you want fuel or do you not want fuel?"

She killed all the enemy bases and grabbed all the fuel, then jetted off into the void, while behind her the planet exploded into jagged, candy-colored shards.

"Why does the planet explode?" I couldn't help asking. "Was...was that necessary?"

"Because it knows there's a triangle out there that can take all its stuff."

Chapter Thirty-Two

I'd long ago noticed that there was a sort of bubble in the middle of the spring schedule not connected to anything else. This turned out to be the five weeks given over to prepping the E3 demo.

Matt and Lisa were hanging out in the Sargasso Sea of office chairs.

"What's E3?" I asked.

"God, I'm glad Jared didn't hear you say that," said Lisa.

"Electronic Entertainment Expo. It's the big industry trade show," Matt said. "Everybody demos their next-gen games for the press. Everybody — Japan, Europe, Australia, whoever. It's a pretty big deal."

"It's more than a big deal," Lisa said. "It's how we get funding. We need all that press to get a publisher. And we need to look like we know what we're doing so Focus won't shut us down. If we kick ass, somebody's going to pay to publish our game."

"Kick ass. You mean, if we look like we're way, way more fun," I said.

"Nobody really cares if a demo is fun, to be honest. It's about whether the graphics look good."

"So at least I'm off the hook."

"Partly," she said. "I think half of it is, are you going to appeal to the hard-core *Realms* fans? But the rest of it's going to be about bells and whistles. Graphics and stuff, showing we have the next big thing that no one else has thought of."

"You mean, your thing. The renderer."

"Yes," she said. "Me. I'm getting us a rough version of the graphics engine at the end of this week."

"What does rough mean?" Matt asked.

"Well, not fully optimized, I guess, but you can load existing data into it. We can play the levels," Lisa said. "It will probably not crash horribly every single time."

"So, um, what does it look like?" I'd long since given up on making my questions sound informed, at least in the leads meeting. At least here, no one was under any illusions about me.

"It's like we'll have the same world, but faster, more detailed, prettier, I guess. Except for a hundred thousand large and small problems that I can't explain to either of you," Lisa added.

"We just need it to look better than everyone else," Matt said.

"It will," Lisa said, but she seemed to be holding something back.

"Yeah, but it's going to have a new engine, too, right?" I said.

"Everyone will. It's one of those years," Matt said. "*Quake* and *Unreal,* both, and whatever Sony's doing."

All we had to do was put up a better game demo than everybody else, a small section of game, five minutes' worth of gameplay, maybe, that would say everything about our game's design, our look, our vision, and most of all demonstrate our crushing technical superiority over the opposition, which is to say everybody else in the world. Against the richest and smartest developers in the entire world, all the bearded arcade-era veterans and pissant teenagers who built their own force-feedback joysticks and all the corporate juggernauts with movie-size war chests and focus groups and market research — against them we would put Black Arts Studios, me and Lisa and Gabby and Don, and our demo.

When the new renderer came online, no one else was allowed to see it at first; Matt had it installed on Don's computer in his office, and the four of us — Matt, Don, Lisa, Gabby, and I — sat down to look at what Lisa had made us.

The renderer is simply the part of a game's software that displays the world; it stores all the data, all the models, all the terrain, all the textures; it knows where they are and where the point of view is, and draws them on the screen in proper perspective. A better renderer will draw more detail in less time — more complex 3-D objects, higher-resolution textures. If possible it will offer a little flash, tricks like mirrored surfaces; silvery, liquid water; translucent polygons; realistic-looking fire, showers of sparks, mists. Multiple light sources, colored lights, moving light sources. Objects that cast shadows. And always, more detail drawn faster. Every year game companies add new features that make the otherworld that much more invitingly, lusciously real. Part of it is just programmers wanting to make other programmers think, "How the fuck did he do that?" Part of it is that sensation, that "pop," every time you see the game world drawn realer than before, that shift to sharper detail that makes everything that was the state-of-the-art ten seconds ago look dowdy, blurry, and a bit sad — it's that "pop" that makes you that year's new hot game and makes it more likely that retailers will stock your game instead of other people's.

Lisa's renderer was…odd.

It was certainly fast. It handled the gnarliest, most convoluted sections of the world without any visible slowdown. Matt panned across a broad, expansive scene of assembled warriors, distant trees and castles, a nightmarish number of polys, and Lisa's renderer just shrugged it off without thinking. It did what we needed it to — it was fast enough to let you forget it was just drawing a bunch of data; it felt like a camera looking into the world we had built, a world you were suddenly part of, immersed in.

But it wasn't the next-gen tech everyone was expecting. It was almost as if it didn't want to be. The problem facing realistic real-time computer games is that the real world isn't a bunch of polygons, it's rounded and rough and lumpy, and computer games do their best to mimic this, even though it's the thing they are basically the worst at doing. They'll

use cleverly drawn textures and soft focus and tricky shading and anything else possible to make their world seem just as curvy and squashy
as the real one. The world Lisa showed us was overtly angular — faceted,
like crystal. The hard planes in the geometry were too apparent. It was
all technology, no art. It looked a little like the graphics demos we
would occasionally receive from autodidact would-be game programmers, a surprising number of whom lived in former Soviet-bloc nations.
They'd have a characteristic look, garishly colored miniature jewel-
toned labyrinths built solely to show off their particular arsenal of
tricks — giant rotating mirrors and fountains of sparks and glistening
waterfalls.

Lisa knew all the tricks, but she seemed to have deliberately turned
most of them off. She clearly had some translucency going, and shadowing and specular highlights (the sharp glints you get off metal or
water), but she didn't bother with some of the smoke-and-mirrors stuff.

But the more I looked at it, the more it seemed to have its own style
of beauty. In its own way, it was like nothing I had ever seen before.

Whatever else it did, it didn't strain for effects it couldn't quite produce. One of the paradoxes of 3-D game technology is that the closer
games get to looking as realistic as film, the more they want to just get
there, and as a result they spend a lot of time in the uncanny valley, a concept that Gabby taught me. The idea of the uncanny valley is that when
you draw people, there are two ways to do it well. You can draw something really simple, such as a smiley face, and it looks okay; or you can
have a very detailed and realistic human face, such as a photograph or a
Renaissance painting, and that looks okay, too. But in between those
two extremes it starts to feel creepy, the way a department-store mannequin does — not obviously unreal or cartoony, but not real enough to
seem like a portrait of a real person. Uncanny.

We'd left behind the world of arcade games, with their tiny little
icons jumping around; and the technology was moving toward becoming as realistic as the movies. But right then, we were hanging around

in the middle, straining to look as good as movies do—good enough to compare ourselves to film, but not looking as real as they do. It was an uncomfortable place to be. Even the flashiest games of any given year only make you want next year's version sooner. In a way, the earliest arcade games were more comfortable being games.

Lisa's renderer showed a world that looked . . . solid. There was nothing it drew that wasn't legitimately there in the game world—no fake foliage, no doors that were drawn on walls that you couldn't open. There was a curious, solemn music to it. It didn't look like anything else. And—thank God—it started up really fast. You ran it and you were in the game.

"Huh," Don said. I could see it through his eyes—or, rather, I could see him seeing it through the shareholders' eyes. It wasn't going to do the job; at least not by itself. The rest of us were going to have to work.

At the end of five weeks, Lisa was curled up in a sleeping bag under her desk. The people working nearby were keeping a respectful silence; the previous night she'd gotten the sky done in a single, heroic fourteen-hour burst of programming. The thing now displayed animated clouds and an incandescent sun that whited out the viewpoint if looked at too long. The sun took ten minutes to pass from one horizon to the other, followed by two mismatched moons that spun overhead through the Endorian night. Both were lumpy and heavily pockmarked, as if battered from too many arcane celestial combats or manifestations of divine wrath.

We were ready, just about. I'd singled out the twenty-minute sequence that ran the engine through its paces, demonstrated at least three of our modes of gameplay (stealth, combat, 3-D movement), and formed its own tidy little dramatic and narrative arc. I'd played through it at least forty times. Not everything was finished, but Lisa and I had hacked together some crude workarounds to make it work as the finished game would. Everything was going to go fine, as long as I followed the script exactly.

I watched a rental car pull into the lot at eight fifty-five, tires crunching the oak leaves no one ever swept out of the lot. With his thick black hair brushed straight back from his forehead, pink button-down shirt open at the collar, and navy blazer, he looked like a high school kid dressed up as an executive for a theater production. But if they wanted, Focus could shut us down tomorrow and cut their losses. I was sure it had been talked about.

"I'm Ryan from Focus Capital. Great to meet you all."

He shook hands with each of us in turn — Don, Lisa, Gabby, and me — and there was a rapid exchange of business cards. I had never given my business card to anybody before.

I wasn't sure how to dress for the meeting. In the end I decided they would want people who looked like a hacker would look in a movie — T-shirt and jeans, unwashed hair. I tried to oblige, but when I checked myself in the washroom mirror I looked more like one of the runaways that hang around Harvard Square.

We went to the conference room, where Matt had set up the demo machine, which was about 30 percent faster than anything we developed on and by far the most expensive computer in the office.

I'd been told that Ryan was there as part of due diligence, mostly just to see if we were there at all or if we had stripped the office of its furnishings and fled in the night. But it was clear that he wanted to see the game. He didn't have any games expertise, but that probably wouldn't stop him from having an opinion, because everyone everywhere has an opinion about whether they're having fun and why. In practical terms, he could tell us, "Make the lead character a lovable puppy or else we'll shut you down."

Don gave a presentation, talking about our strict adherence to the schedule, our bare-bones budget reduction. He ran through a short list of competing games also slated to come out near Christmas, and ticked off the three USPs — unique selling points — that would distinguish us from other games. After hours of discussion we had decided that these were the game's high-res textures, its advanced simulation techniques, and its epic story, set in the award-winning *Realms of Gold* universe.

Don spent twenty more minutes performing the timeworn routine game companies always recite to investors, the story of how they are conquering the world. Precipitous growth of the market through the 1990s, "fastest-growing sector of the entertainment industry," "young male demographic," and the inevitable clincher, "In the coming year, video game revenues will equal or exceed that of the motion picture industry." Everyone had heard it before, but it felt good to say it. He made it sound like—against the evidence of the senses—everyone who had ever touched the game industry was rich. The truth, however, is that games are ridiculously expensive and only the top few games in a given genre make significant money. But whatever happens, we're still the future of entertainment, right?

I walked Ryan through the level, just as I'd rehearsed it, pausing for slow, cinematic pans over the most impressive areas of the city—the palace, the merchant's tower. He watched, as passive as if the scene had been on TV. Exactly twice he gave a tiny nod and a "hm" sound—once when I shot a fire arrow into a group of soldiers and once when we cut to the animation of the princess giving her congratulations speech. He didn't ask any questions.

He thanked us, then he and Don went into Don's office for an hour-long meeting while the rest of us pretended to work. I later learned the meeting consisted of Ryan making two points: "Add more fire arrows" and "Make the girl fall in love with you."

Realms of Golf (1992)

"Oh, Jesus," Don said. "Do you have to play that? We lost so much money."

"I have to," I explained. "I'm playing all of them."

The half elf sliced the fourth hole approach shot badly. "Again!" he shrieked. If only the multiverse hadn't been depending on him.

The game opened on the immortal foursome dressed incongruously for a pleasant day's play, Leira in a particularly fetching miniskirt, all at the start of what appeared to be an ordinary eighteen holes. The initial interface wasn't very different from a normal reflex game.

But starting at the second hole, playing conditions began to degenerate, as the grass thickened and became disturbingly animate. Farther along, a hole was revealed as the eye of a monstrous beast; skeletons emerged from the putting green; fairways twisted and vanished through wormholes or became battlegrounds for contending armies or became boards for absurd alien chess games the characters were forced to play through. In the back nine they began to be dogged by a lone rider who swatted their drives with a broadsword and broke their concentration with arrows. There were bogeys.

No one, it turned out, wanted this game. Golf games were Father's Day presents, by and large, but it wasn't clear whose father this one was intended for. But I dutifully played through, facing down the dark rider, who proved to be Death himself, who had gathered the Heroes there so that they could compete for his favor. At the conclusion, the foursome went their separate ways without saying good-bye, as if to say, "Let us never mention this sorry episode again."

Chapter Thirty-Three

Don lay on his back in the lounge. I sat on a beanbag chair.

"We can't just say, 'Draws prettier,'" he said. "We need a buzz-word, like... GameScaping. TooReal picturation algorithms."

"You can't just make up a word," I said.

"Pentium isn't a word," he replied. "That's why they could copyright it."

"Cineractive immersion. Next-gen caliber market ration."

"The new name for adventure is... Trillionth."

"But... it is going to be better looking, right?" I asked. "Like, better than *Quake II*? And that *Half-Life* thing they're doing?" I'd seen pictures in CGW.

He sighed. "Lisa's working on it. I honestly haven't looked at what she's doing yet. But even if we are better, it's not enough if nobody hears about it. I mean, we could be really fucked if this doesn't work out. People don't know what kind of margin this company operates on."

"Why don't they know? And, um, what kind of margin does it operate on?" I asked.

"It's my job not to tell them. That's, like, half of my job."

"I thought we were next-gen. How are we not next-gen?"

"We are, we are. Sort of. I was just hoping..."

"What?"

"So okay, I have a theory. Simon put us a decade ahead of the competition when he was fifteen years old, right?" he said. "I mean, in a way we've been next-gen for the past thirteen years because of the WAFFLE engine. Simon ported that code but we didn't replace it, ever."

"Simon was pretty fucking smart," I said.

"That's the thing. You remember how Simon was. And you weren't here, but he just got more that way. He was just too smart and too driven to have stopped there. And he worked all the time, he just didn't always show it off."

"Maybe he just burned out," I said. I wanted to tell him about the phone call. Or the dreams, but that seemed stupid.

"I refuse to believe that Simon did his most interesting work as a junior in high school and then...nothing. I don't know what it is, but Simon didn't just sit around. He'd walk around and hack on things, spot-fix issues with the WAFFLE API, tinker with the latest renderer. And then he'd just be in his office coding without an explanation."

"You checked his machine, right?"

"That's just it, there was nothing. Once in a while I'd notice WAFFLE's file size had changed and there were time stamps for recent changes, and maybe it would...feel different, but you could never tell. It's not like Simon had a change log. And he spent a ton of time on his own stuff."

"So maybe...WAFFLE is next-gen right now, and we don't even know about it."

"Huh. I guess we could just say that in the press release. Who'd even know?"

"Have you looked?" I asked. "Hidden improvements? Undocumented features?"

"God, did we." Don sat up and shook his head. "Darren hated WAFFLE. He kept hiring guys to try and replace it. Every six months he'd have a new programmer in — some eighteen-year-old, and you know the way he is, he'd say, 'This is the guy! This is the guy!' He has that way of making you think you're the smartest guy in the room. Guys would drop out of college just for the chance."

"To be the next Simon."

"Like Toby, he was one of those. None of them got it, not even close, and they'd burn out. Not dumb guys, I'm not saying that. But their version was too slow, too random. It didn't *feel* like a world."

"Yeah." I could see it. We all cared about games for our own reasons, but Simon was plugged into something extra. Simon had, in his way, taken on reality itself. He hadn't hedged his bets. I remembered visiting the Pantheon in Rome. The inscription above Raphael's tomb said, as my classics-literate roommate translated, "Here's Raphael. While he lived, Nature herself feared he'd outdo her; but when he was dying, Nature thought she'd die, too."

Before we left for E3, Don confided in me that the only reason Black Arts was still running at all was the money Darren had paid to license the *Clandestine* intellectual property. That night, I dreamed that Lorac the wizard leaned over my bed to whisper in my ear.

He said, "Everything is changing."

Chapter Thirty-Four

We set down at Hartsfield-Jackson airport around eleven forty-five at night. Lisa managed to get some sleep on the plane, but I was studying my speaker's notes for two days from now. At one thirty in the morning we met and walked together down the connecting corridor from the hotel to the convention center. I tried to do a cartwheel and failed. I felt like I was finally living. We were showing at E3 1998. We were really in it. At least there's this, I thought. I didn't finish law school, but I'm part of this.

We finished at six in the morning and woke up twenty minutes before the show floor opened at nine. I sat on the edge of the bed, leaning over, hugging myself. My body kept making these small spasms, a mini laugh or sob or heave. After a minute or two I felt ready to stand upright.

No point in changing one Black Arts T-shirt for another, so I put on my show tags and jeans while Matt did the same. The sunlight on the sidewalk was blinding, but the warmth calmed down the fatigue-shuddering.

I was waved through security and wobbled up a wide flight of stairs to the cavernous Georgia World Congress Center. There were tiny plastic cups of coffee on long tables in the convention center hall. By the time I made it to the show floor I had managed to achieve an almost pleasurable remoteness from whatever I was feeling. I was going to be functional. I made it to the show floor in time, but it took me ten minutes to find our booth, where Don glared at me a little. Lisa had left only a little while ago, after making sure the demo could run for a half hour straight.

We'd convinced Focus to pay for a small plot in Exhibit Hall C, near an entranceway for maximum traffic. We had a space about ten feet by fifteen feet against one wall. There was a plastic-molded-stone archway and two computers inside, one running *Solar Empires,* the other *Realms of Gold*. It had looked a lot larger last night. The hall was, in football-field math, maybe three long and one and a half wide. We were lost in it.

At eight fifty-five, the booths began to power up. What at first sounded like a very strange orchestra tuning up became a long, monstrous, rumbling crescendo, a synthesizer factory sliding down a mountainside only to collide with a monstrous pipe organ next door to a construction site inside an echo chamber. It reached a climactic, thunderous blare not unlike an eight-hour explosion or a daylong cage match between a robot and a monster truck. Every minute it seemed like it must start to die off, but it simply sustained itself, on and on.

I didn't have booth duty until eleven, so I set off to walk the show floor. I could see already how miscalculated our booth was. Most booths had enormous screens mounted on scaffolding along with giant-size cardboard cutouts. Microsoft had a brushed-steel pavilion. Electronic Arts had erected a full-size professional wrestling ring on the show floor. Sony had claimed a mansion-size stretch of territory, upon which twenty-five-foot plastic busts of its signature characters looked down like gods. Several booths incorporated full-size automobiles or custom-built suits of powered armor; many were stage sets of scenes from games—blighted city streets or spaceship corridors. Glittering archways coated in LEDs pulled visitors in. In that company the Black Arts booth looked tawdry and sullen. Guests wandered through like bored toddlers, whipping the mouse back and forth across the pad and gazing up at the screen, disappointed. The games were too complex, depended too much on a long investment in time and attention. No one would stay to watch a colony launch a light-sail barge and wait the few minutes to see it dock at another star. A bearded man in a canary-yellow T-shirt stayed a moment to pan the view across the forest, then dropped the mouse and filed out, ducking eye contact.

"Let me know if you have any questions!" I shouted after him, but no one could hear anything. The booth on our left, an Atlanta company offering children's games, had a speaker stack and a projection TV that played a video short on continuous loop, a shrill cartoon voice saying, "I've got the most star tokens! You can't beat me! This will be the greatest Spin-a-Thon ever!" We heard this once every twenty seconds, which made roughly one thousand and forty times in the course of a day. On our right, four grimly serious Frenchmen had a display of looping CG film noir scenes and a patented way of branching movie narratives they couldn't quite explain to me. Somebody else had licensed "Tubthumping." I kept hearing the phrase "Ocarina of Time." But most of the first day was watching conventiongoers file past, dull-eyed with overstimulation. Lacking as it did a strobe light or flamethrower, our booth didn't even register.

People were aware of us, that much I could tell. It was no secret that Black Arts had lost its marquee talent—not just Darren but the whole upper echelon—and had replaced them with a bunch of no-names hired off the street. The fan community was already clogging the message boards with catcalls, predictions that we were going to turn the hallowed Black Arts name into a joke, kill the *Realms* franchise, and ruin everyone's memories of the early games. There was a vocal minority arguing that this had happened long ago, that anything good about Black Arts ended with Simon's death. It didn't seem as if anyone even knew Lisa's or Don's name. For the fans, Black Arts was the Simon-and-Darren show.

I could sense the world turning. Carmack and id Software debuted *Quake* in 1996 and did the same trick they'd done with *Wolfenstein 3D* and then with *Doom*—they'd again become oxygen, become the standard of high-speed illusion, and their system was either being licensed or cloned twenty different ways, with different tweaks to the DNA. I knew the names of the derivatives because Matt tracked them on a whiteboard: *Half-Life, Prey, Duke Nukem Forever, Daikatana.* And there was already a *Quake II* engine coming.

There was a rivalry I didn't understand but that everyone talked about, in which a designer named John Romero left id Software to form another company. Jared pointed him out to me, a small, long-haired, solid guy, butting through the crowd at the head of an entourage in red-and-white T-shirts. He showed me Carmack, too, who had a Kevin Bacon squint and walked with a stiff bounce, before he disappeared into a closed-door meeting. Ours wasn't the only world whose creators were at war.

Four o'clock came, and even the show floor's manic energy seemed to flag. Matt went out to collect sandwiches. A man and a woman accosted me. It took me a moment to realize they weren't just in medieval dress—they were the first Lorac-and-Leira cosplayers I had ever seen. He was also the youngest man I had ever seen with a full beard.

"What are you shipping on?" he asked without preamble. I soon discovered that encounters with *Realms* fans came with an abrupt and total sense of intimacy, as if we all knew the important things about one another and there was every reason to cut to the chase.

"Windows only." He gave a quick nod, as though I had confirmed a long-held suspicion.

"Who do you play?" the girl said.

"It's a secret."

"Do you meet Lorac?" she asked. They seemed to hang on the response.

"You meet Dark Lorac," I said eagerly. "You meet everybody! It's going to be awesome!"

"Cool, man," he said, and offered me his hand. "I'm Mark."

They nodded and moved on.

On the second day, a couple of journalists quizzed me on the game's release date and system requirements, and copied down my e-mail address. One asked for my feelings about Darren's departure.

"Darren is a legend in the game industry and we at Black Arts wish him well."

"I heard the departure was pretty sudden."

"I'm going to respect Darren's wishes, obviously."

"You're not feeling a little nervous, then, stepping into his shoes?" He leaned in, I guess to express the idea that the two of us were having an intimate chat. I had the feeling he was doing something he'd seen a reporter do on television, and that he was somewhere under twenty years old.

"We — well, I think our product speaks for itself."

Jared had been listening, and he added, "We're pretty nervous that Darren's going to see our game and cry like a little bitch."

The reporter copied it down and thanked us for our time.

"Come back! You haven't seen our weapons upgrades!"

Two or three times, I'd seen a man or woman spend ten or fifteen minutes at one of our kiosks, face carefully neutral. Not playing, exactly, but doing odd maneuvers like looking at the same object at different distances. I noticed their tags were turned around so I couldn't see their name, title, or company, which at first I didn't understand, but Jared explained — these were the enemy, the competition. Whatever Lisa had done, they were taking it seriously. They wanted to find out if we were a threat, if we could actually win.

"I'm just really looking forward to this Spin-a-Thon," Jared said.

Ryan got all of us invitations to the different corporate-sponsored parties. Sony's was in a parking garage and featured a band that I thought seemed addicted to doing Soul Asylum covers, until I realized they were Soul Asylum. Wasn't one of them dating Winona Ryder? I looked around for her. Anything seemed possible. Nintendo had the B-52s.

I was picking up on things everybody else already knew. The booths were built out of marketing budgets to impress the journalists and most of all to attract retail buyers, the representatives for Walmart and Best Buy and Software Etc. Microsoft and Sony and SEGA and Nintendo were at war, rival hardware platforms gearing up to capture the upcoming sixth-generation console market. Activision, Acclaim, Eidos, Capcom, Electronic Arts, and the other big software publishers were fighting over different pieces of the software market. The hardware giants used high-profile game releases as lures to grab market share. *Mario* sold Nintendo game consoles just as *Sonic the Hedgehog* and *Soulcalibur* sold SEGA consoles. I began to see how much money was involved, and that we'd lost control of the whole thing. Not that we'd ever had any. This wasn't about kids trading floppy disks anymore. As actual game developers, we were the only amateurs in the room. We were wandering around, thinking we were the point of it all, when the real contest had almost nothing to do with us. The grown-ups were finally in charge again. No, they'd been there all along, and I was just the last to notice.

Chapter Thirty-Five

The speaker room was just another conference room with slightly nicer snacks. Coffee, bottled water, bagels, and pastries. The other tables were occupied by small groups, mostly huddled around laptops, mostly engaged in serious conversations. All of them looked like they were making deals, or were demoing, secretly, the next big tech advance, or like they at least knew what was going on in the world. It was six thirty in the evening — dinner hour, not exactly prime time for a product demo. But then, I wasn't exactly ready for prime time.

That morning I'd stood in the doorway and watched for a few seconds as Darren ran through his act at the Vorpal press event. Darren was onstage with a headset mike, being interviewed by the editor of a prominent gaming magazine.

"Simon and I were like brothers, you know? And the games we did, they have their niche, right? We love them, we really do." There was a pause, staged or not. There was an industry rumor that Darren could in fact cry upon command.

"But games have changed, it's bigger now. I want to make games for everybody. It's about more than just action, it's about telling a story. It's about character. We're up against the big guys, the movies, right? We're ready to take our place in the world. And we will, and we're going to kick their ass. That's right, Spielberg. I'm calling you out!"

I left as the applause line hit and dissolved into laughter. I knew what I was up against. I knew enough to understand the media narrative they were hoping for: Black Arts Studios sells out, loses the genius duo that made it special, falls on its face. That was the story worth showing up to cover. The presentation hall itself was like an enormous engine specifically designed to leach charisma from the person speaking at the front of it. Pale bald developers dragged themselves onstage to deliver a marketing presentation with the stumbling cadence of a man dribbling an underinflated basketball.

The hall was more crowded than I expected, about two-thirds full—two hundred people, maybe. I guessed it was an even split between hard-core franchise loyalists, people (journalists, particularly) who'd come expressly to see us fall on our faces, and people making sure they got a seat for the Sony press conference that followed us in the same venue. But there was a buzz to it. There was a narrative here, and we were going to get written up. I was going to get written up.

A woman from IT gave me a small microphone to clip to my collar. I typed RoGVII.exe at the keyboard tucked inside the podium and pressed F8. The demo splash screen came up on-screen behind me. I torqued half around, in the awkward characteristic pose you get into, demoing a game on a screen above and behind you. The demo was on two screens, and on a third there was me. I was seeing myself on a forty-foot-tall screen. I swayed a little. I wasn't hungover; rather, I thought I might still be a little drunk.

"The latest game—this exciting new entry—in our award-winning *Realms of Gold* franchise, *Realms VII: Winter's Crown,* is designed to appeal to those new to gaming and hard-core gamers alike. Whether you are new to the *Realms* or a longtime resident, it will offer familiar delights and a few new surprises."

Most of the first four rows of the hall were full, with a few stragglers standing at the edges and back.

"The time…" It seemed a little too soft, so I started again, leaning into the microphone a little. "The time"—too loud!—"is late in the Third Age of Endorian History!"

I gestured up at the screen showing the calligraphed words WINTER'S CROWN as the music built to a climax and the hall lights dimmed.

The screen cleared to reveal a young woman standing in a city square, a crimson-and-violet sunset behind her. The inevitable joker in the audience gave a wolf whistle, but she wasn't much of a pinup figure. She wore a gray cloak over worn and scratched leather armor. Her idle animations were set to "nervous," meaning that if I weren't issuing any commands she'd stand where she was and tap her foot, glance around, touch her sword hilt just to make sure it was hanging right. As the sun set she was illuminated more clearly by light spilling out of a tavern window.

"As you can see here...the *Realms* engine has been enhanced and updated..." I panned across the square and instantly regretted it as the frame rate chugged a little while the renderer choked on all those polys. For a moment I was paralyzed by the thought that I can't take a breath or speak a word that isn't going to boom through the hall. The microphone felt like a bee stuck to my lapel.

"...improved magic system...an array of weapons..." There was an agreed-on and exhaustively rehearsed list of features. In the course of the ten-minute demo I had to hit them all. I was saying something about mipmapping that a programmer had told me to point out. Did other games have it? I didn't know.

I didn't know what it was, but I could feel the collective boredom of the audience. The journalists had been to, at the minimum, a dozen of these press events in the past three days, each one pushing to be bigger than the last, each one in its own way at once technically dazzling and utterly boring. Every year the technology got better but the stories were the same recycled Joseph Campbell or knockoffs of two-years-ago hit movies. When was the last time something surprising happened at one of these?

"We're at a point midway through the game. By the time you get here, a dozen adventures, chance meetings, and decisions brought you to this city. You could be anyone, depending on the life you've led and the choices you've made." I underlined the words by cycling through a few different sets of possible starting conditions for this scenario, each one randomly generated.

"It could be you..."

We saw the exact same scene, but this time it was dawn and rainy and you were a stocky, pale man with a black beard and a battle-ax and an expensive-looking coat, navy blue with brass buttons.

"...or you..."

I switched again and it was a clear, moonlit night and you were a tall, gaunt man in a coarsely woven shirt, with a long sword slung over his back and pointed ears on either side of his scarred and ravaged face, its one remaining eye wanly glowing. Even his posture was different, slumped a little but somehow determined.

"...or you."

It was a good trick, one that Lisa had cooked up, and I heard the murmur as it hit. I flipped back to the initial character, then ducked her into an alleyway. I found a shadowy spot, backed up, sprinted, leaped, and caught the low eaves of a stone building. My feet scrabbled on the wall a moment before I hauled myself up to the peaked roof. Then I was off and running, leaping from one moonlight-drenched slate roof to the next, heading toward a mansion that loomed up in the dark, two stories above its surroundings.

"As you can see, it's a fully explorable environment. Our mission tonight is a bit of intrigue. A young baron has stolen the exquisite Gem Imperial and plans to return it to claim a reward—the hand of the young and beautiful princess R'yalla of the city-state, a path to the throne itself. Our contact in the Thieves Guild learned of the scheme and our job is to steal that gem from the baron and return it ourselves. Young love!"

Was that—? A flash of color in the street, a watchman running past.

I'd done this a dozen times in rehearsal and hadn't noticed it. But this was an unscripted game—these things could vary. I slipped through an open window of the baron's mansion, into an empty storeroom, and then into a silent, dim hallway hung with tapestries.

"Your friend in the Thieves Guild promised it would go down easy. Nobody but you knows the jewel is here. And when you get back to the palace, you'll be able to name your own reward. The source of the information was the Thieves Guild in this case, but it might have been the Faerie Underground or the Sons of Autumn. Cities in Endoria are teeming with rival factions, and your path through them banks heavily on your own choices. You need that gem, maybe to pay off a sorcerer, maybe to court a high-born lady, maybe to hire a mercenary, maybe to feed a drug addiction. All up to you."

I first knew it was going wrong when I heard a guard shout an alarm, followed by a clatter of blades and a shouted, "Who's there?" We'd rehearsed this; no AI should be alert at this point. Matt glanced up at me. He held up two hands in a Ctrl-Alt-Delete gesture and nodded toward the computer—did I want to reboot and start again? I shook my head.

"Looks like they're on to me," I said. I dropped down into a court-yard a level below. My fall knocked off a couple of hit points. Was something wrong with my pants? I was increasingly sure there was a problem with my pants, but there was no possible way I could check.

The guards shouldn't be in search mode. I retreated into an ante-chamber, but it wasn't empty—an elderly servant was on patrol pat-tern. He wasn't a combatant—at the sight of an enemy he'd run off and raise the alarm.

"Okay, I'm just going to—here." The sound effect was unpleasantly meaty. A woman in the front row winced.

"He's fine, everybody," I said, dragging the body into a corner. "Just unconscious."

We were well off-script, but if I hurried there was no reason we couldn't get back on track. Out a window; the wall was tagged as climbable. Maybe the second floor was still quiet.

"We're rendering well into the distance here…" I panned the view out over the moonlit skyline, then instantly regretted it—the frame rate chugged for a second as it tried to draw half the city. But then I was in an upstairs hallway, crouching behind an artfully placed dresser as a chambermaid patrolled past. Silence set in as I waited for her to finish.

"One of our new weapons is the fire arrow—allows you to light a torch from a distance, or set fire to almost anything." There was an unlit torch in a sconce just outside the bedroom. I swapped inventory, aimed, and shot the fire arrow. The torch lit nicely, as did the chamber-maid just crossing the threshold. This time there was an audible gasp from the house.

"So okay, note here that fire is completely procedural, like most things in the game." The maid was now definitely on fire and had gone into her "Help, I'm on fire" response, which meant screaming and running in a random direction. "The fire will spread dynamically in the world depending on what's near it—see the dresser there, and the drapes—degrading objects as it goes.

"Which you'll just put a stop to by—hang on—you can see how the short bow is incredibly effective, even at medium range…and we'll move on to our main object…the jewel! The house will be mostly awake at this point—we track sound propagation pretty well."

The maid's body was still smoldering a little. I sprinted down the hall, a little way ahead of the guards, who had oriented themselves to the maid's shouted alarm.

"And here's the baron himself—we'll see he's a romantic at—okay, I guess he's decided to make a stand. Very—one sec—very brave. He's not really programmed as a combatant. The blood is just a particle system, but we save its location on the textures—spatters pretty well. You'll see he's dropped his inventory—gold, dagger, and...the jewel itself. Nicely done. And I see we have some more servants arriving."

I went to work. By now the audience was actively laughing and applauding as each innocent went down. In a moment the room was covered in blood spatter, bodies, and dropped inventory. It looked like half the characters in the entire level had shown up to make me kill them.

In a dozen playthroughs, this had never happened. When a live press demo is blown, it's one of the great pleasures of E3; that's when the dull, overrehearsed corporate presentation transforms in an instant into a high-wire act, then into a riveting theater of cruelty, the hapless developer squirming, every detail of his fear and desperation called out on the video screen behind and above him. The whole room was awake and watching. I was intensely conscious of the video camera set up at the back of the room. Of Matt in the front row, appalled. I looked out at all the pink oxford-cloth shirts and Dockers and BlackBerries and thought, these aren't even nerds. Who are these people, and why are they trying to fuck me over?

No. No, fuck these assholes and their schadenfreude, this was all going down just the way we planned it, and I'd be damned if I'd admit otherwise. And I wasn't going to get killed in my own demo.

"Right. So there's an inventory system?" I said. Using the camera, I called out a few items on the floor. "Aaaand...you've got a pair of shoes there, a little gold, looks like. Lots of choices for any player."

The audience quieted. Not out of any respect, but because there was obviously more fun to be had here. I was fatally off-script now, with no idea how to get back, but at least I knew the terrain. I ditched out the window onto a balcony and climbed back to the roof. Two guards were waiting.

More ad-libbing. "The guards will have alerted the city watch, and in moments the entire city will be in hostile mode. We've put a lot of work into the AI." This was all supposed to have taken us up to the castle. We were supposed to be getting an award from the king, and then R'yalla was going to smile at us. There was going to be a speech. We'd set it up just the way Ryan wanted.

"Some of this is based on a real city in Scotland. You can see where—hang on, still killing this guy—you can see where there's a northern Gothic feel to the rooftops."

I showed them some close-up fighting moves from the combat system—by this point in the game you're a hardened killer, no longer the untrained naïf of the round tower and the forest. I fenced with one of the guards for a few moments just to show I could, then finished him. I still knew the combat system inside and out. I hooked a leg and shoved the other guard backward off the roof's edge. The interface for this was a sorry, convoluted nightmare that needed fixing—underneath the podium my left hand was holding down three separate keys at once just to maintain the proper combat stance—but nobody needed to know that. It looked fantastic.

It was only when the guards were dead that I realized I was still speaking into the microphone, addressing more than two hundred people. It looked like a few more audience members were slipping in and sitting at the back. Were people already gossiping about this? And what had I been saying this whole time?

"…which is why the old gods never returned to the city." That sounded wildly off-topic, but at least it wasn't offensive. The rooftop was empty. From there we could see the whole city, which was divided by a broad canal.

But by the time I climbed all the way down to the street, a red-and-white-cloaked city guardsman had already spotted me. The guardsmen were deliberately overpowered and more or less telepathic in their ability to coordinate and respond to citywide alarms. They had to be, otherwise players would hang around robbing the city merchants blind.

"As you can see, there's a fully explorable landscape. The city is a living ecosystem." I sprinted down the narrow cobblestone street toward the canal ahead. A merchant's wagon blocked the way.

"Just going to—okay—kill this guy a second." More hilarity as a merchant's headless body stumbled and fell. What was wrong with these people? The wagon rolled a little way forward onto the bridge, but it didn't quite line up, and one of its wheels was left hanging in space.

"Check it out, rigid-body physics in real time," I said limply. I didn't know what it meant.

I scrambled over the cart as the AI guards arrived. Why was the cart on fire? In a few seconds it had set the wooden bridge on fire and one of the guardsmen, too.

I was running out of features to point out that were not on fire, so I stood and let them all see the caravan slowly tipping, then tumbling slowly over into the canal. It fell correctly, thanks be to Crom—I thought of the many, many rehearsals in which objects had hung in midair, or bounced like beach balls, or leaped into the sky and out of sight. The cart began to float downriver, and the fire went out properly. I hoped somebody noticed and cared.

I checked the clock—how had this demo run only eight minutes? The palace was only a few blocks away, but that was a long twenty seconds to fill.

"So—the, uh, Heroes of Endoria are never far. Waiting, watching. All your favorites will indeed appear in *Realms of Gold VII: Winter's Crown*."

Silence in the room.

"Ahem. Note how the sound of footsteps changes when the character goes from cobblestone to mud to wood. Recorded specially."

The palace, at last, was lit up with carriages waiting in front, liveried servants at attention. It was a fairy-tale scene and not at all on fire.

"And you're right on time! This invitation will get us in...and you can see that marble texture is slightly reflective. The ceremony is just beginning and they're calling for the jewel, which is — I checked — safe in your inventory."

The king was speaking to the assembled courtiers and the princess herself.

"It is our pleasure to invite whoever may come forward to redeem the grandest Jewel of Ahr, our Gem Imperial. Does anyone in this room possess it or have knowledge of what has become of . . . aaargh!"

The city watch wasn't even permitted to enter the palace, which made it so especially odd when one of them murdered the flagged-unkillable king with an enormous black runesword. It was the Mournblade bug, and it had been throwing this demo off from the beginning.

"What — what is this foul assassination you witness? We must take our revenge," I said in a hopeless attempt to pivot the narrative midstream. I wasn't really a role player, much less an improv actor. I wasn't actually sure what I said next as the king went down and the watchman began painting the back half of the presentation hall red with noble blood spatters. Then the guard spontaneously collapsed, hit points zeroed out, and the sword was taken up by the next passing unarmed AI in combat mode. I wasn't really aware of too much that happened for the next ten seconds other than trying in vain to talk over the near-deafening levels of hilarity in the room. By the time a demented lady-in-waiting was pursuing me through the Emerald Gallery with her cursed obsidian blade, I was hard put to pull the narrative threads together into anything passably genre-normative.

The canal ran under the palace windows, cool and inviting. Providentially, I could see the floating cart I had tipped in the water earlier. Shortly, I was being borne away on the current through merciful calm, screams fading in the distance.

"There's the water. Specular highlights — see the way the flames reflect? And the moon there," I said.

"So at this point we're halfway through the game. We've come pretty far in our quest to go find a picture of a crown for no reason other than whatever backstory there is. Does anyone even know it? You're spending twenty hours to get a crown that doesn't even affect gameplay.

"Why do you want it? Do you care what happens to any of these people? I mean, Jesus, you killed your own henchman just to get a Helm of Water Breathing. Just to level up so you could get into the Thieves Guild."

The city drifted past, windows glowing orange-yellow against a black sky. The alarm cries of the guards paced me, then fell behind. What now? Standing on a floating wagon wasn't exactly next-gen gameplay.

"The river takes you through the heart of the city," I explained. There was some time to fill. "Then down into the sewer system, farther and farther from the mess you made back in the world aboveground."

The bridge had stopped burning, but the screen still showed a straight line of white smoke climbing into the sky. The canal felt like the loneliest place in the world.

We were in the sewers; no one had expected them to show at E3. No one should be seeing this part. They looked good enough; Matt had at least textured them properly. The audio system modulated background noise into slightly musical echoes. We needed a little narrative.

"Farther from the dead guards and the jewel you lost, and the princess who was waiting for you. Farther from home, farther from your roommate, who doesn't do the dishes, farther from your body, getting softer with each passing year. Overhead, the night sky is pierced by hard white pixels under black glass. You can see your reflection in the screen. Outside it's still midafternoon. God, why aren't you at work? Aren't you twenty-eight or something? Aren't you tired of talking to people through a conversation system that hasn't changed since *The Secret of Monkey Island* came out? That was, like, ten years ago."

Finally, we passed out through a stone archway at the base of a cliff.

The city was far above us now. The moon was starting to set. We were entering a space of open-ended wetlands.

I cleared my throat. "Did I mention that *Realms of Gold* is a mix of indoor and outdoor action-adventure?"

The wagon bumped up against mud. I got out and leaped to the shore, leaving footprints that faded in a few seconds. It was a small, low island hidden in miles of marshland. The night was quiet except for crickets and a bullfrog. At least somebody had tagged this area with the marsh sound palette.

"The cries of panic and alarm have long since faded behind you, and the night's gone still and silent. But in the lands beyond, the world is tilting on its axis. You know it. We all do," I said — where exactly was this coming from? "Everything's changing. You're going to have to find something to hold on to.

"You reflect on what brought you here," I said. "The losses." I made sure they could see the burn scars — unlike regular hits, fire damage in *RoGVIII* leaves a permanent mark. "The victories. The choices." I rotated the camera until we could see the tattoo snaking down the side of Leira's neck. It marked her as a criminal assassin back in her homeland, although they wouldn't know that.

I had lost track of where we were now. Some procedurally generated wilderness landscape no one ever bothered to visit before. I just wanted to find something interesting for people to look at. I zoomed the camera out from its usual close-over-the-shoulder position and upward as we approached the center of the clearing. From overhead you could see now where you were, at the edge of a circle of standing stones. Up and up went the camera.

"The choices you made are the story you told. For better or worse, it's part of you now, and it's your story, not ours. Take it with our blessing."

As the camera kept rising, I could see an ancient plaza, light and dark stone in a pattern I finally recognized.

"Long ago, before the waters came, there was a temple here."

Our character was growing smaller and smaller as the camera was rising. Now you're just a pixelated dot in the center of an enormous rune the size of a traffic circle.

"This is the Sign of Auric, whose temple it was. Auric, the Endorian god, patron of mercy, of late harvests and last resorts.

"*Realms of Gold VIII*, everybody. *Winter's Crown*. Coming this Christmas."

I signaled Matt, and the lights came up. Most of the audience had either left or sat staring expectantly for my next trick as if I couldn't see them, as if I were on TV. I unclipped the mike, shut off the monitor and the computer, grabbed the CD. I wanted to walk offstage, but of course in a conference hall there's no backstage, just a long walk up the aisle to the exit.

Chapter Thirty-Six

I thought it best to remain in my hotel room for the next seven hours. Calls came in on the room phone, four or five before I lost count. The message light blinked and blinked while I watched movies and ate room-service pizza, then a slice of cheesecake and a glass of fairly sketchy white wine, then more cheesecake slices and more and better wines. After the first hundred dollars plus tips, it seemed easier to keep going. The staff and I were developing a cheery rapport, and there was a Cary Grant retrospective on television. I practiced an attitude of amused detachment and thought of how attractive I was becoming. This was going to work.

Around nine thirty there was a tentative knock at the door.

"Russell?" It was Don.

The hotel window was one of the ones that only opens about an inch and a half. I abandoned the tantalizing smell of freedom and answered the door.

"Hey," I said.

"I came to see if you were doing okay. I heard the demo was a little rocky."

Behind me, the bed was covered in plates and napkins and trays, except for a me-size zone in the center.

He looked it over. "I hope you expensed that."

"I didn't think of that." Probably Cary Grant would have said that, especially if he were four or five glasses of wine into the evening.

"Maybe we should go out."

The Hyatt lobby had been colonized by industry conventiongoers on their final night out, and it had become a seething pit of heavy guys in black T-shirts huddled in little clusters of three or four over gin and tonics, exchanging notes and gossip. Here and there a navy-blazered biz-dev type could be seen, generally signing for the drinks. The crowd was about 80 percent men. Like the men, the women were split between the put-together business types, with late-era Rachel hair, and the T-shirted geek tribeswomen. People threading their way through would be hailed every few steps and forced to exchange business cards before they could go any farther.

It was staggeringly loud, but I thought I distinguished an extra buzz and scattered applause when I came into view. Certainly a detectable amount of nudging and pointing.

As we struggled to the bar, one of the suits grabbed Don's elbow and whispered what seemed like urgent information in his ear.

He stopped me before I could order.

"VIP party, room sixteen twelve. Open bar," he said, steering me back to the elevator.

"The demo kind of got away from me," I said.

"I heard. Probably we're going to be okay."

"How so?"

"A couple of people got it. You still gave a good look at the feature set. I've got meetings set up. And a lot of people are talking about it."

"I'm not fired or anything. Or am I?" I said.

The elevator went up one, two, three floors.

"You know, maybe we shouldn't go to this."

"It's a moral imperative," I said.

The suite party was a smaller version of the scene in the lobby, except now most of the people had blazers on. I guessed this was by and large the management layer of things, plus a few star techies. I recognized a few genuine industry moguls—Romero, Molyneux, Spector. Far in the back, a poker game was in progress.

Don was being glad-handed to death, so I plunged into the crowd. I'm five foot eight and a half, which is only an inch and a half below average, but for some reason everyone seemed to be over six feet tall. I got to where the bar was, more or less by mashing my face into the back of three different navy blazers. The bar was unmanned. I stepped behind it, kicking aside empty cans of Red Bull as though they were dry leaves, and rummaged through bottles until I'd united gin, tonic, and a plastic cup.

I turned around and, surprisingly, Lisa was there. I handed her an airplane-size bottle of Jameson that she tapped against my glass.

"Nice demo."

"Thanks."

"Seriously," she said. "You coped."

"How's the party?" I asked.

"Peter Molyneux's fly is open. So there's that."

"So let's get to a corner. I need to ask you something," I said.

"Okay." Her lips compressed slightly and she took her distance, bracing for whatever was to come. It occurred to me that women in tech probably got propositioned a lot.

"So look. We're here at E3, right? You showed up for this," I said.

"There's a lot of tech stuff you don't have to go to, but I do."

"That's exactly it." Another blazered giant elbowed between us, giving me another face full of high thread count. "And I came to run the demo. I slept, like, three hours last night, and I was humiliated in front of hundreds, if not thousands, of my peers. And I would still have killed to come here. Killed. I'm not like you. I'm in a suite party at E3 and that is the center of my universe, and you're totally unaware that this…"

I paused, and noticed again there must have been a hundred people here in a hotel room that legally allowed sixty-three, and apart from Lisa every single one of them seemed to be laughing, or shouting to make a point about video games.

"…this…rules. It actually rules. But you act like it's a complete chore. Like you'd rather be anyplace else in the world. It makes me feel like a loser. Why do you even come here if you hate it?"

"Because," she said carefully, "I like solving problems. And I got into this because the technology is going to be more important than the games. And for a reason I don't want to tell you. You'll laugh."

"Today isn't my day to laugh at people."

"I wanted to make cyberspace."

"Like VRML? That 3-D Web thing?"

"Games. Games were going to be everything. Why doesn't anybody remember what it was like in 1984? We had *TRON*. We had *Neuromancer*. It was logical."

"Wait. Wait. Are you saying you're in games because you think we're building cyberspace? Like in *Neuromancer*? Like *Snow Crash*? For real?"

"It was logical. Everything you do in games are things you want to do in a computer anyway. Manipulate data, change it, look at it. Early text adventures were almost the same thing as command-line interfaces with directory structures. I think real-time 3-D environments are going to be how we do a lot of things with computers.

"We all thought WAFFLE was going to be...the backbone of things. The information infrastructure. It was going to be the Internet, because the Internet was going to work like a game. It made so much sense. Who wouldn't want cyberspace to happen?"

"But...no one wanted—"

"I know no one wanted it. I *know* 2-D was more ergonomic. I *know* no one wants to spend the cycles. Thank you. I know. Nobody wants cyberspace. It sounded great when *Neuromancer* came out, but... nobody wants the Internet to fly around and visit giant spheres and stuff. Heads floating in space. Turns out, if you can just click on bits of text that's all you need."

"So that was how you were going to be rich?"

"That was how I was going to matter."

Chapter Thirty-Seven

The Monday morning leads meeting was unusually solemn.

"I have some unfortunate news," Don said. "It seems there is a major bug in our software."

"You know, we could always spin this as a feature," Matt said. "Darren would put it on the box in big letters: 'Now with Enhanced Mayhem Generation.'"

"I thought of that," Don said. "But that's not even the thing that worries me. Even if it's a feature in a game, it's not a feature in AstroTrade."

"Why do we care about that?" I asked. "I thought AstroTrade went out of business."

"It did. But the way it went out of business was by selling its assets to a company called Enhanced Heuristics, which existed for about ten minutes then sold out to a thing called Paranomics. Which sends us a check every month on the original license, which is one of the major reasons we're still in business."

"Why didn't you tell us any of this?" Matt said.

"Because it was a nice idea to think that Black Arts makes all its money from games. And usually we do, it just hasn't been a great few years. Obviously I didn't make this public, but *Solar Empires III* didn't perform as well as expected."

"I told you not to use that title," Lisa mumbled into her laptop.

"That's what it's called," Matt said.

"I'm not going to argue that point again," Don said. "At this rate, Focus isn't even going to wait for us to publish before shutting us down."

"I've been making a little headway," I said. "It's happening more reliably, anyway."

"That may not be a good thing."

"I've been through the object database for every version of *Realms* I could get access to, and it's just not there with the rest of the magic items."

"I think it's obviously not that simple," Lisa said. "It's not going to be just a piece of bad data. There's code running that trolls the available objects, chooses one, changes its color to black, and gives it Mournblade's powers. The bug is composed of both code and data, and one alters the other to create it."

Data and code are like matter and energy, the two essences that, united, make up the world of entertainment software, a world that is in some basic way broken, misshapen, riven at its core. There was a basic rift in the world, and Mournblade lived in the center of it.

"Great," Don said. "You and Russell and Matt are now the company-destroying bug eradication committee. The fate of the realm, my friends, is in your hands."

Matt was tasked with, among other things, checking in on the various Black Arts fan sites and newsgroups to extract any usable feedback and get early warning on major postrelease bugs. In the days following the E3 demo he was spending two or three hours a day online, occasionally posting under a pseudonym to try to spin the event as positively as possible. He sent me an edited transcript from one of the Usenet discussion groups.

```
rec.games.computer.black-arts.history (moderated) #2988
Subject: Re: poser/wannabe/etc (was: E3 rumors—who saw what?)
```

242 · AUSTIN GROSSMAN

From: "Mandemonium" <man-d@xxxxxxxxx.com>

Date: Sun Jun 07 10:02:30 EDT 1998

> I think at this point we can agree everyone saw it, which
  means at least some of the previous reports of sightings are
  almost certainly true

thank you, belatedly

>...shred of credibility...

snip

I've been playing Black Arts games since *Realms III* and I've
  seen it four times. Twice in *Realms*, once in *Clandestine
  (LNTT)*, once in *SEII*. NPC shows up with a standard weapon
  except MATTE BLACK and it KILLS EVERYTHING. Most of us agree
  that's the pattern.

Approximate sequence is, the weapon appears, whoever wields it
  is driven to attack those around it, lethally, and are
  extremely tough although at least in one case not
  invulnerable.

When all opponents are dead, after an interval the wielder dies.
  It's totally random—I've replayed games the exact same way
  but it doesn't get the sword back.

Works like digger wasp or parasitic fluke? Takes over the host &
  makes it do what it wants. The functionality is the same.

The sword whispers things at intervals but I haven't yet made
  it out. I was a little distracted.

rec.games.computer.black-arts.history (moderated) #2989

Subject: Re: poser/wannabe/etc (was: E3 rumors—who saw what?)

From: "nonborn" <nonborn_king@xxxxxxxxx.com>

Date: Sun Jun 07 11:08:02 EDT 1998

I don't know if it's relevant but I've come across a dead planet
  in *SEIII*, all inhabitants. Gone.

rec.games.computer.black-arts.history (moderated) #2990
Subject: Re: poser/wannabe/etc (was: E3 rumors—who saw what?)
From: "aeris-477" <aeris-477@xxxxxxxxx.com>
Date: Sun Jun 07 11:08:45 EDT 1998
Same here but it was a Mittari trader. Dead.

rec.games.computer.black-arts.history (moderated) #2991
Subject: Re: poser/wannabe/etc (was: E3 rumors—who saw what?)
From: "ender" <ender-bender@xxxxxxxxx.com>
Date: Sun Jun 07 11:17:09 EDT 1998
Screenshots or it didn't happen!!!

rec.games.computer.black-arts.history (moderated) #2992
Subject: Re: poser/wannabe/etc (was: E3 rumors—who saw what?)
From: "aeris-477" <aeris-477@xxxxxxxxx.com>
Date: Sun Jun 07 11:17:36 EDT 1998
pix would be nice

rec.games.computer.black-arts.history (moderated) #2993
Subject: Re: poser/wannabe/etc (was: E3 rumors—who saw what?)
From: "Mandemonium" <man-d@xxxxxxxxx.com>
Date: Sun Jun 07 14:21:21 EDT 1998
as you wish...
[MB1.jpg]

The first attached photo was from the most recent *Realms of Gold*. It showed a 3-D scene of a desert; a merchant caravan in chaos, one of its carts actually on fire. At the bottom left, there was a lizard woman holding a black sword. Behind her, a trail of blood spatters, and the bodies of three men and two horses.

And...

[MB2.jpg]

The next photo showed a very different game in the same graph-ics engine: a pale young man, skinny, dressed in the tattered remains of a blue jumpsuit. He was standing in a steel corridor, and behind him a window framed a starfield. He was holding a sword, too—it had the basket hilt of a saber but was inlaid with glowing lines. The blade was a flat black; it seemed to shed darkness the way a lightsaber sheds light. An older man who looked like a relative was dead at his feet.

[MB3.jpg]

The third photo was of a narrow cobblestone street, daytime, the close-set stone buildings seeming to lean in overhead. But it was a mod-ern city, with illuminated signage in some eastern European language. The street was littered with corpses. In the top right, a black rifle bar-rel, circled in red, projected from the window of a church.

also including earliest shot that I know of [not mine!]
[bug2.jpg]

A rainbow-bright eight-bit game, cartoony little sprites running around in a grassy meadow dotted with flowers, except one of them had a little black stick, and the others were exiting the screen in panic, and about a third of the screen was tiled red with bloodstains.

I admit some of these could have been fakes and I'm just going
to claim that they're not.

There was a long thread of screenshots posted. Most of these were obvi-ous fakes; the authentication thread had a master post that stuck to the top, listing the hurdles any Mournblade screenshot had to pass to be marked as authentic.

Mournblade illuminates itself and the immediate environment to the distance of two grid spaces.

Mournblade takes the form of a high-end weapon in whatever continuity it belongs to; in fantasy context, invariably a two-handed sword. In *Clandestine,* allegedly a sniper rifle.

Weapon appears recolored in black and has a distinctive set of runes running down its length.

These runes had spawned their own thread, which attempted to identify the sword's particular runic language and attempt a translation. This latter discussion had been invaded by a contingent of medievalists and philological scholars, which resulted in a surprisingly uncivil thread on the nature of Futhark, Younger Futhark, Futhorc, Quenya, and Cirth — plus the relative merits of *The Silmarillion* and *The Lord of the Rings* and their respective film adaptations — before the thread terminated unhelpfully in a flutter of warnings and then permabans.

Mournblade flashes white on a successful hit, at which point the target seems to be dealt damage equal to or over its hit points or damage allowance (in the case of objects or golems or robots), regardless of resistances or invulnerability. In theory, Mournblade should not affect an undead creature, but this has not been tested.

An authentic Mournblade shot must include the corpse of an in-game person that should otherwise be unkillable or indestructible by normal means, or at the very least it should include the debris of a plot-critical object.

rec.games.computer.black-arts.history (moderated) #2988
Subject: Re: THE MAN (was: E3 rumors—who saw what?)

From: "Mandemonium" <Man-d@xxxxxxxxx.com>
Date: Sun Jun 14 02:15:28 EDT 1998
UPDATED!!!
I, MANDEMONIUM, HAVE WIELDED MOURNBLADE!!
I got it off an unlucky court guard! I managed to get through
    most of the castle before getting boxed in by dead bodies,
    and I died pretty soon after. But I'm pretty sure King Aerion
    can be killed.

By far the longest thread was a debate about the rights and wrongs and uses of Mournblade itself, which divided the Black Arts enthusiasts into permanently balkanized camps.

The Harvesters (collectively, "The Harvest") were the most vocal; led by a poster called D3athLoom, who gave no name but was tagged with a University of Helsinki address, they just wanted to find it. It was the most powerful item in the multiverse and they just wanted to get their hands on it and run amok for as long as possible. They wanted to kill the fat old king of Ahr, all four Heroes, the princess R'yalla, your old mom and dad back at the round tower, if possible, and as much of the Endorian population as lay in between. As long as you could move fast enough it could be done. A few claimed to have wielded it for a time, but the rate of hit point loss was simply too fast to allow you to survive for long anywhere except a crowded city or a battlefield.

The theory was that with the right combination of elements you could live and kill forever. A ring of regeneration could slow the rate at which Mournblade leached the life out of its wielder, but it couldn't stop it entirely. A ring might be supplemented by a team administering regular healing spells, if NPCs could be compelled to do so. Combine that with a system for ensuring a regular, limitless flow of victims and maybe you would have a chance. How small did a monster have to be before it lacked a soul? A carnivorous ape? A giant rat? A killer bee? Could Mournblade feed on a zombie? Could a necromancer reanimate foes as fast as they were killed? Could Mournblade feed on magically animated golems? Summoned daemons? One of the monsters that regenerates hit points? Could the gods themselves be killed?

And there was no reason to limit oneself to a fantasy milieu—the blight of Mournblade extended across all worlds. The terror of Mournblade might be unleashed in the supercrowded levels of Mexico City or Calcutta, or in the cold industrial cruelty of a Stalinist prison camp. Was there a biotech level in *Solar Empires* sufficient to create a sustenance system that Mournblade couldn't defeat? Or a clone factory that could manufacture victims? Did clones have souls?

The anti-Mournblade faction condemned it as poor game design. When a player gained access to the runesword, the game itself ceased to be meaningful. All that carefully calculated game balance, all the storytelling, all the carefully paced challenges fell apart—all the artistry of any game became meaningless. Mournblade killed at a touch—what was the point of that? Games weren't just about getting as much power as possible, they were about succeeding against nearly impossible odds and, with enough skill, triumphing. What did it all mean with Mournblade in hand? The Harvesters were at best immature, at worst psychopathic.

There was a third group, the Mourners, who were also interested in Mournblade but considered themselves distinct from the Harvesters. They had their own forums, but those were invitation-only.

Chapter Thirty-Eight

It was a Friday evening, which I could remember used to matter to me when I was trying to have a life. I thought about what all my friends were doing this summer. They were interning in D.C. or New York. It was 1998. *Sex and the City* had just started on HBO. People were going out at night; people were drinking martinis. But I had either become so pathetic I didn't even think about having a life anymore or I had fallen so far down in the social world I'd come out the other side into an upside-down place where what I was doing was actually cool.

Either way, I dug up the set of seven floppy disks that contained 1988's *Realms of Gold IV: City of Hope*. They built it the year after graduating high school. Darren and Lisa were at UMass, and Simon was living at home and working at a Kinko's. He made the long car trips west to Amherst. Long Sunday night or Monday morning drives west out of Boston along the Massachusetts Turnpike. By November the foliage had gone, just a few ice-encrusted oak leaves hanging on. The roads were bad; sometimes he'd have to crawl at fifteen miles an hour through inches of slush, but he didn't care. He slept in Darren's room or the student lounge and lived on what Darren could smuggle out of the dining halls—cookies, bruised apples, single-serving boxes of frosted flakes, half-pint cartons of milk. Anything was better than home. In high school he was a loner. Now that he'd graduated he was something closer to a recluse. When he had nothing else to do he just rode the bus around Cambridge, or walked around Harvard or Tufts, passing the kids his age on their way to class.

Once, he was bored enough and lonely enough to go back to our old high school to see the annual talent show. A one-act play, two garage bands; a group of dancers performing to some Prince songs. Simon lost himself for once in the closeness of the school auditorium, the smell of sweat and bodies moving. What made him different from them? How had they learned what he didn't? But it was too late: the Second Age was over. Order and sense had been utterly smashed. Endoria was a cracked, debris-strewn sauna pit of contending factions. He had to begin the Third Age, but didn't quite know what it was.

Lisa had told me that if you dug down into Black Arts code, you'd find that a lot of the functions were just copied out of previous versions. There were chunks of code that had been migrating between versions forever because people never felt like taking them apart and fixing them.

You found a lot of in-line comments, like /*okay but fuck you*/ or /*but why??*/ or just /*IM SORRY*/. Some of them were written for an aborted licensing deal with the Labyrinth franchise, so there were functions everywhere named things like DANSE_MAGIC_DANSE and DRAW_CONNELLY. The more I played Black Arts games, the more they started to feel like they're all part of one huge, sinister rat's nest of fragmented worlds, like bright shards of mirror lost in the tangle.

It was five in the morning and I was playing alone when I got sick of the entire business—the struggle, the mess, the tears of the Third Age.

Leira walked away from the city the Four Heroes had built.

In the long years since *Realms III,* the ocean had risen and the city was a half-drowned island in a wide, shallow inlet. Weeds covered the great statue of Elbas; thieves had stolen his jeweled eyes. I paddled through the streets and the flooded palace.

Then I left the whole point of *Realms IV* behind and walked south.

WAFFLE could generate as much detail in the landscape as I needed, giving it warmer and greener colors.

Later — I couldn't really say how much later — I reached the bottom of the continent itself and looked out over the simulated seas of Endoria. Then I piloted a single-masted boat to islands that became increasingly remote. It was late November, and tacking slowly upwind, watching the bands of orange and purple on the water through the night, was better than sleep.

Even at the eastern limit of the world they'd heard of Mournblade; one man claimed his father's father was killed with it. They said an ancient hermit knew everything there was to know about it. They gave me a map.

I turned when someone sat down behind me; I thought it was Matt but it was only Brennan. He'd been killed a couple dozen times during the past few games, but in the way of video game characters he'd managed to walk it off. Now he sat in an empty office chair with a ridiculous amount of animal grace. He smelled like leather, horses, oil. His hands were dirty.

"Tallyho, gents," Brennan said sleepily, halfway through a bag of Doritos. He wore a maroon T-shirt with a griffin on the front. "For the honor of my house!"

"Hey, there," I said.

"You suck at this game," he said.

"You suck when you're first-level too, you know," I said. I didn't mind Brennan; he'd been through a lot. I'd decided he was in love with Leira, too.

Leira and I found the sage living within earshot of the Last Meridian, where the still ocean picked up speed and slid off the great disk of Endoria and down among the stars. Far out in the mists that rose from below, one could distinguish the Castles of Dawn, where cloud giants lived, but where no one had ever been.

The sage was ancient and wizened but oddly familiar, and after a moment I saw it — it was Brennan, but a different version of him, impossibly aged. I glanced back at Brennan, who was watching himself on the screen in the video game he also lived in. He was mesmerized.

"I was there," the Brennan-sage told us. "We all were, down in the tombs at the end of the Age. Me, the elf, the mageborn, and you, too, Princess. We beheld Mournblade, and it was the wizard who first betrayed the fellowship. He called things from the stone to bind us. After that it was each of us for ourselves, you understand? Mournblade was too much to resist, the idea that we might accomplish all our primary quests and rule the Fourth Age. We fought up and down the levels, hide-and-seek, the four greatest heroes of the age." He spat and continued. He let his gray hair fall to one side and showed his missing eye.

"You gave me this mark, Princess. You thought I was done for — but I was warded. I finished the wizard, held his mouth shut while I put the blade in. He took a few of my fingers with him — the old man showed a little grit in the end.

"After that, I saw what you and Prendar had done to each other, and I ran for it. The Soul Gem took me back in time, all the way back to the start. The black blade is down there in Adric's Tomb, yes, it is, along with a thing that wields it like fury. Don't go, Leira. None of us should. Let Mournblade lie there forever and let the Third Age end in peace."

Young Brennan looked stricken, his stubbly face pale in the monitor light.

"Why didn't you tell me?" he asked.

"I didn't know," I said.

"I hate this game," he said. And I woke to the fluorescent lights coming on at seven. I was asleep at my desk, my head cradled in my arms. I got up and went to the kitchen to find some Skittles and went back to work.

Chapter Thirty-Nine

Lorac and I walked up Oxford Street together. He smelled like jasmine and ash. His eyes gleamed with the unnatural intelligence that could retain twelve different daemonic languages in as many alphabets; he'd done Sanskrit that afternoon. I wondered if he had been born with the talent or if he had paid a price, and what it was.

"Lorac, how does magic work?" I asked. He sighed, barely stopping himself from rolling his eyes a little.

"It depends what kind — they're all different."

"Your thing, then. Conjuration."

He plucked at the hem of his robe. His hands were spotted with age but quick and limber, and they looked strong. He saw me watching and stopped.

"Well," he said, "I bought a level-eight specialization in it, if that's what you mean. But it's ... you have to realize, when the Houses of the Nine were sealed, words were spoken and signs were engraved that cannot now be unsaid or erased. When I speak, when I make the shapes, I take part in ..." He trailed off, muttering in a language I didn't recognize.

"Start again. What's it like to cast spells?" I asked.

"I'll just say — when your body and your voice can shape the world ..." he said. He was more animated than I'd ever seen him. "There are ways in which I have cracked the secrets of creation. The joy, the sense of belonging — I can't explain it to one like you."

"Okay, so why can't I do it?"

"Because you live beyond the end of the Third Age. In your time, magic has retreated and even the ruins of the ruins of the Firstcomers have been dust for aeons, long after their knowledge has been lost to humanity. Long after the last of my kind read the final prophecy of the Earth's Heart and broke his staff across his knee and cursed his art and was never heard from again."

"Great."

"Also because you grew up in Newton."

"So that's it?" I said. "I'll never do magic?"

"There are certain scrolls — of doubtful authenticity, mind you — that claim that once in a millennium, a young person of talent and matchless courage will have the chance to rediscover the world of magic — certain words, at least, and one great sign. This person will bring the return of magic and remake the world in an age of splendor that will come. Madness, yes, but great splendor, too."

"But that's not me."

He laughed. "Ah — no."

"So . . . magic. It's nothing to do with . . . the way you dress."

He was wearing what seemed like a worn maroon bathrobe over a bright blue blouse thing. His long gray hair was tied back with a faded ribbon. He had slippers with pointed toes that curled upward, and they weren't coping so well in the slush and mud of a New England sidewalk.

"The way I dress?" he said, looking puzzled. "No."

"Then how come you dress like that?"

"Because I can do magic."

"So how come you can't use metal weapons?"

"I'd rather not talk about it."

"Lorac, you're really powerful now. Why don't you go back to that fancy kingdom you left? Maybe the king would take you back."

"I did."

"What happened?"

"It's gone; something happened to it while I was away. Nothing there but sand and stone buildings. Empty fountains, beautiful mosaics."

"Shit."

"Let's not talk about it."

"So what happened at the end of the Third Age?"

"I thought I'd explained all that before. Weren't you listening? Magic ended."

He saw me off at the Porter Square T stop. He stood on the platform and waved to me as my train pulled away, the only wizard left alive in our time, if he even was alive. In his robes and beard he looked sad and homeless for a moment, but then he winked at me and mimed a golf stroke.

PART V

CLANDESTINE, OR THE SPY WHO LOVED YOU

Chapter Forty

Clandestine (1988)

Clandestine dated from senior year, the year Darren left high school for good, the year after Simon finally quit his job at Kinko's to live full-time at UMass. He didn't find an apartment. By that time he was a sort of unofficial mascot of the undergrad computer science lab. He'd drift from dorm room to dorm room or to a student lounge. One or another CS major would pretend to lose his access card and pass it on to Simon, who was such a constant presence in the lab that faculty and staff never bothered to ask for a student ID. The students knew who he was, of course—the eccentric genius behind the *Realms* games— and his nascent career as a homeless person only raised him in their esteem. He was a kind of avatar of the hard-core spirit. It helped that he really was brilliant and could defy the conventional wisdom of what was possible on a regular basis.

The *Realms* games were a success but starting to feel like a trap. Darren in particular wanted new worlds to conquer. Fantasy was limiting their demographic.

"People look at a video game and all they see is a bunch of dwarves flying around and purple explosions and nothing makes sense," he said. "So why should a normal person bother playing?"

"It only takes a few minutes to figure it out," Simon said.

"But instead they can just go see a movie, which takes zero seconds to figure out," Lisa put in.

"And movies are about people," said Darren. "We need that. We don't do people, but we will. We'll have better graphics—"

"Better writing," Lisa said.

"—something more like a movie," said Darren. "Like James Bond, or *Casablanca*."

"So how do we do that? Graphics technology is never going to look like a movie," Simon said. He had a point, in 1988. CD-ROM drives were scarcely an idea as a consumer game format, and the first basic real-time 3-D games were at least three years away.

"We can do it. What if players got to be Humphrey Bogart? They get to actually lounge around at Rick's. Looking cool. Everyone would want it."

"I'm picturing a player getting bored," said Lisa. "I'm picturing Humphrey Bogart leaving Rick's to find something to do. I'm picturing an expressionless Humphrey Bogart running through the streets of Casablanca, killing Nazis and taking their bullets and looking for secret doors. I picture Humphrey Bogart ruling a desolate Casablanca he has stripped utterly of life and treasure."

"Everybody wants to be Humphrey Bogart," said Darren. "Right? There must be a way. It's 1987, for God's sake."

With those words the *Clandestine* franchise was born, in the persons of Nick Prendergast, agent of MI6 and cheap James Bond knockoff, scourge of the Soviet security apparatus; the missing Laura, Nick's lost first love, for whom he was on an eternal quest; and his implacable foe, the devious German spymaster Karoly.

Black Arts had a mint-condition copy. I opened the box to find a thick manila envelope containing a game manual, fake period newspaper clippings, a decoder wheel, and a cloth map of Paris showing Nick's apartment, his favorite bar (Le Canard), message drop points, important characters' houses, and an inset giving details of the Paris Catacombs. Finally, a mock classic-noir movie poster showed Nick peering through fog in a trench coat. You could feel it—Black Arts was swinging for the fences on this one, doing what video games had become addicted to doing: challenging the top dog of twentieth-century media, the movies, and trying to beat them at their own game. I wondered if they'd succeed. And I had the fleeting thought that maybe one of them built *Clandestine* with an eye to escaping the black sword, on the theory that it wouldn't leave Endoria to menace Paris.

```
cd qp\clandestine
clandestine.exe
import saved game? (Y/N)
```

It began with a narrow cobblestone street somewhere in Paris, which had high buildings on either side, their plaster facades streaked and dirty. It was a foggy early morning. The sun has just risen as a fortyish man hurries along in a black winter coat and white cravat, his face grim and set at the end of a long night. He glances back once, then hurries on. As his footsteps die away, the title appears over the empty screen:

```
BLACK ARTS
PRESENTS...
CLANDESTINE
```

I remembered, now, playing this one. That summer the game was my failed birthday present to my father, to go with his new PC, but I wound up the only one who ever played it — alone, after the family had gone to bed.

I played obsessively, with no hint book, and I would remain stuck on the same puzzle for days, repeatedly searching a woman's dressing room at the Comédie-Française, or wandering the Catacombs in search of a secret door, or puzzling over a German cipher.

I followed Nick's adventures while wasting the summer driving aimlessly through my area of the suburbs, making my own trip west to visit a girl at Amherst College until she broke it to me that we were only friends. I spent a sleepless night on the floor next to her bed before getting up at six to drive the ninety-five miles back to my Harvard summer-school dorm room, where I would surprise my roommate and his girlfriend, who had expected me to be gone for the weekend. That summer I saw Montmartre and the Champs-Élysées for the first time, I got drunk for the first time on the train to Rome. I decided to become an English major. Years later I happened on one of the source photos that had been digitized for the occupation montage, and was overwhelmed with the memory of that sadness and the sweet smell of my father's tobacco.

I honestly wasn't quite sure I wanted to play the game again, but I knew it would look different this time. I was a different person now.

I had a roommate freshman year who was obsessed with it. I noticed it from the outside as just an unusually pretty game, blues and purples. His girlfriend used to refer to it as "that video game that's, like, not really a video game." And it didn't look like one; it looked like an artsy cartoon crossed with a complex board game, one with the elegance of a deluxe Clue set.

It was a palpable technological step forward. The Commodore 64 was a graphics powerhouse for its day. These were no longer the crayon drawings of earlier games. *Clandestine* delivered lushly picturesque, sixteen-color backdrops of interwar Paris in warm blues and oranges, blocky and vivid and memorable, like an image stitched into a Persian rug.

Nick Prendergast was not really a spy at all, just a twenty-two-year-old fresh from Oxford with a second in Modern Greats who got mixed up with the kind of racy aristocratic set that tended to stumble into intelligence work. Nick Prendergast was still two-dimensional in those days, a lovingly drawn, animated paper doll in his tawdry, fourth-floor walk-up apartment in the cinquième arrondissement.

You could walk back and forth in his apartment, look out his window, and see a tiny piece of the Seine through a crack between two apartment buildings. It's when you're over by the window that you realize that Nick Prendergast is, very definitely, Prendar the thief. He was more human-looking, but he had the same beaky nose, same eyebrows, same blue eyes, and same slightly weak chin. A shabbier, thoroughly modernized Prendar, residing via dream logic (game logic?) in 1937 Paris. Prendar, *voleur,* demi-fey.

Of course, I was there on my own secret mission, which had nothing to do with the German spy ring the game would eventually turn out to be about. My leather satchel should have contained a few francs, a Webley automatic pistol with one bullet, and a telegram with an address on it, from which we gather it is the spring of 1937.

As Prendar/Prendergast/whoever, you leave your apartment for the streets of Paris. You could go anywhere, walk to Père Lachaise Cemetery and visit Oscar Wilde's grave if you liked, but you walk to the address on the telegram, a tailor's shop on the Champs-Élysées, where you find a suit of evening clothes that has been ordered for you by an unknown party. In the vest pocket there is an invitation to an event at the comte de Versailles's house, false identity papers, and a note explaining that someone at the party is a spy smuggling weapons and intelligence to the Reich. The world is on the brink of war, but perhaps one man in the right place can hold back the tide a few moments longer. You're already late for the party.

But this time, it was different. Because when I checked the vest there was an additional inventory item, an object that shouldn't even have existed in this era, in this world, in this genre. A white Endorian flower. It wasn't technologically unreasonable that *Clandestine* could import data from an Endorian saved game — they ran the same code, worked by the same rules. Under the hood, Paris and Endoria were made of the same stuff. But nonetheless it shouldn't have been there. It was uncanny.

At the comte de Versailles's I realized how odd the game was, and why Darren had designed it this way. The game concept demanded intrigue, mystery, glamour, and romance. Accordingly, you couldn't just go around murdering people; there was exactly one bullet in the entire game. Instead, Nick could do things like (F)lirt or (Q)uestion or (W)altz.

The game had a schedule of parties from March to early June, the Paris social season. There was a list of suspects, chosen from the cream of western Europe: artists, aristocrats, and dignitaries. One was secretly a Nazi spy; there was also a Communist mole, an American agent, and a Czech assassin. Darren's trick was to turn the elite social world of Paris into a system of party invitations, weekend invitations, flirtations, cachet, and deceptions, requiring by turns charm, manners, improvisatory brilliance, and the brash self-assurance of the master party crasher.

You wandered around the drawing room, holding a cigarette that you forget to smoke. You were pretending to be someone called the Baron Pemberly-Sponk. A woman named Laura Mortimer, society reporter for a Paris daily, approached. There was a short, surreal exchange about the cinema, which might or might not have been a coded message. According to the decoder wheel, it wasn't code at all, just Nick's native haplessness. Laura looked a lot like Leira with a bobbed haircut.

A young heiress made advances; a mysterious woman in black stared at you, then left the party. What did she want? Did you follow her? The door to the kitchen and servants' wing swung invitingly ajar — did you dare slip out and explore the house? You are dogged and charming; you struggle politely with your cover identity.

I copied the list of suspects down in pencil. I didn't care, but it might help me stay alive while I looked for what I needed. As the summer passed, the challenges grew more difficult. You picked locks and copied letters and scrutinized sepia photographs. You spent a great deal of time creeping through the halls of country houses after midnight. You met Unity Mitford and read Evelyn Waugh's correspondence. The real Pemberly-Sponk put in an unexpected appearance. Laura's passport turned out to be forged. A rumor circulated that Pemberly-Sponk was in fact a world champion practitioner of the Viennese waltz, and an exhibition of skill was required. The list of suspects narrowed.

I noticed one or two more differences. Laura's formal dress was a pale blue-and-white chiffon, not green. My CIA contact, Blandon (a dead ringer for Brennan), wore a white shirt with gold cufflinks and a red satin cummerbund. The AIs knew who they were and who they'd been, although there was no sign of Lorac.

Unfortunately, I didn't care. I was just looking for the homing device Nick was supposed to get access to when he had enough francs stashed away in his cheap mattress — the homing device that would lead us to the cursed sword that shouldn't exist here, but it did, just as it did in all the worlds. And I found it. Nick pawned his best jacket for it, but I got it. From there, I only needed to survive.

I clicked on the flower, and Prendergast looked at it for a moment, then shrugged and put it in his lapel. *Clandestine* was a game that cared about wardrobe, so Nick's character stats reshuffled; a little less intimidating, a little more dashing. The adjustment turned out to have a small but tangible effect. Relationships were all rated on points, and they reshuffled, too.

Laura had been a friend and platonic confidante in the wilds of Paris, but now she gained new conversation options. One night after a party she stopped at the intersection near her apartment.

"Do you love me?" (Y/N)

You stopped for long seconds. Should you? You'd already lied to her. Your name wasn't Pemberly-Sponk, it was Prendergast. Or Prendar. And even that wasn't your real name. Your name wasn't Prendar — was anybody's? You couldn't tell her your real real name; it wasn't in the interface. And should she trust you, the player, who knew she was only numbers? Who just wanted to win the game, to maximize a set of points? Or get a million dollars? And isn't love only for people who can be trusted?

I pressed Y anyway.

You passed a threshold, and a new scene was unlocked. There was a bonus level. Nick and Laura went spinning together through an enchanted Louis Quinze ballroom whose bay windows overlooked the starlit Seine. The graphics were laughable by the standards of even a few years later, but the scene was no less powerfully imagined for that. It worked on its on technological level, just as a Roman mosaic or cave painting doesn't seem less powerful for lacking the realism of a Renaissance oil painting. The camera panned along with them through a seemingly endless gallery. Behind them, through the windows, a cartoonish but meticulously correct Paris skyline scrolled past.

The haunting melody of "Laura's Waltz" had to be one of the finest compositions ever written for the 6581 SID chip. It managed to suggest in three channels of flat eight-bit tones the gaiety and prescient sadness of Paris's lost generation, the waltz's plaintive keening and the warbling of its higher registers soaring over the buzzy, percussive bass.

When I heard it playing, it felt like a sound track to that whole lost sophomore year of college, through and past my first failed relationship. I saw myself growing up, all in a few months going from overage teen to disappointed grown-up, and there was that middle space where it all came together, a sixteen-color Paris between the wars. For some reason, I felt as close to having a life as someone who had no life could possibly feel.

And I was thinking about how catching the spy didn't matter anyway. Maybe I was older, and I knew France was falling, the Reich was coming, history was on its way, and a video-game spy like Nick wasn't going to stop it. On impulse I stopped outside the tailor's and dropped my pistol into an open manhole. I didn't feel like shooting anybody just then.

* * *

There are always trade-offs, narrative paths not taken. Nick finished with a little less money. He missed a bulletin from America he was meant to pick up that night.

And one night in June, you lay in wait on the Île de la Cité for the operation's mysterious ringleader. You were now a trained British intelligence agent, which means that you had spent a weekend in the country with a white-haired old eccentric who taught you to operate a radio, read a surveyor's map, and fire an antique Webley ineffectually at a target across a lawn ("Just keep practicing, laddie").

The evening jacket, which in March you once hugged tight around you against the chill, is now uncomfortably hot. March was so long ago, long days and nights of dances and laughter and so many, many glasses of Champagne. You would barely recognize the man who rang in the New Year walking alone along the Quai de Montebello, shivering, glaring spitefully up at the lighted windows and the laughter trickling down, flinching at the sight of lovers by the Seine. For four months now you lived the life of your dreams.

You heard a voice in the fog say, "Gently, gently now! Or Karoly will murder the lot of us," and the sound of a small boat bumping against the stone landing, and then a rapid exchange in German.

You rushed forward in time to see a long and narrow package being handed down to two men in a waiting speedboat by a third on the dock. The man on shore straightened up to meet you. His scarred, mustachioed face was the one you expected. It was Lord Mortimer himself, Laura's father, alias Karoly, alias (duh) Lorac himself, in his twentieth-century incarnation. "Sorry, my boy, it's finished," he said, and drew a revolver from his satin-lined greatcoat.

If you'd kept your pistol you might have tried to shoot him. Years ago, you did. But this time, he fired, and stepped lightly into the boat while you sank to your knees in the dark, cursing.

He would live on, together with his now-crucial inventory. But whatever choice you made, the first *Clandestine* game ended with Nick watching Laura disappear into the pixelated fog of the Gare du Nord. The *Clandestine* theme played again over a montage of scanned photographs from the Nazi occupation of Paris, now only three years away.

When I last played it, that ending seemed at the time like the height of sad sophistication, the confirmation of all my darkest, most dramatically adolescent ideas of myself and the nature of love.

I saw less and less of Simon that year. I wish I could say I tried harder, but it made me uncomfortable. It was a time in my life when I was trying to join the prelaw fraternity and convince myself I was going to be the kind of virile corporate lawyer who appears in thriller novels, who plays rugby and can fly a small plane and might someday run for Congress.

And then, Simon was a more and more marginal-looking character. He was living in a shabby group house in Amherst, inhabited by maybe a floating third of the CS department. I was there once, stopping in before we went out to dinner. It seemed furnished entirely with beanbag chairs and carpet fragments; they'd broken open the drywall to expose the first-floor wiring. They had three different generations of game console in the living room, and there was a commotion upstairs that I guessed to be an improvised sport involving an ottoman, a Wiffle ball, and approximately three to five grown adults. It seemed at the time like all of Simon's friends, men and women, played ultimate Frisbee and dressed like the nerd auxiliary of a biker gang. Not only could they field-strip a hard drive but they also carried the necessary tools in their pockets. They juggled when I didn't want them to, and were opinionated about manned space exploration, and seemed to be building a medieval siege weapon in the back yard. And it didn't help that Simon seemed happy; annoyingly, he seemed almost cool. He told me stories about outwitting campus security, and parties where they did weird things with dry ice. He even had a girlfriend for a year, who, judging by the little contact I had with her, was an unbelievably nice person. Whereas I constantly felt like I was auditioning for my grown-up life. In fact, I felt like a bit of a schmuck.

Six weeks after *Clandestine* was released, Simon woke under the conference-room table to Darren shaking him.

"I got a call from EA. They tracked us down. They want to publish us. They want to buy *Clandestine*."

The conversation that followed was long only because it was so hard to agree on a company name. Blast Radius, AwesomeStrike, and Quantum Pony were considered. Quarterstaff. Primeworld Optimization Services. Panjandrum. Hyperdream. Nekropony. Dimension Door. Cybermantix. Monumental Games. Rat Giant. Fire Giant. Storm Giant. Wizard Panic. Black Arts.

They'd need another new graphics engine and a whole new approach. The industry was pivoting away from graphic adventure games. *The Legend of Zelda: A Link to the Past* came out, *Civilization* came out, and *Street Fighter II,* and *Sonic the Hedgehog.* Parallax scrolling was ancient history compared to what was coming. The technology was progressing almost faster than they could keep track of it. The only question was what to do with it.

Black Arts got itself a real office, a sunny penthouse loft that could have fit the company three times over, with a wraparound view of downtown Boston, free snacks, a private game arcade, and a life-size plastic sculpture of Brennan. Darren bought the Rolls; Simon probably bought some new T-shirts. Darren roamed the office with a BB gun, stopping to sight down the hall at shelves full of Game of the Year trophies. At the end of the day, the cleaning staff swept up the BBs and put them in an urn for the following day.

Chapter Forty-One

"Can I talk to you for a minute, Russell?" Lisa was standing behind me. I wondered how long she'd been there.

"Sure."

"Privately, I mean."

"Okay," I said. Private talks weren't part of Black Arts's open-office design, so when anybody wanted to chat confidentially it meant walking all the way to the End of the World. Black Arts wasn't anywhere near large enough to fill the space we occupied, so half the office was just a trackless desert of blue carpet. We checked to make sure nobody was trying to sleep in any of the unused cubicles nearby.

"So what's up?" I asked. There was no place to sit, so we both just leaned against the wall.

"So I've been thinking. Let's say I knew more about Mournblade than other people. Would it be okay to talk to you about it?" She wasn't looking at me, just back toward where the working area was. At this distance it glowed like a city on the horizon.

"You mean, would I tell anyone else?"

"Yes."

"No, I wouldn't," I said. I hadn't thought about it ahead of time, but it was true. "I would feel bad keeping secrets from Don, though."

"Let's say sooner or later I'll end up telling Don."

"Okay. Agreed."

"Okay. So we can't get Mournblade out of the object database because that's not where it is, right?" she said.

"According to you."

"Right. But it is…someplace in the world. The code that generates it also puts it into the world. There's a room where it exists."

"Then why can't we find it on the map?"

"Because the engine generates that room, the same way it generates the object," she said. Dealing with people who knew astronomically less about a subject than she did was just ordinary conversation for her. "It builds the space when the game is running. This is why WAFFLE is such a weird program. It generates data procedurally, the same way Mournblade comes into being. WAFFLE can make things up; that's what makes it so interesting to play."

"So you could go to the room and find it if you knew where it was."

"And if it was accessible, yes."

"But you think it might not be," I said.

"Or it's really, really hard. Now we can't fix the code per se…"

"But…"

"But maybe we can produce a version of the universe in which Adric's Tomb is free of the curse," she said. "Export a saved game with the changed version, issue it as a patch. I'm not sure how hard that is, maybe impossible. But we know it was done once, right? Because Simon did it in the *Realms* final."

"I've been thinking about that," I said. "Are we just dealing with the fallout of Simon cheating in the tournament?"

"He didn't cheat."

"Yes, he did," I said evenly.

"He just realized no one ever took Adric's Tomb out of the map, so maybe he could find it. That's not cheating."

"It's specialized knowledge."

"What happened wasn't even about the tournament. It was just a systems test. To see if it worked," she said.

"Whose test? Simon's?"

"Mostly."

"Who else knows this?"

"Darren," she said after a moment. "But I don't know where the thing is, okay? That part's yours."

"I don't know why you know any of this."

"The thing about Simon…" she stopped, sighed, began again. "The funny thing was, he thought he was a hacker. I mean he and Darren used to grab cracked games off BBS'es and stuff. There was a lot of underground trading going on at KidBits. I did it, too."

"You did?"

"I had a *Dragon's Lair* habit. Those were different times. The problem was, we got caught."

"It can't have been that big a deal."

"Don't you remember how they treated Simon? They were literally talking about kids starting a nuclear war from a phone booth. They didn't make any distinctions. There were real people who could have crashed the nine-one-one system of a major city—how did they know that wasn't us? Darren freaked out the worst, of all people. You could probably go back to KidBits and find all the cracked copies of Apple II games he threw into the lake one night. So what the fight was about…"

She stopped for a moment, looked away, then went on. "We were all guilty—whatever that means—but Darren wanted to try and put it all on me. He wasn't even that much of an asshole, you know? He was just scared. I was scared, too. I was a straight-A student. It was my whole life. I couldn't afford to have people know. You don't remember what it was like, I bet."

"Yeah, I do. I was probably the most terrified person you could possibly imagine. But why didn't any of you tell me?"

"Russell, how could we? Nobody trusts you." She said it without hesitation, but it took me a second to process it, to replay it in my head, to let it settle, to comprehend it as inarguably true.

"What? What did I ever do to anybody?" I said after a while.

"Nothing, nothing. God. Do you remember one night, like late in camp, Darren was going on and on about UMass and how awesome it was going to be, they'd both major in CS and room together and do games and it sounded perfect, you know how he could do that. He made you want to live forever, somehow. And then, just casually, he asked you where you were applying next year, and you just mumbled and looked away, the way you do when you don't want to answer something—you think no one notices?—and then said you'd probably be going to Dartmouth if you could get in. And so, you know, bye-bye, nerds. And that's what you did. And now you're back a decade later saying, 'Hi, nerds, where's my job?'"

"That's not how it was."

"Really? So you didn't spend the next summer in Washington at a fancy internship, trying to learn to smoke, finding out about sex, going to parties where you laughed about how you were 'such a nerd in high school'? So yeah, we didn't tell you. We didn't tell you anything. It was so obvious you couldn't wait to be done with Simon."

"Simon was not that easy to deal with," I said.

"You think I don't know that?" she said, louder. Could anyone hear us? "At least he wasn't slumming it. At least he didn't ditch everybody to go hang with the cool kids."

"What?"

"Well, it's what you did, right? None of us heard from you that whole senior year. You didn't even say hi to him in the halls."

"I was busy," I said. "I had to get into college. You don't know—"

"I don't know. Like I didn't have college? Is this what happens after we ship? Are you going to be busy again? When you get tired of hanging with people like Matt and laughing at them?"

"That is fucking bullshit." I was angry, but Lisa was more so; she was shaking. I don't know why people thought she didn't have emotions. She just kept them in weird places.

"You live off Simon and you didn't even know him. At least Simon knew what friendship was."

In actual fact, that was my summer in Paris, and I'd talked up the idea that I was prelaw, and I wouldn't have had the gumption to tell anyone I was a gamer, not that I got anywhere by not mentioning it. I'd shed the whole dorky thing, like a juvenile delinquent whose court records were sealed forever at sixteen. But anyone could see that a person like Simon would carry his dorky youth with him for his whole life. That he might be out of juvie but he'd never lose that memory of the first night, the bars clanging shut and the taunting in the dark.

Chapter Forty-Two

Lorac, do you think Lisa likes me?"

"Like-likes you?"

"Yeah."

"This seems more like a Brennan question."

"Can't you do magic to figure this out?"

He sketched a quick little figure in a puddle with the tip of his staff and frowned at the ripples. "You don't know her that well, do you?"

"No. She's pretty hard to read."

I wondered if Brennan wouldn't indeed have been a better person to ask.

"Should I ask her out?"

He shrugs. It's not really a Lorac question, but he's the only one around. "Why not?"

"But what would happen?"

"I can see the future, but only in parts and only under third-edition rules, the augury and divination spells."

"All right. What do they do?"

"This is augury: Caster may dwell on a proposed course of action and receive a general sense of its outcome, positive or negative." He mumbled a few words under his breath and drew a complex polygon in the air with one finger.

"Well?"

"Basically it turns out all right, I suppose. Mingled essences of relief, bliss, regret, anger."

"What? That sounds like it sucks. What about divination?"

"Divination: Caster may dwell on a proposed course of action and receive specific images, clues, and impressions regarding the short- and long-term outcome and consequences."

"Okay, so try that."

He hesitated.

"Very well." He pushed a few chairs apart then dimmed the lights. He knelt without apparent difficulty for a sixtysomething magician, fished a piece of chalk from within his robes, and began sketching a complex figure on the floor, a bit like a crab.

"I'm drawing a little diagram of what time looks like if you're looking straight into it—like looking down a tunnel and seeing a circle, if the tunnel were an angry ten-dimensional crab, which is what, in vastly oversimplified terms, we mean by the human word *time*."

He rapidly sang an arcane song under his breath—the words weren't in any human language; the melody was close to "California Girls."

"What does it show?"

"Not sure," he said.

"Come on. I thought you were a wizard."

He sighed, then he looked at me with eyes that had seen the top three levels of the abyss, that had looked out across countless battlefields and into the eyes of the Lich King. "If I tell you, will you swear to stop bothering me?"

"Fine."

"First of all, I can't really tell if she like-likes you," he began. "But she's lawful neutral."

"And?"

When he was done, I knew a bit more than I wanted to, and none of it answered my question.

Some of it I already knew. I knew that Lisa's mother was a librarian, her father was a paleontologist. She was an only child.

I knew she was five feet tall for most of high school and carried a huge backpack, so she had to walk looking up a little. She got beaten up by a group of older girls once, and didn't tell her parents.

She got crushes no one knew about. She drew in her textbooks. When her father bought an Apple][Plus, she didn't know girls weren't supposed to use it. She played Sierra On-Line games and solved *Mystery House* in a long weekend.

Her first serious boyfriend was in freshman year of college. He was notionally a playwright. For six months they were that couple that was *always* making out in public. Then later you just noticed they were never in the same room together.

After sixth grade she stopped having friends for a long time. Lots of people joked that she was a witch or a lesbian. She thought about whether she should be a witch. Her parents had all kinds of books in the house. She read *The Anarchist Cookbook* and the *Whole Earth Catalog*. Her dad died.

Somehow everybody at school knew about it, and they were surprisingly decent. She started eating lunch with a circle of people from honors English. She didn't actually hate people. She sang second soprano in the school choir. She had a short, intense friendship with a tall girl named Sarah that ended abruptly.

A lot of boys who went to high school with her developed severe retroactive crushes on her in college, all around the end of sophomore year.

Computer science is a good discipline if you like to be left alone.

She last got in a fight in fifth grade. It didn't stop until two teachers pulled her off, a fact no one at school ever seemed to forget. The other girl has a tiny discolored patch near her right cheekbone from where her face rubbed against the asphalt. They never became friends.

She wrote stories in a notebook in a big looping hand that her teacher let her turn in for extra credit, a lot of which were about time travel. She even wrote a rambling novella stretched over several spiral-bound notebooks. She made a graphic adventure game based on it and gave it to her mother as a birthday present. Her mother kept it on a shelf but she never played it.

Junior year of college she started hanging out in the twenty-four-hour computer lab more. She tried smoking pot. Her roommates stopped seeing much of her. They'd see her sleeping in a pile of clothes during the day. That spring she had a series of one-night stands, mostly with people she met at parties at the campus radio station, where she was interning as a sound engineer. She started hanging out with the same group of CS majors a lot. Some of them knew Simon. She went on elevator surfing expeditions, and smoked even more pot. She started collecting copies of building keys. She got a semiregular boyfriend that her roommates hated. She threw up from drinking for the first time. At Christmas her mother asked her if she thought she needed therapy.

She started drinking more. She had a line of green Jägermeister bottles on the windowsill of her dorm room. She still slept a lot during the day. That fall she failed a class. Her honors thesis was entitled "A Closed-Form Solution to the Radiance Transfer between Two Distant Spheres," and it drew a lot of attention from the faculty. In January, she started avoiding her adviser. One night her roommates heard a sound, half sobbing, half screaming, and found her with a bunch of 3.25-inch disks she had snapped in half.

Her roommates finally told her boyfriend to stop calling. She finished her thesis and graduated late, with honors. Simon offered her a job, which she turned down. That summer, fall, and spring she lived with her mother in her old room, which was probably the last happy period in her life. She applied to the Columbia grad program in computer science, got in, and moved to the city. She was the kind of person old people in her building liked and the people at the bodega said hi to every day. She still smoked pot sometimes; she went to department happy hours and campus *Star Trek* marathons and contra dancing. She had her last name legally changed. She did research on natural language processing. She quit after a year and a half. She e-mailed Simon and asked him for a job and moved to a big group house in Somerville with a mix of software engineers, IT workers, and engineering students.

She had dinner with her mother twice a week. She saw a therapist who made notes about low affect and a thing called dismissive-avoidant attachment style. She got asked a lot about the period around her father's death. She stopped going after four months. She still read a lot of science fiction.

Chapter Forty-Three

The crucial fact of whether or not a particular area is player accessible was hard to determine. The WAFFLE engine tended to generate unexpected scenarios. In the very first puzzle I built for *Winter's Crown,* I learned this lesson. You were on a narrow road leading north through the Celestials, a mountain range that cut diagonally across the continent. You needed to cross a river. This was an easy one. The drawbridge was up, but if you fired arrows you could cut the ropes and it would fall down to your side.

I handed this one to Jared, who proceeded to knock over a tall tree so that it lay across the chasm. I reset the level and told him not to do that. He then spawned a wizard and levitated himself over the gap.

"Let's just say you don't have levitate."

He threw a grappling hook across the river and yanked until the ropes gave way.

"And you don't have a grappling hook."

He then froze the river.

"No freeze spells."

He cast Lava Storm; the flying lava blobs struck the water and congealed. Soon there were stepping-stones of solidified lava.

"No lava!"

He took off his armor and swam. He pushed rocks into the water until he had enough stepping-stones. He cast Three-Second Invulnerability on himself, then cast Fireball; the explosion threw him over the chasm and a ways down the road. He polymorphed himself into a giant eagle and flew across. I gritted my teeth.

"So what if you didn't have any items or spells?" I told him. "Just a bow and arrow."

He thought about it for a while, and then shot arrows across the gap until he'd cut both of the ropes holding it up. The drawbridge wobbled, leaned, then fell with a crash. Problem solved.

"Nice puzzle." He went back to his desk.

I could see why some designers thought of players as the enemy. As a designer I could see a perfect scenario playing out in my head, but players didn't care about it in the slightest, they just followed their own script. In the WAFFLE engine, this was more true than elsewhere. It gave players a great many tools that interacted with the world and each other. Used creatively, or in combination, these tools could enable a player to do almost anything. I'd seen a playtester climb into the sky by startling a flock of birds, casting Stop Time, then leaping from bird to bird to land on the back of a dragon that took him so high he could see the false sun was a thin yellow disk pasted to the ceiling of the world.

I made a local copy on my laptop and met Matt in a scrubby café in Davis Square. I ordered a coffee, and he got a large slice of day-old Key lime pie on a paper plate. I showed him the bugs Lisa had assigned me, then he spent half an hour going through the data while I stared at impressionistic paintings of electric guitars. Most of the people there were our age but had apparently learned different lessons about how to spend their lives. Behind me two men and a woman discussed different brands of racing bicycle.

"I don't suppose — is there any way to just not care about this?" I suggested.

"So I'm going to guess that you haven't looked at your bug list lately."

I opened my laptop and looked, and there was a brand-new one.

```
Reporter: rlamber
Version or Build: e3
Module or component:
Platform / Operating System: whatever was at e3
Type of error: design
Priority: 1
Severity: 1
Status: open
Assigned to: RMarsh
Summary: e3 demo error
Description: fix soonest please
```

It was now a P1S1, also known as a showstopper. We couldn't ship with a P1S1 in the active database. In some cases you can't even leave the building with an open P1S1 attached to your name. And "rlamber" was Ryan Lambert at Focus, which meant I didn't even have the authority to DNF it. Not even Don did.

"Oh."

"If it helps, Vorpal's got it, too."

"Really?" I said.

"They licensed WAFFLE along with *Clandestine*. Their public event went okay, but I've heard there was some epic mayhem in a closed-door press event."

"More — epic — than ours?" I asked. "How'd you hear about their demo?"

"Some people out there are still big fans of Simon's. They think Darren's screwed up a lot of what made Black Arts good."

"Why didn't this ever come up before? We can't be the first ones to see this happening."

"It's definitely happening more often, but yeah, that's one of the mysteries," Matt said. "QA should have got it if nobody else."

"Is somebody covering it up? Taking stuff out of the database?"

"It wouldn't be hard; it's not like there's any security. Anyone can delete anything at any time, and playtesters are used to being ignored. But I don't get the reason."

"Maybe somebody screwed up and they're trying to keep from getting fired," I said.

"I can't see it. Bugs are just a fact of life. It has to be on purpose, but that's almost as weird."

"Sabotage? Or just an odd sense of humor?" I suggested.

"An Easter egg, sure, but usually those don't actively break a shipping game."

"What if it was industrial sabotage? Like it was planted there. Somebody at KidBits, even? I was just thinking, it's a good thing Focus didn't know about this when they bought the company; they would never have paid that much for it. Maybe Darren cashed out because he knew it'd get found out."

"Maybe. But remember, all the code got reviewed before it was checked in. So Simon or Darren or Lisa would have had to okay it."

"Isn't this the kind of thing Darren likes? People getting killed, blood everywhere, chaos? I thought that was, like, his aesthetic."

"Yeah, but look at all those *Clandestine* games he made. He likes story. He basically wants to do movies!" Matt said. "And when Mournblade shows up it tends to break the plot. It can kill the character you need to start the next quest, or break the sacred diamond you spent half the game finding. Darren cares a lot about controlling events within a given framework, because that's what you need to get a story told. You subtly hem players in and push them forward through the story as they play. But you have to keep control of the events around them to do that. The blind seer has to show up on cue to give a speech; a bridge has to break at exactly the right moment — these are the big plot events you plan out in advance. With Mournblade around, everything goes haywire."

"Maybe that's what Mournblade is all about," I said.

"What do you mean? What's it about?"

"It's not a weapon for killing characters. It's a weapon for breaking games. Think of how a griefer plays—they don't win the game, they play against the game; they break it. The designer sets up constraints—the way you're supposed to play—and they say no. It's not just vandalism or perversity, it's a war of liberation. Whose story gets told—the designer's or the player's?"

"Basically, let's say Simon was going to put something where you can't get to it, like a room with no doors, a puzzle with no possible solution in the rules. The game just won't let you, unless you make it, or trick it."

"So what's there? What do you find?"

"I don't know. Whatever the gods have hidden from you. Hidden from themselves, maybe. At the very least there must be an off switch for it. A way to reboot the WAFFLE engine, fix it."

"Can we do it?"

"Griefers aren't the only ones who break games," Matt said. "I used to work for Quality Assurance."

Beta had its own signature routine, the morning bug meeting, where Don read out whatever inexplicable disaster the QA guys logged the previous day.

July 3: "I went down a particular corridor and turned left. Game froze. Repro x3."

Data! We'd check out the corridor and report back.

July 8: "I dropped my short bow, then picked it up, then dropped it, then picked it up again. Game froze. Doesn't work with other objects. Repro x2."

Art! a programmer would shout, and he might be right—a flaw in the 3-D model.

July 12: "I ran the game and pressed New Game. Game froze." No repro, but P1S1 anyway.

"..."

"..."

"..."

"I'll assign it to you for now, Lisa," Don would say, as kindly as possible.

He tried to keep a light tone at the meetings, but most mornings they went by in an atmosphere of sullen, petulant rage, a roomful of black-T-shirted, pale twentysomethings clinging to self-control, faces puffy and slack with sleep deprivation.

Programmers, designers, and artists had long since learned to hate each other with the pure and unflagging hatred orcs reserved for elves, but they were brought together in their hatred for Quality Assurance. A game tester was obliged to report almost anything that didn't work right — one measure of their productivity was simply driving up the number of bugs reported. They'd report design flaws, textures that weren't detailed enough, or anywhere the frame rate lagged a little bit. Better safe than sorry.

But of course the goal of every other department was to lower that number. This was where I most came to admire Don's seemingly inborn ability to suck the maniacal hatred out of the room when it flared up, or at least to soldier on through the tension until it dissipated.

Insufficiently detailed bugs were ruthlessly kicked back to Quality Assurance. At least a quarter of the time, Don would get only halfway through reading a bug and someone would angrily shout, "Fixed! As of the lunchtime bug." Or they'd shout, "Dupe!" for "duplicate," a bug that had had the same root cause as another open bug but manifested in a different context. After weeks, five persistent crashes in five different areas were proved to be the same bug after one tester finally noticed they all took place when the player was carrying one of every type of currency while attempting to switch between primary and secondary weapons within thirty meters of a horse, pony, donkey, or unicorn.

Don congratulated people for particularly clever fixes, or, failing that, for committing particularly colorful errors. The best of these went into a permanent hall-of-fame list kept in red dry-erase on a superfluous whiteboard. Gallows humor, but hilarious.

July 14: "Texture-mapping error makes Prendar's pants the same color as his skin ergo appears to be wearing no pants." 100% repro for that build. "REPEAT PRENDAR HAS NO PANTS."

July 18: The thermomantic spell Ice Storm had a bug in which it tried to reference the Giant Hailstone object and instead found the Pony object, which resulted in the spell Pony Storm, in which the caster fires a spray of between six and eight ponies at the target. Fixed, although we kept it open as long as we possibly could.

Lisa hid a secret spell in the necromantic arsenal. By combining elements of Poison Fog and a reversed Cure Disease, the caster could initiate a plague that could potentially depopulate the world. Not a bug, we decided, and hid the formula deep in the library of an abandoned castle half consumed by ocean.

Most bugs were more prosaic. "Fell through world ($x = 65.7$, $y = 3809.1$)." This one was a constant for months. No one ever stopped falling through the ground. I'd find it, too, constantly—one minute the world is a solid thing, the next you're watching it disappear into the distance above you while you fall through white space, never to return. For an instant you'd see nearly a whole kingdom above you, then you'd splatter against the ultimate lower elevation limit of the world and the sad truth that all of Endoria lives inside a colorless rectangular box.

I walked by a machine that was doing nothing but showing split-second glimpses of *Realms* levels. It would appear, look around for a second, then vanish and appear somewhere else. I watched it for a while. Forest...dungeon...mountain...too fast to follow. Lisa had written a script to render a single frame of the game, teleport, and render another frame, logging everything that happened until the game crashed. Longest duration so far, sixty-one minutes.

Endoria was being atomized until it was hard to think of it as a place at all—the long, haunted walk north after the mountain pass, which seemed like an endless, grueling rite of passage in the extended play-throughs, seemed like an obvious trick when you knew you could tele-port from one end to another in an instant. There was no ten-league stretch of forest, it reminded you; there was just a set of numbers. It was just data. In the same way, playing hide-and-seek with the marauders who have sailed upriver, it could take hours, days, to find your way through to the Endorian coast, where at last you reach the Lonely Tower and find the eerie Plutonian Dagger still gripped in the dead, unfeeling hand of the wielder who came before you. But the dagger was just a check box on a spreadsheet you could pull up in the editor. A click of a button and it's yours.

It started to feel like a miracle every time you took a step and found solid ground, or every time anything in Endoria behaved like the coher-ent reality I once imagined it to be. The secret truth was that the thing we had created had a gossamer delicacy, and any given piece of it had a hundred options as to how to behave in any given situation. It would only pick the correct one if half a dozen different systems coordinated exactly correctly, systems typically maintained by people sitting in dif-ferent parts of the building who might or might not be speaking to one another on a given day.

The sword was coming more and more often. After E3 we saw it at least once a week. Todd watched it destroy all the life in a crowded city, an hour and fifteen minutes to bare streets and empty houses. Even the rats were gone. Afterward, he reformatted the hard disk twice before reinstalling everything.

"I just...didn't like it," he explained.

I came into the playtest room to find them crowded around a single machine; we watched a berserk halfling on the far side of a metal grat-ing; it bobbled back and forth for a few minutes, then chopped through the grating. Everyone flinched as the screen flashed red; another player character down.

"Not supposed to do that," a long-haired tester muttered.

We had nine weeks to get through beta, which was an arbitrary length of time that had been set with no actual regard for how much work it represented. We fixed hundreds of bugs a day, which seemed impressive until I realized that the number of bugs was still increasing. We couldn't even think of bringing the bug count down until we tamed the rate at which new bugs were discovered. Black Sword bugs were all assigned to me, as the original owner, but I noticed no one was asking me about it.

Chapter Forty-Four

My bug list was flooded, and it wasn't until the third weekend in September that I found time to play through the rest of the Nick Prendergast games. I had to; there was no other way to find Mournblade. But it also meant facing the fact that first-person shooters ruined Nick Prendergast. The debonair, slightly hapless spy became a hardened one-man killing machine, fully capable of storming through a division of Russian infantry and leaving behind nothing but well-searched corpses.

In 1992, id Software shipped *Wolfenstein 3D,* the first game that let you sprint through three-dimensional corridors, killing anything that moved. I can only picture Darren and Simon sitting at their monitors partly inspired but mostly aghast that they had been so massively, atrociously scooped. Every advance in video game graphics looks definitive; everything before it looks pathetic. They stared into the hacked 3-D perspective sliding past them. No more cartoons; this was an enchanted mirror, and Simon felt the otherworldly breeze blowing through it. Holy fucking shit.

Simon stayed up until dawn three nights in a row taking apart what John Carmack had wrought and reverse engineering it. It wasn't that difficult when he looked at it. It cut every possible corner. You were looking into a flat maze; there was no variation in floor heights; it was all walls and ninety-degree angles; there was no looking up or down, and the floor and ceiling were featureless planes. It minimized the number of problems the computer had to solve, but in a clever way. Simon worked rapidly, knowing that everybody else interested in the problem was thinking the same way.

There was going to be a land rush into the third dimension of virtuality. As soon as he had the engine in hand, Darren lost no time in putting it to use. They would need to occupy and monetize, get their brand and their reputation out there. Nick Prendergast was the logical choice; he'd sold well, and he fit the context. The poor man was called back into service, his license to kill renewed and then some.

Clandestine II: Love Never Thinks Twice (1992)

Gone was the quaint two-dimensional animated figure ambling across colorful backdrops. Prendergast had disappeared — or, rather, you saw the world from his point of view. The new Nick was simply a gun hovering in midair, scanning the world.

Gone was the slender, slightly schoolmasterish, and, let's face it, virginal Nick. He was done with fooling around picking locks and making chitchat with this or that baroness. There was no apparent plot. Nick was deployed like an infantry brigade to sterilize any square mile of rooms and corridors his spymaster deemed a threat. It would in general have been more humane to carpet-bomb a given area rather than to dispatch Nick Prendergast in first-person shooter mode. Enemies made just as little sense. They'd pop out of dead-end alleys or closets or basements as if they'd been living their whole lives there, waiting for Nick to walk past. In between, there were colorful graphics of Nick indulging his new interest in sports cars and East German strippers.

Clandestine II outsold every Black Arts game in history, and for a few years Black Arts turned into a factory for *Clandestine* sequels. One thing didn't change, and that was the untouchable spymaster Karoly, who would dog his steps for the length and breadth of the franchise. Karoly was obsessed with ending the Cold War by acquiring a weapon of transcendent destructiveness, which he was always on the edge of obtaining. He was the Wile E. Coyote of the Soviet intelligence apparatus.

Love Never Thinks Twice began with the now-familiar prompt:

IMPORT SAVED GAME? (Y/N)

The flower appeared, and the tracking device. I couldn't help feeling that an obscure payload was being passed forward along with them, up the technological ladder. I wondered how much data was in there, and how far it had been relayed. From the third *Realms of Gold*? The second? From *Adric's Tomb*? How far were my choices going to be tracked? What else was coming with it?

When I started the game it felt a little less responsive than it should have. Movement speed was slightly off, the easy, flick-of-the-wrist feeling of playing a first-person shooter, the machine gun on oiled casters. Like a concert pianist forced to play on a second-rate grand, I was experienced enough to feel the difference.

I thought back to the first *Clandestine,* that flower that crossed the gap from Endoria. It wasn't too much of a stretch to think of Lord Mortimer's bullet still lodged in Nick's shoulder, triggering a metal detector and slowing him up when he reached for a new clip on his semiautomatic.

The tiny loss of speed resonated the same way the flower did. A slower, weaker Prendergast skewed the game away from its original run-and-gun flow. It was a little too hard to simply gun down brown-suited heavies one after the other. The tiny delay forced a slower, sneakier Nick, one who chose his shots, one who had to think, one who seemed rather more mortal. It edged the game over from action-adventure to suspense. A quarter-second difference changed the feeling; it even changed who Nick was. The Nick who chose to drop his pistol in a sewer rather than bring it to a party, who took a bullet from his true love's dad, was a slightly different brand of operative.

Clandestine III: Mirror Games (1993)

Clandestine IV: On American Assignment (1994)

Clandestine V: Axis Power (1995)

Clandestine VI: Deathclock (1996)

Clandestine: Worlds Beyond (Limited Edition) (1996)

Clandestine VII: Countdown to Rapture (1997)

Sequel followed sequel, and Mournblade didn't show. Meanwhile, you haunted every theater of the Cold War, lived a thousand adventures, and loved a thousand women under a thousand assumed names. You fought:

A) A Colombian drug lord

B) A sleazy, expensive-suit-wearing Czech Eurotrash war profiteer

C) A sexy female Stasi agent

D) A Mafia kingpin (your "American assignment")

E) A sexy female former Vietcong you never *quite* got around to mentioning to the sexy female Stasi agent

F) The inevitable ninja-assisted yakuza crime lord

G) An alien bounty hunter in the Congo from *Worlds Beyond,* but nobody believed you — but YOU SAW WHAT YOU SAW

H) A former teammate who was just like you but lacked your moral boundaries and ended up GOING TOO FAR

I) Karoly

Only Karoly persisted, skipping from continent to continent, from PC to PlayStation, always fading away as Nick came onto the scene, erased, absented, always already absconded.

I don't think Simon's life changed much. He slept at work at least half the time. With Darren and half the company churning out sequels, he could carve more time out of his schedule for engine research.

Darren was the public face of Black Arts; he was the one challenging all comers to online multiplayer *SpyMatch* throwdowns. He was the one boasting in print about their next-generation technology, which was going to make id's next outing look like a Lite-Brite. He showed up to gaming trade shows and conventions and made calculatedly inflammatory statements, teased fans with hints about the next release, and exuded a kind of cocky, precocious anger that nerds loved in their celebrities—anger they could take as their own.

Darren and Simon posed back-to-back, arms folded, ready to take on the world. Darren wore wire-rimmed glasses, a polo shirt, and a carefully honed smirk. His sandy hair looked blow-dried. Simon seems to have perplexed whoever was behind the camera; he just didn't have a glamorous angle. Pudgy, unsmiling, hollow-eyed, he exuded a desperation that brought to mind van Gogh's self-portraits.

Clandestine V: Axis Power (1995)

The graphics engine that had once made *Clandestine II: Love Never Thinks Twice* cutting-edge was in its last days as a competitive tech. All the graphics cards in the world couldn't hide Nick's blocky, dated look, his helmetlike hair, and his mittenlike hands, with their sketched-in fingers. In the games, you could see Nick trying to top himself with bigger and bigger set pieces, while Simon withdrew more and more into his own work. When you looked at the bug database, this was when the Mournblade sightings started their slow climb in frequency toward the present day.

This was the game where I discovered a scrap of hand-lettered text on the stationery of the old Hotel Raphael, an intelligence dispatch from the CIA. It was in code, and I had to root around in the library to find the old decoder wheel. NICK MY FRIEND LAURA REAL NAME EVA KA-ROLY STASI REPEAT STASI SORRY TO BE THE ONE BRENDAN

Nick's plastic face showed no reaction. It was three in the morning and I wasn't in a state of mind to examine my feelings about this.

Clandestine VII: Countdown to Rapture (1997)

Karoly again, and by this time it was well into Sunday night and the game had become somewhat hallucinatory.

Nick's a superspy, used to waking up at odd places and times, handcuffed to odd things. As Nick, you wake up tied to a chair in a featureless room more days than not at this point. Or else you wake up on a white sandy beach, faceup in the surf at the high-tide mark. You wake up in an alleyway behind a hotel in Monte Carlo, pockets full of thousand-Euro chips. You wake up at the controls of a stalled F16 at 10,000 feet, ears ringing and tasting your own blood. You wake up with a stranger pointing a gun at you, or you wake up alone. This time, it was on a submarine.

Karoly was at bay far out on the northern rim of Siberia; a shivering, wet-suited, jet-lagged Nick Prendergast surfaced by moonlight at the base of a cliff before the ice-slick entrance to a natural cave system. The year was, notionally, 1989, and this version of Nick had a sort of *Baywatch* styling.

He crept inside and began garroting and poison-darting his way through Lenin-era subbasements crammed with rusty, brine-crusted filing cabinets. Up through caverns with vast, slowly cycling turbines, breaking necks and cutting throats and ducking the occasional electrical arc. For Nick this was, after all, only a Tuesday.

Eventually Nick made it down the hall and ducked into a restroom. As Nick you stare into the bathroom mirror. Nick stared back, haggard after a sleepless Monday night getting drunk, beaten up, driven around, and tortured. He was dressed in what was once a nice semiformal look, but tie and dinner jacket were long gone. If experience was anything to go by Nick would likely go on to kill every single person in the building he was currently inside. Nick did a lot more killing than what was considered professional in the real intelligence community, but in fairness he got handed some pretty difficult assignments.

Lisa watched as I went through at a leaden, bureaucratically deliberate pace; I hoarded health packs, conserved ammunition, and dutifully dragged guards' bodies into supply closets, where they'd never be discovered. Life went on, knife to garrote to pistol to shotgun to light submachine gun to chain gun to sniper rifle to rocket launcher.

"Are you having any fun whatsoever?" Lisa asked me, materializing from the shadows with a bowl of ramen.

"Fun takes many forms. And no. I'm just trying not to die."

"Weren't you already here?"

I'd crept around a corner to find three Soviet guards already dead.

"Can't be. Just got out of the stairwell."

We exchanged glances. I sprinted ahead, then pulled back. The next room was crowded with alert guards. I heard a sniper rifle ping and one of them went down. Mournblade had returned.

"So...did you have a plan for when this happened?" she said.

"I've killed, like, nine hundred seventy-seven guards in the past forty-eight hours."

I ducked out and back. The sniper had an annoyingly good position at the top of a wide cylindrical shaft. We were at the base of a missile silo, I realized.

"This one's going to be eating souls for a while with his magic sniper rifle," she said. I'd kept Nick Prendergast alive this long; I didn't want to step into that kill zone.

"I know."

"Can he suck their souls when they're already dead?" she asked.

"No. Ew. But no."

I stood back and started rolling hand grenades through the door. Booms and recorded Russian screaming started up. Above, the demented sniper reloaded. Souls for the accursed rifle! Then silence as the last guard died. I turned the sound up.

"What?"

"Wait for it," I said. Silence, a faint groan, then a far-off clank. I sprinted through the doorway and up the metal stairway that spiraled up the side of the shaft. Mournblade's wielder was dead. I reached the rifle just before it disappeared. I clamped the tracking device I bought in Paris in 1937 to its black barrel, and it vanished.

"It worked."

"So where did it go?"

The tracking device had a monitor I carried that could tell me where the beacon went. Unrealistic, especially for a device built when we were still trying to figure out radar, but it made perfect in-game sense.

A line on the display pointed in a precisely vertical direction. Below were the words DISTANCE: 9.85E24. So it went up.

That night I dreamed of a final encounter with Karoly, the one that finally ended it. It couldn't last, after all. Nick couldn't keep looping back through time forever. Karoly stood on a catwalk in the missile silo, arrayed in a Soviet space suit and helmet, which he tucked under one arm.

"Hello, Nick Prendergast. You are rememberink me, yes? *Da?* Today glorious Soviet state is winnink space race. It is 1989, yes? Not a moment too soon, I am thinkink."

Little puffs of steam emerged from the rocket's sides.

"I am to be goink to space now."

I was only two levels beneath him. A Klaxon warning buzzed on and off; spinning red lights tracked across his face. A gangplank began extending out from the side of the shaft toward the rocket itself.

"I am envyink a long time now your life in the West, Comrade Nick. But twenty thousand years after your death I will wake up amonk the stars and where will you be? I will do the Great Comrade's work there. And I will be havink the weapon I need at last."

What weapon? Mournblade? A plus-five intercontinental ballistic missile? A new and unfailing disinformation campaign?

A technician beside him finished programming a row of coordinates that appeared on the wall.

"Or — who is knowink? — perhaps Workers' Paradise is already beink there, looking down on us."

I hope so, friend.

"A great war it was, you are agreeink? But for now it is no more questions. The future is not ours."

This game was written in 1995, Karoly. If you even existed you'd have lost the Great Game five years ago. The future is mine but I'm not sure I want it. Maybe it should be yours, after all. You'd know what to do with it.

"I am thinkink, we are belonk dead."

He lowered his helmet and stepped onto the rocket. His assistant turned to input the final launch command. I saw very clearly — past two generations of game technology and half a dozen platforms — that it was Laura. She turned and left as the interstellar rocket roared away. We'd always have Paris.

Even in the dream I remembered it was the last game Simon made.

Chapter Forty-Five

Late on a Tuesday night I was trying to set up three boulders just right to fall on players as they came up a trail. But they fell too soon or too late, or not at all, because the simulation had no interest in my wishes whatsoever. Lisa knocked on my desk.

"Come here," she said. "I want to show you something I got running."

"All I want to do is kill," I said. "It's all I want now."

"Come on." She grabbed my sleeve and pulled.

"Okay, okay." She led me to the outskirts of the cubicle settlement, where a table was piled with ugly-looking hardware. Virtual-reality headsets; bulky, dorky motion-sensing goggles.

"Why do we have these?" I asked.

"We get them free for supporting them. I've got it running now, try it out."

I picked one up. "This weighs, like, ten pounds. Who buys these?"

"As far as I can tell, nobody ever in the history of the world," she said. "Come on, I spent two days on this."

"I'm going to look stupid."

"Everybody does. Even the models on the side of the box do."

I put it on. The display was like having a pair of tiny, low-resolution TV screens two inches from your eyeballs. It was showing bright static. "Jesus," I said. "Just tell me when I can open my eyes."

I heard her typing. "Now." I opened them.

"So?" It was Endoria on a tiny low-resolution screen.

"Turn your head."

I did, and my view turned, too.

"I...oh, my God." It was stuttery and low-resolution, but it was as if the borders of the monitor had fallen away and the rendered world spread to engulf me. I looked down at myself, half expecting to see a medieval tunic. I looked up into the blue sky and right into the sun, which gave fake lens flare, as if seen through a nonexistent camera. The air of the office felt Endorian. The hair on my arms stood up; a part of my brain was afraid and yet very, very happy.

"How come nobody knows about this?"

"Because everything about it sucks."

I felt weightless. It felt like —

"Did Simon ever get to try this?" I asked.

"No."

"Where are you?" I said.

"Here." Somewhere back on earth I felt her take my hand, tightly. For a minute, I felt like Simon wanted to feel.

Chapter Forty-Six

I couldn't see anything promising in falling in love with the heroine in a video game, but there it was. And that I was designing her latest game raised questions of conflict of interest. But I was in love—I couldn't help it. It was an occupational hazard and didn't do any harm. So what if I had a fantasy girlfriend? She was smart and confident and had amazing hair, and she was a princess. At least she was a playable character. Or did that make it worse?

After much hesitation I'd asked her to have dinner with me at a Vietnamese restaurant in the Garage, in Harvard Square, on our awkward first date (at least, I thought it was a date; there were cultural differences to consider). I sipped my bubble tea while she fidgeted in her seat. She was in her alternate outfit, the one you unlocked by finishing *Tournament of Ages* without losing a single match. It was like a cherry-red sheet-metal corset. It wasn't built to sit down in. It didn't look much good at stopping arrows, either.

She leaned the NightShard, her signature weapon, against the scarred wood paneling behind her. It was a long wedge of dull gray metal with a two-handed hilt. The weapon was named for the chip of obsidian mounted at the top, allegedly hewn from the scales of a nameless dragon-god. The blade was bare of runes or any ornamentation, but that would change if it tasted blood tonight. No one tried to take it.

"Are you cold?" I asked. "I have a jacket." The armor left her arms bare, not to mention her midriff.

"No," she said. She tapped a silver armband against the metal table. This might not have been the best venue. The Garage was crowded with college students on Thanksgiving break.

The waitress brought our menus.

"Just order anything," I said. She looked at the menu for a few seconds before laying it back on the table.

"I can't read," she said quietly.

I ordered a Diet Coke for me, plum wine for her, and pho for both of us. Leira wore her black hair up in a topknot tied with braided cord. She was physically intimidating, perfectly muscled, except that up close she had the beginnings of crow's-feet near her blue eyes. She looked beautiful, although at life size her poly count was a little low.

"So," she began. She looked around the room. I guessed that she was a little uncomfortable with noncombat situations. "What is it you do? You're a scholar? Or a clerk?"

"Formerly." I hedged. "I'm still figuring it out. I'm only twenty-eight."

"Ah," she answered. "I'm twenty-two." I guessed that in a medieval world, twenty-eight was a pretty advanced age. I should probably have my own township by now. Leira, of course, had been twenty-two for a dozen years now. She'd also killed about a hundred thousand people.

"And then you're a, um, warrior princess?" I asked.

"That's right."

"And how did you get into that line of work?"

The food arrived; she ate like a princess turned nomadic warrior, and then we chatted. Adventures she'd had; which weapons she liked (cavalry saber, compound bow) or hated (morning star, crossbow); the current stealth system (hated it). She told me her origin story, the real one, the one that doesn't show up in any manuals or cutscenes. I paid for dinner. She offered, but the waitress wouldn't accept rubies or gold armbands.

Afterward we walked down to the river and looked at the moon. "Only one?" she said.

"Only one," I said. They'd given Endoria three. They'd made Endoria better. It *was* better, I thought.

"Leira, what do you know about Mournblade?"

"They say that when Mournblade is destroyed, this age will come to a close and the world will be reborn."

"But what happens then?"

"The Fourth Age, silly. The Age of Humankind."

"That sounds a little sad, actually."

"Well, Prendar's not a fan."

I walked her back to the portal: a flat oval that hung next to the Harvard Square T stop. On the other side, blocky white clouds drifted past on a summer's day; green polygonal hills adorned the horizon.

"So. This is good night," I said. "Is that home in there?"

"I can't go home, you know that. They'd never take me back. Also, my men burned it down."

"What do you want, Leira?" I asked. "Really want, you know?"

"I used to want to get married," she said.

"I'll marry you." I said it without thinking, but I would have.

She shook her head.

"I don't want to marry you. I want to keep robbing and murdering the people who should have protected me in the first place. I want to burn things. Can't we just do that?"

We shook hands. Her palm was small and rough, like a workman's. She was silhouetted against the bright Endorian day with the warm wind coming from behind her.

"Look for me," she said. She kissed me on the cheek, then stepped through the portal and vanished, onward to the next adventure.

Walking home, I remembered a story Lorac had told me months earlier. Late one night, sitting up over a skull-shaped chalice of wine, he'd claimed that long ago, human beings and video game characters were all part of a single mighty race of glowing, immortal wizards and warriors. Even the gods feared us, so much so that one day they joined forces against us and after a long struggle defeated us.

To forestall any future threat, the gods decreed we should each be separated into halves, and each half hurled into a separate dimension. There was a human half, weak but endowed with thought and feeling, and a video game half, with glowing and immortal bodies that were mere empty shells lacking wills of their own. We became a fallen race and forgot our origins, but something in us longed to be whole again. And so we invented the video game, the apparatus that bridged the realms and joined us with our other selves again, through the sacred medium of the video game controller. The first devices were primitive, but every year the technology improved, and we saw and heard and sensed the other world more clearly. Soon enough we'd be able to feel and smell and taste and live entirely in our own bodies again. And on that day, he finished portentously, we'd challenge the gods once more.

"First of all," I said, "you ripped that whole thing off from that story in Plato. Except it's supposed to be where love comes from, whereas yours only explains video games. Second of all, video games weren't even invented until 1965. How could there be video game characters before video games existed?" Lorac only shrugged and looked at me through the darkness with his glowing eyes, which was a surprisingly effective retort.

Leira and I couldn't get married, not even in Massachusetts, although I could ask Toby to write the code. But I suspected in my heart it wouldn't work. Maybe I was only really attracted to Leira because I liked ranged combat and procedural fire, and because I wanted to kill and kill and then ride for the horizon as she did, hair streaming in the wind. Maybe we were two halves of a sundered whole, a single eternal hero for the ages, till death do us part.

* * *

The conversation was happening on the other side of the cubicle wall.

"So AstroTrade disappeared, but its assets were bought by Paranomics. They say they found our name in a text file in the software package and tracked us down."

"But how did we manage to lose their hundred million dollars or whatever the fuck?"

"They were using prediction markets to drive high-frequency trading software. You know, the stuff that does trading without you. The funny part is that it was kind of working, but now it's not. What?"

There was a noise that at first I thought was a chair creaking, or maybe a record skipping. I got up and rounded the cubicle divider to see Lisa sitting in her chair, bent over and hugging her stomach, her long hair brushing the carpet. She was, I guessed, laughing, but she wasn't very good at it.

After a few moments she managed to croak the words, "It worked. It worked."

"What worked?"

"I guess now we know why Darren sold his shares," said Lisa.

"Let's go into my office," Don said.

We did. Don closed the door behind us, which must have been noticed. A closed-door meeting at Black Arts was almost unheard of.

"Oh, God, I think I'm the only person now who knows this," Lisa said, leaning against the door. "You don't even know what the funny part is."

"I would love to know about the funny part," Don said.

"AstroTrade didn't just lose its money on Black Monday. I think they may have caused Black Monday. And that's even not the funny part."

"That's impossible," Don said.

"We have to go back. So AstroTrade...1987 was the early days of automated trading programs. You know, people think they have software that knows when the market is right to make a particular trade, and can do it faster than a human can. A hundred times a second if it wants to, way faster than a person can keep track of. Everyone was excited. All you need is the magic algorithm; you set it loose in the markets and it generates money. It would be like the philosopher's stone."

"So they just let these things run on their own? They can do anything?" I asked, picturing one of our dwarves buying and selling on the stock exchange trading floor.

"It all happens in its own little world, an electronic trading platform, and it has software that regulates trading activity in case one of these algorithms starts to make things crazy. They all have their own strategies, and they do all kinds of things — set up fake bids and drop them — it's a dirty business with its own rules."

"How can you make fake bids?" Don asked.

"I can't believe you're in charge of money. It's the kind of behavior people like to simulate with, um, agent-based simulation software. Which I know, because I helped Simon put ours together. Agents being, in this case, things like dwarves. The Endorian version was like a platform, and the dwarves were the trading programs, strategizing away. Meanwhile, people have learned that trading programs can fuck up the market faster than any human can spot them. When trading starts to spin out of control — like when algorithms get in a loop, selling the same item back and forth thousands of times a minute, or if everybody starts to sell at once — that can cause what's called a flash crash. The market can go up or down hundreds of points in a few seconds. You blink and millions of dollars are just gone."

"In a minute," Don said, "I'm going to ask you how you know this."

"If there's a big market shift and the programs start to panic, regulatory software will clamp down. Pause trading till everybody settles down and resets. If you're curious, in our sim there was an archmagus in each town who would cast Mass Sleep and everyone would lie down for a while. So that's how the sim worked. Now, who sees the problem?"

"That elves have sleep resistance?" Don said.

"Not to a ninety-eighth-level caster. Go again."

"So it's all really happening in the game. But dwarves and elves don't like each other. What if a fight starts?"

"We recast Improved Harmony every few minutes. No one fights in cities. Not normally."

"Does anybody know if Mournblade confers sleep resistance?" I asked. "Did anyone ever try that?"

"Mournblade gives the wielder complete and total magic resistance, superseding all other bonuses. The sword is in fact designed to create exceptions in whatever agent-based simulation it's a part of. That's what I wrote it to do."

"I think I have another question now," said Don.

"Do you still have the stock program, Don?" Lisa asked.

"Yes. I was thinking I should get rid of it."

"Run it, please. In debug."

He did.

"Maybe the ultimate game," Lisa said, "is when there stops being a difference between the world and the game. It's all the same data with different pictures on top."

She hit a key.

"Look, it's Endoria." In Endorian Chicago, the elves, dwarves, and gnomes ran back and forth, wheeling and dealing.

"Look, it's America." She pressed a key. In stock wizard mode, it displayed an official-looking set of spreadsheets.

[Tap]

"Endoria."

[Tap]

"America. They're the same."

"That doesn't explain the sword," said Don.

"Oh, I thought that was obvious. Well, we thought it wasn't just going to be a game. In 1984 we thought WAFFLE was going to be the basis of everything. That cyberspace was only a few years away."

"Like VRML? The 3-D Web thing?" Don said.

Lisa winced. "Like cyberspace! The matrix! All cubes and pyramids—floating heads—people flying around in digital space, and that's how business would happen, socializing, everything. We were like the people who thought there would be a moon base in 1980, or flying cars, or jet packs. Cyberspace was our jet pack. But that was the funny part, the first funny part. We thought we were making the future, but we were just making a stupid game."

"But if there was going to be another world, then Simon was going to grow up and be Elric. Mournblade was hidden in the fabric of space-time, and when the moment came, Simon would have it. I built it, he hid it where only he could find it."

"Like he did in the *Realms II* finals," I said.

"The finals were a weapons test. He passed."

"Now in theory—in theory—AstroTrade's entry into the Hong Kong stock exchange somehow loosed Mournblade into the electronic trading platform and then some day trader's automated software got hold of it and ran around spilling the guts out of any poor hedge fund that got in its way. If that happened, it could happen again. Except now we have a much faster and more globalized system. In 1987 it was just getting started. Now you don't have to be on a stock exchange to trade electronically. Now—it's everywhere."

"When was this supposed to happen?" Don asked.

"In the Ninth Age."

"The Ninth Age?"

"Didn't you ever hear about the Ninth Age?" she said. "Matt knows. In the Ninth Age, the old gods return and Adric's the harbinger, he emerges from his tomb to lay waste to the world that betrayed him. Most of the Tenth Age is him laughing on top of a pile of skulls, and taking breaks to go hunt the survivors."

"But when in reality?"

"Oh, soon, I guess. Once it gets harbinged, which should be soon—Simon wrote the date into his future history, nine nine ninety-nine. So that's the actual funny part, it happened after all. Simon and I forged the magic sword that will bring on global financial apocalypse. If that's not funny, I don't understand what funny is."

We left Don alone trying to think of a way to explain this to Focus Capital's in-house counsel. The bug was still assigned to me. We retreated to the kitchen.

"How do we fix it?" I said. I dropped quarters into the snack machine, but I didn't have enough. Lisa handed me some more. I just wanted something sugary.

She paused, thinking. She didn't answer.

"What, you're a supervillain now? You're not going to tell us how to save the world?"

"No, that's not it," she said. "I don't get all of this. We shouldn't be seeing the sword at all. Mournblade should be in its hiding place, waiting for Simon to get it."

"Can't we just go there and look?" I said.

Lisa shook her head. "I was in charge of making the sword. Simon worked out how to hide it. I've looked since then, and I never worked it out. In theory, if we find it, we could maybe neutralize it, and save out a game where the world's been changed. All Paranomics would need is the new build."

"He didn't leave any clues?"

"It wasn't a treasure hunt. He didn't want anybody to find it. It's not anywhere in the data, though, because that changes every game. Something in the code generates it and stashes it. Something must have gone wrong there."

"But it's in the game. I know it's physically manifesting in the game. I have the saved game where there's a tracker attached to it."

"Okay." She looked surprised. "Then let's go find it. Where is it?"

"Very high up."

"So build a rocket ship. Why do I have to think of everything?"

PART VI

THE SOLAR AGE

Chapter Forty-Seven

I would walk home from work at two or three or four in the morning, breathing in the heat after sixteen hours of shivering in the office air-conditioning while editing the glacial landscapes of northern Endoria.

I had two jobs—the first was making and testing a fantasy role-playing game, and the second was extracting a cursed sword from the Milky Way galaxy. The next night Lisa stopped by my desk.

"So just make sure you import the last saved game or this whole thing is pointless. How far away is it, actually? What did the tracking device say?"

"Pretty far up, I guess." I showed her the slip of paper on which the number was written down. She took it and walked away without saying anything. Five minutes later she came back.

"What units are these?"

"It's an MI6 device, so...I don't know. Yards? Furlongs? Is there going to be a problem?"

"Probably you should start working on a way out of the solar system."

She went away again.

There were hard limits to how high you could fly by magic in *Realms;* in *Clandestine* you were limited to pre-1989 tech (the alien spacecraft being, I found, nonoperable), so Nick Prendergast rarely made it past low earth orbit. It was time to take matters into the twenty-second century.

SOLAR EMPIRES (1989)

```
se.exe
IMPORT SAVE GAME? (Y/N)
Y
LOADING...
```

The screen cleared, the Black Arts logo appeared, then the title screen appeared over a stylized view of the solar system, the player peering in from just past the orbit of Saturn, its ecliptic tipped at a jaunty, inviting angle. This would be Black Arts' science fiction franchise, of course. Matt sat down to watch, taking a break from updating the bug database.

I pressed NEW GAME and was given a choice of identities from among the Heroes' far-future analogues: Brendan Blackstar, Loraq, Ley-R4, or Pren-Dahr. To whom would I give the future of humanity? I chose Ley-R4.

The screen cleared, and words began scrolling slowly up from the bottom of the screen:

```
It is 2113, and the Second Terran Empire is coming apart. At the
    same time, humankind stands on the brink of expanding into a
    universe of mystery, danger, and vast wealth.
YOU are one of the four reigning personalities of the age locked
    in a desperate struggle to be the first to launch an inter-
    stellar colony ship, thus becoming the guiding spirit of
    humankind's expansion into the galaxy.
It is time to wage interplanetary war! It is time to begin the
    Solar Age!
It is time to build...
SOLAR EMPIRES!!!
```

* * *

In a map of the solar system, planets appeared as king-size marbles, sliding achingly slowly around the sun as a celestial chorus chanted faintly in the background, a Philip Glass touch.

I heard Lisa sit down behind me. "Ley-R4 again."

"Does that matter?" I asked.

"It's just predictable."

Lisa leaned past me. Her black T-shirt smelled like clove cigarettes.

"You've got Saturn's moons. Shitty for metals, but all the hydrogen and methane you'll ever want. Get your fusion tech up and running fast."

"And then what?"

"It's a four-*X* game."

"A four ... ?"

"It's what you do. Explore. Expand. Exploit. Exterminate."

She left us alone with the cosmos.

"I thought she didn't play these games," I said to break the silence.

"You didn't know? She designed about half of it herself; the rest is from Simon's notes. That's why it doesn't play like a Darren game," Matt said.

"I thought Darren did everything."

"He did a lot. I mean, it was his idea to start using Simon's sci-fi material, but the *Clandestine* games were making so much money he just focused on that. It was more his kind of thing anyway. Plus he was, I don't know, deal-making, partying with investors, I guess. He was good at a lot of stuff."

Looking back at the screen, I realized I was seeing Lisa's cosmos. The stars had a faint shimmer, as if seen through the soft air of an evening cookout. The vacuum of space wasn't a flat black; it took on an illusion of depth, layered with dark gray and ultradark browns and purples, the downy fur of an immense, velvety night beast. It made you want to explore; it made you feel that the cosmos was a glittering jewel box.

The display zoomed in to a set of three dirty-white spheres huddled in space underneath the sublimely enormous expanse of Saturn's cloud layer, which was mottled like a made-up fantasy ice cream flavor.

Your tiny ships are blue-and-white spheres studded with antennae, and your bases are like little cartoon college campuses under glass domes; grassy quads and white neoclassical buildings fronted with tiny flights of steps leading up to tiny fluted columns, and—at maximum zoom—tiny faculty and tiny students.

History holds its breath while you ponder your options. You begin scooping ammonia out of Saturn's upper atmosphere. You receive a communication marked DIPLOMATIC — URGENT. It's Pren-Dahr, future incarnation of Prendar/Prendergast. His familiar long face and tufted red hair poke out from a sparkly gold toga draped over a purple leotard. He is an elongated native of zero gravity. The sun bulks overlarge in the view screen behind him—he is on the planet Venus, which he owns. Pren-Dahr's ships are tiger-striped in blue and green; his bases are gold pyramids. He is, fittingly, a corporate overlord. He is friendly, flirtatious even, as if recalling his brief, disastrous marriage to Leira in the Third Age.

You grab for territory. Ceres is dotted with grim concrete bunkers, and a little tail of debris emerges from a mining operation at one end. This is the domain of Brendan Blackstar, a military leader and privateer, who seeks to crush the galaxy beneath humanity's five-toed feet. His spaceships are maroon with gold highlights, blocky, as if they were made of LEGO, with wide, stubby exhaust jets.

You set about starving him of resources. Maybe he'll forgive you later; you're both going to live a very, very long time. Somewhere deep inside the bunkers, under the Hellas Planitia, under layers of Martian sediment and the fossil bones of ancient beasts, a tiny Brendan Blackstar must be yelling at his tiny general staff, just as a tiny Pren-Dahr coolly teleconferences with his board of directors. Loraq's got his network of temples on Mercury. Maybe Karoly got there after all. You, Ley-R4, lecture your recalcitrant department heads.

When the meeting ends, you linger on in the fourth-floor meeting room, looking out over the frozen surface of Saturn. You wear a silver-and-blue skintight leotard, your raven hair floating in the low gravity like a mermaid's. You wear horribly anachronistic glasses.

Why are you in charge? You came up through the classics department, for heaven's sake. The Milky Way looms, mysterious and welcoming, an unattainable bonus level that lasts forever. Will you ever get there? Will you get there first, or will one of the others?

It's only a matter of time before a dirty war breaks out. Pren-Dahr and his board of directors declare that for the sake of the stockholders, more stringent measures must be taken, and so ends the First Terran Commonwealth.

And so now, creaking, antiquated spaceships roam the system, some still marked with the names of obsolete Terran nationalities. Their grizzled pilots breathe stale air from groaning compressors and fight with ballistic repurposed mining equipment — rock cutters and mass drivers. It is a war of orbital mechanics, fuel economy, and terrible, violent decompression events. You can take control of individual craft whenever you want — sometimes it's necessary to execute a plan that the ship AI is just too dim to grasp, or sometimes you might just want the kinetic thrill of piloting an ailing craft through an edge-of-possible near-orbit maneuver.

In the middle of a mission it comes to you what you're doing — you're playing *Lunar Lander,* a game you played on the Commodore PET, the first time you put your hands on a computer keyboard, the first time you felt yourself touch the phantasmal world of simulated reality through that conduit, however primitive. You remember the feel of tipping that little Apollo lander back and forth in a sad dance that always ended in the little craft, its fuel zeroed out, its tiny astronauts probably saying good-bye to their loved ones, plummeting to the lunar rock, shattering on impact, or just as often cannoning into the side of a crag in a burst of poorly judged acceleration.

And it came to me in a flash that Simon must have marched down the same hall to the same computer. I pictured Simon in the same scene, seated in front of the PET. He sensed this was it for him, a portal into the future—into his own future, into the only adult life he could bear to have. They'd handed it to him, saying, in effect, "We don't know what this is, and we don't even have time to figure it out; we're busy being grown-ups and operating the mimeograph machine and pretty much making your lives possible."

And Simon got it. He recognized its rigid limitations and its endless possibilities at the same time, and the daemon inside him told him how to answer the grown-ups: "Don't worry. I know this doesn't make sense to you, but it does to me. In fact, it's the thing I've been waiting for, the thing that makes my private obsessions, all that thinking I do about numbers and other worlds and all of it, it's the thing that makes it all work. Trust me, this is going to be great. And thank you." Of course nobody said those things—it would take years and they'd never remotely understand each other anywhere near this well—but that's what happened nonetheless.

Until now you didn't realize. You were staring right at this thing, thinking it was a simulation game about a vicious four-sided intrastellar war. Whereas now you see it is a letter to the future.

I was combing the cometary halo for clues when Lisa came back with a number on a piece of paper.

"So that's a big number," she said. "Do you know how big?"

"I know that numbers with an *e* in them are big, but that meters are not big."

She said, "It's just short of a yottameter."

"You're saying nothing. These are just sounds."

"A septillion meters. Yottameters are the largest unit in the metric system. It wouldn't be inside the solar system. It wouldn't be inside the galaxy. You'll have to get farther."

"Why don't they need anything bigger than a yottameter?"

"Because the universe is only nine hundred and thirty yottameters wide, of course."

"You're making this up."

"Why would I make it up?"

"Why would you know it in the first place? Consider yourself appointed to the intergalactic travel initiative. I have a war to fight."

When you pile up enough Research Points, you get to choose a new technology to develop. Starting with Basic Fusion, you can move on to Biosphere Design, Holographic Computer Interface, Stellar Mechanics, Improved Social Engineering, and so forth. Every technology unlocks new choices about what you can learn next, so that if you take Fusion it leads to Improved Fusion or Gamma Radiation Beams or Pin-size Nuclear Missiles or Ultradense Matter Manipulation, and those open up more choices. It's called the Technology Tree. Every technology allows a new kind of building or spaceship or ability. There's a building tree that works the same way — basic buildings like biodomes and electric generators and factories are prerequisites for building more specialized production facilities, which allow new and different units, and so forth. Everything is interconnected in a complicated web. Some technologies are prerequisite for some buildings, and vice versa, and it all gates on other factors, like what materials are available — there's no fusion without plutonium, for example.

So you lie in an empty cubicle by the far wall, a down sleeping bag pulled to your chin. It's an old sleeping bag you lugged from home to college to your first apartment to the next to the next. It's a pointless exercise, since you never go camping anymore, not since the seventh grade, and you never go to sleepovers or lie out all night in the backyard.

The bag has probably never been washed in its entire lifetime, and it seems to smell like campfires and basement damp and sweat and the pee from a long-ago cat.

As you lie there your mind wanders in the darkness in a sleepy train of thought, in which the tech tree just keeps going and going, on past fusion and neural interfaces and planet-busting missiles into force fields and teleportation and hyperdrive, and then you're falling asleep, and now you invent hypermancy and neuro-French and conceive of factories for s'mores and manifestos and you can breed superintelligent cats and fix the family station wagon, and then you even build your old elementary school and in the back of the principal's office you find the portal to Mars that was so obviously there — why didn't I think? — and you step through to Mars, where it's the summer of 1977 forever, and you want to go back through the portal and tell everybody that guys, guys, this is it, I finally found it, but now the lights are on and it's morning and the early-morning programmers are already at work.

The Dark Age passes, and the Second Terran Empire, and the Solar Tetrarchy emerges. Brendan Blackstar and Pren-Dahr fight to a stalemate. You discover the buried relics of a Precursor civilization at the Martian north pole. Tech bonus!

By this time you can speak the language of *Solar Empires,* a rock-paper-scissors exchange of moves and countermoves. You learn to deduce hidden information. You learn that, underneath it all, the world is just a way to turn water, minerals, and sunlight into spaceships and soldiers and scientists.

It's time to leave. You build an enormous freighter and add a cylindrical biosphere whose construction costs a third of your resources per turn. When it's ready, you sling it away from the sun. Your enemies make a last-ditch effort to knock it down before it passes Jupiter orbit, but they can only scratch the hull. Ley-R4 is on board, dreaming in stasis sleep as the system collapses into chaos behind her.

The Solar Age is at last over; the Pan-Stellar Activation begins.

* * *

It's dawn, and in my mind I imagine Simon at work a decade ago, grinding out *Solar Empires* against the pressure of a Christmas deadline, stopping only when he's half blind from tracing through his own code. "I'm never going to forget what this feels like," he thinks, breathing the blue dawn air, stumbling once in the dirty, snow-crusted parking lot, "not if I become a famous movie star, not if I have a hundred hundred friends." His car is the only one in the lot, the last ugly chocolate in the box. His hands are cramped, and at first he can't really grab the steering wheel properly, he just kind of hooks his hands on. He starts the car, lets it run a minute before blasting on the heat, and crunches packed snow as he tears out of the lot.

He drives home, passing commuters going the opposite way, all part of a routine he's become unstuck from, gone out of sync with, like a dimension traveler whose fantastic machine has jammed. This is what he wanted, isn't it? To stay up late every night? To cut his own path, to laugh at the ones who didn't have the imagination to invent their own lives, who were too afraid or too dim, the ones who didn't know how to burn? But just at that moment, he remembers how much easier it had been the other way, like in high school, when he at least shared a temporal rhythm with the rest of humanity. But, he reflects, I hated that, too, hated it so much I learned C++, for heaven's sake. He returns at five that afternoon, as the sun is setting on his last day.

I don't know what happened. I don't think Simon was trying to kill himself, or do anything else crazy. I think he had problems, but making games was probably the sanest thing he could do for himself, or for the rest of us. It's probably stupid for me to feel this bad about someone I didn't know that well, someone I had every chance and more to get to know. But he was never a dick to me, and the overwhelming likelihood is that he just didn't have any experience having close friends, and I had no way to show him where to start. It was good that I now have the chance to see how cool he was. It's possible that Simon may have saved my life.

Alewife Station, built in the late seventies at the northeastern edge of the subway system, includes a giant concrete parking structure to accommodate commuters from the suburbs. The construction took years. It was a fixture of my childhood, a slow-growing, labyrinthine edifice wrapped in scaffolding and plastic tarps glimpsed from the backseat through rain-spattered car windows on our rare trips into the city.

Dark Lorac walked beside me, tapping the bricks with the Staff of Wizardry, a black rod five feet long surmounted by a small goat skull. We watched cars pull up, moms dropping off kids, dads picking them up. He made a gesture with his staff that seemed to include the garage's rain-darkened monumental spiral ramps, its sevenfold stack of concrete parking lots, its handicapped access ramps leading underground.

"This is neither the first nor the greatest Dwarven empire."

Chapter Forty-Eight

Solar Empires II: The Ten-Thousand-Year Sleepover (1995)

Cinematic Intro

A. We see a black starfield, then the camera (but it's not a camera, because it's all computer generated, just a point of reference) pulls back until the field of view takes in an enormous (although it's hard to judge the scale) cylindrical spacecraft, a metal hulk the color of dirty ice whose meteor-scarred hull and dim, flickering navigation lights give an impression of great age. The point of view moves back and back to take in more of the ship, and then we see that the image is framed by a porthole. The porthole is in turn framed by a metal wall decorated with graffiti and posters for musical groups, and then we see a hand gripping a bar fixed to the wall, a hand wearing black nail polish, anchoring its owner floating by the porthole. This, you realize, is you.

You're about fourteen, and you're a girl. You are dressed in a gray jumpsuit with the sleeves cut off, and your pink hair is cut in a short, messy pageboy. There are tattoos on your arms and shoulder and throat and cheekbones, curved designs and numbers in a futuristic font.

Your face is hidden from view as you peer out the porthole at the looming craft, until you turn and appear in profile.

Your character design is an anachronistic mess, a nineties Goth girl in space. You imagine the rest. You are in space, where you have lived all your life. The tattoos are indicative of your home asteroid, your training, and your lineage. You have acne scars and a strong jaw.

You hover over the scene. Added detail comes to you unbidden, from your native instinct to make narrative sense of it. You think you are a chieftain's daughter. Evidently you have been crying.

B. The next image we see is you again, this time in a bubble-helmeted vacuum suit, plunging like a skydiver toward the drifting spaceship, which now occupies the whole background. Your own craft holds position above you — it is a one-person skimmer, a rounded pop-art fantasy in candy colors. You see yourself grow smaller as you drift down away from the camera (as we inexorably surrender to the metaphor), falling toward the spaceship, until on-screen you shrink to a few last pixels against the immense hull that drifts slowly from bottom left to upper right. The craft is slowly spinning.

As you see yourself dwindle, your sense of the ship's scale grows by an order of magnitude, then another. You make out features on the surface, towers and canyons marked with green and red and amber lights, and a line where, evidently, a piece of space-borne debris impacted the ship at a shallow angle and plowed along the hull for hundreds of feet, or perhaps miles, for all we can tell.

At the upper right-hand corner is a patch of white, which you mistakenly assume is frost until a piece of blue rotates with cosmic slowness, pixel by pixel, into view, revealing itself as one claw of Ley-R4's iconic blue falcon.

Not heard is the crackle of static on the radio transmitter back in your ship, and the voice that asks, "Honey? Lyra? I'm sorry." Or the subvocalized words inaudible even in the close air of your helmet. "Don't look for me."

C. The last image is the inner surface of an air lock door. A bright spot appears that travels along the line where the door seals itself against the hull, a conventionalized image of an outer-space break-in. But near the outer edge of the image there seems to be trouble, a burn mark on the wall, piled-up garbage, and what is perhaps the toe of a shoe. The bright spot completes its circuit and the door begins to swing open, and here the cinematic intro ends and the game begins.

Looking out through the portal, you can see a planet, a banded gas giant with a red spot. Last thing you knew, you'd bitten and scratched and fought your way out of the solar system. A thousand years later you were still mired in the solar system, and in the body of a teenage girl. What the hell happened?

"Seriously, Matt, what the fuck happened?"

"So, um, *Solar Empires II* takes place in what Simon's notes call a pocket interregnum between the interplanetary and interstellar phases."

"So we're not leaving the solar system at all?"

"Not in this one," he said. "I mean, yeah, the idea is there was an accident in space and all, but the relevant part is that *Solar Empires* didn't make that much money so they thought they should try and spin it as an innovative first-person shooter, which turned out to make even less money."

"So is this a game that sucks?"

"Well, uh, it wasn't my thing," he said. "And it got great reviews. I mean, people still talk about it constantly—like, it was ahead of its time and people are still learning from it. Just…no one bought it. Everyone said it was because it starred a girl, until a year later *Tomb Raider* came out, which of course made a zillion dollars. I guess it was a little different, with, you know, how the model was—"

"The rack."

"Right. Oh, and one last thing—the whole thing was kind of Lisa's idea? So…kind of don't mention it to her, ever?"

Level Descriptions

Maintenance Deck

The air lock cycles. And the girl, the you in this world, steps into the scene. The suit registers breathable air and she pops the suit's seal, slowly takes off her helmet.

Absently, you escape out of the tutorial and sweep the mouse from left to right. The viewpoint shifts and the figure on the screen turns to follow.

The room is apparently an antechamber where mechanics prepare for debarkation on routine maintenance missions. It is lined with empty hooks; a few discarded gloves and most of an antique vacuum suit lie haphazardly on the floor, as if the room has been looted in haste. There is a strangely damp smell. The sliding door to the room has been wrenched off its track and lies in one corner.

You should be traversing the space, sucking up weapons and keys and trying switches. Instead you stand still in the half-light. There are at least three layers of sound underneath the silence. A steady buzzing of fluorescent light; a subliminal roar of what might be air circulation. A far-off beeping that could be an alarm.

No one builds like this anymore. With its neo-Barsoomian lines, brutalist exposed surfaces, and big metal planes, it is decadent and utilitarian at the same time, distinctly a ship of the late Solar Wars. That puts it way way back in Simon's time, just after the Solar Tetrarchy fell and the system-wide Dark Age began. Its solid metal construction would not be remotely practical in the current era. It might be three thousand years old, its mass uncountable tons. Jovian-class, at the very least.

Of course. It's not a freighter at all, it's your colony ship, the one you built. It never made it out of the system at all, and nobody knew — for a thousand years the solar system's inhabitants warred over dwindling resources but believed that at least a better world was being built elsewhere. But the solar exodus never even happened; we're still stuck in the Dark Age, and humanity's future has been drifting derelict, half-lit, its biosphere way past its projected life span and probably slowly leaking out through a dozen minor hull breaches.

You step over a shattered barricade of piled-up lockers and pace down the corridor. A skeleton lies slumped against one wall. It wears scraps of blue and gold braid, and bits of colored metal lie among its ribs, the trappings of a lieutenant junior grade in the navy of the Second Terran Empire. It shows no obvious cause of death. Nearby there is a gray card, thin as a fingernail, chased with pulsing blue lines. A locked door, likewise outlined in blue, can now be opened, admitting a blast of warm, moist air.

Sewage System

You're in a sewer, because what would a video game be without a sewage level? In the medium of your heart's choice, dim lighting, mossy corridors, and aggressive rats are eternal artistic verities. This one just seems to see more use than a derelict spacecraft's should.

You are just a few tiles from the exit ladder when a trap closes around you, walls that slide into place, obviously a designer-driven effect. So much for interactivity. There's no way out.

"Hello?" a boy's voice calls. "Don't you know not to go in there?" he asks. He sounds angry. The grating overhead gives a squeal of neglected metal workings and starts to open. You hear the quick slapping of sandaled feet running away.

Hydroponics

Climbing against the centrifugal force of the spinning ship, you see the geometry where a long-ago explosion ripped into one great metal-lined swamp. Brackish water drops past you, outward to the stars.

It's a fallen ecosystem of genetically warped felines and avians and simians, arachnids and carnivorous plants. You learn to harvest toxin sacs from mutant koi in the shallow ponds. You learn where the security cameras are, and the exact range of the door's proximity sensors.

The boy returns occasionally. He says he's a prince; he calls you an idiot.

Recreation Commons

Water-damaged carpeting, silent ranks of anachronistic arcade cabins. You are attacked by a robot that once taught fencing; its untipped foil is caked with old blood. You knock it into a hot tub, where it sparks out the last of its misspent life.

You find a library containing old mocked-up news photos of the ship, called the *Concorde,* as it was being built, exposing the honeycombed space inside. The *Concorde* should take 800 years to reach a destination 4.37 light-years away; it should have been there already. You should be combing the galaxy for Mournblade and kicking bugs off your to-do list. Instead, the ship has now been adrift for three thousand years, almost four times its expected life span. The tolerances engineered into its biosphere and its flight capabilities are strained beyond imagining.

And in the office it's late, eleven o'clock, and you already know tomorrow you'll regret the lost sleep and the wasted time when you could have been working out or reading, but you're too distracted. The world is broken; you have to fix it.

The prince paces you on the far side of a metal grillwork, so you can talk but not interact. He's afraid of his older brother, who stands to inherit the mantle of king, who plans to go to war against a tribe two decks in. His brother dreams of reuniting the world under one ruler. He doesn't know what the *Concorde* is; no one does.

A thin trickle of water flows through a damaged seal overhead and forms a silty pool on the deck plating. There's an object at the bottom, a gray steel disk with blue plastic inlay, stamped with a long serial number. On-screen, your HUD morphs to become more complicated and dangerous. You can't believe they waited this long to give you a gun.

'Tween Decks

A cramped world of palettes stacked with spools of thick metal cable, dormant terraforming machinery, prefabricated huts, farming equipment, fertilizer, seeds, and water purification units. An Emerald Green Key-Card sits at the center of a giant web strung all the way across the entry to a disused dining commons. You do not find the spider.

You don't know why you left home. You don't even know why you sat down to play this game instead of going home or getting work done. But definitely life in a mining colony sucked; as a chieftain's daughter, you knew you'd have to marry whomever your father said to marry, and the day was coming. And you looked at your mother's face and saw that she wasn't going to save you. She wasn't even going to fight for you. You stole a one-person ship, and as you felt the acceleration subside and you drifted in the black nothing, you felt the absence of a pressure you'd been feeling without knowing it for all your fourteen, all your twenty-eight years.

Where would you go? Ganymede? Jovian orbit? What if things are just the same there? You warmed up the engines. You rotated the ship to point in-system, toward forbidden Mars and devastated Earth, Venus, and Mercury, or straight into the sun if that's what it took to feel anything different. There were stories of long-dormant defense systems from the days of the stellar siege, of rogue mining robots gone sentient, of ancient Martians returned, of old-world technologies long forgotten.

You were asleep when the proximity detector sounded and showed you a ship where no ship should have been, in the darkness between Mars and the outer planets. The largest ship ever built, maybe, straight out of the legends of the Second Terran Empire.

Shopping District

A chalked symbol informing you that the last sailors of the Second Terran Empire Fleet hold the territory beyond, although they're a little hazy about what they're doing there. In the end you are permitted to boss-battle the prince's older brother with stun weapons for the right to live and enter the sacred refrigeration and storage deck and look upon the Sleeping Ones.

The crowd lines an arena that was once the sunken floor of a two-story food court. The prince is watching; you feel his sense of fear, sense of awe. You're a girl and you're about to fight the brother he could never match. You face him across multicolored tile.

Normally you hate boss battles, a highly conventionalized way of staging a climactic moment that is purportedly dramatic but that usually devolves into hitting a supertough enemy's weak points over and over again until he disintegrates or his head flies off and becomes a rocket-powered helicopter with its own special weak point; repeat as necessary.

The brother's head does not turn into a helicopter. You throw chairs, scale the side of the food court, dodge through the crowd. You reactivate the sunken fountain and roundhouse-kick him into it. Press N to decline his offer of marriage.

Stasis Tanks

The prince's brother shows you the secret treasure-house of the world. Inches under the glass, you can see a teenage girl who looks maybe a year younger than yourself, but she must have been born well over two thousand years ago. You see Ley-R4, queenly and unmoving; you see Pren-Dahr, her captive, who elected to come with her. She doesn't even know the empire's fallen or that her ship got lost. She'll never even know you or the prince were there. You must save her.

Spinal Tramway

You see now that you originally landed two miles up from the aft engines. If the ship were Manhattan, you'd be walking from Houston Street to the Bronx, block by block. The ship is big enough to have its own seasons, which work their way up and down its length with the stale air and recycled water. It creaks and sighs. It's getting colder. You have a lot of walking to do.

The tramway flooded when the ballast tank in the middle of the foredeck was breached. As you watch, a monstrous vertical fin taller than a man breaks the surface, followed by a column of gray-green muscle. You'll have to find another way around.

You don your space suit and traverse a silent, dark, hull-breached section to reach the foredeck. Grisly corpses of men and women lie mummified in the cold. Jagged holes in the floor show a brilliant starfield and a distant lonely sun. A black shape stirs in a corner.

Playtesters claim that once in a while they'll enter a sealed level and find it decompressed, its diamond-hard portholes shattered.

Command Deck
You turn inward. This side of the breach it's cooler and drier. The Violet Key-Card is in a circular room where four corridors meet. Bones are crushed under heavy robot treads. A captain's hat; the Second Terran Empire's falcon in gold. The card opens a security gate, and the prince emerges, ready to do what must be done.

The Bridge
You go up and up. Gravity decreases as you climb upward and inward through concentric cylinders toward the ship's core, and one day you're out in the clean cool air of the bridge, and there you can finally see the shape of the world as it turns around you and hurtles on from a forgotten, ruined past to an unknown future.

The prince is this little world's last computer programmer. He's the only one who can fix the world. He glances up at you to see if you're watching, if you notice how well he's mastered the interface.

The prince fixes the ship's mad AI, brings peace to his tiny empire, and sends the *Concorde* on its way to the stars. Your heart skips a beat as you watch the ship unfold a translucent lavender web a thousand kilometers across, the solar sail, and begin the long acceleration push to Alpha Centauri. You and your inventory go with it.

You've walked, fought, bled, schemed your way to the threshold of galactic exploration, but at the moment it's a gray dawn, a thing you've seen far too often lately. You didn't notice the time passing, as if it flows differently on the other side of the glass screen, but in two hours the early-rising Black Arts workers will arrive to start the day, having slept away the time you spent rescuing the world of the *Concorde*.

You switch off your monitor, grab your bag, and speed-walk down the hall, unable to bear the idea of meeting anyone coming in. You exit into the chilly air outdoors. Your hands are so cramped you can barely grasp the steering wheel, so you drive with your fingers hooked around it, desperate just to get home and sleep. You could get five hours and make it in by eleven. This isn't the first time you've done this, or the fifth or tenth. I guess it's time to think of it as your life.

Chapter Forty-Nine

Like the Third Age itself, late beta was a grim and demoralizing slide into barbarity punctuated by rare moments of heroism. Like the time the build went oversize by 10 KB and couldn't fit on a double CD. Lisa and I were bickering about map size while Gabby went to her desk, did something to a map tile with the blur tool in a paint program, came back, and rebuilt the entire game. It was 14 KB smaller.

The bug count dwindled, except for the obvious one. Everyone was being polite about winnability, Mournblade, and the rest of it. I told them it was under control, that I was just prioritizing. I needed sleep.

"We can close out the series in a day or two," I told Lisa. "Thirty-six hours if we push it."

"So you're still thinking of it as a series?" she said.

"What do you mean?"

"I mean, it's all just one game. We're playing through the largest, longest game ever made, the Black Arts game that's been running from the start. And I think it's ending."

Lisa and Matt sat behind me as I ran *Solar Empires III: Pan-Stellar Activation*.

```
se3.exe
IMPORT SAVED GAME? (Y/N)
```

Y
LOADING...

Black Arts had a new logo for this one, a skeletal figure cupping a ball of light in its hands. The splash screen echoed the one for the first *Solar Empires,* with the Milky Way's spiral form swapped in for the solar system; looking closely, I saw that it rotated in slow, epochal sweeps.

Character selection was skipped; as the winner of the long-ago Solar Wars, Ley-R4 presided.

    It is the year 4113. Humanity has gained a fragile foothold
        among the stars, a tiny outpost at the edge of a perilous
        dark continent.
    YOU must guide the human species through its last and greatest
        era of expansion, facing a galaxy fraught with wonder and
        wealth, unknown danger, and the strangest of destinies.
    Let us now wage interstellar war! Let us now claim the stars!
    Let us initiate...
    PAN—STELLAR ACTIVATION!

Another strategy game, but on a grander scale. The starting view took in ten light-years, showing the first three colonies of Homo sapiens. Zoom in to see tiny starships so detailed you can read their histories in their battered, refitted hulls. Fractally generated continents on planets, moons, and stranger celestial objects. I felt a slight pull in the guts. It was Black Arts' crowning achievement: they were simulating an entire galaxy's economic, military, ecological, political, and—in a sense—narrative life.

At first it seemed like just another facade applied to the same old WAFFLE mechanics, swapping solar systems for cities and starships for galleons while keeping the underlying machinery the same.

But science fiction and fantasy aren't perfect analogues of one another. Only space exploration features this blinding expansion of scale, the abyssal blackness between stars; the dislocation, the multiplication of months into years, centuries into millennia, the concept of geological change and of deep time. Going from Endoria to the Milky Way mattered — it reenacted the shock of the Enlightenment, the first bruising contact of the human imagination with the scale of a scientifically defined universe.

Moreover, even if far-future technology looks like magic, it isn't the same thing. Science admits of no consciousness in nature, and knows that language and reality have no sacred connection. In *Solar Empires* games, there were no magic words, no jinnis, no wishes. Which made it all the stranger to find, in the cargo manifest for Ley-R4's flagship, both an antique twentieth-century tracking device and a dried flower of a species unknown to terrestrial science.

The Colonial Age

As promised, the first *X* stands for "explore." Stellar colonization is slow; even with solar sails, rail-gun launches, and fancy orbital mechanics, you are still crawling along at well below the speed of light. It turns out that one yottameter equals more than 105 million light-years.

Colonists board their generation ships, eyes shining with fear, ambition, and regret before they are frozen for the long trip. One in three ships disappears into the dark forever. You build and build, playing the ruthless odds. Stasis fields can collapse, letting colonists awaken a hundred years from arrival. Many arrive to find their target planet uninhabitable for one of a hundred reasons — it's too hot or cold, its atmosphere contains ineradicable traces of poison, or nothing grows. These colonists must chart a new course and face the grim attrition rates associated with a second stasis. Centuries later, ships are found gutted or irradiated or mysteriously empty.

A handful of worlds prosper. Alpha Centauri, Procyon A, Sirius, Tau Ceti. In relative isolation, their cultures diverge. The Centauri develop a militarized culture, shadow successors to Brennan's regime. Tau Cetans revert to an agrarian culture — like the Achaeans burning their ships outside the walls of Troy, they set their spaceships to self-destruct, and within three generations Earth becomes a legend.

Procyon holds a mystery, a stone temple in the equatorial jungle, built (your scientists tell you) approximately the year the Beatles recorded *Revolver* and made from stone native not to the planet itself but to the planet's second moon. You find one like it on Epsilon Indi's second planet, another on a planet orbiting L5 1668. They contain carvings that, when compared, yield a coded schematic for a machine that can pull on the space between stars and very slightly condense or wrinkle it. Your people call it a warp drive.

Crossing the centuries at one bound, you move to the next historical phase...

The Cosmopolitan Age

It is three centuries later, and your ships go faster. Humanity's reach spans 250 light-years. There are fifteen hundred stars now, more than you can name personally. There are four warp-capable alien species whose volumes of influence interpenetrate with your own. You know of two dozen other sentient life-forms in industrial or preindustrial phases of civilization.

Outside, the leaves are starting to turn, and you're a year older, and the incipient chill and the smells of rain and rotting leaves bring on an involuntary sense memory of the expectation of school and book bags and new teachers. Or is part of that memory buried in the code itself, in the mind that made it, in the cool fall air of the garage, the new possibilities that grew from the summer of 1983? You don't know. But the second X means "expand."

As Ley-R4, you continue to rule, empress, sage, and justice in perpetuity. The other three Heroes serve as your ministers, immortal figureheads of the fields of human endeavor they represent. Loraq is the philosophical and religious head of the empire. Pren-Dahr administers economics (well, exploitation) and diplomacy, and Brendan Blackstar, of course, handles the military.

Rogue colonies, border wars, and piracy trouble the empire's peace. And stranger things happen—ships go missing or turn up empty or hull-breached. You find, once, a ship's crew butchered as if by a preindustrial weapon. And from time to time a colony or a world goes dark and is found depopulated, whether by disease, environmental failure, an uprising of indigenous flora or fauna, or simply with no explanation at all. Even the occasional star explodes. You wonder if Mournblade's reach is this far.

The galaxy is a large and strange place, and it's only a matter of time before monsters come out of the darkness. That's how the age ends, with the arrival of a vast and ancient fleet that swallows a quarter of the empire overnight. The Cosmopolitan Age is over, and the Spindrift War begins.

The Spindrift War

The view scale jumps again, and humanity's existence is threatened, and it's time to exploit, which is the third X. Asteroids are quarried into massive fleets equipped with the Improved Gravity Splice. Combat is now too fast to follow on a tactical level, so you learn to program artificial intelligence systems. The weapons are terrible: entire planets are shattered and stars implode on your orders. By the time the Terpsichore

Myriad (for so they call themselves) is exterminated, the human dominion comprises six hundred million stars (out of the galaxy's two hundred billion) and thirty thousand light-years, almost a third of the way across the galaxy, but still far short of your goal. The war has paved the way to a Golden Age.

The Golden Age

Now the galaxy blazes with life from its core to the outer reaches, incomparably great and ancient. The view scale pulls back to encompass sixty thousand light-years at its farthest zoom, and the galaxy's large-scale forms finally come into view — the fuzzy logarithmic spiral, the globular clusters at the rim, the long bar, which passes through the central disk.

The breadth and variety is extraordinary and never-ending. The sensation is one of an inner fullness, limitless wealth, the barely remembered feeling of needing to hug yourself and jump up and down in the effort to contain sheer happiness. You start to see, as never before, the scope of Black Arts' achievement. You can't believe they've given you this gift. It's a very, very, very nearly perfect game.

The game can end in many ways, but each character has its own special ending, which you may or may not be able to achieve.

Brendan Blackstar

If you're Brendan, there is an extra subphase late in the Golden Age when a challenger emerges, a nemesis triggered by your own aggressive philosophies, a master politician and strategic genius. The military victory occurs only when you have driven your opponent's forces back to their home planet and dueled him yourself on the marble steps of his palace. You fight as a white-haired general, vibro-sword to laser ax, and throw his severed head to the crowd.

Pren-Dahr

Pren-Dahr's victory is more of a statistical threshold triggered by careful management of production and trade, which, as they reach a certain level of productivity, obviate the need for wealth itself. Our last view of Pren-Dahr shows him as an old man in retirement, gazing out over a golden city, one of a million cities in a galaxy that will know an eternity of plenty.

Loraq

Loraq attains victory as a galactic philosopher-king who, as head of the Galactic Council, is empowered to adjudicate border disputes, enact various galaxy-wide rulings—such as caps on weapons production or mining or expansion—and set the penalties for violating them. In time, it's possible to play with the way various species-wide AIs react and realize a galaxy-wide peace. If it can be maintained for a full galactic rotation, the conditions are met and the result is an eternity of peace and wisdom as the formerly disgraced vizier is at last allowed to rule in his own right.

Ley-R4

If you're Ley-R4, you may at long last decipher the Precursor technology. Then, if you have the requisite technologies, you can invest resources to create the reality engine, the hidden apex of the game's broad and deep technology tree. When activated, it triggers the Science Victory, the creation of a new parallel universe to explore. The game ends, but you finish knowing that, for Ley-R4, the cycle of exploration need never end.

There are other moments that go unseen, fragments of the Heroes' long, long lives that will never enter the histories. Eleven-year-old

Loraq lying on his flowered coverlet looking up at the ceiling and listening to bootleg cassette tapes of *The Hitchhiker's Guide to the Galaxy*. Pren-Dahr delivering the valedictory address at his college and finding, looking down at the familiar bored or smiling or nervous faces, that he feels nothing. Brendan Blackstar straying from the path on a summer-camp hike and finding himself alone for the first time in weeks.

The game doesn't end. A millennium passes, and then another, with nothing but a long, extended moment of peace and vitality. All victory conditions have been met, but the game won't end — the galaxy's golden moment continues while outside days pass, a wet summer to a dry autumn.

You comb through the galaxy's wonders for anything you've missed. Cities of white towers, jungle cities dripping long tangles of vegetation, undersea cities, cities in hollowed-out moons. You catalog all the Precursor temples — what was going on there? You think you've got all of them — you ended up glassing a few planets from orbit back in the Spindrift (a couple dozen, if we're being honest with ourselves), and one of them might have been important, but you make do with what you have.

The temple complexes are all unique and beautifully modeled. Each one has its own style and carvings, and each one has been artfully smashed to pieces by time and weather. Someone toppled those columns and distributed those pieces. One temple is at the bottom of an ocean. Another is cut in half where a river collapsed its base. Pieces have been washed for miles downstream. (Matt pointed out that all the temples are made of porphyry, a material component for the Dimensional Portal spell in *Realms*. Dork.)

You realize the planets form a pattern, a shitty, useless zodiacal configuration, as jumbled and abstract as any other constellation. From one angle it might be a three-masted galleon; from another, a giraffe. From a third it looks very, very much like a giant hand giving you the finger.

What would Lorac say? The real one, the wizard, but he doesn't seem to be around. Or Karoly, either.

The tracking device points you up and out of the galactic disk, a line that seems pointless, bound for the edge of the universe. But at the far reach, far, far beyond the galaxy proper, barely detectable on Ley-R4's telescopes, there is a dim, dying star.

"You're telling me the planet is too far to get to?"

"Even at the top of the FTL drive tech tree, using ripplewarp technology with all the trimmings, and pushing the time scale all the way up, the sixty-thousand-light-year span can be crossed no faster than exactly one hour, which is what Darren decided is the maximum attention span of a human being. It's already thousands of times the speed of light, and they designed it so that's all any technology can do. Which means that to travel nine point eight five yottameters——" Lisa broke off. She always had to do math in her head.

"I'm waiting," I said. I watched her work. "Just use a calculator."

"Shut up." She mouthed a word repeatedly while she thought. It looked like maybe she was saying, stupid you, stupid you, stupid you. Then, finally: "Sixty thousand light-years in an hour, and a yottameter is a hundred and five million light-years, sort of, so vaguely, like, seven hundred twenty days minimum."

"So we'll get there, and meanwhile we'll hoard glass beads to be ready for the bold posteconomic era."

"I think in the game mechanics you have to carry fuel, too," said Matt. "You couldn't do it anyway."

"I hate this game," I said. "I hate this game so much."

We went back to the message boards. Surely someone had been there, or someplace similar. But there was no mention of it; no strategic or narrative reason even to look in that direction.

Matt called me over, a few hours later. "I think I've got it. The Big Bump."

"Tell me."

"A bug. It's mentioned only three times, in three reports, widely separated. All three times, a starship running on reactive drive was in midbattle when, in an instant, it found itself halfway across the galaxy. Usually in pieces, but it had traveled faster than the sim said it could — much, much faster. But no one knows how to trigger it."

It stumped us for days, until one day Lisa plunked herself down in a spare Aeron chair and wheeled herself up to me. Neither of us had bathed in a few days, but it didn't matter.

"I think I have a thing to try, anyway."

"Tell me."

"I've always hated reactive drive. It's the worst thing in the game."

"I thought players loved it."

Reactive drive was a tech you discovered when you got maybe two-thirds of the way through the game. It let you start and stop spaceships on a dime, just zero out any velocity and park it, motionless. Or start it up the same way. It was a good trick in a dogfight, but that was about the last time when individual ship-to-ship combat meant anything. After that, things like antimatter clouds and starbusters came into play.

"Players do, yeah," she said. "It's for players who like games and who are too lazy to make orbital mechanics work. That kind of start-stop bullshit is how people are used to things moving in games. It's intuitive, it's point-and-click. It's clean."

I felt a little guilty. I always hated how in *Asteroids,* once you fired your jets it was almost impossible to bring your ship to a dead stop again. Realistic, but annoying.

"Yeah. No one but you really likes calculating fuel burns. It's a pain."

"Right. But you know who else hates reactive drive? The physics simulation module. The physics system hates it. It spends all day making things behave all proper and Newtonian, and Darren writes this spec saying, 'Okay, this tech makes ships start and stop instantaneously, because that's fun.' And it is, but it's nonsense physics. In the real world, if you want to decelerate, you have an equal and opposite force, and you stop, over some distance that is not zero. It may be a millimeter, but it is definitely not zero."

"Who cares? Doesn't the programmer just write, um, 'velocity equals zero' and leave it at that?"

"No! No!" she said, her voice cracking a little. "Sorry, really need to sleep more. But no. The point of a physics model is that it takes over all that stuff for you. Where stuff is, how fast it's going and in what direction, what's touching what. You've put it in charge, and if you go in and micromanage it starts to get confused and snappish and doesn't know where to put things. Plus you can't even always do it." She did a gesture, blinking and waving both hands as if to disperse the very thought.

"So reactive drive is part of the physics bug?"

"You call it a bug, I call it physics justice. Just listen. I tried to think how reactive drive works at all. So I went to the actual code, which is by—" She glanced around and whispered, "Todd," then went on. "It's a total mess, a lot of different ideas commented out, a lot of just 'fuckety-fuck this code'–type comments. Bottom line, they can't just set it to zero, and there's a limit to how much they can just drop the kinetic energy of these starships right out of the universe. I mean, it's a mile-long chunk of titanium, potentially, up among the high-end Angel-class ships. So they ended up with this horrible, horrible hackery. Just for an instant, they set the starship's mass to a number so small it's as close to zero as the physics universe will tolerate. It's a lot easier to bring it to a dead stop when it weighs about as much as a neutrino. But just for one tick of the clock. Then it's back up to its usual gigaton self, and hopefully no one notices."

"So...fine?" I offered.

"It's not fine! That's the thing. For one cycle of the simulation, its mass is near zero. That means—" She stopped altogether and wrote on my whiteboard F = MA. "Okay. God. Force equals mass times acceleration, right?"

"Okay, okay, yes. I'm not totally hopeless," I said.

"You'd better not be. Reactive drive wants mass to be small, so force is small. But then if mass is just about zero, what if we're trying to work out acceleration?"

She wrote another equation: F/M = A.

"Acceleration. Now we're figuring out what force divided by mass is. So if force is anything reasonable and mass is virtually zero, anything divided by zero is..."

"Infinity."

"Yes! Acceleration is infinite!" she said. She actually struck my desk with her fist. "And that's what the Big Bump is. Those ships got hit exactly when they weighed nearly nothing. And boom, they went right to nearly infinite velocity. Nothing to stop it."

"Wait...did you just invent hyperdrive?"

"I call it Enhanced Reactive Travel, but yes, I did. And you're welcome."

You remember the days when you were working so hard to figure out how to act normal and attractive, so hard it was killing you, so hard you moved to Portland. How did you get tricked into believing that that was all there was?

For all that I understood Lisa's equation, I had no idea how to make it happen in a game. I called Matt and Don and had her explain it to them.

We set up in the conference room with the amp-up demo machine and hooked up the projection screen for Matt to use. This was, after all, what he used to do — re-create the precise, heartbreakingly specific set of conditions that will strike an apparently beautiful simulation along its hidden logical fault line and tumble the world into nonsense again.

I watched, fidgeting protectively, as he took command of my galactic shipyards. I'd forgotten how sad and primitive life was back in the Cos-

mopolitan Age when reactive drive was fashionable. I'd even forgotten
I had few reactive-capable cruisers still in service, but Matt found a few
out in the backwater colonies. Somehow, in the six hours since I built
them, the Bishop-class light cruisers—with their stage VII warp
drives, their DeVries full-reactive bootstrap drives, and their front and
rear fully upgraded particle accelerators with the Overload option—
triggered a nostalgia reaction in me. I'd rolled them out, the techni-
cians in their white jumpsuits still scrambling over the red-and-white
striped hulls, and they seemed like the crowning achievement of an
ancient spacefaring race. But only a few short centuries later I was ram-
ming them into Kun-Bar capital ships just to save on upkeep.

I watched as Matt created a custom-built ship with reactive drive and
the best force field available and bags and bags of small, very weak
magnetic mines. Launch a mine stupidly close to your own ship and let
it hit you. Then, on the moment of impact, turn on reactive drive.
Bump.

Next, he flew the ship to Mars, now the capital of the entire Impe-
rium. The planet's red sands and pressure domes had long since yielded
to terraforming and macroengineering. Mars was one-third hollow now.

Ley-R4 stood on a mile-high tower, where Olympus Mons once was,
and thought about what she'd made. The millennia had aged her
gracefully into her early forties, but she was recognizably the same pale,
raven-haired princess I'd ordered pho with long ago. Now she was
empress of the galaxy.

She'd be coming with us. She'd always been a mobile personnel unit,
but she was one you'd be insane to put into the field. Now she boards
the light cruiser IGV *Spickernell* along with the other three Heroes.

It must have been an awkward reunion onboard. There are two
failed marriages between the four of them, one child (turned time-
traveling undead tyrant), four or five era-defining wars, countless battles and duels, countless adventures. No one will ever forget Dark
Lorac, or the war for the Mournblade Splinter, or the truck bomb in

East Berlin, or the dirty bomb over Venus, or the whole knife-fight-in-a-phone-booth Solar War, or their first meeting in a tavern, where they swore that false vow they never bothered to keep. Mournblade still lived. I looked at the four heroes on the bridge, watching breathlessly as they attempted to cheat the laws of their world: Brendan Blackstar stoically indifferent, Loraq wincing each time a mine went off, Pren-Dahr rapt with the thought of redeeming his cosmic crime.

Matt's face had the eternal blankness of a gamer facing a monitor. Only his hands moved, clacking and thumping the keys over and over, as if he were playing a rhythmic piano suite nobody could hear.

"Shit." The mines turned out to be tricky to predict. They launched, then curved back in an elliptical orbit Matt had to match. Then he had to guess how close he had to be to set off the mine.

"Shit."

"Shit."

"Shit." The *Spickernell*'s force field degraded to half and had to be replaced or else we'd risk losing the whole game. Don ordered pizza.

"Shit."

"Shit."

"Shit!" Matt typically played with beatific calm; playtest had inoculated him against gamer frustration, but we were nearing the three-hour mark. Finally, I tried it. Lisa tried it. Don tried it.

Don cleared his throat and said, "I just had a horrible thought."

"Me, too," said Lisa. "Who wants to call?"

Don sighed. "It's what they pay me for. I don't know if he'll come, though."

"Hey! Fuck, yeah! Black Arts!" Darren said as he came through the door twenty-five minutes later.

It was really, really hard to keep from being happy to see Darren while still being aware of the interior voice telling you not to be. I'd missed him, I knew that. Nobody else at Black Arts had his skill set, which was to make whatever he was doing become charged with excitement and meaning. It made Black Arts fun again. We'd all forgotten — for how long now? — that we were in the goddamned games business, and we were rock stars and doing the most exciting thing on the planet and getting paid for it.

As business talents go, Darren's was as close as I'd ever seen to that of a genuine superpower. Whatever its origin in trauma or mutation, it was supremely adaptive for its entrepreneurial moment in history. When Darren was there, people worked hundred-hour weeks; he moved the hands of sober, dead-eyed businessmen to write and sign eight-figure checks.

Also, unlike the rest of us, he was a tournament-level player. It's common to assume that game developers are ringers when it comes to playing games. In reality, most of us are good but not great; video game excellence is its own skill, and almost none of us can do the things our fans can, even on our own games. Darren was the exception. He was barred (unjustly, in my opinion) from official competition, but I'd seen him place high in informal aftermatches.

I explained as much of the situation as I could. I didn't know how much he knew, so I couched the problem as a showstopper bug and explained the logic behind the Big Bump. He nodded his understanding at once.

"I love it. Who figured that one out?"

"Lisa."

"Well, all right," he said. He was impressed, and good at showing it. He was looking right at her, and she blushed. I knew what it felt like. I knew Darren had that trick of knowing the version of yourself you most desperately want to believe in and playing to it shamelessly. From outside, you could see how easy and how nasty it was, that he was casually exposing an infantile and uncontrolled and crushingly obvious hunger. I still missed it; I always would.

It took Darren twenty-two minutes to set off the Big Bump. When it happened, we didn't see the ship move, only the camera snapping back to its maximum zoom to try to keep the ship on-screen. Darren tapped the space bar to activate reactive drive, and the ship stopped.

"All right, this time we try aiming."

It took eighteen more jumps to get to the place where the tracking device was.

Darren stood to give me his place at the keyboard.

"Go ahead," he said. "It's your turn. You're the man." Which was a little annoying, and that was the moment I realized I had been listening to Darren wrong. Why didn't I ever realize that nobody was as vulnerable to Darren's dirty trick as he was? He needed to believe that the person in front of him was a genius, and he needed that just as badly as you did. Once upon a time, his best friend had been a genius.

I sat down, conscious of the silence in the room and that it was slightly weird to play with people watching. Normally you're alone, drifting free in your own story, letting your unconscious go its way, no witnesses, no script, and nothing at stake.

PART VII

ENDGAME

Chapter Fifty

Somehow you always knew. From one hundred miles up, you have a beautiful view across the Western Mountains to the Savage Ocean and beyond, to nations you've never discovered in all your time with Endoria's champions, and it still stirs your spirit to know that there are lands yet to be explored.

You descend from orbit, and the barriers of time, space, and genre fall away at last. Diegetic conventions shred and transform at the sight of a Terran atmospheric runabout hovering on a jet of blue-white fusion flame above the stillness of the Pendarren Forest, itself the echo of Kid-Bits' scrubby pines, now grown to enormous size and trackless extent. The Heroes file out onto the surface, inhaling the illusory digital scent of their long-ago franchise. See that it is Pren-Dahr who sinks to his knees; it is Loraq who curses aloud.

SOLAR EMPIRES EXPANDED
CAMPAIGN SETTING: ENDORIAN ANOMALY

Black Arts Studios brings you a gaming experience like no other!

An adventure for slightly-too-advanced characters, Endorian Anomaly pits the galaxy's rulers against an ancient evil.

Note: Characters from a science-fiction milieu may find this context particularly unnerving, portraying as it does a preindustrial civilization with annoying mystical abilities. They may draw their own conclusions. For some, a sufficiently advanced form of magic will prove indistinguishable from technology. For others, it will stir strange sensations of other lives lived and emotions forgotten, or mayhap deliberately pushed aside, on the not unreasonable premise that magic is for the primitives, the losers, and the gaywads of the galactic backwater. It matters not; the Endorian Anomaly scenario contains all game items and all game rules.

Note: *Solar Empires'* Embarkation mode allows you to leave your ship and play as an individual unit, so you can board an enemy ship or venture forth onto the surface of a planet. In fact, it's an inheritance from the game engine's original function as a dungeon adventure game, repurposed to add an exciting gameplay mode to your *Solar Empires* experience.

You consult the tracking device. There is a clear signal coming from far to the east. The group is silent as they fly over lands where they fought on horseback, moving a thousand times faster than the fastest horse ever could. Down below it is somehow still — still! — the fucking Third Age, its final end delayed for long, long eras as the Heroes busy themselves elsewhere. As you travel, the landscape below you changes from forestland to grassland to dark ocean. From high above you can see the shadow of a leviathan surging in the depths. At these speeds it is only an hour before you set down on the pebbled shore of an unknown continent. Outside, the day is warm and muggy, but you can smell the not unpleasant smells of grassland and forest and ... adventure.

"Is this ... what anybody was expecting?" Lisa asked.

"All that matters is we find it, right?" Don said. "And we can fix it?"

"Yes," Lisa said. "It's just weird."

Darren shook his head and said, to no one in particular, "Simon, what did you do?"

Wise adventurers prepare for danger. The orbiter's loadout includes a pair of blasters. Galactic empress Ley-R4 carries the ceremonial blade of her office even though she hasn't drawn it in centuries. Loraq, of course, scorns all conventional weaponry. Pren-Dahr leads the party inland, flaunting his overland movement rate. It's been so long since he's had a ground movement rate, let alone an armor class! Brendan Blackstar lingers on the beach, trying to recall a half-remembered prophecy. A warning, wasn't it? Well, it's too late now.

It is not long before you encounter...

THE TOMB OF DESTINY
BY
SIMON BERTUCCI

What lies in the depths of Black Arts' oldest and shittiest dungeon?
BACKGROUND

The Four Heroes reunite after many wanderings to discover at last the resting place of the legendary warrior-magus Adric and the accursed sword Mournblade. The Fortress of Adric lies in the far northern reaches of Endoria, amid the half-melted bones of the Great Ice Serpent, who lived far into the Third Age. The site has been abandoned for untold millennia, ever since the long-ago Correllean empire fell (see *Correllean Dreams,* various authors, Orbit, 1994).

Warning: This adventure is for high-level characters only. Naught but doom and defeat await you below! So you know.

KEY TO DUNGEON MAP

Starting Location

Aboveground, a mere two dozen slabs of stone in the mossy ground sketch the outline of what was once the mightiest fortress in the known world. Alert players (INT check at –4) will observe a small crater a few hundred yards to the east containing a half-buried capsule bearing the markings CCCP and the decayed shreds of a parachute. The capsule is empty. Loraq lingers at the site a moment longer than the others.

After a search, characters will notice a dozen stone steps leading down to a pair of doors built of the same stone as the rest of the fortress. A dwarf or experienced thief—although either would be an odd choice to go on vacation with—will observe that the gates have been opened and resealed several times.

Level 1: The Shallows

The stone complex is a simple maze built to no obvious purpose, terminating in a set of stone stairs leading downward. The air is dry and cold; the rooms are lit by gaps in the ceiling. Its ornamentation is sparse. There are crudely carved mossy granite and marble gargoyles and dry fountains in the larger rooms. The maze is empty and silent. Its floor plan resembles what you would draw in the last fifteen minutes of Western civ, which ought to at least have some cool castles in it, but what do you expect? Things never turn out the way you think.

Level 2: The Maze

Similar to the first level, but the walls and rooms form a more complex pattern, presumably a second layer of defense or the work of a more confident designer. You see the bodies of four or five ampers piled in one corner, mummified in the dry air. Once they were mysterious items of punctuation crawling through the dark; now, in color and three dimensions, they are, disappointingly, revealed to be thuggish bald men with tusks, wearing vaguely tribal leather gear. They were slain long generations ago, evidently by fire.

Level 3: Hall of Pillars

An airy hall of open construction punctuated by two rows of broad pillars that lead to a pair of white marble thrones on the far wall, the seat of absent monarchs. The air is growing warmer, with a hint of moisture. There are more dead ampers here, but these have rotted away to broken skeletons.

This may once have been an audience chamber, although not a very conveniently located one; maybe it's there to congratulate people who can get through two pretty easy mazes. This marks the last point where anybody remembered constructing what was supposed to be a historical building rather than just going and drawing whatever they wanted.

Level 3: Inscription

You emerge into a set of corridors that form the puzzling words *Darren Rules* in cursive Roman characters (far away, its designer high-fived an associate producer). The hallways are mossy, and the air grows humid. Here and there a trickle of water flows down the walls and forms a running stream along the corridor.

Here you see what may be your first living ampers. It is unlikely they will stand up well to blaster fire. Ley-R4 draws her sword, which hums menacingly, a vibro-blade from the days when dueling was a deadly feature of life among the Martian aristocracy.

At the base of the second cursive *e*, adventurers will encounter a figure sitting upright against one wall. It is a corpse, long decayed, wearing a dark robe that survives, stiff with age. A staff surmounted by a broken animal skull lies a few feet from its outstretched hand. Players knowledgeable in the history of the *Realms* will recognize this as Dark Lorac, once the most feared wizard in this plane of reality. Characters of above-average intelligence may spot (20% chance) an additional set of small finger bones at rest nearby.

[I was startled by a cold pressure on my left hand. Lisa was handing me a Mountain Dew.]

Level 4: Pentagram

The passages form a five-pointed star surrounded by a circular corridor. This area of the complex has no obvious purpose other than to make it slightly more badass and reinforce the popular association between fantasy gaming and satanism. Observant adventurers will become aware that your grandmother is an insane bitch and even after a year your mother is not any closer to getting her head together, and

354 · AUSTIN GROSSMAN

the later you can stay at Darren's each night the better the chance they'll all be asleep when you get home, or maybe they'll be dead or they'll forget you ever existed (does that happen?) and you can live at Darren's forever or maybe get your own place.

Another skeletal body is here, lying facedown at an angle where a point joins the circle. The bones lie across a charred patch on the stone. Pren-Dahr kneels down and picks out a pair of modern spectacles and a short length of wire. There is no weapon. Deep in the angle of the jaw you see what is either a small round pebble or a cyanide capsule.

Level 5: The Guardian Figure

The shape of this level forms a crude representation of a human body (Adric?), similar to the Long Man of Wilmington or other hillside chalk figures. It is very evidently male. It makes you wish someone would stop fucking around; truly, this dungeon holds great evil.

Level 6: The Lady

This level has been built in the stylized image of a female face, architectural verisimilitude having been abandoned several levels ago.

The first body you find here lies on its side, with a long dagger resting between its third and fourth ribs; it displays tallness and slightly elongated fingers, toes, and cranium. Fifteen feet farther down the corridor, a skeletal hand still holds the hilt of a long black sword, the NightShard (artifact longsword; +5 to hit and damage; 4% chance of Soul Drain; wielder's Altruism, Loyalty, and Mercy scores immediately fall to zero). The hand evidently once belonged to the human female whose skeletal remains lie on the very top step of the stairway down to the next, penultimate stage.

Ley-R4 may pick up the NightShard if it is found. She now has the option of remaining in Endoria, walking away from her job as empress of the galaxy, and returning to terrorizing the unjust from horseback. If she does, she will relinquish her ceremonial blade and the title to Brendan Blackstar, the true king of Endoria.

Level 7: A Giant Penis

Here, the walls form what we just might as well say is an image of an erect phallus. The three disconnected rooms to the west of the main complex were originally thought to be sealed burial halls. It is time for archaeological scholars to admit they represent airborne ejaculate.

"Oh, Jesus," said Lisa. "Really?"

"What, you never saw that?" said Darren.

"Yes, but I deleted it."

"I wondered if that was you. Yeah, I put it back."

"Did you ever think that maybe that was why we got a B plus? Which is why I wasn't class valedictorian?"

"Did you ever think of getting over it?"

There is one body, that of a large human male dressed in scraps of denim and a canary-yellow shirt emblazoned with the words SOUL ASYLUM. Nearby you find the remains of a fiberglass skateboard, its rear wheels sheared off. Brendan lingers, baffled at his doppelgänger's choice of weapon.

Level 8: The Antechamber

From the base of the stairway a single corridor zigs and zags, then terminates in a large room, one hundred feet square, empty except for a low square altar built of stone. The only other item in the room is a skeleton wearing the gray cotton fatigues of a senior intelligence officer of the Soviet Union. It rests, propped against one wall, in a sitting position, hand extended toward the altar.

You always thought this was the bottom level, but the altar has been pushed to one side to reveal a set of stairs leading down. You check the tracking device: Mournblade is exactly five meters below you.

Level 9: Adric's Tomb

The final level is a network of natural stone caves plainly much older than the rest of the complex. You see here the skeleton of an enormous beast, half hound and half dragon, a long row of vertebrae encircling the room.

356 · AUSTIN GROSSMAN

At the rear of the room is an archway built of porphyry, which any competent mage or an associate producer who could stand to broaden his horizons a little will recollect is the primary component of any portal spell. It is sad that they know this, but they are correct — any player present will see through it to another place entirely, a random location in space and time.

Here you see Adric himself, seated on a black throne and dressed in shreds of chain mail. His skin is pearl white and his mouth sneers, even in his sleep. He is slender and beautiful and tragic, just as he is on his book covers. He is, without any doubt, what Simon looks like in his deepest, most private fantasies. At the sound of a living being on his threshold, he begins to awaken. His eyes, when opened, are green and soulful. The Artifact-class greatsword Mournblade is visible on his person.

This is the end of the Endorian Anomaly module. Any further material included is of abstract interest only. It is here that the players will die, regardless of whether they rule the galaxy and can't believe they are being knocked off by a pissant artifact on a backwater planet in an unfashionable genre.

"So is this it?" I asked.

"Okay, okay, I get it," Lisa said. "Simon said he'd put it in a place no one would ever find, but I didn't understand the scheme exactly. The room runs simulated all the time, and sometimes Adric gets activated and wanders out into the world. Or an amper picks it up, maybe. So the sword is out there, and then very occasionally the wielder runs into somebody and kills them. Or the wielder dies and another creature picks it up and the rampage starts."

"Why's it happening more often, though?" I said.

"Simon wanted it to, I guess. He had some theory about the year 2000, how there should be some big computer failure. Probably it just checks the system clock, spawns wandering ampers more often."

There was a scuffling sound in the corridor outside Adric's chamber. I whipped the camera around to see what could only be a Dreadwarg, the terror of the First Age. A Dreadwarg looked like a standard wolf, but, like that of Mournblade, its palette was wiped to black.

I was at the controls. Select all Heroes, target the warg as an enemy, attack! Pren-Dahr's blaster didn't seem to damage it. Ley-R4 cut at it with the NightShard, but for some reason it rushed past her to attack Brendan Blackstar. It took 75 percent of his hit points in one bite, but Brendan's riposte with the Martian blade cut it in half. A gimmicky black wolf had almost managed to kill the rulers of the galaxy. A howling noise came from the passageway outside. Perhaps they could smell the royalty in Brendan Blackstar's blood.

I paged through the Heroes' inventory for the first time. Nothing much, only their few weapons and useless imperial money, until I reached the weaponless Loraq, who turned out to be craftier than the rest. He possessed a number of odd items, some of which he spawned with, some of which he had looted from corpses as we passed. A Soviet-era codebook, the Tentacle of the Over-Mind (purpose unknown), and an antimatter grenade, far more powerful than anything these Iron Age fucks had ever considered.

Purely from the point of view of gameplay, it was my option. I had him start the timer on the grenade, proceed into the corridor, and shut the door behind him. The blast was well in excess of its targets' toughness. After a thousand millennia of shame, Loraq had found a way to give his life for his true king.

We turned to see Adric shambling toward the portal, as he had been doing for millennia. As we watched, Adric passed into the world of American finance to kill and despoil. When he passed through, a metal door closed behind him and locked. I had the Heroes try to break it with the blaster, the NightShard, and the Martian vibro-sword, all without result. On the far side, Adric would kill until the sword consumed him, and then a luckless character would pick the sword up and wield it after him, until at last the sword ran out of wielders and tele-ported back. In a city as dense as the AstroTrade level, the carnage would be indefinite, a building wave of panic and fiduciary bloodletting.

"Adamantium," said Matt, looking over my shoulder. "Nothing cuts it."

"C'mon, nothing? That's bullshit. This is a plasma gun or some shit."

"It's just a rule — there had to be a thing nothing could cut so we could keep players from breaking out of the world entirely."

"Can't the thief pick the lock?" Don said. He pointed at Prendar. "Isn't that a thief?"

"Uh, right," said Matt. I set Prendar to working on it. It took about five seconds. It was a hard lock, but Prendar had been a thief since back when doors were made of stone.

"Weren't you going to cut the thief class?" said Matt. "Something about their being useless."

The door opened, and, as Brennan, I went through. Brennan wasn't dressed for it, but he had a sword from the future and melee skills superior to anyone except maybe Adric himself. The door slammed shut behind me. I wouldn't see the others again.

Beyond the portal, it was spring in Endoria the Electronic Trading Platform. I stood in a city square next to a dry fountain. It had rained recently, and there were puddles among the cobblestones, puddles that reflected the sky beautifully. Lisa had written a really, really pretty renderer.

Adric stood there, looking around for souls to drain. Around us, trading continued; with their combat instincts suppressed, the innocent dwarves, gnomes, humans, and elves would go on with their speculation and arbitrage until they picked up the cursed sword. The stage was silent. Brennan faced Adric. The vibro-sword buzzed; the black runes-word moaned.

Darren got up to take my place. "I should probably do this part."

"Let Russell do it," Matt said. "We kinda tweaked things after you left. Added a couple of things."

"Okay," Darren said, but he sounded dubious, and I decided Matt was right.

One way to think about game design is in terms of verbs — what is the array of verbs available to a player? Obviously, there must be fighting, because otherwise (at least for many of us) why play a video game? But what verbs does that involve, exactly? Matt and I considered the previous game's system too simplistic, too dumbed-down, and Don agreed. We set to work to change that.

First, we prototyped the combat system as a card game using 3-by-5-inch note cards to stand for actions. A player could choose to attack high, attack low, block high, or block low. Once the cards were turned over, a high attack against low block, or low attack against high block, dealt the most damage. Simultaneous attacks resulted in less damage. Each player had a limited supply of hit cards and block cards, so by counting cards, players could guess at each other's strategies. Not terrible. We demonstrated it at the next company-wide meeting, to modest applause.

It wasn't enough. I'd had a semester of saber fencing in college and had a green belt in hapkido. Matt had an extensive knowledge of the writings of Robert E. Howard, Fritz Leiber, Roger Zelazny, and Michael Moorcock, plus he had seen all the Highlander films in their original theatrical release. We agreed that a really good sword fight wasn't about just choosing one of four options. We needed panache, daring, and creativity. We needed more note cards.

We began to build out the system. What if a strike that directly followed a successful block did extra damage? Now the simple matching game acquired a new rhythm, and just a tiny element of drama. Thrust, parry...riposte!

It wasn't enough. Encouraged, we did what any self-respecting game designer does: we added a gratuitous number of features. Forehand and backhand attacks; long-range thrusts; sweeping cuts. Directional parries, first . the basics — tierce (right), quarte (left), and quinte (upward)—then prime, seconde, sixte, septime, octave. Corps-à-corps! En garde! We shared the conviction that a simulated universe that could not express these things was not a universe worth simulating.

Still, it wasn't nearly enough. The minutiae of footing and weight changes, obviously. Stances, hit location, armor, unarmed combat, different materials. Flint ax heads shattered against metal plate. Bronze weapons could be hacked to pieces by carbon steel blades.

After ten weeks of work, we could play out an altercation between an eighteenth-century French mercenary with a short sword and buckler (a saucer-size shield with a pointed spike—as Eskimo language is to snow, so archaic English is to "metal objects designed to cause harm") and a Roman legionnaire from the age of Marius, with his gladius, scutum, and pilum. *Vae victis!*

I felt the three of them watching while I tried to work through the variables in my head. I would play Brennan, a tall muscular human with high skills across the board, but he favored a heavy blade. To his disadvantage, he now held a delicate saber, light and whippy, with a fiftieth-century keenness. My opponent, Adric, I judged to be a maxed-out Scottish greatsword artist wielding a four-foot blade.

I had a great deal of speed, but he had the longer reach. I was unarmored; he wore chain mail and a fancy helmet that flattered his cheekbones. In addition, Adric was a First Age Correllean noble, which involved a long string of modifiers I didn't know about, although I could assume it meant he was a badass. He suffered from a long-term Byronic depression, although that might not translate tactically.

Adric advanced forward without ceremony, the massive sword held out in front of him, vertical and tilted slightly back, just as it was in the Renaissance fencing manual we'd taken the moves from. When the blade descended, its moaning dopplered up and down the scale. He made three looping overhand strikes that I backed way the hell away from, because I wasn't sure the cursed sword could be blocked at all. But I had to at least try. I blocked the third one; when the blades touched, the sound suggested a dying god impacting an electrified high-tension wire. Adric's pale horse face kept its signature expression — the weary, sophisticated sneer of a man who has forgotten how many souls he's taken, who pities the world that must contain him.

I ran at him and struck at him over and over, fast and sloppy, thinking to outpace him, but his defense seemed immaculate. He waited for a break, then stepped behind himself and pivoted all the way around for a low backhand. I fumbled at the keyboard for a split second, no idea what was happening, and wound up blocking in a crouch. Then Brennan wouldn't stop crouching and shuffled around parrying until I realized the Caps Lock key was down. I wished Darren weren't watching.

I made mistakes, but I knew the system, or I knew what to try. I slithered in and cut up Adric's forearms. I ducked under sweeping cuts and jabbed for the belly. I started to remember the little tics of posture that led into his special attacks, and anticipated them. I nicked him a few times — his blade was unquestionably slower — but he had the hit points of a bull elephant. He had a guard stance that made him almost unhittable, a stance I let him take until I realized he was regenerating hit points. I switched stances, too, to a slightly precious-looking saber stance, body sideways, left arm tucked behind the back. I nipped hit points off of him. Brennan could do a lot of things. He had nifty forward roll and upward thrust. He had a countercut off a parry in quarte that popped back in the opponent's face. But Adric had responses ready. I circled around Adric, and he sidestepped to cut me off. It was hard to commit to a real attack when I couldn't risk taking even a minor cut. I had the fleeting thought that in all this, some part of me was learning a lot about game design.

Fighting games, Jared once explained to me, are about yomi. Yomi is a concept popular with game theorists, tournament-level fighting-game players, and people who like having Japanese words to throw at you. It means, literally, "reading." Figuratively, it means understanding your own and your opponent's options in a given situation while simultaneously knowing that your opponent knows those things, too, and then trying to predict what he will do, knowing that he may know what your prediction might be and change his mind accordingly.

Sword fighting has its yomi. There is a thing fencers call the tactical wheel — the strategic laws that decree that each attack has its own specific countermove, the way scissors beats paper, paper beats rock, rock beats scissors. Our combat system was no different, it just came with a great many more options and more ways to predict the outcome. Strong cuts committed a fighter's weight forward; countermoves took advantage. Certain maneuvers had to be set up by a specific prerequisite move. Some attacks required a recovery phase, leaving the combatant tragically vulnerable. Every choice set up the next set of possibilities on both sides. It was a complex decision tree that both fighters were constantly trying to think their way down, down to the place where their opponent didn't have a winning option.

Adric — I couldn't guess how — fought as if he knew his advantage. I gave him false openings and he didn't move. He fought as if he knew he was fighting a coward. He feinted and jabbed and played with me as I backed up, practically chasing me around the square. I really did look like a coward. I very possibly was a coward.

"Don't forget, if he can't recharge he's going to die," said Matt. I tried waiting for Mournblade to drain him, but he smoothly decapitated a passing dwarf. It flashed white, which meant another soul gone to power Mournblade's wielder, who was now back at full strength. He could do that forever.

Lisa said, "Just kill everybody in the city and then he can't recharge."

"Isn't that a little counterproductive?" I said. "Plus, Brennan can't fight indefinitely. Not since we added the fatigue model." And Brennan was already getting tired, fighting two-handed now. I was getting a little tired, too. "And stop helping me," I added.

Brennan started to do his "I am very fatigued" animations. He panted; he staggered when blocked. I tried to rest him by getting out of range; when I did, he'd lower his sword and let the point drag on the ground.

Meanwhile, I was trying to yomi Simon's own AI, even though everyone knew Simon was smarter than I was and had always been smarter than I was. I could feel—with an inner certainty—that everyone wanted me to give somebody else the controls. Darren, a world-class player who would already have taken Adric's head off. Matt, who knew the system and the entire world better than I did. Lisa, who understood what was happening and why, and whose nerve wasn't going to break.

But I knew that Adric would live forever, a walking curse on the world. That was his story. He was a loner, an outcast, an eternal, pretentiously sad fantasy douche bag. Simon had already written his story for him and given him the AI and the devastating magic sword to make it happen. There had to be a way out of that story. That's why we had video games, which were an enormous amount of trouble to make. So you could do that.

I wasn't going to win inside the tactical wheel. Screw the tactical wheel. Endorian Anomaly enabled all the game functions, all that code kicking around. I could probably play golf in there if I wanted to, not that that seemed productive. I backed up and watched Adric advance to keep me in range.

Then I turned and ran, sheathing my sword as I went. Probably people were yelling at me, but I didn't listen. Why should I? The sun had almost set, turning the puddles gold and orange and purple. It seemed just right, the last moments of a warm evening before it gets chilly and you think of going home. It was, in fact, an excellent moment to shred.

Yes, my board had no back wheels, but not all the moves needed them. In point of fact, the lack of back wheels just made me more hardcore. I reached the fountain and tried a little minigrind, balancing on the board as it slid along the rim. It worked just fine. In fact, the camera even knew to run a 180-degree pan to show off the move—which, incidentally, revealed that Adric was closing in, runesword ready to strike. Brennan landed and transitioned, prepping the move I had in mind. It was one of those moments when you're good enough to forget there's even a controller. I got into the handplant, feet up, one hand on the rim, and the point of view revolved around me to catch the setting sun, a beautifully thoughtful piece of programming. I triggered the second stage, and Brendan whipped his sword out with his free hand. As he came down, he swept it in a showy circle. It even did the sound effect, a surf-guitar sting and a deep-voiced, heavy-reverb roar as the true king struck home.

ENDORIAN ANOMALY: GAME MASTER'S SUPPLEMENT

1) If Adric is killed and the game is saved out, a new version of the world-state will be exported and further playthroughs of all WAFFLE games will include the Tomb of Destiny in its revised state. In games that import this state, Adric will no longer be a character in the Black Arts universe, and Mournblade will no longer menace this or any other world, ever (note that these effects may be reversed by the use of the Wish, Limited Wish, or Resurrection spell. We're just saying).

2) Adric's inventory contains the following items, available upon his death:

   a) An antique suit of chain mail

   b) 495,000 gold pieces, contained in (one assumes) a Bag of Holding

   c) The First Age Artifact-class greatsword named Mournblade (+10 to hit, ignores dodge attempts, force fields, intangibility, and other varieties of magical, technological, and psychic protection. Successful hit destroys target creature or object with no possibility of resurrection; Mournblade's wielder receives bonus hit points equal to the target's at time of death. Wielder invulnerable to sorceries, enchantments, glamours, conjurations. Hit points decrement by 5% each minute held. Once wielded, Mournblade cannot be dropped).

d) A crown, but you find it is not the one you expected, not the Crown of Winter at all. It's the Crown of Summer. It is, quite simply, the last crown anybody in Endoria really, truly cared about, but you forgot that, didn't you? What it felt like when the long summer ended and you had to go home to the life you planned for yourself, the one that didn't work out the way you planned. But for a brief moment the crown existed, to honor the King of KidBits Camp for Young Achievers for 1983. ["He wanted you to have it," Lisa whispered to Darren. "He really did."]

e) Finally, there is the secret of the ultimate game, inscribed on a series of crumbling scrolls in a language that is no longer well understood. But partial translations suggest that the secret of the ultimate game is that you're already in the ultimate game, all the time, forever. That the secret of the ultimate game is that the ultimate game is a paradox, because there's no way to play a game without knowing you're playing it. That games are already awesome, or else why are we making such a fuss? That the secret of the ultimate game is that at the very least we're going to have voice recognition and 3-D body-sensing interfaces and augmented reality and generated narrative and, really, much better writing, and that it would help if people would just notice that it's going to be pretty fucking great. And the secret is also that you've always been fatally slow on the uptake, and that you're sitting with a girl who is smarter than you and almost anyone else you've ever met, and that she's spent eighteen months in your company without completely despising you, and in fact was willing to stay up till four in the morning with you watching you play a video game, and that it would help to be a little more relaxed about things.

Or the secret is that in the winters when the snow fell deep enough, ten-year-old Simon used to take his family's one battered pair of cross-country skis from the chilly, oil-smelling basement, painstakingly wedge his feet into the plastic boots, clamp them in, and set off awkwardly up the snow-covered street, sweating already, breathing hard into the scarf wrapped across his face, pom-pom of his blue-and-gray wool hat swaying. The snow was still falling, still only two or three inches deep, and the skis grated on asphalt every few yards. He would turn off the road along a path into the woods, and scrubby maple and birch would give in to tall white pines, and he'd reach the thin strip of cleared, undeveloped land along the power lines. They marched in a line across his neighborhood, through forests and behind backyards, the tallest structures for miles, arrow-straight, and then across the highway and north to parts unknown, Canada and then the North Pole, a dimly imagined winter country of villages and wolves that he'd envision until the snow turned blue and pink in the sunset — whatever was at the end of the line of metal pylons and humming crackling wire. A few years later, he'd be coming back with Darren and his older brother and his friends to learn to get drunk on summer nights and, as long as the weather held, in fall. And on some nights Simon learned to code in his garage, but on others they laughed and threw empty green and brown beer bottles at the rocks. Even when they were ten the halos of sparkling brown glass were already a constant feature, spreading out from those same rocks among the pine needles and dead grass, as if they had been deposited there by the glaciers as they melted rather than left there by the previous wave of Rush-shirted teenage boys and the ones before that, all having the same conversations about friendship and music and the ultimate game in whatever form it takes and their asshole parents and all other matters of consequence that lie between the Second Age and the Fourth and beyond, all things then known to elves and men.

Chapter Fifty-One

I came in the Saturday after we shipped to look at the game we had finished, right at the last possible instant. No matter what happened, I wanted to see what we had before they took it away.

WAFFLE was so legally radioactive at that point that we'd be releasing it as shareware — all the tools, all the source code, a game construction anthology for the ages. Focus had, sadly, become the prey of Bain Capital, which managed to make a modest profit from its assets, either because of the unexpected value of cask-aged intellectual property or its superfluity of high-end office chairs.

Matt, Don, and I were forming Magus Games, a start-up stealth-funded by Vorpal, now flush with cash. The film rights for *Clandestine* had sold for more than what I would have believed possible. Hollywood had decided to start taking notice of video games; I could almost believe we were beginning to scare them a little. Darren immediately packed up and moved to a house in Pasadena, and was reportedly "in meetings." Lisa walked into an MIT doctoral program after a lengthy interview and presentation of her work, and the discovery that very few people could keep up with her in conversation.

For now, I just wanted to look around with the virtual camera and see what this place was. I let it spawn in at a random location. Take me anywhere, I thought. I don't care.

We wound up on a hillside far out on the eastern continent. A half-elven prospector looked out in the blue early dawn over a misty virtual pine forest. Water condensed in tiny drops on his leather armor. I could see him breathing as his standing-still animation cycled; I could almost feel the moist air in his hybrid half-faerie lungs, his narrow eyes watching the pixelated trees in the far distance.

This was Simon's vision brought to life as truly as I could make it. Display technology didn't matter; who cared how many polygons the trees had? I could feel this world breathing.

I drew the camera back, kicked the time scale up, and watched days and then years pass. Smoke ascended from a solitary woodcutters' camp in the ocean of pine. Every few turns there was a low-percentage chance the forest would spread out and become fields, or die and become desert, or a tribal people would settle there and form a village.

Clouds gathered, herded around by a rough climate model, towering over plains in jagged cubical stacks, shadowing castles and armies on the march, piling up against the mountain ranges that ribbed the continents. Rivers and streams trickled from the mountains' heads and shoulders, through bumps and ridges, down into the plains. There was no geologic time per se, but we registered a few types of terrain-altering events, the rare earthquake or volcano, the once-in-an-era feat of earth-shaking high magic or divine retribution.

Simple probability pyramids governed the world's production. Fields generated crops in appropriate proportions, more staples and fewer luxury goods; regional imbalances generated trade. Forests generated x amount of game, and $x/10$ predators, and then rarer exotic or magical fauna, populations swelling and shrinking by Malthusian logic. The seas generated fish and whales and, in the depths, the leviathan and kraken and the odd stranger things, ancient things that belonged on other planes but found their way into the deep ocean. When a dragon, our apex predator, appeared, it automatically aggregated treasure and laid waste to the surrounding countryside. (It is a privilege of my profession to know where dragons come from.)

In our toy economy, all the world's wealth started at the top of the supply chain, as gold and wood and leather and food. Dwarves and humans dug for minerals in the deep folds of the irregular crust, and so jewels and metals and rarer things propagated along caravan routes and clogged in the cities then radiated outward as crafted goods. X number of ingots became a dagger or a sword, so many hides became a cloak or a suit of leather armor, and so forth for all the myriad daggers and bridles and lanterns and helmets and vestments and statuettes and bowstrings and scroll cases that equip and ornament the world.

The supply chain had a top, and it also had a bottom — a benthic sludge of used boots, misfired arrows, torn surcoats, sunken ships, blunted weapons, and burned siege engines that simply vanished from the simulation after a set time. The economy worked, but we were long past understanding why, because every employee who had ever touched the system — which was almost every designer or programmer in the building — had added their own little algorithmic tweak to it, and by now the price-setting algorithm had fifty different half-remembered undergraduate versions of Keynes or Weber or Adams feeding into it. Add to this the nonlinear fluctuations born from player behavior — tweaks to the magic system revalued every magical herb and powder, and every infusion of treasure every adventuring party hauled up from the depths, to upset the markets like a diver cannon-balling into a neighborhood pool. It still worked suspiciously well. In fact, I suspected that large sections of the economics programming were a front, and that Lisa ran it all from a little console, four or five sliders controlling pricing and production as though it were a tiny Soviet-style command economy.

Cities and settlements held together in fanciful political congregations — the lands sparkled with barons and dukes, viziers and khans, elven kings, orcish warlords, dwarven magnates, tribal elders, Lich Kings, robber-chieftains, matriarchs, regents, god-emperors, and petty lordlings who ruled a stockade and five or six men-at-arms, an underground convocation of thieves.

After much overpromising and backtracking from Toby, we agreed that yes, there would be a day-night cycle running at eight to one, roughly three hours per twenty-four-hour day. Things were a little hacked at night, colors were wrong and nothing shadowed correctly, but there were three moons and they were beautiful.

Elves (high / wood / dark) lived in dark forests or fanciful spun-sugar Bavarian castles. Dwarves lived in caves and forged things. Orcs lived their economically ineffectual tribal lives in the wastelands. Humans did their bit, filled up the map with farmers and thieves and priests and castles. Lizard men lived in deserts and swamps and carried on their biologically doubtful lives in isolation. Exotic horrors lurked in the darkness. Daemons, devils, spirits, giants, benevolent jinn. Extraplanar magi and ethereal predators that intruded into the world from extraplanar civilizations, through gates or summonings or natural rifts. We'd get to these other worlds in fourth- or fifth- or sixth-edition rules. The toughest adventurers would still be killed — by undetectable traps, by unpredictable monster types, or, if necessary, by mobs or armies of midlevel monsters. There would be epic deaths, throw-the-controller-across-the-room deaths. Where necessary, there were gods.

History progressed, blissfully free of historical or political or technological progress. Kingdoms rose and fell over the millennia, but there was no trend toward democracy, no Enlightenment, no industrial modernity, no Luther, no Hume, and absolutely, definitely, no gunpowder. No *Principia Mathematica* or Declaration of Independence. We held certain truths to be self-evident, but those truths were that elves hate orcs and wizards can't wear metal armor.

What we had instead was world history frozen in an eternal thirteenth century — or, rather, something more complicated than that. It's more as if history had paused forever during eighth-grade study hall, a Thursday afternoon free period stretched out into countless millennia, where knights and castles mix in with fantasy novels, fairy tales, vague orientalist fantasies, Arthurian kitsch, Norse mythology, *Star Wars,*

Paradise Lost, medieval travelogues, heavy metal album covers, and dimly remembered historical trivia.

I felt it then, Simon's victory. We could indeed make a world. Chess is a game with simple rules and pieces, a small sixty-four-space board, but there are more possible chess games than there are atoms in the universe.

But in the middle of all this, there's you, a person playing a video game. For fun, for a challenge, for reasons hard to understand. Some of it is just cognitive burnoff, something to take up the mental cycles you aren't using and, frankly, desperately don't want, because a lot of it is just compressed, impacted sadness.

But there is only so much you can do about it. Your character is always going to be you; you can never ever quite erase that sliver of you-awareness. In the whole mechanized game world, you are a unique object, like a moving hole that's full of emotion and agency and experience and memory unlike anything else in this made-up universe.

You can't not be around it; it's you, even though "you" might be the last person you want to be around. But when the game, the second-person engine, starts again, it tells you about yourself, and maybe this time you will get it to tell you the thing you've been waiting to hear, the mighty storytelling hack that puts it all together. You're lost in a forest, surrounded by mist-shrouded mountains. You're in command of a thousand gleaming starships in a conflict spanning the galaxy. You and the machine, like Scheherazade and her king mixed up together in one, trying over and over to tell yourself your own story, and get it right.

CODA: RULES SUPPLEMENTAL
Introduction

Simon's original paper-and-pencil role-playing game notes were left in his old bedroom until his mother sold the house, at which point they went into storage for a few years and wound up in the Black Arts office. I'd seen them long ago, sat reading them sometimes during sophomore year, waiting for the school bus, waiting for the long afternoons to end and my dad to get home. I read and read them, but we never ended up playing them even though I'd gone through all the dungeons in my head.

There are two main rule books. There's the one with the red dragon on the cover, a picture of a dragon rearing up and breathing fire down on an armored figure whose upraised shield divides the stream of flame. REALMS OF GOLD is written across it in gold letters. And then there's the Creatures and Items catalog, the cover of which depicts men and women in medieval dress posed stiffly around an overflowing treasure chest, their eyes wide in greed and wonder. There were also many, many supplements and photocopied articles, and the maps to all the dungeons and lands, with accompanying descriptions.

You got the books for Christmas when the game was first popular, and maybe your parents didn't know what to get for you, but heard this was a good gift. The sample character sheets are marked up and erased in a bunch of different places, with joke character names written in and doodles in the margins.

(It's hard to explain to Lisa how some of this matters; it helps that she used to play bridge a lot. Also that she is a good listener.)

Basic Rules

It's a game, but there's no score and no winner, and too many rules to remember properly. There are six terrain types: Town, Forest, Ocean,

Mountain, Ruin, and Sky. There are five public character attributes: Fortitude, Acumen, Nimbleness, Resolve, and Folly; these cards go faceup. There is also a sixth secret attribute that is different for everyone. It goes on a card you hold facedown on the table.

Town Zone

The way it starts is that you meet an ancient traveler in a village inn who tells you a tale about a lost ruin deep in a mountain fastness; beneath it lies the gateway to a fantastic underground empire containing fabulous riches. At its very center is a treasure of untold value.

There are four of you. You listen, spellbound. Things aren't going well at home, not for any of you. Barbarians sacked your village; your master was killed before your eyes; you were jilted by a lover. A usurper stole your rightful kingdom, and you stood around and let it happen. Somewhere out in the world there's got to be a fix for this. You've got to find it.

As you exit the Town Zone, there is a rush of feeling, a mixture of relief and regret as you leave your backstory behind.

Forest Zone

On the map, the Forest hexes are cool and green, with darker green trees, like lumpy pillows, sketched in. The elf ignores movement penalties here, but it's not like he cares—according to the manual, elves live for a thousand years.

As you wander the trails, there's too much time to think. About whether the old man was lying, about why you didn't just do something about that fucking usurper. It was all you had to do, deal with one guy in a velvet chemise. Why couldn't you have been just a little bit brave? You imagine pushing him off a balcony; the crowd below cheers, the king and queen smile approvingly. You walk a little faster—can't we get this over with?—and the track of an ancient road leads through miles of underbrush to a break in an ancient stone wall. There you make camp, crouching in the dimness like coders from Lisa's graphics team.

You wonder who built the wall — dwarves or orcs or humans. Certainly not adventurers like you, who pause at places like this to search them for treasure but who never figure out how to stop and build a city. People like you only hoard the spoils, dividing it among sons who fight among themselves then ride off into the wild. Nobody learns to weave or make bricks or anything; there are just men in furs on horseback, bows and arrows and swords, and at night it's cooking fires to the horizon.

Ruin Zone

A nameless, deserted fortress stands alone, deep in the wilderness. Once upon a time, this was the center of a great kingdom surrounded by a forest without end, a vast swath of Town terrain that stretched the length of the map until, long ago, it was annihilated in a strategic-scale campaign. When the kingdom fell, its terrain type modified to Ruin; one day, centuries from now, it will change to Forest.

(Ruins can contain multiple specialized terrain types: Cavern, Corridor, Debris-Strewn Corridor, Door [Standard and Secret], Room [Large and Small], Stairway, Pit, Special.)

A) Dungeon

Under a wooden trapdoor in the courtyard, stone stairs lead downward into a narrow space smelling of earth. At first, tree roots poke through the ceiling and stray sunbeams come in through the cracks, but after a few hexes, sunlight and the sounds of the forest disappear.

Skeletons hang from manacles in rooms and corridors of damp stones coated with algae. Goblins, giant rats, vicious animals roam the otherwise empty halls. A false wall at the back of a cell opens to reveal stairs leading still farther down.

(There's a picture showing the ruined hall; Lisa says the artist could stand to learn a little about stonework, not to mention where to place load-bearing elements.)

B) Tombs of Terror

Were these built at a later date? The workmanship is much finer, although poison spikes and mocking inscriptions ward explorers off from the graves of the honored, eternally pissed-off dead. In the Tomb of Lorac, there is a cache of gold and precious magic objects surrounded by the bones of luckless adventurers who came before you.

This is as far as the old kingdom builders ever dug, but a crack in the tomb wall gives access to the Glowing Caverns.

C) Glowing Caverns

A rough landscape of towering stalagmites and luminous, overgrown fungi. Colored crystals protrude from the cavern walls. A pool of shimmering rainbow liquid yields random magical effects—invisibility, telepathic powers, hallucinations.

Your pouches are now full of rubies and emeralds dug from the walls; you are all wealthy enough to live comfortably for the rest of your lives. You think fleetingly of going back, but no one mentions it aloud. Why would you? This is the best part of your lives—the four of you together against the darkness and the unknown, a quest that could last forever without your ever wanting to leave this basement.

D) Underground Stream

The distant sound of running water beckons you forward to the place where a swiftly running stream of black water has carved a channel in the stone that leads downward into the earth, through a series of narrow tunnels and larger chambers. An Ancient Giant Cave Pike swims just beneath the surface. Farther down, the stream becomes a river that drops then drops again, then cascades down into a cavern so vast you cannot see the far wall. A fresh breeze blows through it, smelling of salt water and carrying the sound of...crowds?

E) Goblin City

The Goblin City has always lain beneath the kingdom and was perhaps the secret agent of its downfall. You follow the river as it winds through crowded streets and markets to a dock where a skiff is moored, and the party stops to camp by the dark waves of a mysterious underground sea.

Probably everyone's pretty tired by now, and outside the sun has long since gone down and you're going to need a lift home, or else you're going to have to ride your bike a long way on a cold March night, your back wheel sliding on wet leaves as you pass the lit windows of houses and wonder what it's like, how you'd be different if you lived there. You're way too much inside your head, and other people notice, but you won't realize that for another ten years, maybe more, and by then maybe it's too late.

F) Subterranean Ocean

As you cross the subterranean ocean, shadowy, enormous forms move beneath your boat, lit from below by phosphorescent algae. Nautical movement rules apply.

G) Maze of Wonder

Those who journey to the far shores discover the gemlike Maze of Wonder, where corridors bend at impossible angles and the rules of space and time become less certain. The monster population becomes more exotic—outré, whimsically lethal inventions out of rare rules supplements. Lorac himself lurks here, now an undead being of near-infinite power. He warns you to go back. He, too, was once a prince and a twenty-sixth-level magus, until he opened a portal to the Burning Worlds and was lost.

Here and there portals lead off into other dimensions, where you can fight angels or mutants or space aliens or Nazis for as long as you want to, but the quest remains here.

H) The Base of the World

Few indeed have seen the silent chamber at the base of the world, which is littered with the most flagrantly unfair traps available—soul traps, contact poison, portals leading into doorless chambers filled with water.

Each of you will find a hidden treasure inside, and it's the one thing you always wanted. The royal signet ring; your master's sword; a lock of hair; a seed to regrow the forests of your homeland. But now that you think about it, you're not sure if your origin makes sense anymore. Has it been weeks since you left home, or months? Years? It's getting late and everybody's tired and you can barely remember what was said at the start that meant so much, about a girl in a muddy village or a third-level barbarian chief who threatened your tribe. Seems like inventory could just about buy that town by now.

Town Zone (2)

But when you get home, you find that everything has changed. While you were away the town grew into a sprawling city. They built walls around it, then the city expanded past them. It sent roads into the outlying fields, past new farms and over the borders to other lands. The old king died, and in your absence the false prince took the throne. He sent the kingdom deeper and deeper into debt until he in turn was replaced by a council of merchants, and that's it for the royal family.

More time passes, and the palace you grew up in is now a museum. The forest is cut down; the city spreads along the river to the sea and establishes a port where ships come from all over the world and bear people away to countries you've never heard of. The ships bring back textiles and jewelry and gunpowder. New character classes appear, some playable and some not, artisans and musketeers and gangsters and astronomers, which are explained in still more supplemental rule books, *Realms of Gold: Age of Sail* and *Realms of Gold: Sages and Scientists*. You pack away the lock of hair, the signet ring, and the sword. All that stuff was long ago.

Decades go by, faster and faster, and now, of the original party, only the elf survives. He has aged only fractionally through the years, and his accumulated experience points have taken him far off any of the level charts. He spends the day lounging in cafés on the cobblestone street where the old tavern used to stand; he pays his rent with jewels and odd coins that ring strangely against the table. He owns a horse and carriage and half a dozen houses in town. He's an eccentric guest at dinner parties, the subject of society talk and gossip. You—and somehow it's still you — can invest in merchant caravans for profit. You can finance other adventurers if you want, for a share in the returns. You never marry or have children. You collect old books, a few of which make reference to your early adventures, but only as legends.

One day a hot air balloon passes over the city. It only costs five gold pieces to ride in it. An amusement for gentlemen and ladies of quality!

Sky Zone

You ascend. The Sky Zone was never meant to be playable, so now what? You scrounge up a Xeroxed page and a half of sketchy guidelines. Rules for movement, suggested cloud maps, lightning-strike table.

It's raining hard outside the office this evening, too, there's lightning here, too, and past nine o'clock it doesn't feel like work. You're hanging out late in the break room with Matt and Lisa and you're trying to steal soda from the machine using adhesive tape, which doesn't work but is hilarious.

The Sky Zone contains air elementals, floating eyes, yellow lights, storm giants. Giant Erl from the Legendary Adventures supplement in a cloud castle. All areas of the Town, Forest, and Ruin maps are accessible. You find portals to all the elemental planes. You may reach the Starlight and Ethereal Zones from here.

You order new rules through the mail from an address in the back of *Dragon* magazine, rules not published officially, to describe galleons that sail between planets and starfish with arms that span continents. You resolve to reach the center of the galaxy, the center of everything, if you can, and that's where the game ends, now not a game at all but a campaign that's going to go on as long as your life does, no matter what you think of me now, because we are graduating from high school, from college, getting married, and now it's time for all cards to be turned over, all items identified, all secret areas revealed. And now at last maybe we can score this thing properly.

A Selective Time Line of Video Game History

1971: The *Chainmail* tabletop strategy game is modified to include rules for person-to-person combat, rules that would ultimately be used in *Dungeons & Dragons*.

1975: *Adventure* (a.k.a. *Colossal Cave Adventure*)—the first text-based computer adventure game—is created by Willie Crowther and Don Woods.

1979: The first Choose Your Own Adventure book—*The Cave of Time,* by Edward Packard—is published. *Adventure* for Atari 2600, containing the prototypical video game Easter egg, a secret room showing the name of its creator, is released.

1982: The hit single "Pac-Man Fever" by novelty act Buckner and Garcia reaches number 9 on the *Billboard* chart.

The movie *TRON* is released.

E.T. the Extra-Terrestrial, widely accepted as the most loathed home video game of all time, is released for Atari 2600.

1983: *Ultima III: Exodus,* often cited as the foundation for the computer fantasy role-playing genre, is released.

Realms of Gold I: Tomb of Destiny is written in Mr. Kovacs's intro to programming class.

The movie *WarGames* is released.

Electronic Arts runs the famous "Can a Computer Make You Cry" advertisement in *Creative Computing*.

Realms of Gold II: War in the Realms is written at KidBits computer camp.

1985: The Nintendo Entertainment System (NES) is released in the United States.

1987: *Realms of Gold III: Restoration* is released.

1988: *Clandestine* for the Commodore 64, Black Arts' first commercially published title, is released.

1989: *Solar Empires I* is released.

1990: *Realms of Gold IV: City of Hope* is released.

Super Mario Bros. 3 is released for NES.

1991: *Black Karts Racing* is released.

1992: *Realms of Golf* is released.

id Software releases *Wolfenstein 3D,* introducing the first-person shooter genre.

Clandestine II: Love Never Thinks Twice is released.

1993: Cyan releases *Myst,* an artistic milestone and the first mainstream hit on the CD-ROM platform.

Realms of Gold V: Aquator's Realm is released.

Realms of Gold's Worlds of Intrigue: High Society is released.

Clandestine III: Mirror Games is released.

1994: *Clandestine IV: On American Assignment* is released.

Realms of Gold VI: Far Latitudes is released.

1995: *Clandestine V: Axis Power* is released.

Solar Empires II: The Ten-Thousand-Year Sleepover is released.

Pro Skate 'Em Endoria: Grind the Arch-Lich is released.

1996: *Tomb Raider,* featuring the first successful female action hero in a video game, is released.

Clandestine VI: Deathclock is released.

Clandestine: Worlds Beyond (Limited Edition) is released.

Tournament of Ages is released.

1997: *Clandestine VII: Countdown to Rapture* is released.

Ultima Online, the first massively successful multiplayer-only role-playing game, is released.

Solar Empires III: Pan-Stellar Activation is released.

Founding member Darren Ackerman leaves Black Arts and founds his own studio, Vorpal, which will continue the *Clandestine* franchise.

1998: Mike Abrash publicly reveals the technology behind the *Quake* game engine in a talk at the annual Game Developers Conference.

The Legend of Zelda: Ocarina of Time, one of several games often referred to as the greatest video game of all time, is published.

Clandestine: World's End is released.

Realms of Gold VII: Winter's Crown is demonstrated at the Electronic Entertainment Expo.

2000: The Sony PlayStation 2 is released.

2006: The Nintendo Wii, the first mainstream motion-sensing console, is released.

2008: Gary Gygax, principal inventor and popularizer of *Dungeons & Dragons,* dies.

Austin Grossman is a video game design consultant who has worked on such games as *Ultima Underworld II: Labyrinth of Worlds, System Shock, Flight Unlimited, Trespasser: Jurassic Park, Clive Barker's Undying, Deus Ex, Tomb Raider Legend, Epic Mickey,* and *Dishonored.* He is also the author of *Soon I Will Be Invincible,* which was nominated for the 2007 John Sargent Sr. First Novel Prize. His writing has appeared in *Granta,* the *Wall Street Journal,* and the *New York Times.* He lives in Berkeley, California.

MULHOLLAND BOOKS

You won't be able to put down these Mulholland Books.

YOU by *Austin Grossman*

OVERWATCH by *Marc Guggenheim*

THE SUSPECT by *Michael Robotham*

SKINNER by *Charlie Huston*

LOST by *Michael Robotham*

SEAL TEAM SIX: HUNT THE JACKAL
by *Don Mann with Ralph Pezzullo*

ANGEL BABY by *Richard Lange*

MURDER AS A FINE ART by *David Morrell*

WEAPONIZED by *Nicholas Mennuti with David Guggenheim*

THE STRING DIARIES by *Stephen Lloyd Jones*

THE COMPETITION by *Marcia Clark*

BRAVO by *Greg Rucka*

DEATH WILL HAVE YOUR EYES by *James Sallis*

WHISKEY TANGO FOXTROT by *David Shafer*

CONFESSIONS by *Kanae Minato*

Visit mulhollandbooks.com for
your daily suspense fiction fix.

Download the FREE Mulholland Books app.